ONE CALL AWAY

EMILY GOODWIN

One Call Away
Copyright 2017
Emily Goodwin

Cover Design by RBA: Romantic Book Affairs
Cover Photography by Lindee Robinson
Models: Travis Bendall and Ali Abela
Editing by Lindsay at Contagious Edits and Ellie at Love N Books

~

❀ Created with Vellum

To my girls. I love you to the moon and back.

PLAYLIST

Unsteady- X Ambassador
Never Say Never- The Gray
Mad World- Gary Jules
Say Something- A Great Big World
Let Her Go- Passenger
Breathe Me- Jasmine Thompson
Never Let Me Go- Florence + The Machine
Trust- Christina Perri
Say You Won't Let go- James Arthur
Cosmic Love- Florence + The Machine
Back to You- Alex & Sierra
Even My Dad Does Sometimes- Ed Sherran
Life of the Party- Shawn Mendez
One Call Away- Charlie Puth

SIERRA

THEN...

$\mathcal{M}$y phone clatters to the ground, and the smiling faces of Hermione and Luna stare up at me from the back of my Harry Potter phone case. I exhale, and as the breath leaves me, so does part of my soul. I close my eyes, refusing to process what I just heard.

Time stops, yet everything is swirling around me at a dizzying rate. Panic rises in my chest, and my knees threaten to buckle. A strangled sob escapes my lips and I pitch forward, catching myself on the counter. Tears burn behind my closed eyelids, and I'm struggling to breathe.

"Sierra? Are you all right?" Mrs. Williams' voice comes from behind me, sounding miles away as if it's echoing through a dark and harrowing tunnel. She's only a few yards to my right, putting a new shipment of children's books away on a display. "Sierra?" she calls again and the floorboards of this little, old bookstore creak beneath her feet. "Honey, what's wrong?" There's a bit of panic in her voice, but she does her best to hide it.

"Jake," I whisper, and the tears start to fall. "Jake…"

Mrs. Williams picks up my phone. There's a fresh crack down the middle, but I don't care right now. It's just a phone. It can be replaced. She carefully puts it to her ear and says something, and then listens to what the liar on the other end has to say.

I want to swat the phone out of her hand. I want it to fall and break into a million pieces on the cold, hard ground. Because none of it is true.

It can't be true.

Jake can't leave me.

The blood drains from Mrs. Williams' face. She nods as she talks, then lowers the phone. "Sierra," she says softly, voice full of pity. Her hand lands on my back and if I weren't frozen still, I'd jerk away. I don't need sympathy. Because that means something is wrong. That means something bad happened.

And nothing did.

Things are good.

I'm good.

Jake's good.

We're good.

"I'll drive you to the hospital."

The panic is back and everything inside me aches. I need to be there. Now. "The store," I start, brain going into survival mode. It's only me and Mrs. Williams running this place, and we have our first customer of the morning in right now, shyly flipping through a dirty romance novel.

"The store can wait," Mrs. Williams says gently. "We won't miss too many sales anyway." She gives me a small smile, eyebrows pinched together with worry. "Come on, honey, grab your purse."

I blink and realize that tears are streaming down my face like rain. I can't make them stop. My chest tightens when I turn, and all I can do to keep from coming apart is to focus on putting one foot in front of the other. I make it into the little room in the back and take my purse from the hook. There's no air conditioning back here, and the humidity is high today, normal for late spring in Mississippi. The world spirals around me and the liar's words echo through my head.

There was an accident.

I'm sorry.

We've done all that we can do.

There's not much time left.

Hurry if you want to say goodbye.

"Sierra?" Mrs. Williams calls. I can hear her keys jingling in rhythm with her limp as she hurries to the back. The weather makes her bad hip hurt. "Come on, honey."

I look down at my sunshine-yellow ballet flats, tears blurring my vision. Forcing myself to go numb, I follow Mrs. Williams out the back of the store and get in the passenger side of her car.

The fully restored 1971, cherry-red Chevelle that's detailed to hell with rims so shiny you can see them from space is the last thing you'd expect an eighty-something-year-old woman to be driving. But those who know Mrs. Williams know restoring old cars to perfection was her husband's hobby that turned into his career. She has a garage full of these things, and she and her son take great care of them.

I stare straight ahead at the dash, not allowing myself to think. Or feel.

But I do.

My mind goes back to how it all began, to that first night I saw Jake at a party in college. He was drunk and had his hands all over some blonde with boobs pushed up to her chin. Yet for some reason, he left her and wanted to talk to me. I thought he was a pig. He asked me out and I told him no.

After a bit of a cat-and-mouse game of him asking me out and me telling him no, things changed when he kissed me on my birthday, and we've been together for nearly two years now. I moved back home to Summer Hill after graduating college, working to save for grad school and waiting for Jake to finish his residency and become a doctor.

We're nearly an hour away from the hospital, and each bump in the road, each mile that passes, makes things feel more real. I curl my fingers into the leather seat beneath me, eyes wide and jaw tense. My heart is beating so fast it hurts, with each beat echoing loudly in my ears.

They're wrong. Jake is going to be fine. I can't lose him. I won't lose him.

Not a word is spoken on the way to the hospital. Mrs. Williams stops at the front and suddenly I can't move. My fingers won't work to open the door. My legs are lead and are much too heavy.

"Do you want me to come with you?" she asks.

My jaw begins to tremble and I shake my head. "I don't know." I blink and the sight of the large, brick building takes my breath away all over again. Vomit rises in my throat and the panic comes back in a fury. Without another word, I get out of the car and rush to the desk in the ER.

"Hi, how can I help you?" a young girl asks with a smile that slowly disappears from her face when she takes in my desperation.

"Jake. Jake McLeland," I start, voice trembling. "I got a call that he was…" I can't finish the sentence. The girl behind the desk nods and types something into the computer. Her face softens more when she reads whatever the file is telling her.

She grabs a phone and calls for an attendant to take me to the ICU.

Everyone looks at me with pity. Smiles gently. Talks softly. Like they're afraid I'll break at any moment. But if what they say is true, I'm already broken.

The smell hits me first. It's a typical hospital smell: a mixture of disinfectant, ointments, and blood. I know it doesn't make sense. There aren't pools of blood left to fester, yet it's what I smell. The lighting gets to me next. The waiting area is dark, contrasted by harsh lights in the nurses' station and over the patients' beds.

I'm directed to a room at the end of the ICU. Curtains are drawn around the glass walls and it hits me; there's no need for the nurses to be able to look in on Jake. It's that moment that defines me, that moment when I know I've lost my faith.

And I haven't even seen Jake yet.

Unsteady, my legs shake. My fingers tremble and I reach up to the cat charm hanging from my necklace, rubbing my thumb over the smooth metal. It's a nervous habit, but the gesture brings no comfort.

A nurse comes to greet me. Her eyes are gentle, and she explains things to me like it makes sense. Like anything makes sense. I look up at her, wondering how she's able to do this day after day. How's she's able to say things like 'no brain activity' and 'unstable blood pressure' without breaking down herself.

She puts her arm around my shoulder and opens the door. The sight of Jake, my sweet Jake, lying motionless in the bed, hooked up to more IVs and wires than I can count, with tubes in his mouth and his neck in a brace, sends me backward into a dark spiral of despair I know I'll never be able to claw my way out of.

Tears fall from my eyes and everything inside me breaks. I go to Jake, taking his hand. His skin is cold.

The beeping from the heart monitor isn't rhythmic. Isn't steady. It's nowhere near the rate it should be. His heart beats once for every three of mine, but that's okay. I'll give him my strength. My heart is already his.

"I'm not sure what your beliefs are," the nurse softly says. "But a lot of people believe the soul or spirit remains until the last heartbeat. He might still be able to hear you."

Words meant to comfort me bring on an icy chill, and I collapse onto the bed, unable to control my sobs.

The last heartbeat.

"Jake," I cry, lacing my fingers between his. An IV tube gets in the way, but I ignore it. "Jake, please don't leave me. Don't leave. Please."

I wrap my other arm around him and rest my head on his chest. Instead of the warm comfort of his muscles, he feels stiff and cold, covered in wires. Faintly, I can smell his cologne underneath the stench of hospital that's stained his skin.

"You can't leave me," I sob. "We're not done yet, remember? You left me a message this morning about finally putting in that garden." I press my head into him, crying harder than I ever have before. "And the cat shelf," I say, looking up at him. He's going to open his eyes and laugh at me. Any second now, he'll tell me I'm crazy for wanting to install a row of shelves along the ceiling in the loft for the cats. "We still have to put up the cat shelf."

I swallow the lump in my throat and wipe my tears.

"Come on, baby. I know it hurts. But you can do this. You can fight this. Please, don't go. You can fight this, I know it."

But he doesn't. His eyes don't open. His fingers don't twitch. The beeps from the heart monitor grow further apart.

"Jake!" I call, shaking his hand. Tears stream down my face and fall onto him. I lift his arm and put his hand over my heart. "Take mine! Take anything you need. Take it all. Please…please, baby." I hang my head, sobbing.

A hand lands on my shoulder. "Your mother is on her way," Mrs. Williams says. She stays there, hand on my shoulder until the nurse comes back in, asking if we had more contact information for Jake. Always prepared, Jake had the proper documents folded and kept in his wallet that listed me as his emergency contact and power of attorney if need be. Seeing situations just like this in the ER made him prepare for the worst.

The worst wasn't supposed to happen.

Mrs. Williams leaves the room to help the nurse get Jake's mom's number. I hug Jake tighter, willing him to come back to me.

"I'm not going to give up on you," I whisper through my tears. "You can pull through this. I know you can. I love you so much."

The heart monitor gives off a series of rapid beats. I shoot up and look at it. The line spiked three times. Oh my God. He's coming back.

"Jake, baby!"

I wait. *Come on…come on…*

But nothing comes.

Nothing, except the last heartbeat.

~

MY HOUSE IS on our family's property, same as my sister's, but unlike hers, mine isn't new. It's the original Belmont farmhouse, the one all nine of my ancestors crammed into when they first took up farming and made a name for themselves. It's not fancy like the historic plantation house my parents reside in. It has no ostentatious facade, no grand staircase or granite kitchen island big enough to seat a dozen people.

It's small yet quaint, and I wouldn't have it any other way. You can feel the history when you walk in, pressing on you from all sides of the brick house. The necessary updates have been done to make the space livable, of course. The entire first floor is modernized, with the latest update being a total kitchen remodel that Jake and I did ourselves this past Christmas. Well, mostly ourselves. And by that, I mean I picked out farmhouse kitchens on Pinterest and he approved the final design. We ripped out the old cabinets and let the professionals take it from there.

Walking into the house alone isn't out of the norm. Jake stayed at school most weeknights when he was taking classes, and now that he is—*was*—in his residency, the drive to the teaching hospital was just too far to take on a daily basis. But this time, when I stick my key into the deadbolt, the weight of the world crashes down on me.

Jake will never walk through these doors again. I'll never wake up in the middle of the night to a call from him, telling me he loves me or filling me in on the nightshift drama at the hospital. Some nights I'd be too dead asleep to hear the phone ring, the curse of a sound sleeper, I suppose, and would wake up to a wonderful message. I'd call him on my way into The Book Bag and leave him a message to listen to as well when he got done with his rotation in the ER.

I'll never see his name on my phone again.

I'll never hear his voice again.

Feel his arms around me.

Get annoyed with him for putting plastic in the garbage instead of the recycling.

I step into the house and a wave of grief washes over me, pulling me under the surface. I'm caught in the undertow and there's no way out. And right now, I don't want a way out. I'm drowning, but once the water fills my lungs, everything will end.

I make it to the couch and fall, curling up into a little ball. I bring my knees to my chest, pressing against my heart. It hurts so much I can feel it in my bones. I cry and cry and cry until there are no more tears left to fall.

And then I cry some more.

"Sierra?"

"Mom," I choke out, looking up. The house is too dark, and my eyes are too swollen to see, but I know her voice. She comes to the couch and sits next to me. Doesn't turn on a light. Doesn't tell me things will be okay. She just holds me and lets me cry. She cries too, both over the loss and over my heartache. She stays with me until I fall asleep, and is there when the early light of the morning filters through the windows. My dreams of Jake kissing me escape me, leaving me naked and cold in harsh reality.

My heart, mended in my sleep by dreams that will never come true, rips in two again. The break is so deep it vibrates through my entire being, bringing pain to my whole body. My head throbs. My throat is sore and thick from crying. My eyes burn. My stomach is sick. Yet nothing is as bad as the heartache. The pain intensifies, and I feel like I'm dead too, yet they forgot to bury me.

Yesterday, my world ended. I lost Jake yesterday. *Yesterday*. And waking up, remembering it all, it's like I lost him all over again.

It's going to be like this every day for the rest of my life.

~

MY SISTER GRIPS MY HAND, giving it a reassuring squeeze as she opens the door to my little brick house. I've been staying with my parents the last week, just trying to survive. I feel like I've failed, yet here I am, still breathing. Heart still beating. My body is betraying me. I want it to give out and let the quiet peace of death surround me, taking me into the dark where I can be with Jake again.

But I'm still here.

"The cats are fine," Samantha tells me, opening the door. "I came by every day to feed them and I scooped their box a few times too. You had a load of laundry in your washer that got a bit stinky from sitting there, so I rewashed it and put it in the dryer. And I loaded your dishwasher."

I nod and for the first time am thankful for my older sister's no-nonsense personality. Today is Jake's funeral, and she's come to the house with me to pick out clothes. Sam closes the door behind me, and my cats come running. I drop down and run my hand over a pretty calico cat who's purring and pressing her head against me. Tinkerbell, a gray and black tabby, meows and twists around my arm.

"Hey, girls," I whisper, voice shaking. Everything is the same. The house looks like it did that night. Smells the same. But it's so very different. This house is no longer a home.

"Do you want me to pick something out for you?" Sam offers.

"I don't care."

"Okay. I'll bring options."

Dolly, the calico cat, nips at me as she demands more attention. I had her before I met Jake. He wasn't much of an animal person, but he tolerated the cats for my sake. And it was him who brought home Tinkerbell, and the memory of him coming in the door with a little wet ball of fur makes me choke up. He found her shivering in a puddle along the driveway to our house, no doubt separated from its mother and littermates from the large barn behind my parents' mansion.

"Do you want me to do your makeup?" Sam asks, voice

coming from the bedroom.

"I don't care," I repeat. It's been one of the few things I'm able to say. Because I don't care. Clothes...makeup...what to eat for dinner...I don't care. It's all so trivial.

Both cats are meowing now, and I know they want treats. Using the coffee table to pull myself up, I shuffle into the kitchen to get them. I toss them on the floor, watching the cats playfully chase after them. Going on autopilot, I wash out their water bowl, refill their dry food, and open a can of cat food to split between the two. Then I go into my bedroom, eyes going to the bed that Jake and I shared.

He'll never be in it again.

I'll never wake up to his arms around me.

He'll never complain about me sticking my cold feet under his legs to warm them up.

The bed is made, and I want to get mad at Sam for messing it up. She should have left it how it was, though it's not like Jake woke up that morning. He hadn't been home in over a week, going on a long stretch at the teaching hospital we joked he was temporarily married to.

I don't remember what he was wearing the last time I saw him. I had the day off and was still in bed, half asleep, when he left. He kissed me goodbye and said he'd call later, which he always did. Two days went by just like normal, and then... tears are back in my eyes, and it's a wonder I'm not dehydrated from crying so much.

The clothes I wore that day are still on the floor, hastily strewn about. The yellow skirt, blue tank top, and a red headband, stand out against the dark hardwood floor, reminding me how fast things can change. I got dressed that morning in an outfit that vaguely resembled Snow White, and went to work like my life would continue to coast along like normal.

"What about this?" Sam holds up a black dress. "Oh, never

mind, those are skulls. I thought it was just a design." She frowns and puts it back, then thumbs through my clothes again. I make a move to the closet, about to tell her that I own exactly one appropriate dress, and the last time I wore it was for a job interview two years ago. I have what most call an 'interesting' fashion sense, but the way I see it, everyone else is way too boring. Clothes can be a way to express yourself, just as much as tattoos and makeup.

Then I see Jake's side of the closet, with his clothes organized by color and type. It hits me hard, and it takes every last ounce of strength I have in me not to come undone. My sister looks at me, tears in her own eyes, and grabs the skull dress and a black sweater, and rushes over, wrapping her arms around me.

We cry together, and in that moment, I've never felt closer to my sister. She's five years older than me and my polar opposite. She got her degree in agriculture, married a nice guy with a head for business and a background in farming, and popped out her first kid exactly ten months after their wedding. They're set to take over the family farm, carrying on the Belmont traditions and doing exactly what they should.

I'm not good at following the path. I've been an outside-the-lines kind of person my whole life, which isn't always easy in a small town, one whose rumor mill is bigger than the actual mill.

There were times when I was the only one marching to the beat of my own drum, and the loneliness got to me in moments of weakness. And then I found someone who loved me despite that, someone who supported my decision to follow my own dreams and not just go through the motions and become a farmer's wife.

"I'll help you get dressed." Sam goes into the bathroom and returns with a brush. She combs through my long brunette hair before braiding it and then lays out my clothes. The black sweater is a slightly different shade of black than the dress, which would normally drive me crazy, but seeing them together makes me feel nothing at all.

I run my fingers over Jake's pillow and then get dressed. Everything begins to feel surreal and time escapes me. Sam fills a black clutch full of tissues and takes my hand. We step outside into the bright sunlight and walk down the old stone path from my little porch to the gravel driveway, where the rest of our family is waiting in my dad's black Escalade.

My brother Scott, who I only see on special occasions since he got an engineering job in Orlando a few years ago, welcomes me in a tight hug. I sit in the back of the SUV with him, and once we get going, he pulls out a silver flask and offers it to me.

I blink my tear-soaked eyes and take it from him, taking a big gulp. And then another. And another, until he takes it away from me. My body shudders in a sob and he puts his arm around me. I rest my head on his shoulder, trying to disassociate from everything for the hour-and-a-half-long drive it's going to take to get to the cemetery.

I've been told that the grief will come in waves, and over time, the crash on the shore lessens. I'll still feel the spray of the ocean, but it won't feel like a constant battle to stay on land and not be washed out to sea. The only problem is, the waves haven't started yet. I'm still in the middle of the sea with no land in sight, desperately treading water. My heart feels like it's about to give out, that it can't beat another beat because of the pain. So I stop. I become still. I welcome the cold darkness that wraps me up and pulls me below the surface.

And then I open my eyes and I'm above the surface again and have to go through the whole thing over and over again.

Dying, every single day.

2

CHASE

I bring the beer to my lips, take a swig, and look at my father. It's been years since I've seen him, and even longer since I've been back to Summer Hill. My father's wife—the one he cheated on and the affair resulted in me—isn't too keen on the sight of me. I'm forever the Jon Snow of the family, since looking at me reminds her of her husband's infidelity and all. I can't blame her for that since I am the product of dear old Dad getting lonely on business trips.

My half-brother, Josh, claps his hand on my back. "It's good to see you again, Chase. I just wish it was under different circumstances."

I nod. "Yeah. It has been a while."

"It's been too long. Are you staying this time? For a few days at least, right?"

"Uh, maybe," I start, trying to think of a polite way to say 'hell fucking no,' though really, I have no reason to rush out of here and get back to my life in New Jersey. Josh takes a

14

step back and helps his pregnant wife to her feet. She winces, putting her hand on her back, and slowly comes over. They're good people, who have gone out of their way to include me as family.

Josh and I share a slight resemblance, one we get from our father. Hazel eyes, wavy brown hair. Tall and muscular. But that's where the similarities end. I look back at our father, noting how we got those characteristics from him, and realize how fucking old Dad looks.

It probably has something to do with the fact that he's dead.

After years of drinking, his liver finally shut down and he spent his final days on home hospice care. The wake just ended, and just the family is here to say our final goodbyes before his body is cremated.

Moving to the casket, I take another sip of beer and hold up the bottle, silently toasting my father. A weird sense of guilt creeps over me. I don't feel sad. I don't have a longing in my heart for the man who sired me and left me without a second look back. I got cards and money over the years every Christmas and birthday, and a few visits mixed in there, but he was really just a stranger.

~

"I MEANT it when I said you should stay a while," Josh tells me, wiping down the counter. I lean back on the barstool and pick up my whiskey, ice clinking on the glass. "Melissa and I could really use the help. It's tough enough working with one kid at home. Adding twins into the mix is going to make things…interesting."

I finish the whiskey and nod. "I don't know. I don't want to impose."

"You won't be. I actually do have to hire someone soon,

15

before the babies are born. You'd save me from interviewing people."

I run my finger around the rim of the glass and shake my head. "How do you know I'd be any good at the job?"

Josh laughs. "Can you pour drinks? Take orders to the kitchen? I know you bartended before at swankier places than this. Most of our drink orders are beer and straight whiskey. It's not that complicated."

The kindness Josh always gives is welcome but unsettling. I'm not used to it, and I'm sure as shit not used to family doing favors for each other. Hell, my own mother started charging me rent the day I turned sixteen and could legally get a job.

I look around the bar. It's seven o'clock on a Wednesday night, and it's starting to fill with regulars. Located on the outskirts of Summer Hill, The Mill House is home to both locals and those coming from the neighboring towns and gets a fair deal of customers coming off the highway.

It's definitely not as busy as the bars I worked along the boardwalk back home, but it's busy enough to maintain a steady cash flow and give me something to do.

"There's an apartment above the bar," Josh starts. "It's been empty since Melissa and I got married. She didn't want to live above the bar." He chuckles. "It's yours if you take the job."

"I can't—"

"Yeah, you can." Josh tosses the dishcloth into the sink and comes over, still on the opposite side of the bar, and grabs the bottle of whiskey. He pours more in my glass and then some for himself. "I don't think I ever told you this," he starts and downs his shot of whiskey. "When I was a kid, I begged Mom and Dad for a baby brother. And then when I found out I actually had one, I was elated. But it didn't turn out the way I hoped, and I've always regretted that."

I divert my eyes to the bar top, studying the many nicks and scratches in the wood. Total honesty and baring my emotions isn't something I'm used to either.

"Dad was an asshole, I know," Josh goes on. "But now that he's gone, I feel we need to take what remains of this family and hold it together. Stay. Dakota is excited her uncle is finally here. She wants to get to know you."

"Right. I suppose I could stay for a while."

"Consider this a fresh start. I know you could use one."

I meet Josh's eyes again, wondering how the hell he knows that. And then I remember the last time I was arrested, someone paid my bail but I never knew who.

"That was you?"

Josh gives a half-smile and turns, washing out his glass. "I can't let my little brother rot in jail, now, can I?"

"I'll pay you back. I have the cash."

He shakes his head. "No way. You can, however, work it off."

I finish off the rest of the whiskey, smiling as I shake my head. "When do I start?"

~

I'VE ALWAYS LED a transient style of life, moving from place to place, never fully settling down. I'd go where the work took me, which usually required traveling anyway. It's not that I never wanted to settle down, I did, but I never found a place that felt like home.

Some nights, after a long day full of chasing, running, and usually a side of breaking and entering, I'd lay alone in whatever motel bed I was staying in for the time being and think of life. Of the big picture. I'd wonder what it would be like to have visions of the future on the horizon, to get by on hopes and dreams, and not on a day-to-day basis.

I could easily convince myself that wasn't true, that I went after the high-dollar jobs for the payout in the end, along with the thrill and the danger of course, but if I thought about it, there was nothing I was saving for. Hell, I blew through a decent amount of the cash I got paid. I lived for the moment, not wanting to accept the fact that there was a growing pit inside of me, one filled with darkness, resonating with the pain of never fitting in or feeling like I belong.

Sweat rolls down my brow, and I wipe it away with the back of my hand. I take the last box down to the parking lot and head back up to the apartment above the bar. It's been four years since anyone has lived in here, and while that doesn't sound long, in theory, the place has its fair share of issues.

Starting with the non-working air conditioner. The morning after I agreed to stay, I flew to the place I was staying in New Jersey and drove back here, Mustang loaded with everything I own, minus the furniture. Not having a home of my own has resulted in a minimalist lifestyle, and I've always had the attitude that things are just things and can be replaced. But my car is my most prized possession. It was the first thing I bought when I got my first-ever large payout, and I've put in a lot of the under-the-hood work myself. The thing is badass if I do say so myself.

Not having a garage is killing me, and I just arrived back at The Mill House. There is an old barn behind the bar, but it's full of junk. I plan to clear it out so my car can have shelter, but I'll get to that later. I've been clearing crap out of the apartment all morning, moving my own few things, and have a big order from Amazon coming tomorrow.

I go back up the rickety stairs and into the apartment, and stop in the entrance. The building used to be a mill house back in the day, hence the name of the bar. It's been a few things over the years before it became the bar my brother bought, but the history has remained despite the many renovations.

The apartment is a decent size for the age of the place and boasts a large floor-to-ceiling glass window in the living room overlooking the river that once powered the mill. It's dried several feet since then, but the soft sound of running water in the distance is calming.

Through the living room is a kitchen with dark cabinets and stone countertops. A rustic farmhouse table sits in the center, and behind that is a door that leads to the only bedroom and bathroom. Nothing is fancy, but it's a hell of a lot nicer than places I've stayed in the past.

The gentle sound of running water comes in through the open windows, and leaves rustle together with the breeze. The air comes in, welcome against my hot skin. I feel an odd lurch inside of me, almost like my heart skipping a beat the same time my stomach flip-flops. It's because it's hotter than hell up here and I haven't eaten all day. Not because I think with a little TLC this place could become a home.

I spent a few more hours rearranging things until I like the layout, hook up my TV and gaming system, and then move on to the bedroom. Someone knocks on the door and immediately enters, calling my name.

"Uncle Chase!" Dakota's little voice echoes off the brick walls. "We brought you food!"

Thank God. I ball the sheets I'd just stripped from the bed and leave the bedroom.

"Daddy, it's hot in here," Dakota says, making a face.

"Yeah, it is," Josh agrees guiltily. "The electrician is coming tomorrow. Sorry about that."

I shrug. "It's okay."

"Hungry?" Josh asks, holding up a white CorningWare dish. I can't see what's inside, but it smells amazing. "We can eat in the bar." He looks at his four-year-old and laughs. "It's closed now, so I suppose it's okay. It's better than being in this sauna."

We go down into the bar and dig into the casserole Melissa made for me. Dakota fires off question after question as we eat, then announces that she's going to help decorate my new room. She thinks a princess theme is best. I laugh but don't argue with that. She's too fucking cute.

"Are you settled in?" Josh asks as we finish eating.

"As much as I can be. I ordered the rest of what I need online and it's coming tomorrow. Oh, what kind of cable do you use?"

Josh laughs. "We don't get cable out here. I'll set you up with the guy to install the satellite though."

"Thanks."

"You might be without TV for a while."

"It's okay. I have my phone for entertainment, and I have books." I have a box full of my favorite paperbacks but read mostly on my Kindle. Moving around a lot makes it hard to keep all the hard copies of books I've read. And I've read a lot. It might sound stupid—and I'll never admit it to anyone —but for the time when I'm immersed in a book, I don't feel lonely.

And I'll never admit to anyone that I'm lonely. Not even myself. Because I'm not. I've been on my own most of my life. It's what I'm accustomed to.

"The last time you were in Summer Hill, you were too young to drive."

"Legally," I say with a smirk.

"I do remember you driving." Josh shakes his head. "Not much has changed, but I can show you around tomorrow. I assume you'll need to go to the store and get groceries. The Walmart has become a Super Walmart, and we finally got a movie theater. It doesn't play current movies, though. A tour won't take too long."

"Thanks."

We finish eating, and I tell Josh that I'll wash the dishes. It'll give me something to do and an excuse to stay in the air conditioning, after all. Dakota wants to see the apartment again, so she knows how many princess pictures to make. I cover the leftover casserole and take it upstairs with us, sticking it in the old fridge that thankfully still works.

Josh pokes around the apartment a bit, taking notes on things that need to be fixed or replaced. I assure him it's fine and I can take care of it all, but he insists.

"Baking soda and vinegar," he mutters, seeing the red ring in the bathtub. "That should take it out. Melissa uses that on everything. Seems to work."

"I'll pick some up tomorrow."

"I should have cleaned this place before offering it to you. I assumed it would be in the same state I left it."

"Don't worry about it. You offered it to me, and you didn't have to."

A crash comes from the bedroom and we both bolt in there. A rickety bookshelf toppled over and is laying in pieces on the floor.

"Dakota!" Josh screams and scoops up the crying toddler. I check her over while he holds her, trying to quiet her sobs.

"I don't see any blood," I say, and then move my hands to her head, gently feeling for bumps. "Did you get hurt?"

"It didn't hit me," she hiccups.

"What were you doing?" Josh asks harshly, his fear coming out in disciplining the kid.

"Trying to measure."

"You can't climb on stuff like that. You know better than that! You could have gotten seriously hurt, Koty."

21

"I'm sorry, Daddy. And Uncle Chase. I'm sorry I broke your bookshelf."

"It's okay," I tell her. The shelf didn't look in the best shape when I loaded it with my books anyway. Dakota quiets and moves to the bed while Josh and I upright the bookshelf.

"Oh shit," I say, then shake my head and look at Dakota. "Sorry." I pick up my phone, which thankfully is looking like the only casualty in this mess.

"Shit," Josh echoes. "Sorry. I'll get you a new one."

I look at the shattered glass screen. The phone itself still works, but I can hardly see past the cracks, and know one swipe across the screen to unlock it will result in a sliced-open finger. "I can take it in for a repair. There's not an Apple store around here is there?"

"Hah. Funny. You'll have to send it in."

"That's fine."

"You need something in the meantime. It could take weeks before it comes back. Dakota, you broke Uncle Chase's phone. You really need to listen and not climb on stuff."

Dakota starts crying again, and maybe it's because I'm not a parent but I want to just give in to her to make her stop. Crying makes me uncomfortable.

"There's one place in town, and if I leave now I can get there before they close."

"You really don't have to. I can order a new one and—"

"You need a phone, and I know how long a brand-new phone can take to get here. Let me get you something in the meantime."

"Fine," I say, seeing how there's no point in arguing. And I really don't want to wait to have another phone. What the hell did people do for entertainment before smartphones? We leave together, driving into town. An hour later, we're leaving with an iPhone. It's secondhand, but it's the best the little phone service store had to offer and will be fine for the time being. Being assigned a new number was a little surreal. Seeing the area code for Summer Hill feels almost like a trap. Since it's getting late, Josh drops me off and heads home to get Dakota in bed.

With the sun sinking low in the sky, the air begins to cool. I pick up the rest of the broken bookshelf and then sit at the kitchen table to set up the phone. It was activated at the store, and the guy told me I should probably switch to this network provider anyway since they had better service here than what I was previously using.

I run into an issue when I go to set up the voicemail, and discover that the mailbox is nearly full. The first message is from over a year ago, and all the messages are from the same number. The phone has sat in the shop for months, or so I was told. And no one thought to do a factory reset?

I roll my eyes and wonder if I can easily recover deleted photos since whoever took this to resell obviously didn't know to clear out the voicemail box. Curiosity gets the better of me, and I hit play on the first message.

"Jake." The voice is female, and she doesn't say the name. She breathes it. "A strange thing happened today. I saw an infomercial for cat shelves you put by your window. Someone stole my idea. I knew you'd get a kick out of it, and I wanted to tell you. I picked up the phone and everything. Then I remembered...I remembered that...you're...that you're dead."

Whoa. I was not expecting that.

"That's the first time I've said it out loud," the woman whispers, voice full of emotion. "I miss you."

Too intrigued, I listen to the next message, which was left just a day after the first one.

"Calling you makes it feel like you're still alive," the woman says, and the sadness in her voice pulls on my heart.

"It's like you're away at work and you'll listen to this message when you're done with your shift. Like we're only one call away from talking to each other. I keep waiting for you to call me back. It's been a month, and I keep looking at my phone hoping to see your name. I don't know when that will go away. I don't want it to go away. I just want you back. I want us back. I miss you, and I love you. Always."

I play the next message right away, which was left just days later. "People tell me that I need to get out and enjoy life. Because I'm alive. But I don't feel alive. Everything hurts all the time, but at the same time, I feel nothing. How can you feel nothing and everything at the same time? It doesn't make sense, I know. It's like…it's like I died and they forgot to bury me. I'm not sure what to do. You'd know, but if you were here…" She breaks off crying, and the line goes dead.

I don't think as I press play on the next message, which is from a few days after the last. "Jake," she breathes his name again, and I feel a weird stirring inside me, and it takes everything I have to repress the truth. I'd give anything to have someone say my name with such longing, which is totally fucked up. The woman is grieving the loss of her loved one. "It's been raining all week and everyone is worried about the river. They say these things can happen fast and the currents are strong. Scott called today and asked me to stay with him for a while in Orlando. He said he'd take me to Disney World. I'm tired of people treating me like a child, even though you know I love Disney."

I find myself smiling at her words, heart breaking at the same time.

"Maybe I should go," she continues. "Because I feel like I'm drowning, like I'm caught in the muddy current of the river and I can't get my arms and legs to move to fight it. Because I don't want to fight it."

The message ends and I bring the phone away from my

ear, letting out a breath. I blink and stare at the window, listening to the river in the background. The pain in this woman's voice is hauntingly beautiful, awakening the dark parts of my heart and making me feel.

I haven't felt anything deep in years.

I look back at the phone and scroll through the messages. The voicemail box has to be close to full, but since there's nothing else on the phone taking up memory, it's able to store them all. For now. Once I start using the phone I'll have to delete the messages, which seems wrong for some insane reason.

Her words are spoken in heartbroken whispers, not meant for anyone to hear. And yet I can't stop listening.

The next message is from two weeks after that and is considerably shorter. "Mom made me see a therapist today. She also told me to write down how I feel on a piece of paper. I left it blank. She seemed annoyed, but that's how I feel. Empty."

"Fuck," I mutter and lock the screen on the phone. No more messages tonight. My mystery woman's words hit a little too close to home. I set the phone down, shower, and get into the uncomfortable bed, which instantly makes me eager for my new mattress to arrive tomorrow.

I pull out my Kindle and try to read, but my mind keeps drifting to the woman who left the messages. Collectively, I've heard her speak for only a few minutes. Yet it's not the time, but the depth of her words. The emotion in her voice. I can't get her out of my mind and I don't know her name or what she looks like.

If we ever met, I'd be fucked.

3

SIERRA

"*I*'m not taking no for an answer. It's my birthday."

I pick up a box cutter and carefully slice through the packing tape. "I don't know, Lisa," I say to my cousin, who also doubles as my best friend. "There's a lot to do here tonight."

I don't have to look up to feel her incredulous stare.

"Really?"

"Yeah, I mean, we just got this shipment in and I have five-hundred dollars to spend on new orders tonight."

"Tonight?"

Her one-word questions further prove how little she believes me. "And this has to be done on a Friday night? Don't most places not process orders over the weekend?"

"No, lots of places ship every day of the week. And it's going to take time going through the catalog, plus I've been slowly convincing Mrs. Williams to stock more indie books." Since Jake died over a year ago, I haven't felt like myself. It's like part of me died with him, and all that remained was the part of me that does day-to-day tasks, surviving, getting by and fooling those around me.

But not living.

I flick my eyes up from the box of books in front of me and see Lisa's face. She's annoyed and concerned, like everyone else close to me, though Lisa is one of the few who didn't put a time limit on my grief. But I know it won't last forever, and I don't want to throw away a lifetime of friendship.

"Sierra, please," she says softly. "I miss hanging out with you."

I remove packing paper from the box of books and close my eyes in a long blink. Lisa is my only remaining friend. Everyone else ran out of patience, it seems, and didn't feel comfortable hanging out with me. I don't want to lose Lisa too.

"I guess it could wait," I start.

"Fuck yes!" Lisa exclaims and then winces. "Sorry," she says to the customers milling about the store. "We've missed you, Sierra. So much."

"Who's all going?" I ask and try to ignore the instant regret I feel for agreeing to go. Though even before I became the shell of my former self, I wasn't much of a going out person. I enjoyed quiet nights at home reading or binging a show on Netflix.

"The usual crew: Katie, Bella, and Heather. But not Francine. I can't stand that bitch."

"I can't either. She's too judgmental."

"She's worse than me, and I'm a very judgey person," Lisa quips.

"What's the dress code?"

"Sexy." She lifts her hand and points at me, pushing her eyebrows together. "Don't think I forgot what a total

27

knockout you are. I'm still jealous you broke the Belmont curse of the flat chest."

I laugh and shake my head. "Trust me, I'd trade with you any day. Especially in this heat. The sweat dripping between my boobs all day is so lovely."

"Well, put those suckers to good use tonight and get us some free drinks. Flirt a little and have some fun. I want to see you enjoying life again."

I smile at her words but feel the dull edge of the knife in my heart. "I do too." And I do, but I fear the void inside is too big to ever be filled.

~

I sit on the edge of my bed looking down at my multi-colored pastel heels. It's the only thing I've put on so far other than a bra and underwear, and am having a hard time picking out an outfit for tonight. I ordered these shoes the week before Jake died, and since the flower design is hand-painted, they didn't arrive until after his funeral. I've never worn them until tonight.

Standing, I go to my closet and look through my clothes. I settle on a white sundress with flowers stitched onto the thin straps. I put it on, and go into the bathroom to do my hair and makeup. I keep things simple and add big, loose curls and just a bit of eye shadow and mascara.

When I step back and look at myself in the mirror, it's like I'm looking into the past, and I'm overcome with longing again. But this time, it's for the woman I used to be. I want to be her again, though the thought of laughing and going out with friends, of *moving on*, makes me feel guilty.

Lisa calls to say she's in the driveway waiting for me, saving me from thinking about it too much. I double check to make sure I unplugged my curling iron, then hurry through the house and go out the door.

"You look amazing!" she gushes when I get in the passenger side and buckle up.

"So do you," I say back and hand her a wrapped box. "Happy birthday."

"Sierra, you didn't have to get me anything!"

"It's not much," I say. "And is kinda lame."

"You're always lame," she says as she tears into the paper. "I don't expect much from you, you know."

"Keep the expectations low, that's my motto."

Lisa laughs and pulls a picture frame from the box. "Awww, this isn't lame at all." She blinks away tears and looks at the photo of us, arms wrapped around each other. We were six years old in that picture and were matching Disney princesses for Halloween. "Oh my God, look at how cute we were! This makes me feel so old! Thanks, love!"

"There's one more thing."

Lisa unfolds the tissue paper and screams. "Chainsmokers tickets! Holy fuck, Si!"

"So, I take it you're excited?"

"Yes! Oh my God, yes! Thank you!"

I smile, feeling my heart warm. It's such a strange feeling, one I forgot how much I missed. "I figured you and Rob can go. Assuming you haven't gotten rid of him yet."

Lisa laughs. "What about me and you? Oh, uh, yeah. Rob would love to go." She looks at the tickets, no doubt seeing the date of the concert and not pushing the issue. She leans over the center console and hugs me. "Thank you so much."

"You're welcome. I'm glad you like it."

"I love it." She packs the frame and the tickets back in the box, sets it in the backseat and puts the car in drive. "I'd offer to buy you a drink tonight, but I think *the girls* will do all the work for you." She raises her eyebrows and looks at my breasts. "Seriously, it's not fair."

"Try running with these things. Or riding horses. Or just laying down and being comfortable."

"Like you'd really give them up."

I shake my head. "Never. But I can humbly brag about how annoying having big boobs is all day."

"Exactly my point."

We both laugh and things almost feel normal on the short drive to The Mill House bar. The bar is busy tonight since beer is half-off on Friday nights. Katie, Bella, and Heather are already there and have already started drinking.

"Happy birthday!" they cheer and embrace Lisa before turning to me.

"We're so glad you came out!" Katie says and wraps her arms around my shoulders. "I've missed you!"

"I've missed you ladies too," I say, not wanting to make a big deal about anything. Though in truth, I can't remember the last time I saw my friends. Christmas, maybe? They've made no effort to connect with me, but to be fair, I haven't made any attempt either. Time's gone by fast the last year and has crept along at the same time.

"We got a pitcher of margaritas," Bella tells us, and pours two glasses and hands one to me. I take a small sip and slide into the booth. "And it's karaoke tonight. Who's singing with me?"

"Me! Just let this sink in a bit," Lisa says and takes a big gulp of her drink, then makes a face from the rush of cold. We all laugh. I slowly nurse my drink just to blend in but don't want to drink it. An hour passes, and I'm not miserable. I'm talking with my friends, laughing at their jokes, and fully mixing in. It's almost like I'm having a good time, but this all feels pretend, like I'm just playing along, acting but not feeling.

They go through another pitcher of drinks, and Lisa and Bella get up to sing "Wannabe" by the Spice Girls. I get up to go to the bathroom, and come back to find Rob, Lisa's on-and-off-again boyfriend sitting close next to her in the booth. He has friends with him too, and overall, they're all nice guys who grew up in Summer Hill.

"Sierra," he says, blue eyes widening. "Hey. It's good to see you out again. I mean, not again. I, uh…" He turns to Lisa, who rolls her eyes and shakes her head.

"Don't mind him, he's an idiot."

I smile. "It's okay. I know I haven't been out in a long time. You guys don't have to sugarcoat it."

Rob gives me a curt nod. "Good. Hey, you've met my friend Talon before, right?"

"Yeah, a few times." I take my seat, which is subsequently next to Talon. He's a few years older than me and is an attractive man with dark skin and expressive eyes. "Hi," I say to him, feeling awkward.

"Hi, Sierra," he says back, giving me a kind smile. "So, Lisa couldn't get you to go up and sing?"

"No way. I don't do singing in public. Or speaking." I shudder and shake my head.

"I bet you'd be good at it."

"Not at all." I reach for my glass and slide it in front of me. I watch a grain of salt fall down the side, stuck in a little bead of condensation. The watermelon margarita is delicious, and getting drunk and crazy with my friends would do me some good. But the last time I drank, it brought out the emotional side of me, and that's the last thing my friends need to deal with right now. No one wants to claim responsibility of the drunk girl in the bathroom crying about her boyfriend, no matter the circumstances. So I take a small sip and put the glass down, careful not to even let myself get tipsy.

I turn and look at Talon, admiring his muscles and the

clean-cut lines of his jaw. He smells good, looks good, and I want to feel something toward him.

But I don't. I don't feel anything, and the more I watch my friends enjoy life, the more panicked I feel that something is irreplaceably broken inside of me.

My friends finish off their drinks and grow restless, and decide to move the party to Rob's house for a bonfire. I decline, saying that I'm going to order food and head home, taking Lisa's car back to my place.

I used to love barn parties like that, but can't right now. I can only hold up the front that everything is okay for a little while, and my soul is tired. I'm going to stumble and fall soon, dropping the facade and revealing to everyone that there's nothing left inside me.

4

CHASE

I stand in front of the vent feeling cool air blowing in my face. It feels fantastic, and couldn't have come at a better time since the summer heat index is rising daily. The air conditioner repair guy left only an hour ago, and I turned down the air as cool as it can go in an attempt to get the apartment down to a comfortable temperature. I need to put away everything I ordered online, including bringing the old mattress downstairs.

I don't want to move away from the air, but I have shit to do and am hanging out with Josh at the bar tonight. I told him I can jump right in and take over, but he insisted on one day to 'shadow' him and then another few for training. It's the proper way to do things, I suppose, and the pace of life is slower here in Summer Hill than what I'm used to.

And I should stop taking risks.

I've been running on luck, and luck runs out. One day shit is going to hit the fan and I'll get hurt beyond repair. I close my eyes, inhale one last breath of cold air, and then go into the bedroom and heft the old mattress down the stairs and over by the barn that's full of junk. I opened the barn doors earlier this morning only to promptly close them, overwhelmed by the sight of things. I'm going to need multiple dumpsters to get rid of all that shit.

I stop by the river, watching the water rush by, and think of the woman's words from her message about the river flooding. I stand there a moment longer than I planned, summer sun baking the back of my neck, lost in thought about her. I woke up thinking about her and had to listen to one more message, which was left a few days from the previous. All she said was that she took Tinkerbell and Dolly to the vet, and he liked her idea for the cat shelf.

I went back and listened to the older messages again, not able to get enough of her poetic words.

It's insane.

It's weird.

I'm wasting my time.

I need to mass-delete all the messages and set up my own voicemail. If I'm going to be staying in this town for a while, I should start to establish some sort of life for myself. But I can't bring myself to delete the messages. I need to listen to them all at least.

Like a good book that keeps you flipping pages, I want to listen to message after message and hope for a happy ending for this woman. Which is weirder and more insane than the curiosity of listening to the messages in the first place.

I wipe sweat from my forehead and go inside, taking solace in the whirl of the air conditioner. I spent a few hours setting up the rest of my stuff and washing all the dust-covered dishes that were left in the cabinets. Hunger takes over and I finish off the casserole Melissa cooked.

Having no food left, I grab my keys and get in my Mustang, using the GPS to find my way into town to get groceries. Summer Hill is a small town but has a decent amount of stores for a town of its size. I get groceries and head back, hustling to get everything done in time to shower before going down to the bar.

Fridays are busy with discounted beer and karaoke. I stay behind the bar, trying not to cringe at the country music, and watch Josh talk to the regulars, filling drink orders without even having to ask. I've always been a bit of a people watcher, and am able to get a good read on most within minutes of meeting.

The night goes on and the crowd remains steady. I'm getting bored, and being bored usually leads me into trouble. Because being bored means my mind has time to wander, and when you stumble around in the dark, it's easy to trip and fall. And falling into the truth of why my life feels so unsatisfying isn't something I want to do.

I tap my fingers on the bar, half-listening to Josh and an old man named Joe talk about a cow being found with its stomach ripped open by mountain lions. A group of girls walks in, dressed in shorts and tight skirts, looking like they belonged in a club, not a hole-in-the-wall tavern like The Mill House. They go for a booth in the back, and Erica, one of the waitresses working tonight goes over to take their order, returning with a pitcher of margaritas.

A table that emptied minutes ago still has dirty dishes on it and seeing as I have nothing else to do, I go over and pick them up, taking them into the kitchen. When I come back, I see another group of women walk through the door. Two walked in, but my eyes go to one.

Her brunette hair blows back from the draft created by the open door, and her white dress swirls around her long, lean legs. She's not dressed like her friends—the girls in clubbing clothes—but rather looks like she should go to a fancy tea party with the Queen of England. I watch her for a moment, unable to get a read on her and decipher if she's stuck-up or a bit eccentric to be dressed like that in a place like this.

Josh catches me staring and raises his eyebrows.

"Who is that?" I ask him.

"Sierra Belmont," he says like the name should have some sort of impact on me. "Right, you have no idea who anyone is. Her parents pretty much own the town."

"They own the town?"

He nods and turns, filling a glass with beer. "You had to see the big, white plantation house on your way into town, right?"

"Yeah, it's hard to miss."

"That's their house. And most of the farmland in Summer Hill belongs to them. They sell their crops to big manufacturers. They're loaded."

I narrow my eyes, looking at Sierra's pretty face. She seems too unsure of herself to be stuck-up, though the fact that she hails from a rich family would lead me to believe that to be the truth.

"But they're good people," Josh goes on. I'm fairly certain everyone is a 'good person' to him. He has a tendency to see the good in everyone…including me. "Sierra doesn't come in here often, though. I honestly can't recall the last time she came in."

"It's one of her friend's birthdays," I say, reading the lips of the woman in tight black shorts and a leopard-print top.

"Oh, I should give them a free round," Josh says.

I just laugh and shake my head. I already planned to tell him that half-priced beer on the busiest night of the week is a huge loss, but I'm biding my time. The night goes on and I keep watching Sierra. She's quiet, smiling when her friends are looking, then retreating inside herself as soon as they look away.

When a group of guys shows up and one slides into the

booth close to her, I give myself a mental slap in the face. Sierra is pretty, with large breasts and a nice figure. I need to get my imagination under control. I go into the kitchen and help with some cleanup for a while before going back to the bar.

I'm surprised to see Sierra sitting there, Kindle in front of her, and a slight scowl on her face.

"I told you," she says to the guy next to her. "I have a boyfriend, and he'll be here any minute."

The guy next to her is on his fourth beer—I know because I saw him get served three and then he took one from his buddy—and doesn't believe Sierra. I don't either, and can tell right away she's a bad liar.

"I'm not worried about your boyfriend, baby," Beer Guy says and leans forward. "He's not here yet and I don't think he's coming."

"He is." Sierra pulls her shoulders in, looking uncomfortable.

"Why you gotta be like that?" Beer Guy goes on.

"I'm not being like anything," she shoots back.

"Just talk to me, sweet cheeks."

She shudders and shakes her head. "No, thanks."

"You know what, I took a chance talking to a pretty girl and you gotta go and be like that. You don't have a boyfriend and you don't have the balls to tell that to my face."

Sierra looks exasperated. The 'I have a boyfriend' line might be the oldest line of shit in the book, but it's said to let someone down gently. Hell, even I'd rather hear that than a blatant 'I'm not into you.' Beer Guy takes a swig, and turns, obviously checking out Sierra's breasts.

"I shoulda known you'd be a bitch," he mutters.

I rush forward but stop myself before I throw a punch and start a fight. And for some reason, I don't think Sierra wants to be rescued. She's looked uncomfortable being here since she walked through the door, but not scared or weak. So I play her game instead.

"Hey, babe," I say, coming up behind her. "Sorry I'm late. I got held up at work."

She turns around and looks into my eyes. God, she's gorgeous. I give her a small smile and an even smaller nod, then flick my eyes to the guy trying to pick her up, letting her know what's going on. A second passes and I'm regretting what I just said, thinking Sierra is going to get up and walk away, assuming I'm even worse than the guy next to her. Then her full lips pull into a smile.

"Oh, hey, *boyfriend*. I'm so glad you finally made it."

I would have laughed at her obviousness if I weren't well-versed in bullshitting. "Me too. Work was crazy. Being the CEO of a Fortune 500 company keeps me busy." She laughs, and I take the barstool next to her.

"You work too much. I think we should put that private jet to use this weekend and get away."

"Good idea. We can go to Hawaii?"

She lets out a dramatic sigh and shakes her head. "We just went there two weeks ago. How about Paris instead?"

"Too cliché. Iceland?"

"Too hipster."

Now I laugh. I put my hand on the counter and Sierra slides hers forward, so our fingers are touching. The gesture is small and is the last thing I expected to send shivers down my spine. "There's a little island in Scotland," I start. "Everything is rocky and green, and you feel like you're the only people left on earth when you stand on the cliff overlooking the ocean, feeling the spray of the waves on your face. Legend says mermaids gather in the coves on the cliff. Maybe we'll see one."

Her smile turns genuine and she looks at me like she's seeing me for the first time.

"It sounds lovely."

"It is. I've been there before. For business, of course."

Beer Guy leans over, eyeballing me. "You're her boyfriend?"

"I am," I say. "You got a problem with that?"

Drunk enough to say whatever is on his damn mind, Beer Guy widens his eyes and looks at me, taking in my muscles and tattoos, then runs his eyes over Sierra. "I didn't think a pretty lady like her would go for a guy like you."

"But you thought she'd go for a guy like you?"

Beer Guy lets out a snort, laughing for a second before realizing I insulted him. He finishes his beer, sets the bottle down, and gets up with an indiscernible huff.

"Thank you," Sierra says, taking her hand back. She leans in when she talks, having to speak over the music. Her brunette hair brushes over my arm, and we lock eyes again. Something passes through me when we do, almost like a faded memory being brought back to life.

I don't know this woman.

I have no memories of her.

So why does she feel so familiar?

"No problem. I'm Chase, by the way."

"Sierra. Nice to meet you." She puts her hands on her Kindle but doesn't turn it on. Her posture changes and she's back to looking uncomfortable.

"So...are you from around here?" I ask, acting like Josh didn't give me the rundown on her entire family mere minutes ago. The question perks her up. She's used to people in this town knowing who she is.

"I am. Are you?"

"I am now. I just moved here."

"Oh, nice. Welcome to Summer Hill. How do you like it?"

I shrug. "It's different than what I'm used to."

"It's like its own little world here. Where are you from?"

"A few places," I say with a laugh. "I was in New Jersey before this. And New York before that for a year. LA for a few years too, and I really have been to Scotland."

Her head tips as she looks at me with curiosity, letting her eyes wander over my body. It's obvious, yet innocent. It's like she's looking at a work of art, just taking it all in before she makes a judgment. I can't tell what the verdict is.

"Why did you move so much?"

"I was trying to find a place that felt like home." The words leave my mouth before I have a chance to think about it. The honesty shocks me since I've worked hard to deny it to myself. I'd told myself I moved around a lot because I didn't like being tied down, that staying in one place too long creates expectations and attachments to people, two things I did not want.

Sierra's green eyes soften. "Did you ever find a place that felt like home?"

I slowly shake my head. "Not yet."

"Maybe you'll find it here."

Behind us, the bar is full of life. The music is loud. Drinks slosh on the floor. The smell of cigarette smoke wafts through the open doors, carried in on the fresh night breeze, making the air stale. But all I see is Sierra.

"Maybe."

Josh sets a to-go bag on the counter in front of Sierra. "I see you've met my brother," he says to her.

Sierra looks from Josh to me. "Oh, I didn't know you were related."

Josh laughs. "Took me years to finally get him here. I had to use a guilt trip," Josh whisper-talks to Sierra, pretending like I can't hear. "He's going to take over for me after my wife has the twins."

"You'll have your hands full for sure. And you have a little girl already, right?"

"Yes. Dakota. She's enough of a handful on her own."

"She's cute. I saw her in church a few weeks ago." Sierra puts her money on the counter and slides her Kindle back into her purse.

"Thanks," Josh tells her. "Have a good night, Sierra. It's good to see you out again."

"You too. Good luck with everything." She slowly slides off the bar stool. "Thanks again, Chase. I appreciate it. That guy was rather persistent."

"No problem." I fight the compulsion to kiss her. "See you around."

"Yeah, I'm sure I will. Bye."

She pulls her keys out of her purse and heads out the door. I watch her leave, getting swallowed by the sea of people before disappearing out the door. Right as the red door swings closed, I see him.

Beer Guy.

He's staggering as he walks, cigarette hanging out of his mouth. Sierra's back is turned, and she doesn't see him coming. He's headed right to her, and he doesn't look happy.

5

SIERRA

*I*t's been well over a year since I felt even the slightest inkling of attraction to a man. The moment I set my eyes on Chase Henson, everything changed. Tall and muscular with tattoos covering his arms, he's a tall drink of water that I don't need but desperately want to sip. His well-structured face didn't help my case. The strong jaw, full lips that promise to give the best kisses, and deep, hazel eyes were enough on their own to make me have dirty thoughts.

But there was something else about him, something I could relate to but couldn't exactly put my finger on. Maybe it was the way he said he was trying to find a place that felt like home. Things changed this past year, and while I love Summer Hill like an old friend, the sense that I belong has vanished like whispers in the wind.

I press the unlock button on Lisa's key fob, then remember the battery has been dead in this thing for the last six months. It's turned into a bit of a running joke between us since she complains about it all the time but has yet to put in a new battery.

The sounds of the bar echo behind me, getting louder for a few seconds as the door opens before becoming muffled again as the doors swing closed.

"I knew you lied."

The gruff voice makes me jump and I drop the keys. I whirl around and see the guy from the bar taking fast and unsteady steps toward me.

"You don't have a boyfriend. Why you gotta be like that?"

"I'm not being like anything. Leave me alone."

"That guy with the tattoos isn't your boyfriend."

"It doesn't matter what he is to me." I push my shoulders back, trying to stand my ground. If I look him in the eye and don't show my fear, he'll back off, right? Or does that only work with bears? Shit. "I'm not interested, so go away."

"You like bad boys? I can do you one better and be a real bad man."

I roll my eyes and shake my head. "Does that line ever work?" I swallow, take a deep breath, and mentally debate kicking him in the balls or the stomach.

He advances, taking another drag of his cigarette, exhaling the smoke in my face. "What do you say, little lady? Want to get out of here?"

"Hey!" A loud, male voice reverberates off the parked cars surrounding me.

The drunk guy quickly turns, wobbles, and falls on his ass. I look past him and see Chase rushing out.

"Are you okay?" he asks me, gravel crunching under his feet.

"Yeah, I'm fine." My heart is in my throat, but I really am fine.

"Did he hurt you?"

"No, just annoyed me."

The drunk guy gets to his feet and looks at Chase, sizing him up. Realizing he'd lose that fight, he shakes his head and says he's getting out of here. Chase takes his arm and guides him to his truck, pushes him in the driver's seat and closes the door.

"He really shouldn't be driving," I say slowly, not taking my eyes off the truck.

Chase holds up a set of keys. "He won't be."

"You picked his pocket?"

"It's one of my many talents. He'll be passed out in a few minutes. Sleeping it off is the best thing for him."

"Good thinking." I readjust the strap of my purse and bend over to pick up the keys.

"Are you sure you're all right?" Chase asks again.

"Yes. I had it handled."

A smile plays on his lips like he doesn't believe me. "Sure."

I cock an eyebrow. "You think I can't handle myself?"

He holds up his hands innocently. "Oh, I think you can. In fact, I bet you're great at handling yourself."

I purse my lips. Is that supposed to be a sexual innuendo? And more importantly…do I want it to be?

I do. I think I really do.

"Sorry then," he goes on. "But from where I was standing, you looked a little, well, *frozen*."

"I was debating how to take him down without dropping my food," I tell him and then realize how ridiculous that sounds. We both laugh, and I shake my head. "But thanks. It was very chivalrous of you."

He takes a tentative step forward and shrugs. "Dealing with that guy isn't like slaying a dragon or anything."

The soft and haunting hoots of an owl come from the trees surrounding the parking lot. Chase turns, staring into the woods before he moves his gaze to the sky above us.

"I forgot how much I missed the stars," he says softly, almost as if it's a confession instead of a conversation. "Until I saw them again."

My heart is beating fast again. "I guess you don't see them well in the city."

"Not at all. The stars over that island in Scotland were the brightest I've ever seen. And when the sea is still, you can't tell where the water ends and the sky begins. You really do feel like you're the only person left in the world."

"Is that a scary feeling?"

He moves his eyes to me and shakes his head. "I don't know. I'm used to being alone." Then he blinks and looks away, almost as if he's embarrassed by what he just said.

"It sounds amazing. Were you there with someone?" I cringe at my words. Can I be any more obvious? The fact that I want to flirt with him sends a jolt through me, followed by a heavy crash of guilt. It's like I'm betraying Jake. Besides, I have nothing to give Chase. My heart is sitting in a shattered heap inside my cold, dark chest. I worked so hard to feel nothing that I've permanently broken myself. I don't think I'm capable of feeling anymore.

"No. I was there to steal a boat."

I blink, unsure if he's trying to be funny or not. He looks serious and doesn't offer a smile or a laugh to let me know he's joking. I tighten my grip on the bag of carry-out, and the paper crunches under my fingers.

"Thanks again, Chase," I say. "Have a good night."

He looks right into my eyes again, and for a moment, I don't want to go. "You too, Sierra."

$\sim$

"GRAN," I begin, setting my tea down. The delicate cup clinks against the saucer, and I carefully turn it, lining up the flowers on the cup with the matching ones on the saucer. It's Sunday evening, and I'm sitting on the large covered porch sipping tea with my grandmother until dinner is ready. I don't like tea, but I like talking with Gran. A true southern woman, my Gran is well-mannered and well-versed in Summer Hill's latest gossip. "Did you know that Josh Henson has a brother, Chase?"

"Chase Henson. I haven't heard that name in years," she says, adding another sugar cube to her tea before gently stirring it with a porcelain spoon.

"So you know him?"

"I know of him," she says and gracefully lifts her tea. "Why do you ask, dear?"

"I met him the other night at The Mill House."

She tries to hide her smile behind her teacup. "You went to a bar?"

"Yeah, for Lisa's birthday."

"Good for you, honey." She lifts an eyebrow. "I take it that's the reason Lisa is late for dinner."

"What do you know about Chase?" I ask, bypassing saying anything about Lisa. She's not here yet because she and Rob had another fight Friday night, broke up, then got back together this morning. They're busy making up.

"If you recall, Josh and Chase's father was a truck driver."

"I remember," I say, though I can't remember the last time I saw Mr. Henson. He bordered between the town drunk and the town outsider. He was a big burly man, and Lisa and I always found him scary when we were children.

"Apparently he couldn't handle the long trips away from his wife, if you know what I mean."

"I don't—oh. He had an affair."

Gran nods and takes another drink of tea.

"So Chase…he's Josh's half-brother. That explains why I'd never seen him before. I wonder why he's here now."

"His father passed last week. I assume he came for the funeral."

"Oh my God." My eyes go wide and I suck in a quick

breath. "I had no idea. Josh and Chase both seemed so... so...normal."

"I don't think either boy was particularly close with their father, and he'd been sick for years, not that it makes it any easier."

"Right." I reach for my teacup, feeling horrible. If I see Chase again, I'll tell him I'm sorry for his loss. That I know how losing a loved one feels like you've been ripped in two and stitched up with a rusty needle, pieces hanging together by weak threads, ready to rip apart and tear open at any second.

If I see him again.

6

CHASE

I sit on the edge of a large rock, dew soaking the bottom of my jeans. I squint and look at the river, watching the sunlight dance off the rushing water. The Mill House is closed on Sundays, and the lot is empty except for me.

I can pretend I'm the only one in the world again.

Except I can't get *her* out of my head. I reach into my pocket and pull out my phone. I haven't listened to a message since Friday, and the want to hear her poetic words and the harrowing emotion in her voice weighs on me. I unlock the screen and bring up the messages.

The next message was left just hours after the previous one. I bite my lip, look out at the water again and then press play.

"I can't sleep," she starts, and her voice sends a jolt of familiarity through me. I'm a visual person. I remember faces, can pick up on the slightest mannerisms and expressions, but when it comes to matching voices to faces, I lack.

"Which isn't unusual," she goes on. "But tonight, it's worse. Tonight, I feel like the waves are too much to take, that I'm struggling to keep my head above the surface. Sometimes I let myself sink under and think about how easy it would be if I just slipped down to the bottom. No more struggling, no more fighting the current. I go under and then it's even harder to push back up. It's just darkness. Above me. Under me. Around me. And it hurts."

Again, her words are too close for comfort. Yet that's exactly what they bring: comfort. Because I feel it too. The darkness closing in on me, threatening the life inside of me. I haven't suffered a great loss like my mystery woman has. Her darkness comes from the outside.

Mine resides within.

~

I FOCUS on the space ahead of me, feet pounding on dry earth. It's weird to be running without music, and since all my songs were stored on the phone Dakota accidentally broke, I'll be without them for a while. I could put music on the new phone, but that would take up precious memory, and I need every bit I can get to keep the messages.

My pace slows as the trail thins. I've been following a deer path in the untamed woods and assume I've gone three or four miles away from the bar. The path has stayed near the river for most of my run, but a few paces ago it took a sharp turn away from the water. The trees grew sparse and the bright sun is now beating down on me. It's not as humid today as it has been, which helps make running in the afternoon bearable.

Staying in shape is important to me, mostly because a fast getaway was crucial to my survival before. And when I couldn't make a fast escape, then I needed to fight my way to freedom. I've never lost a fight.

The overgrown weeds make way to a neatly planted field,

and my mind flashes back to Josh's words about the Belmonts owning most of the farmland in this town. I stop and take a few minutes to stretch, looking at the acres of crops. Something crashes through the woods several yards behind me, and I whirl around, fists clenched.

A deer stops, staring at me with wide, black eyes. I let out a breath and unfurl my fists. Going on the defense, ready to fight, is second nature to me. This—the peaceful small-town setting—is so fucking weird to me.

I stand still and watch the deer, having a bit of a staring contest. The thing doesn't move an inch. The sound of a tractor starting up makes me turn, and when I look back, the deer is gone. I take a deep breath, wipe away the sweat that's dripping into my eyes, and continue my run, going along the outside of the field until I find what I assume is another deer path, though this one is much wider than before. Thankfully, it veers away from the field and the sun and into the woods again. It goes along the straight edge of the field, continuing for what has to be miles. I can't hear the river anymore, and the sounds of birds become almost deafening.

The path becomes more defined, with large rocks and fallen logs moved to the side. I jump over a pile of manure and notice the horseshoe imprints. I keep going, wondering how much farther the trail will lead before I come to an opening in the woods and then someone's barn.

Not knowing what lies ahead has never bothered me. People like to plan, to be prepared. But you never know what's going to happen. So why bother? I live my life day to day because hoping for anything more becomes an expectation. And disappointment goes hand in hand with expectations.

I continue running, feeling the burn in my legs from the changes in terrain. I go up a hill and pause to catch my breath. Then I hear it.

Music.

Softly drifting through the thick of trees and weeds.

Going slow, hardly making a sound, I move forward until I see the large barn through the forest. A white fence runs alongside it, stretching for miles. Lush green grass fills the pasture, and a small herd of horses stand close to each other in the middle, tails swishing away flies as they graze.

The music is coming from the barn and someone leads a tall gray horse into the pasture. The large animal hides her face. They stop as she opens the gate, gives the horse a hug, and then turns him out. With a kick of his heels, he takes off, running toward the others. They look up, and one whinnies a greeting. Another pins his ears back and lets out a sharp whine.

My experience with horses is limited, but I've always found them fascinating. I move my eyes away from the horses and back to the woman who let the gray horse out. My breath hitches in my chest.

Sierra.

She's walking back into the barn, stopping when a black cat crosses the pasture. Sierra sits on the ground, petting the cat. It steps right into her lap, pressing its face into her hand. Another comes running, and the two barn cats fight for her attention. The wind blows Sierra's hair around, and I can't help but find her beautiful.

Then I feel like a creep for just standing here, watching from the woods. That was never my intention on this run. I tear my eyes away and head home.

~

"I SHOULD HAVE DONE THIS SOONER," Josh says, parking his pickup along the street. "Better late than never, right?"

"It's fine," I tell him. "I've only been here a week."

"True."

I get out and stand on the sidewalk, looking at the two-story courthouse in the center of the town. Josh is giving me my official tour of the town today, which includes introducing me to some of the locals. People talk, he warned me, and are probably wondering about me. We start at a hardware store since I need to pick up a few things to continue fixing and improving the apartment above the bar.

A children's boutique is next to the hardware store, and we go so I can pick something out for Dakota, who's only four but loves fashion. Since I don't know the girl well, I have Josh grab an outfit she'd like and I buy it. Marissa, the owner, smiles and bats her lashes at me the whole time she wraps the overpriced dress in purple tissue paper.

"It's so nice to meet you, Chase. This town needs more handsome young men in it," she tells me, leaning over the counter to hand me the hot pink shopping bag. Freckled-covered cleavage threatens to spill out of her blouse, and Josh is dying next to me as he tries to contain his laughter.

"Uh, yeah." I take the bag and offer a small smile.

"Don't be a stranger," she coos. "It's so nice you want to shop for your niece. I can help you pick something out next time."

"Thanks." I give her a nod and take a step back, then quickly turn and follow Josh outside.

"You've made quite the impression on her," he laughs when the door closes. "She's single, you know."

I shudder and shake my head. "She reminds me of my grandma. My mom's mom," I add since Josh and I have different grandparents. "Which is weird, since I've only seen her like half a dozen times and she was always drunk."

Josh's pace slows and I wish I could eat my words. I know he feels bad for not standing up for me in the past. We were kids. I didn't expect him to. I don't reveal much about my past to anyone, and I'm careful not to let Josh know how shitty it was. He's a good person. There's no reason to upset him or further his guilt.

"Melissa works at the bank, right?" I ask, changing the subject.

"Yeah, she's a manager."

"Is she still working?"

"She wants to work as close to her due date as possible. Well, if she can make it that long. She's pretty uncomfortable already and still has several weeks to go."

"I can imagine."

"We can stop in and say hi, if you don't mind. She told me her co-workers keep asking about you."

I shake my head. "This town is weird."

We cross the street and enter the bank. A big plaque next to the door informs me of the historic significance of the building and was home to a standoff between an infamous outlaw and the sheriff over a hundred years ago.

"Hi, Josh," the security guard says to my brother. He's leaning against the wall, cell phone in hand, and looking bored.

"Hey, Wyatt. How are you doing today?"

Wyatt shrugs. "Same old, same old. You?"

"I'm good. Have you met my brother? This is Chase, Chase, this is Wyatt."

"Nice to meet you," Wyatt says and holds out his hand. He's tall and thin, with sandy blonde hair and sunburned cheeks. He looks at me then diverts his eyes, which has been common today. Seems everyone in this town knows me as the product of my father's affair and they've clearly sided with Team Judy Henson, though I can't really blame them. My father was a selfish asshole who got another woman pregnant while he was married to Judy, the kind-hearted schoolteacher.

"Y'all here to see Melissa?" Wyatt asks.

"Yeah," Josh says. "We were in town anyway so I thought I'd check on her. Her back was hurting bad this morning."

Feeling eyes on me, I turn and see the friend Sierra was with Friday night looking out at me from behind the counter. She has shoulder-length dark hair and has her brown eyes heavily rimmed in black liner.

"Hey, Josh," she calls. "Want me to get Melissa?"

"Only if she's not busy," Josh says and takes a step over to her.

"She's not. It's been slow today." She looks past Josh at me. "So this is the brother I keep hearing about?"

"Yeah, this is Chase."

"Hi, I'm Lisa. Sierra told me what you did," she starts. "Thanks for watching out for her."

I shrug. "It was nothing."

"Well, I appreciate it. And she does too." She gives me a smile. "I'll go get Melissa."

"What the hell happened?" Josh asks as soon as Lisa goes into the back.

"Some guy was bothering her. I made sure she got to her car all right. Really, it was nothing."

"Thanks," he says heavily. "I'd probably be forced to close if something bad happened to a Belmont at my bar."

"She seems pretty capable." My mind flashes to her face, set with determination as she told me she could handle herself. "I think she would have been fine."

"Either way, I'm glad you made sure it didn't get to that point."

Melissa waddles out of the backroom, and I swear she's bigger than the last time I saw her. I'm impressed she's still up and on her feet at this point. The doors open and close behind me, and out of habit I turn.

A cop walks in, going right up to the counter. I recognize

him as Lisa's boyfriend, who she was hanging all over at the bar Friday night. Lisa says something to him, and he gives me a smile and a wave.

Josh and I get lunch after that, and he orders a to-go box to take to Melissa, who was craving a burger and fries. Having spotted a bookstore on the way to the café, I tell him I'm going in while he runs the food to the bank. I stop before I cross the street, needing to get my fix. I look around, making sure there is no one around to interrupt me and pull my phone from my back pocket. That alone should be enough to make me delete all the messages. The mystery woman won't stop occupying my brain.

I need to delete and move on. But I can't. Not until I hear the last message.

"I'm not okay," she says and starts to cry, voice tight and hard to understand from all the emotion. Her sobbing is soft and almost beautiful. "Everyone keeps telling me that I'll be okay. They want me to be because they don't want to deal with me not being okay. I wish they knew that sometimes it's okay to not be okay."

I listen to the message again and move onto the next.

Wind blows through the speaker, masking her voice. I press the phone to my ear to hear better. "I keep thinking about the garden. I even sketched up a plan. But then I looked out back and realized how much work it's gonna be. I'm standing there now, looking at all the weeds that I don't want to deal with. Maybe next year."

It's the most normal message she's left, and it hits me the hardest. This woman desperately wants her loved one back and is calling as if he's going to answer. It's heartbreaking. I put my phone back in my pocket and walk across the street. A faded sign that reads *The Book Bag* hangs above the store. A little bell rings when I open the door and step inside, getting hit right away with the familiar smell of ink and paper. The store is small, packed full with as many books as possible. It's bright and airy in here, and the large windows along the storefront let in sunlight. Sierra is sitting behind the counter, nose buried in a book. She looks up and blinks.

"Chase." Her voice is welcome and familiar.

"Hey, Sierra," I say back and spy the cover of her book. "That's a good one."

She carefully slides a bookmark into place and closes the book, running her fingers over the cover almost as if she's caressing a beloved pet. "You've read it?"

I nod. "I read the whole series."

"Oh." She doesn't try to hide the surprise on her face but instead looks at me with curiosity. "This one is pretty dark."

"They get darker. But in a good way."

"That's what I've heard." She slides the book away and slips off the stool she was sitting on. "Are you looking for anything in particular?" Her question is innocent, one she probably asks all her customers, but I feel like she's testing me.

"What do you recommend?"

"Depends on what you like to read. Do you only read epic fantasy?"

"I'll read anything if it interests me."

"Even romance?"

I give her a grin. "I did read *Fifty Shades of Grey*."

"No way." She smiles right back at me.

"I mostly wanted to see what the fuss was about. Once I start a book, I tend to finish."

She laughs. "Did you read the other two?"

"I can't say I did. But thanks to the internet, I know how the story ends."

Sierra laughs again and her green eyes sparkle. She pushes a curtain of thick hair over her shoulder and comes around the counter. She's wearing denim shorts and a white T-shirt. Her long hair hangs straight around her face, and she's not wearing makeup. She's just as beautiful as the first time I saw her.

"I've been meaning to read this," she says and picks up a copy of *The Fake Wife* and hands it to me. "The movie came out last year, but I haven't seen it yet. I try to read the books before I watch the movies."

"The books are always better. And I haven't seen it or read it either. I'll take it."

She nods and goes back to the counter to ring me up. "Chase," she starts, saying my name slowly. It sounds so good coming from her lips. "I'm sorry."

"For what?"

"About your dad. I didn't know and—"

"It's okay. And thanks."

"So...does it feel like home yet?" she asks as I pay for the book.

My heart lurches in my chest. "No."

"Maybe it'll take time."

"Yeah, I'm sure it will."

She gives me my change and motions to the window. "What you see is what you get here. It's simple, but I like it. Life is complicated enough, right?"

"That's for sure. At least it won't take me long to figure out where things are."

Sierra smiles. "Very true. You can do a tour of the town in just a few hours. Or less. Probably less. Though there are rumors we might get a Target. People already come all over to go to the Walmart here. I can't imagine what a Target will do. Especially if it's one with a Starbucks inside."

I laugh. "I do miss getting coffee in the morning."

"Suzy's Cafe has the best coffee," she tells me. "I get a cup almost every morning before work."

"I'll have to try it. What about places to eat? Living in the city made it easy to never have to cook."

"Uh," she starts, smiling again, and I realize that I'll do just about anything to make this woman smile. "There are a few places. But if you're looking for something to take home, my go-to is Suzy's again. We do have a Pizza Hut, too. And Paragon has decent Chinese."

"And that's probably all the restaurants in town, right?"

"We do have a few sit-down places, and then The Mill House, of course."

"Of course." I look into Sierra's green eyes, trying to figure her out. She's guarded and it's almost as if she's shy. From what I saw Friday night, she's not. It's not often I come across someone I can't figure out, especially when they're not trying to fool me.

"Do you want to go out sometime?" I ask Sierra before I have a chance to overthink it.

She opens her mouth, but no words come out. She blinks a few times and shakes her head before looking down. "You don't want to go out with me."

I chuckle. "I do. Or else I wouldn't have asked you."

She takes a hold of her necklace, rubbing her thumb on a little cat charm. She takes in a shaky breath then looks back up, eyes meeting mine. For a split second, her walls come down and I see it.

Pain.

The same pain that's ricocheted its way through me, leaving scars on my soul.

"How about this," I start, giving Sierra my best smirk, the one that always works for me. "I take you out and then I'll decide if I want to go out with you or not."

"What if I decide I don't want to go out with you?"

"That won't happen."

"You seem rather sure of yourself."

"I am," I tell her. "I've never had any complaints before."

She lifts an eyebrow, and I can't tell if she's amused or annoyed. Dammit. Leave it to Sierra Belmont to get under my skin. "There's a first time for everything," she quips and flips my receipt over. "Call me then, and I'll see if I'm feeling it." She sticks the receipt in the bag and hands it to me. "Or text, because I actually don't like talking on the phone."

"You're honest. I like that."

"See if you still like that when I give you my honest opinion after you take me out."

I give her a smile again, shaking my head. The door opens, and we both turn to see Josh walking in.

"Hey, Sierra," he says then turns his gaze to me. "Ready? Sorry to rush you. We have to open soon, though."

"Yeah." I pull the bag off the counter. "Thanks for the recommendation. I'll call you."

"Bye, Chase."

Josh and I leave, making a beeline for his truck.

"You're going to call Sierra?" he asks once we're in.

"Yeah." I reach into the bag for the receipt, wanting to put her number in my phone before I lose it. "I got her number."

"Seriously?"

"I'm gonna pretend the shock in your voice isn't insulting."

"It's nothing personal," Josh starts, and I unfold the receipt. I recognize the number immediately. The blood drains from my face and my chest tightens. No. Fucking. Way. Sierra is the mystery woman. It all makes sense now and I feel dumb for not recognizing her voice. Though, in my defense, most of her messages were left when she was crying or emotional, distorting the way she sounds.

"Sierra's always been a little odd," Josh goes on, and I immediately feel defensive of her. "I didn't think you'd go for her. Though, I know a good-looking woman when I see one.

And those Belmonts are very selective. Don't tell Melissa, but I used to crush on Sierra's older sister, Samantha."

Josh's words go in one ear and out the other. I can't take my eyes off the number written on the thin strip of paper. Sierra's handwriting is big and loopy, messy yet neat in its own way. Shouldn't I be happy to find out who my mystery woman is?

"Chase?" Josh asks. "Is something wrong?"

Yes, something is terribly wrong.

"No, not at all." I force a smile and fold the receipt, shoving it back in the bag. Josh starts the truck and I turn, watching The Book Bag grow smaller and smaller out the window, heart in my throat.

I can't call Sierra.

I wanted this mystery woman to have a happy ending, to have found her second chance and started over. And that's why this is all wrong.

Things never end well for me.

7

SIERRA

"*I* gave Chase my number." I run my hand over Tinkerbell's sleek fur. She's purring like mad and cuddling even harder.

"You better not be joking." Lisa turns away from my closet that she's raiding and stares me right in the eyes.

"I'm not."

"I need details. Now." She comes over to the bed and sits at the foot. Dolly, who was lazily grooming herself, glares, growls, and then gets up. She's such a friendly cat, I know.

"He came into the store yesterday and—"

"This happened yesterday and you're just now telling me?"

I look down at Tink, admiring her black stripes against her soft gray fur. "Yeah."

"Go on."

"He asked for a book recommendation and then asked me out."

"And you said yes? That's awesome, Si! I'm so happy for you!"

"Don't get too excited. I told him I might go out with him, and I might not answer if he calls."

Lisa purses her lips. "Why?"

I shrug. "I just don't see the point. I don't want to go out with him." Or anyone, and I think it's a safe bet I'll always feel that way.

"Have you seen him? That man looks like he sprang from the pages of those bad-boy romances you're always reading. Take a chance."

I wrinkle my nose and shake my head.

"Don't be nervous," she goes on.

I bite my lip and think of what to say next. I'm not nervous. Or scared. Or excited. I don't feel anything.

"I'm not."

"Then what's the problem?"

I shake my head. "He's kind of irritating."

"Good!"

"How in the world is that good?"

She looks out the window and pulls her lip over her teeth, considering her words, which is very unlike say-it-like-it-is Lisa. "You were sad for so long and then shut down. You never went through the rest of the grieving process. You need to get irritated. Get mad. Hell, a full-out screaming match would be good for you at this point."

I keep my gaze on Tinkerbell, not knowing what to say back. It's true, and I didn't think anyone had noticed. "It's only been a year and a half."

"I know. And I know how hard it's been for you but it's time to move on."

"If you think I can move on then you have no idea how hard it's been." Tears pool in my eyes and anger wells inside of me. Tinkerbell jumps out of my arms and runs down the hall. My jaw trembles and I shake my head, trying to push back the tears. "Everyone is giving me a time limit and I'm sorry I can't follow it. I'm sorry to inconvenience you with my grief," I spit and angrily wipe away tears.

"I'm not giving you a time limit, but you're not the only one this has been hard on." Tears roll down her cheeks. "Jake was my friend too. I lost him and then I lost you."

"I'm still here."

"But you don't want to be." She stands up and waves her hands in the air as she talks. "I talk to you but you don't listen. We go out and it's like you're not even there. I know losing Jake hurt. I know it's been hard on you. But it's been hard on me too. I never know how to act around you. I don't want to be too happy. And when Rob and I have a fight, I feel like I can't go to you because I know you'd do anything to have one more fight with—" She cuts off and closes her eyes. "I feel like we're drifting apart and I don't know how to stop it. Because no matter how many times I reach out to you or throw you a rope so you can pull yourself to shore, you just let it go. I don't want to imagine how you feel, Sierra, but I know it hurts. And letting yourself get carried out to sea isn't the answer. You'll still hurt, but you'll be alone."

Her words are like a sucker punch to the stomach. I don't deny it. My throat thickens and what's left of my broken heart thumps in my chest.

Lisa takes in a slow breath and brings her arms in around herself. "Listen," she starts. "You're family *and* you're my best friend. They told me not to say anything, but I can't sit back and watch you wither away. I love you, Sierra, and I miss you."

"I miss you too," I croak out.

"Please don't be mad at me."

"I'm not."

Lisa flies around the bed and wraps her arms around me.

"I don't know what else to do, and it makes me feel like I'm failing you as a friend."

I hug her back, not knowing what to think. I want to be angry at her, to tell her to get over herself and not make me feel guilty on top of everything else. That it's bullshit to make my grief out to be a burden.

But at the same time, I see merit in her argument. I've shut down. Stopped feeling to spare myself the pain.

I don't want to go through life like this. Jake wouldn't want me to go through life like this either.

"I'm scared if I move on, I'll forget," I whisper, tears falling.

"You won't."

I move my head up and down, but don't believe her. How can she promise me that? She gives me one more squeeze then sits up, taking my hands. Lisa and I grew up together, so naturally, we fought like sisters, but we always made up fast, and none of the fights were serious.

"So." Lisa wipes her eyes and smiles. "When Chase calls, answer. Let him be a fling or even your first bad date. And if it gets serious, go with it."

I smile and nod like I'm supposed to. "Okay."

"Now…the concert Thursday night."

"What about it?"

"Please tell me you changed your mind and want to come with."

"Even before…" I let out a breath and shake my head, trying to center myself. "You know I'm not a fan of crowds. And didn't you just say that Rob took off work just to go with you?"

Lisa makes her face. "Yeah, he did."

"You're stuck with him then." I lean back against my pillows. Six months after Jake died, I stripped the bedding we'd picked out together, packed it away in bags, and stashed it in the cave of a basement this old house sits on. I drank a bottle of wine that night, and the alcohol flooded my emotional walls and I couldn't take it anymore.

The bedding I had before Jake moved in is back on the bed, and the little smiling tacos that are printed on my sheets stare up at me.

"I'm starving," Lisa announces and stands. "Want to go into town with me and get something to eat?"

"No, I don't want to get dressed." I look down at my sleeper shorts and tank top. "But I will go to my parents' and see what they're having for lunch."

Lisa grins. "Now you're talking my language."

We get into Lisa's truck and drive the mile-long gravel driveway connecting my house to the family mansion.

"Want to take bets on how long before my mom comments on my outfit?" I ask Lisa as we walk up to the front porch.

Lisa turns, dark hair blowing around her face in the wind. "I'm gonna give her ten minutes."

"I'm gonna go with one minute. I'd say less, but the shock is going to hit her and leave her speechless." I point to a Lexus parked in the breezeway. "Isn't that the Vanders' car?"

Lisa squints in the bright sun. "Yep. They have that douchy custom license plate. This will be fun."

The smile comes back to my face. "If I'd known they were going to be here I'd have changed into something even worse."

Lisa laughs and links her arm through mine. "Now this is the Sierra I love. Want to run home and get your 'my ideal weight is Dean Winchester on top of me' shirt?"

"Sadly, it's in the laundry. I dropped blueberry pie filling on it the other day." More like two weeks ago, and I'd forgotten about it. It's probably ruined now. "Which is rather fitting for a shirt about Dean, now that I think about it."

I open the front door and step in, kicking off my flip-flops. Melinda, my parents' housekeeper, rushes over to get the door, face flushed. Seeing that it's just Lisa and me, she relaxes.

"It's good to see you again, Ms. Sierra," she greets. "And Ms. Lisa. Always a pleasure."

"Hi, Mel," I say. "Is my mom around?"

"Yes, she's in the sunroom with Mr. and Mrs. Vander. Was she expecting you?"

"No, we're just here to raid the kitchen," I confess.

Melinda nods. "I'll let her know you're here."

"Thanks." Lisa and I go into the kitchen. It's one of my favorite rooms in this large plantation house. It was newly renovated a few years ago, updating the previous renovation from the early 1900s. Now the kitchen is huge, looking like something you'd find on Pinterest or on the cover of *Southern Living*.

My parents have a chef who cooks for them six days a week. The meals are perfectly proportioned, so there aren't usually leftovers. But we get lucky today and dig into the spread that's still out from lunch that was served to my mother and the Vanders. I fill a plate with fried okra and sweet potatoes, saving room for at least one beignet.

Lisa pours herself a full glass of wine and offers me the bottle. I decline and take my food out to the rear veranda. I'm able to eat all the fried okra—which is one of my favorite foods—before Mom comes out.

Lisa looks at her watch then up to me, raising her eyebrows.

"Oh, Sierra, darling," Mom gushes, smiling as soon as she sees me. Her excitement is genuine. I don't come over as often as I used to, even though the main reason was always for the food. "And Lisa! What a treat to have you girls over. And what perfect timing. The Vanders are heading out and you get to say hello before they leave."

"Hi, Mom," I say, setting my fork down. I stand from the patio table Lisa and I are sitting at and start to go over to give my mother a hug. Her eyes bulge when she sees me, and Lisa snickers into her wine glass. "And it's nice to see you again, Mr. and Mrs. Vander."

"What on earth are you wearing?" Mom whispers as she hugs me. "Are you not feeling well? You're not slipping into —*that*—again, are you?"

"I'm fine, Mom," I say, knowing she's worried I'm becoming depressed again…as if the heavy sadness ever left in the first place. My mind flashes back to what Lisa said not that long ago. How many times have I said, 'I'm fine' over the last year? Each time was a lie.

Mom doesn't know what else to say, so she goes on autopilot, being the perfect hostess as usual. Lisa and I make small talk with the Vanders before they go. I finish my food, then go inside to use the bathroom. The Vanders are slowly walking through the corridor that leads to the front door, and don't know I'm behind them.

"It's been long enough you'd think she'd be over it by now," Mrs. Vander says to her husband. "They weren't even together that long to begin with."

"It's a shame," Mr. Vander agrees. "She used to be such a lovely girl."

Mrs. Vander shakes her head, clicking her tongue. "There's no coming back once you've let yourself go that far."

My stomach twists and I take a sharp turn, entering a sitting room. I perch on the edge of an impressive hand-carved replica of a Victorian settee, and close my eyes. Should I be mad? Should I run out there and demand an apology? They are guests in my family's house and are gossiping about me. Should I be upset, sad, or embarrassed?

Probably. But right now, all I feel is tired. I inhale as I open my eyes and start to feel something else, something I haven't felt in a while. It starts deep within, rising from my bones and wrapping its cold, cruel hand around my broken heart.

Fear.

8

CHASE

I pop the top on my can of beer and sit back on the porch swing, pushing off the wooden boards beneath me just enough to sway back and forth through the air. A cool breeze comes from the north, bringing with it the heavy scent of rain.

The screen door opens and shuts, and the porch vibrates with each step Josh takes.

"That wasn't too awkward, was it?" he asks, leaning against the railing.

I let out a snort of laughter and bring my beer to my lips.

"I'll talk with her," Josh offers.

"It's fine. I get it, and I get that the wound is still fresh." Josh invited me over for a family dinner, one that included his mother, who goes through no trouble to cover up her feelings for me. "Sometimes people need someone to hate. To look at as the bad guy. Life is hard, and making someone be the villain makes you forget that your entire existence is just a crapshoot. Bad things happen to good people. Bad things happen to bad people. It's random chance. But blaming someone makes it easier." I take a glance at my brother. "And she needs me to be that person right now. So let her."

"That's wise. I didn't know you had so much infinite wisdom in you."

I shrug. "When you screw up enough, you learn shit."

"Screw up and learn shit." Josh laughs. "That's a good motto."

"It's been mine for years. Lord knows I've screwed up a time or two."

"Still, I feel like I should apologize. She's acting like a child, and honestly, it's embarrassing."

"She is, but don't worry about it." For the first hour I was over, Mrs. Henson pretended like I wasn't there. Didn't look at me, didn't acknowledge my presence at all. Even Dakota noticed and said something.

And I really do get it. Looking at me reminds her that her husband was unfaithful, that he sought comfort elsewhere, essentially making her feel like she wasn't good enough. I'm not the one to blame for my father's actions, but now that he's gone I'm the *only* one for her to blame.

Well, besides my mother. But that requires seeing her. Finding her. Knowing what the hell state of mind she'll be in that day depending on what drugs she pushed into her body.

The front door opens and a beagle runs out, tail wagging so hard his whole body shakes. I reach down and pet the dog, who jumps into my lap and licks my face.

"Hey, guys," Melissa says, coming out after the dog. "I had an idea since it's not every day I have two strong men in the house."

Josh gives her a look, but can't hold the fake anger for long. His face breaks into a smile, and I can't help but feel a slight twinge of jealousy to see the way he's looking at her. Not because I have the hots for Melissa, that's not it at all. And I'm not jealous of Josh per se, but of this whole situation.

A wife.

A family.

A stable home full of people who love you.

Living in the same town, surrounded by the same people day after day.

And being happy with it.

Maybe unsettled is a better term to use than jealous. Because seeing him like this is making me want something similar too.

"What do you have in mind?" Josh asks.

"We should switch Dakota's bed to her big-girl bed before the twins arrive, so it's not a bunch of change at once. We've had that new bedroom set for over a month now and haven't put it together."

"That is a good idea." Josh looks at me. "The set was delivered into the barn, so we'll have to carry it up, assemble it, and take her old furniture out. Do you mind?"

"Not at all." I take a long drink of my beer and get up.

"You sure? Saying it out loud makes me realize how awful it's going to be."

I laugh. "I have nothing else to do. And you're family. It's what we do, right?"

～

It's nearing ten o'clock when I finally leave Josh's house. We ran into a bit of trouble putting the new bed together since several small parts were missing and we had to improvise. Mrs. Henson left not long after we started moving furniture, and Melissa stayed downstairs with Dakota, leaving just Josh and me to do the heavy lifting. It might sound weird to say I enjoyed it, but I did. Having that time to just hang out with my brother, helping him with something as mundane as a new bedroom set for his daughter was nice. Normal. Maybe I can get used to this after all.

The bar parking lot is full, and I slowly drive through the uneven rows of parked cars and trucks—mostly trucks—and park around back near the rear entrance to the place. I shut off the car and grab my phone, hesitating for a moment before getting out.

I haven't listened to a single message since I found out Sierra was the mystery woman. Moral dilemmas aren't things I typically waste time with, but this time I don't know what's right. On one hand, I've already listened to a handful of messages. What's the harm in listening to more? But on the other, the messages are intimate. Not meant for anyone to hear, especially not me.

I open my voicemail and look at the display, noticing that the next message to listen to was left exactly a year ago today. I don't believe in fate, but come on…this is a pretty big coincidence. With no hesitation, I press play.

"Happy birthday," Sierra whispers. "I just…I wanted to tell…" She starts crying and the phone goes dead.

There are few things in life that I regret. That's not to say I've never made a bad decision—I do those almost daily—but I deal with it and move on.

Right now, I'm regretting listening to that message. Because now I know today is Sierra's dead boyfriend's birthday, and the hurt is still there. Hearing her cry, even when it was a year ago, upsets me for some reason, and I can't get the ball of dread to leave my stomach. The sick feeling rises, tightening my chest.

I'm so fucking stupid sometimes.

I get out of the car and exhale. A shining blanket of stars covers the night sky. Around the back of The Mill House, the sounds of the bar are muted, like distant memories escaping with the breeze. The woods are alive with a chorus of bugs, and the steady sound of rushing water from the river soothes my soul.

And I still can't get Sierra out of my head.

Instead of going right up the stairs to my apartment, I go into the bar with the intention of making myself a Jack and Coke before trying my best to pass out and *not* think of her.

Turns out, going into the bar was the second stupid mistake of the night.

She's there.

Alone.

Sitting in a corner booth with two empty glasses in front of her. Her eyes are glossy. She's sad. And I know why.

Dammit.

Corey, a large man with small, dark eyes and a friendly smile, brings her another drink. I watch Sierra slide it in front of her and gulp a fourth down before taking a breath. She needs to slow down. Drinking away your problems —*your feelings*—isn't the way to go. Trust me. Been there, done that.

I cross the room and go behind the bar, finding Corey working on another drink order.

"Hey, Chase!" He gives a wave. "I thought you were off tonight."

"I am. Just passing through. How many drinks has Sierra had?" I ask, cutting right to the chase.

"Uh," Corey looks up as he thinks. He's one of the nicest guys you'll ever meet but is definitely not the smartest. "Three."

"What is she drinking?"

"The first was a Long Island. Second was a mint Julep. And I just brought her another Long Island."

"Jesus. Why didn't you cut her off?"

Corey gives me a blank stare. "She ordered them."

"That's a lot of alcohol for anyone, let alone someone

Sierra's size." I shake my head. Now's not the time to scold Corey. Rayne, the head cocktail waitress, was supposed to be helping him with stuff like this tonight anyway.

I fill a glass with water and grab a plate of French fries from the kitchen, and weave my way through the crowd to the back of the bar. Sierra is gone. Her drink is still on the table, half empty. Panic rises inside of me, knowing what she's going through and how drinking alone is the worst thing for her. I whirl around, sloshing the water down my hand, and find her standing with some random couple, who just ordered a tray of tequila shots.

"Sierra!" I call over the music. A song about a red Solo cup comes on and everyone goes crazy. My voice is lost in the cheers. I shove past someone and call her name again.

Sierra turns, lowering the shot from her lips. "Chase."

"I brought you food," I offer, able to tell right away that she's wasted. She's wearing another interesting outfit, though I'd be lying if I said the tight pink skirt didn't look good on her. The tank top she has on hugs her curves as well and shows off her large breasts perfectly. It's the big screen-print of a cat on the front that throws me.

"I'm not hungry," she says and turns away. I set the food down and take her arm. She looks back, eyes going to my fingers gently wrapped around her skin.

"I thought you said you were here alone," the guy from the couple says gruffly. He has his arm draped around his girlfriend, and is eyeing Sierra with obvious lust...and so is the girlfriend. I don't like the look of either of them and know their intentions with Sierra aren't noble.

"I am. Alone. Very alone," Sierra slurs. "Chase works here and brought me food. But," she starts and holds up her hand, closing one eye as she tries to look closely at me. "He doesn't know I like to dip my fries in cheese and not ketchup."

"No." I shake my head. "I didn't know. Let's go get you some."

Sierra shakes her head. "Nah. My friends bought me shots."

"I don't think you should take that," I say quietly. "You've had enough."

"Pshhh," she waves her hand in the air. "We're celebrating tonight. It's their anniversary. Isn't that amazing? People… people…" She closes her eyes for a moment then shakes her head. Fuck. I need to get her out of here. "She's giving him a surprise present. Isn't that so romantic?"

"Very," I say when it dawns on me that the surprise is a threesome. That's why they're shoving shots in Sierra's face and both looking at her like she's an all-you-can-eat buffet. Physically speaking, they made a good choice, but no one is taking Sierra home when she's drunk like this. I won't fucking allow it.

"Want to know what else is romantic?" I blurt.

"Yeah," Sierra says eagerly.

"I, uh, have to show you." What the hell is wrong with me? I'm usually a good bullshitter and an even better liar. There's something about Sierra that's causing me to panic in a way I never have before.

Because I care about her.

The guy steps forward and puts his hand on Sierra's shoulder. She shies away, moving closer to me for comfort.

"Come on, sweetheart," he says, voice thick like gravel. "We ain't got all night."

"Right." Sierra smiles and nods, then brings the shot glass to her mouth and downs the tequila with a shudder. Not even a minute later she looks at me, eyes wide. "I think you were right. I shouldn't have done that."

"Let's get some air." I take her arm, grab the water, and look at the couple. "Good luck finding somebody else."

The girl looks shocked, and the guy is pissed. Sierra wobbles on her heels, holding onto me for balance. We leave out the back and I offer Sierra the water. She takes a small sip and lets out a breath.

"I want to feel normal and not be sad," she breathes. "For one night. Is that terrible?"

"No," I tell her. "It's not."

I take her hand and lead her down to the river. We sit on a rock, and Sierra rests her head on my shoulder, eyes falling shut. We stay like that for a few minutes.

"Do you want me to take you home?" I ask.

"Not yet. I like listening to the water."

"I do too."

She shivers and inches closer.

"Do you want a jacket?"

"That'd be nice," she slurs.

"I can get you one. Don't fall into the water and drown while I'm gone, okay?"

She slowly moves her head up and down. I stand, take a step, and decide leaving her drunk on a riverbank is a terrible idea. "Come with me."

I extend my hand to help her up. She takes a few paces, then stops, doubles over, and throws up. I spring forward, pulling her hair back just in time. She retches again and the smell of tequila and stomach bile permeates the night air.

"Better out than in." I try to comfort her.

"I'm sorry," she tells me, wiping her mouth.

"Hey," I say and look into her eyes. There's a good chance she won't remember a thing in the morning. But I don't leave things to chance. She has no idea I know about her past, and it needs to stay that way. "It's okay. Don't feel bad. Come inside and get some water and lay down."

She wrinkles her nose. "I don't want to go back into the bar. The smell of smoke…"

"We won't go into the bar."

"Oh. Okay."

On shaky legs, she comes up the stairs to my apartment with me. I turn on the lights and take her to a kitchen chair. She puts her head down on the table, groaning. I get her water and a damp rag to wipe her face.

Sitting next to her, I gingerly lift her head up and run the rag over her chin. She takes another small drink of water and looks around the apartment, tears filling her eyes.

"Is there someone you want me to call?" I ask.

"No. Lisa is at a concert tonight. I'm just tired."

"You can lay down here if you want."

She takes in an unsteady breath and nods. "Okay."

I help her up and lead her to the bathroom, then take her into my room, tossing a T-shirt and boxers onto the unmade bed in case she wants to change.

"I'll, uh, come in and check on you."

She nods and starts to pull her shirt over her head. My dick tells me to stay and watch because seeing Sierra strip would be one of the hottest things I've ever witnessed. Then another part of me speaks up, a part that usually keeps its mouth shut.

My heart.

It tells me that Sierra deserves respect, that she's unlike anyone I've met before, I know the real reason she drank herself into oblivion tonight. Before I catch a glimpse of her perfect tits, I turn and shut the door.

Realizing that Sierra didn't have a purse on her when she left the bar, I hurry down the stairs to look for it, knowing that it's already too late.

"Chase," Rayne calls, seeing me look under the booth Sierra had previously occupied. "Looking for this?" She holds up a little pink purse.

"I think so. Is it Sierra's?"

"Yeah. I grabbed it the first time she dropped it. I haven't seen her though." Rayne gives me a worried look. "Have you?"

"Yeah. I took her home," I say.

"Thank God. Want me to put this in the safe?"

"I'll take it to her. Thanks, Rayne."

She gives me a smile. "No problem."

I rush back upstairs and look in on Sierra. Her skirt and shirt are on the floor, and she's in my bed, curled up under the blankets, fast asleep. I leave the room again, keeping the door cracked in case she wakes up sick or something.

I sit on the couch with a weird feeling growing in my chest. I've never taken care of anyone before. And I don't know if this weird feeling is stemming from doing a good deed—another thing I'm not used to—or something else.

Something I don't want to admit to myself.

That I'm starting to have feelings for this woman, a woman I've only talked to a handful of times.

But there's so much more to Sierra than that. Her messages spoke to me before I could put a face to the voice. I knew I shouldn't have listened to them.

Screw up and learn, right? What the hell am I going to learn from this?

9

SIERRA

I wake with a dry mouth and a pounding headache. If it weren't for the need to use the bathroom, I could go back to sleep for the rest of the afternoon. Slowly, I blink open my eyes, squinting from the bright sun shining through the large window.

I'm in Chase's bed, and I remember everything from last night. I think. Maybe? Crap. I push myself up and realize I'm wearing his clothes. Okay. Don't remember that. I close my eyes and think backward and finally recall him leading me into his room and leaving. I changed and passed out. From there, my mind is blank. I assume I stayed asleep the whole time, but I can't be sure.

Before I get up, I take a minute to look around the room. It's long and narrow, and the wall the bed is pushed up against is exposed brick. I touch it, feeling the rough stone beneath my fingers. We're above the bar, and I had no idea an apartment was up here.

Chase's bed is plain with white sheets and a dark blue soft, down comforter. A bookshelf is against the wall next to the bed, and it looks and smells new like it was just put together. The bottom two shelves are full of books, and the rest of it is empty. He wasn't lying when he said he reads anything. The books vary from thriller to historical fiction. Epic fantasy seems to be his favorite.

Across the bed is a dresser and there is absolutely nothing on it. A single lamp sits on the nightstand next to the bed, along with a glass of water, a bottle of Advil, and a hand-written note. I pick it up and unfold the paper.

Sierra-

Thought you might need this.

He didn't sign his name, but I know Chase wrote it. I read his simple words twice. Why does his compassion surprise me? I try not to judge people before I get to know them, but there are some snap judgments I can't help.

And tall, muscular men with tattoos and eyes you can drown in are usually nothing but trouble. Usually. I've been wrong before.

I take an Advil and drink most of the water before getting up and gathering my clothes. I think there is vomit on my skirt, and a wave of embarrassment comes over me. I haven't thrown up from drinking too much since I was nineteen. I shake my head and fold my skirt so the mysterious stain is safely tucked inside and away from my hands. Then I go to the bathroom, pee, and do my best to remove my smeared eyeliner.

The house is silent besides the quiet hum of the air condi-tioner. Holding my breath, I tiptoe out, wincing when the floorboards creak beneath my bare feet. A floor-to-ceiling window in the living room gives an impressive view of the river below. But an even more impressive view might be Chase, looking uncomfortable on the couch, still asleep. The book he bought days ago is resting on his chest.

Carefully, I move down the hall and shiver. What does he have his air set to? Arctic? He's wearing only boxers and has to be cold. I go back to his bedroom and take the comforter off his bed, set on covering him up and trying to sneak out of here without being seen.

I furtively move to him and pause, noticing a long scar that runs the length of his thigh. It's straight and neat, looking like the result of an operation to fix a broken bone. I tear my eyes away and raise the blanket. The moment it touches his skin, he startles awake so suddenly it causes me to jump back. The book falls to the wooden floor with a thud.

"Sierra. Sorry, didn't mean to startle you. What are you doing?" he asks, wide-eyed and fully awake. It takes me a few blinks, some stretches, and at least one eye-rub before I can form a coherent thought.

"I was going to smother you in your sleep."

Chase blinks, looks at the blanket and then me. "That wouldn't work, you know. Go for a plastic bag next time. Get it around my head and tie it at the neck."

"Noted."

He shifts his gaze and smiles. "What were you really doing?"

"I thought you were cold. I was going to cover you up."

"Oh," he says as if that's more shocking to hear than me trying to murder him. "Uh, thanks. It is a little chilly in here, I suppose."

"A little? What do you have your air set to?"

"Sixty-two."

I blink. "That's freezing."

"Trust me, I know. But this place isn't well insulated and doesn't retain the cool air well. By the afternoon it'll be twenty degrees warmer in here. I try to get a head start by keeping it cool at night."

"Oh. That makes sense, I guess."

He stands and pushes his shoulders back. There are scars

on his chest, but are harder to see since they are hidden beneath the ink of his tattoos. Which I'm not looking at. And not finding incredibly sexy.

"How are you feeling?" he asks and runs a hand through his hair, made messy from sleep.

"I'm not sure."

Chase laughs. "Maybe you're still drunk."

"No. I'm not. My head hurts and I'm dreading the stomachache that's going to come on later in the day." I pull my arms in around myself and look into Chase's hazel eyes. "Thanks for everything last night."

He gives me his trademark shrug, a move I assume he's perfected over the years. One that says he doesn't care, that he's not invested, and he doesn't feel anything toward the words spoken.

It's something I tried to learn and tried even harder to make myself believe. I didn't want to care. I didn't want to be invested in anything. And mostly, I didn't want to feel anything toward anything at all.

I failed.

"It was nothing," he says casually, and then smiles. "Were you really going to have a threesome with that couple?"

"What?"

"They wanted you to join in on their 'romantic surprise'," he laughs.

"That's what they wanted?" My hands fly to my face. "Oh my God."

Chase is laughing even harder. "You didn't know?"

"No!" I can feel the blood rushing to my cheeks. "I thought they were just being nice."

"Oh, they were being nice. Nice enough to get you to go home with them and then be bad. Very, very bad."

"Oh. My. God." I shake my head, not sure if I can look at Chase ever again. "I guess I owe you even more now."

"You don't owe me anything, Sierra."

I like the way he says my name. Slowly. Softly. I raise my head and meet his gaze. "Okay."

"Are you hungry? You really should eat, even if you don't feel like it."

"I am, but the thought of food is very off-putting."

"That's a typical hangover."

I shake my head. "I haven't had a hangover since college."

Chase steps closer and a chill runs down my spine, one so deep into my bone I'm unable to hide the shiver. Chase picks up the blanket and wraps it around my shoulders, letting his hands slide down my arms.

Is it completely crazy that I want to step into him, to rest my head against his chest and listen to his heartbeat? Yes. Yes, it is.

"Why were you at the bar last night?" he asks quietly, almost as if he already knows the answer and is waiting for me to tell the truth.

I take in a breath. Last night was a bad night. I went through a maelstrom of emotions last night. It was Jake's birthday, and I woke up not thinking about it. I made it through breakfast and a shower before it hit me. Guilt took over, and I pulled out old photos of the two of us to look at, reminding me of what we had. I spent the morning crying and was late to work because of it.

Then regret for not going to the Chainsmokers concert hit, and then I remembered I gave Chase my number and he hadn't called.

"I was going to yell at you," I confess.

Chase's eyebrows go up. "At me? Why?"

"You said you'd call and you never did. Why didn't you call?"

His face falls and he looks at the floor for a moment. He opens his mouth, contemplating his words, looking as if he's about to confess something. Then he shakes his head and looks back into my eyes.

"I thought about what you said. That you're not the type of girl I'd want to date. You were right, but you had it the other way around. I'm not the kind of guy you want to date."

A beat passes between us, and my heart is hammering away in my chest. He's making me nervous. Irritated. And a little turned on.

He's making me *feel.*

"And now I understand how insulting it is to be told who'd you want to date."

"Right?" he quips. "I'm sorry. I should have called."

"It's okay." I pull the blanket tighter around myself and look out the window. Beams of sunlight bounce off the water, and shadows dance along the shore. A deer emerges from the woods to get a drink.

"She comes almost every morning," Chase says softly.

"She's beautiful."

"Yeah," he agrees, but he's not looking at the deer. "She is."

Not making any sudden movements, we inch to the window to watch the deer. She takes her time getting water and then leaps off into the woods. A few more follow, moving so fast they're just blurs of fawn amongst shades of green.

"Do you want to get something for breakfast?" Chase asks. "I'd offer to make you something, but I'm still adjusting to this whole 'I have to cook for myself' thing like I told you about."

I smile and turn to him, appreciating the full beauty of his stubble-covered face. "Yeah, I'm getting—wait. No. We can't."

"Why?"

"If we go out for breakfast together, especially with me dressed like this, people will think we slept together."

"Is that a bad thing?" He flashes a grin and I struggle to hold onto my resolve.

I lower my gaze. "People talk."

"Then give them something to talk about."

I stare at a knot in the hardwood floor under my feet, wondering how many people walked over this in the years this building has been here. People who watched the river with sharp intent, needing the water to remain steady to keep the mill running. "Take me home and I'll make you breakfast as a thank you for taking care of me. I'm not a master chef or anything, but I'm not terrible either. I do have stuff to make beignets, actually."

Chase gives me a blank stare.

"You've never had a beignet?" My voice gets high-pitched from sheer horror.

"I don't even know what that is."

"Oh, you're in for a treat then. I won't tell you what it is either. You'll have to be surprised."

Chase laughs. "It's some weird southern food, like the fried lobster everyone around here loves, isn't it?"

"Crawfish," I correct. "And if it were, you wouldn't try it?"

"Not unless you want to hit me with an EpiPen minutes later."

"Oh. You're allergic to shellfish?"

"Very."

"Good thing you told me. And no, beignets aren't fish. It's a dessert-ish food."

"Dessert-ish?"

"Yeah."

"That's not a word."

I raise an eyebrow. "I just said it, so it is a word."

"I'm pretty sure it's not."

I hike an eyebrow. "It's not like we're playing Scrabble

here. Dessert-ish is a word and I'm going to use it every chance I get. Just to annoy you."

Chase watches me, smile growing. I shake my head, but end up smiling too. He moves away from the window. "You left your purse at the bar." He picks up my little pink clutch and hands it to me. "One of the waitresses saw you drop it which leads me to believe she got it in time, but check to see if anything is missing."

"Shit. I forgot about it." I take the purse from him and open it. I don't keep much in my purse, just my wallet, phone, keys, and lip gloss. "It's all here, thankfully." I pull my phone out and see the battery is dead. The only person who'd call me overnight would be Lisa anyway.

Chase opens the fridge, pulls out orange juice, and pours himself a glass. "Want some?"

"Yeah. Just a little bit though."

He pours half a glass and hands it to me. We move to the couch and sit in silence, watching the early morning sun shine down on the river. Minutes pass in silence, but it's anything but awkward. As if Chase and I have some sort of unspoken understanding between us, sitting next to him is comforting.

I finish the orange juice and feel sluggish again. I lean back on the couch, eyes growing heavy. Chase rests his back against the cushions too and lets his head fall to the side so he's looking at me. I inhale and smile, searching his deep eyes for answers about him.

"Tired?" he asks softly.

"Yeah. It's hitting me all at once."

"You can go back to sleep. I'll let you take the blanket." He gives me his crooked smile again. I thought it was deliberate before because no one has a smile that cocky and sexy without trying. He looks tired too, and I don't think he's trying.

"You only have one blanket?"

"Yeah. I usually sleep in my bed with it, so it's never been a problem."

"But what if someone stays over?"

"I've never run into that issue before. When attractive women sleep in my bed I'm usually in there with them."

I roll my eyes and pull the blanket out from around my shoulders. I cover us both up, and Chase leans in, reaching out and tucking my hair behind my ear. Our eyes lock and I think he's going to kiss me.

I want him to, though in the back of my mind I'm well aware that I threw up last night, passed out, and have yet to brush my teeth.

A knock on the door interrupts us and Chase's brow furrows. It's early. No one comes over this early with good news. He springs up and strides to the door. I stand, loosely holding the blanket in my hands.

Chase opens the door, revealing his brother. My heart lurches in my chest, and I'm sent backward through time and space and it's like I'm standing in The Book Bag listening to that phone call all over again. Josh has bad news. Terrible news. Someone died. Chase's sister-in-law lost the babies. His niece was in a horrible accident.

"Sorry, didn't mean to wake you," Josh starts. "The shipment that's supposed to come at five pm is here at five fucking am. I hate asking but can—" he cuts off, noticing me. Josh looks at me, taking in what I'm wearing, then back at Chase. He raises his eyebrows, tries not to smile, and fails.

No one is dying. No one is hurt. The only thing that's wrong is a delivery service not knowing the difference between AM and PM. So why am I teetering on the edge of a panic attack?

"I'll be right down," Chase tells him. "Let me, uh, get dressed."

"Sure. Sorry to interrupt. Morning, Sierra."

Chase closes the door and turns, grinning. "So that thing you were saying about people thinking we slept together..." The smile disappears from his face. "Are you okay?"

In an instant, he's here, in front of me. I squeeze my eyes shut, pushing back the tears. My hands shake and my stomach flip-flops. Suddenly I can't breathe and I desperately try to suck in air.

"Sierra?" Chase whispers and takes my trembling hands in his.

"Something's wrong." My voice comes out breathy and uneven. "I don't know what. But it is. Really, really wrong."

"You're having a panic attack. Nothing is wrong. It's okay," he soothes. moving closer and wrapping his arms around me, gently cradling me to his chest.

His skin is warm. Comforting. I don't want to move, but a few of the broken pieces of my heart scream for me to shove him away. I shouldn't find solace in another man's embrace.

Not yet.

Not now.

Not ever.

He slides his hands down my back and pulls me closer, holding me still for a minute before reaching up with one hand and stroking my hair. I'm still shaking, heart still racing. Still struggling to breathe.

Chase shuffles us back to the couch. My feet get caught in the blanket that's loosely hanging from my left hand, and I start to fall. He catches me, sitting heavily on the couch and pulling me with him.

"Hey," he whispers. "It's okay. Take a deep breath."

"I...I can't."

He puts his hand to my chest, fingers gently touching my collarbone. "Inhale," he instructs.

I take in a deep breath and my breasts rise, pushing

against the palm of his hand. I know what the touch is doing to him and he fights against the struggle so he can help me.

"Hold it. One…two…three. Now slowly exhale."

My eyes close as I let out my breath, and he has me repeat the process three more times. He pulls me into his lap and wraps the blanket around my shoulders. I close my eyes again, fighting against everything inside of me that wants to be close to him. I'm still shaking, still feeling like the world is closing in around me and there's nothing I can do to stop it. Chase holds me, not saying a word until my trembling stops.

I let out a sigh and feel embarrassed. I've never been a shy person, but I've never dealt with anxiety well and having people see me freak out is the last thing I want.

"Sorry."

"Don't be," Chase whispers. "Are you okay?"

"I am now. Thank you. Again. You must think I'm a total basket case."

"I think the opposite."

I let out a nervous laugh. "Between being unable to get that guy to leave me alone at the bar, drinking too much, and then *this*, you can't be thinking I'm a winner or anything."

"Panic attacks aren't anything to be embarrassed about."

I shake my head, agreeing with him yet not believing him. Because I am embarrassed, and my life has been one mess after another. "You seem to be familiar with them."

"They're not all that uncommon in my previous line of work."

"What did you used to do?"

"That's a story for another day."

I lift my head off his chest and stare at him.

"What?" he asks.

"Nothing. Just trying to decide if you're full of shit or not."

He holds my gaze for a few seconds, and his eyes darken. "I kinda wish I was."

I tip my head and study him, but as hard as I try, I can't figure this man out. I'm not the best at reading people, but I can usually tell when I'm flat-out being lied to.

Chase isn't lying.

I rest my head on his chest again, eyelids feeling heavy. Chase folds his arms around me again and lets his head fall against mine. Maybe I'm more dehydrated than I thought or suffering from exhaustion, but laying here with Chase feels *right*. I forgot how good it feels to be wrapped in someone's arms.

Someone *else's* arms.

"Your brother is probably wondering where you are."

"Yeah," he mumbles and then gives me a cheeky grin. "He probably thinks we're having a quickie before I go down."

"He probably does. Like really, he's down there rolling his eyes and checking his watch."

Chase laughs. "I'll make sure to tell him you overdid it on tequila and the puke in the yard is yours."

"Thanks," I say flatly. "But really...thanks."

"You're welcome." He brings his hand down my arm, stopping when his thumb rests on the pulse-point of my wrist. My eyes shut again and I yawn. "You can take the bed and go back to sleep if you want."

"I should go home and shower then try to get a few hours of sleep before work."

"Ouch. When do you go in?"

"Ten-thirty, so it's not too bad. We open at eleven on Fridays. So I guess we'll take a rain-check for breakfast."

"Deal. Just to be sure, does that include you spending the night again? Because if it does, I have a different idea on how to pass the time."

"No."

"You mean not yet."

I just shake my head and sit up. Pulling myself away from Chase is harder than I expected, and once the heat of his skin is away from mine, I shiver.

"Drink a lot of water," he says and steps away, picking his jeans up from the floor. "It'll help with the hangover." He gets dressed and I'm not sure if I should look away or not, which doesn't make sense since I'd been looking at him in only boxers all morning. But there's something intimate about getting dressed like this because it implies we're comfortable enough around each other to get *un*dressed.

He turns to get his shirt and I see yet another scar on his back. It's small, but I can tell the wound was deep. My first thought is that someone stabbed him in the back—literally.

"I'll walk you out," he offers and pulls his T-shirt over his head. I grab my clothes, step into my shoes, and pull my keys from my purse. "Thanks again," I tell Chase when we near my car, which surprisingly isn't the only one left in the lot.

"You don't have to thank me, Sierra."

"I want to."

"I'm glad you do." He tips his head down, blocking out the early morning sun. "I'll call you. For real this time."

10

CHASE

"You move fast."

"Is that supposed to be a compliment?" I ask my brother. We just finished unloading the truck that showed up twelve hours early and are sitting in the bar having a drink.

"It's an observation. You just got Sierra's number and you already slept with her."

"Actually," I start and pull the tab off my Coke can. "I didn't."

Josh looks across the bar top at me, waiting for me to explain.

"She drank too much and needed a place to crash. That's all."

"Oh."

"You look disappointed," I say.

Josh shrugs. "Nah. Just, uh, surprised."

I set the Coke down and cross my arms. "You're a terrible liar, you know."

Josh sighs. "I might have hoped that if you got involved with Sierra it would make you want to stay here."

"I am here."

Now it's Josh's turn to stare at me incredulously. "For now. Come on...we both know you don't stay in a place too long. It's been hard trying to keep in contact with you because I never know where you are, what you're doing, or if you've been arrested...or worse. I know I can't convince you to change professions, but maybe a woman can."

My go-to response to a statement like that is to get offended, defend myself, and probably say something shitty. Josh is my brother and probably the only person in the fucking world who actually gives a shit about me. So I bite my tongue.

"You know I don't believe that nothing happened," Josh goes on. "You take a girl home and *nothing* happens..." He arches his eyebrows and shakes his head. "You two looked pretty cozy this morning."

"I am serious," I say with a laugh. "She was pretty far gone, so I took her upstairs to lay down with the intention of taking her home later. She passed out until this morning."

"So noble."

"Shut up."

Josh snickers. "You like her."

"She's all right."

"Just all right. Sure."

"She's hot," I admit and press the sides in on my can. "I'd fuck her if I had the chance."

Josh raises an eyebrow. "Didn't you have the chance last night?"

I did have the chance and it would have been easy to put the moves on Sierra and have her begging for more. But I didn't. And it didn't even cross my mind.

"She was wasted."

"You do like her."

"Not like that."

Josh's face turns serious. "Why would liking someone 'like that' be a bad thing?"

I take a drink, buying myself a few extra seconds. I don't get emotionally involved because I don't want another human being to impact my happiness. Giving a person that kind of control is the dumbest thing we can do. I don't depend on anyone. Never have. Never will.

"Like you said before, we're different people."

Smarter than he lets on, Josh just nods, not buying it for a second. "Thanks again for helping this morning." He finishes his drink and gets up, stretching his arms above his head. "I need to get home to watch Dakota before Melissa has to leave for work. See you tonight."

Once Josh leaves, I go upstairs and crash in my bed. Sierra's sweet floral perfume clings to the sheets, and the scent calms me and turns me on at the same time. I toss and turn for half an hour before giving up. I grab my phone and go right to the voicemail.

I stare at the unheard messages, heart lurching at the thought of hearing her voice again. I should have told her. Confessed it all and gotten it over with. She might not have wanted to see me again, and I didn't want to risk that. Because I do have feelings for Sierra.

I press play on the next voicemail and a rush of adrenaline goes through me. My heart swells in my chest at the same time. I close my eyes and bring the phone to my ear. No one has ever made me feel this much.

"I dreamed that I died," Sierra starts, voice flat and void of emotion, "and when I woke up, I was disappointed. What the hell is wrong with me? I want to live but I feel guilty for wanting that. I try to think what you would say, but if you were here to give me advice, I wouldn't be in this situation. I know what's right isn't easy, and what's easy isn't always right. But right now...right now I feel like I have nothing left inside of me."

Her words hurt and I feel a maddening desperation to make everything better. I play the next messages, pulse racing. Eventually, I'll get to a message where she says she's okay. That's she's moved on and is enjoying her life again.

But—fuck—I know she's still struggling. Still hurting. And I hate it.

"Your voicemail changed," she starts, and this time she's trying not to cry. "I knew it would happen, but I didn't expect it to happen so soon. It still feels familiar to dial your number though." She lets out a heavy sigh. "I went to the hardware store and got stuff to work on the garden today. I drew out a plot of how I want it to look and everything. Now I just need the motivation to actually do it."

Lacking all self-control, I play the next message. "Mrs. Williams fell today. She sprained her wrist and is all bruised up, but she'll be okay. Her son called me from the hospital. I wanted to go, but the thought of walking through those doors...I haven't been there since...since...and I couldn't do it. I feel bad. She said she understood though. And I'm working the rest of the week so she doesn't have to come in."

I exit out of my voicemail and open the internet, doing a search for this Jake guy. It's a bad idea, and I'm well aware. It takes a few keyword changes to get his obituary and an article about the accident pulled up. Jake McLeland died from complications of an accident when a truck failed to yield and struck the driver's side of his Jeep. He was taken to Mercy Hospital and died from his injuries several hours later. No wonder Sierra can't go to the same hospital. She must have been there with him.

From what I can tell from the article on the accident, he was alone in the car and on his way home. His way home to Sierra. According to his obituary, he was doing his residency at another hospital, lived here in Summer Hill with Sierra, and was from a nearby town. A list of his accomplishments follows, and Jake was a model fucking citizen, not counting the fact he was on his way to becoming a doctor.

He went overseas and volunteered his time and medical skills to children in Africa. He led activities with the Boy Scout Troop he was part of as a child. Worked at a free clinic in a poverty-stricken town in the bayou.

There's no fucking way Sierra would go for me. Not that it matters. Because it doesn't.

~

I STOP BY THE RIVER, slowing so I can catch my breath. I'm not a morning person, but going for a run this early was nice. Not as hot. Though standing here in the sun I can feel the heat.

I followed the deer path this time and found another direction to follow instead of going along the Belmont's field. I'm back at The Mill House now, looking at the rushing water that Sierra and I sat by last night. The river is about ten feet wide here and takes a slow curve wrapping around the brick building. The old wooden wheel that used to roll in place from the current of the water is rotting at the bottom, and I can't help but think it's a shame something so historic has been left to just rot away.

The surface of the water is a good foot and a half below where it was back when the mill was working, and the erosion along the bank leaves tree roots exposed, dry and hanging over the water, like hair on corpses. I pick up a hard lump of dirt and chuck it into the water. It breaks apart as it hits, sinking down and becoming mud. I sigh and go into the apartment to shower.

Exhaustion hits me once I'm out, so I eat and lay on the

couch. It's only nine in the morning, and already the sun coming through the large window is heating up the room. I strip to my boxers and flip through Netflix, and eventually fall asleep.

Four hours later, I wake, startled by a dream. I don't dream often. Or if I do, I don't remember them. The dream started well, with Sierra back in my bed and this time I was next to her. She was naked and her perfect tits pushed up against me as we kissed. I moved on top of her, ready to fuck, and suddenly I was inside a casket buried deep in the ground, yet was still able to see what was going on above me.

Nothing.

People carried on with their lives. No one missed me. No one even noticed I was gone. Sierra stood on top of the grave, crying, and her tears penetrated the earth and dripped inside the casket. I thought she was crying for me, but then I realized I was inside Jake's grave.

I woke before things could get even *more* fucked up. Dream interpretation is a crock of shit...or so I thought. Figuring out exactly what that messed-up dream means requires me to think about it, and I don't want to. It's just a dream. A stupid dream.

Feeling groggy, I take my time getting up and dressed. I'm out of food again so I grab my keys and head out. I make it to my car when I suddenly stop.

"What the fuck is wrong with me?" I mumble aloud. I've never been one to back off when the odds are stacked against me. I like a challenge. Change has never fazed me.

But Sierra...Sierra is a force to be reckoned with.

SIERRA

I yawn for the fifth time in the last ten minutes. I reach for my water and regret sleeping in the extra twenty minutes after my alarm went off. I'm still just as tired as I would have been if I'd gotten up, and I didn't have time to run to Suzy's for a coffee. Time is crawling by, and business has been slow as well. I have an hour to go until my lunch break, and I'm honestly unsure if I can keep my eyes open for much longer.

Nothing makes you feel old like a hangover, right? I roll my neck—yawn—and try to wake myself up by stretching my arms above my head. That doesn't work. Getting up and moving might, but that requires energy, which I don't have.

The bell above the door rings, and I lazily turn my head, questioning my decision to work in retail and having to deal with the public.

"Hey, Sierra," Chase says with his famous grin.

"Chase. Hi." I blink, mind going to the lack of makeup and messy bun sitting like a rat's nest on the top of my head. Wait, what? Why do I care? "What are you doing here?"

He holds up a bag of takeout from The Mill House in one

hand and a drink holder with two iced coffees in the other. "I finished *The Fake Wife* and need something else to read. And I figured you could use this."

He sets the coffees down on the counter. Still in a bit of shock, it takes me a few seconds to realize he got my usual.

"That's what you like, right? I can get something else if not."

"Yeah. It is. How...?"

"You said you get coffee from Suzy's Cafe almost daily. So I asked them what you get."

I stick a straw in my cup and bring it to my lips, closing my eyes as soon as the cold liquid hits my tongue. "French vanilla is my favorite. And I didn't have time to get one this morning. Thank you, Chase."

Our eyes meet, and I get hit with the strangest feeling: I miss him, and he's standing right in front of me.

"And I don't know about you, but after a night of drinking too much, junk food for some reason makes me feel better." He gets a box of fries out of the bag, along with poppers and wings. A little plastic tub of cheese dip is inside the French fry box, taking place of the ketchup. "You said you like cheese."

"I do." I bring my coffee to my lips and push books out of the way. The man brought me coffee and bar food. Why is it making me so emotional? "Thanks, Chase," I say and realize that I've thanked him already. "Want to stay and help me eat this? It's too much for me to eat on my own."

"I can do that. For the food."

I wave him around the counter and pull out another stool. He smells good and looks even better. His jeans and T-shirt cover up the scars but don't hide the tattoos that decorate the skin on his arm.

"Did you get much sleep?" I ask. "After I left, I mean."

"About four hours. Which is probably more than you, I'm guessing."

"I showered as soon as I got home and slept until about ten-thirty. I think I slept more than you did, but I still feel tired," I say with a small smile and dip a fry into the warm cheese. "What about you?"

"I'm okay," he says. "I went for a run after we unloaded that truck, which helped. Though I wasn't the one who drank enough to kill a whale last night." He playfully nudges me with his elbow.

"It wasn't *that* much."

He raises his eyebrows. "Don't make me remind you of the threesome that almost happened."

"You just did."

He laughs and I shake my head, smiling. "Maybe I should say sorry for intervening. Those two looked like they'd be a good time."

I shudder and laugh. "Ew. No way." The door opens again, and I turn to see Wyatt walking in. He smiles when he sees me.

"Good afternoon, Sierra." His eyes go to Chase and his face falls a bit. "And, uh, Chase, right?"

"Right," Chase says. "And you're Wyatt, from the bank where my sister-in-law works."

"Isn't she your half-sister-in-law? Josh is your half-brother, right?"

I stare at Wyatt, wide-eyed, and then slowly turn my head to see Chase. He looks amused, not offended, and doesn't bother responding. He grabs a fry and dips it in the cheese.

"Are you looking for a book?" I ask Wyatt and wipe my hands.

"Uh," he starts, still staring at Chase. He wanted to offend him, and I have no idea why. Chase's non-response is irritating Wyatt. "Yeah. I need to get my grandma something for her birthday. You remember her, don't you, Sierra?"

"Yeah," I respond, giving Wyatt a look. I know most people in this town. Why is he acting so weird? "We just got some new cozy-mystery novels in this week. I ordered a few from indie authors too so she wouldn't be able to get them just anywhere."

Wyatt leans in and gives me a forced smile. "It's sweet you remember what she likes to read. I guess she made an impression on you like you did on her."

"She's nice," I say and walk to the display of new books right in front of the counter. "And she's a regular customer."

"She talks about you, you know, and still brings up how nice it was to have you around the house."

"Aww, that's nice. I always enjoyed talking to her. She had such an interesting past." I grab the book and give it to Wyatt. "Make sure you tell her I said 'happy birthday' then."

"You can say it yourself. How 'bout you come to her party tonight?"

"Uh," I start, mind blanking on a way to politely make up an excuse not to go. "Tonight isn't good." Each word comes out slowly, obviously a lie.

"You got plans?"

"Yeah. I do. I have a, uh, a thing…"

"I'm taking her on a date," Chase says, sitting up straight. He brushes salt off his fingers and meets my eye. "I have a very romantic evening planned for us. If Sierra didn't go, I'd have to cancel the helicopter and I won't get my deposit back."

How he says everything with such sincerity and a straight face, I'll never know. I blink, look away from Chase and back to Wyatt. "Right. So, uh, sorry."

Wyatt nods, gives Chase a quick glare and then pays for

the book and leaves. Standing behind the counter next to Chase, I turn, hands on my hips, and inspect him.

"What?" he asks, taking another popper and putting it in his mouth.

"I don't know what I find more curious: the creativity of your lies or the ease at which you tell them."

He smiles, finishes chewing, and says, "Either way, that's a compliment."

I shake my head. "A helicopter, really?"

"Hey." He holds up his hands defensively. "You seemed to enjoy the Mr. Grey vibe the first time we met."

"Christian Grey is pretty damn sexy," I agree. "And thanks, but I really don't need to be saved like that, you know."

"Oh, I know. We already established how well you handle yourself. You'd get out of the party, I'm sure, but he'd be back. That guy has a serious school-girl crush on you."

I shake my head and let out a breath. "I know. I was friends with his sister and went to prom with him when he was a senior and I was a sophomore but only because he had no one else to go with and underclassmen couldn't go to prom unless a senior asked them. And I really wanted to go to prom. It was the classic Under the Sea theme that year."

"You used him for a theme night."

"I totally did. I've always had a girl-crush on Ariel."

Chase laughs and then slowly runs his eyes over me. "I should take you out tonight. You don't want to get caught in a lie, do you?"

I stare back at him and bite my lip. Part of me really does want to go out with him. He's funny, confident, and so damn hot. There was a time in my life not that long ago where Lisa and I would gush over a man like Chase, admiring his fine physique from a distance. We could look, but not touch.

I *can* touch.

I'm single.

I can touch whoever I want. Whenever I want. It shouldn't feel wrong.

Yet it does.

"Sierra?" Chase asks softly and reaches out. His fingers sweep over my wrist, and the tenderness of his touch makes me want to melt into him. I crave the touch of a man, the way it feels to be wrapped in someone's arms.

"Sorry," I say and bring my arms in and around myself. "Chase," I start, only to let out my breath and shake my head. "When I said I wasn't the kind of girl you'd want to date, it wasn't a lame attempt to blow you off."

"Then what was it?"

"The truth."

Chase's eyes soften, and he gently curls his fingers around my wrist. "It's okay," he whispers, and it's almost like he knows. I twist my arm in his grasp and slide my hand up, so my fingers intertwine with his.

"Before this," I start, feeling my chest tighten. "My boyfriend…Jake…" I say his name and the same pain that hurts my heart is reflected on Chase's face. "He died." Tears fill my eyes and my bottom lip begins to tremble. I pull my hand out of Chase's grasp and turn. "Sorry."

"Don't be," Chase says and stands. His hands land on my shoulders, and he gingerly turns me around, pulling me close. "Don't ever be sorry for feeling, Sierra. It's what makes us human." A tear rolls down my cheek and Chase brushes it away. "And don't worry about going out tonight."

"I want to," I whisper. "I find you interesting, Chase. I want to go out with you but it's…it's…" I let the words die in my throat. Because I don't know what it is. Too soon? It's been almost a year and a half, yet the hole in my heart is still fresh. The edges of the wound are still seeping blood. It's thickening and beginning to scar, but the oozing hasn't stopped, and I'm weak from blood loss.

"Your heart was broken," he fills in.

"Yes. But it was because...because he died."

"I'm so sorry, Sierra."

"And that's why you shouldn't want to be with me. I have baggage."

"Everyone does," he replies and slips his arms around me. I step into his embrace, soaking in the warmth of his touch. "There aren't many people I'm willing to pick up the baggage for, but you're one of them, Sierra. I don't know why," he confesses. "But there is something about you I've never seen before. And I want more of it. Go out with me tonight. Give me a chance."

I look up at Chase and see it. The momentary slip in his tough exterior. It's not the first time I've seen it, and right now, I hope it's not the last.

"Okay."

～

"SPILL," Lisa orders, leaning on the counter.

"We close in five minutes, you know?"

"I already locked the door."

"You can't do that!"

She shrugs. "But I did. Now fucking tell me everything! Wyatt came back all huffy saying you're going on a date with Chase tonight."

"I am. Kind of."

Lisa leans back, waiting for me. "Don't make me beat it out of you."

I look at the clock, decide we're close enough to closing, and pull the cash drawer out of the register. "You know yesterday was Jake's birthday."

"Yeah, I do."

"Let's just say I didn't handle it too well. I was all emotional, and then got mad that Chase said he'd call and never did. So I went to The Mill House to yell at him, but ended up drinking too much, puking by the river, and passing out in Chase's bed."

Lisa's jaw drops. "Are you being serious?"

"I am. And no, nothing happened, sorry to disappoint you. He was the perfect gentleman last night. But this morning..." I wiggle my eyebrows, teasing Lisa. "Nothing happened this morning. I thought he was going to kiss me, but then his brother came over because they had a delivery at the bar, so whatever vibe we felt was over." I pull out a handful of pennies and start counting.

"Do you want him to kiss you?" Lisa asks after I counted and sorted.

"I think so."

Lisa waits until I count the rest of the change. "That still doesn't explain why Wyatt says you are going out with Chase tonight."

"He brought me food and coffee this afternoon and stayed to eat with me. Wyatt asked me to go to his grandma's birthday and you know I'm terrible with excuses, so Chase said I can't go because I'm going out with him." I shake my head. "He really is irritating. It's like he thinks I can't take care of myself. Socially, I mean. He probably thinks I'm socially awkward."

"You *are* socially awkward."

I give her a look. "I'm usually better at hiding it."

"So you're not actually going out with him tonight?"

I quickly count the dollar bills. "I am. I think. Maybe. I shouldn't." I bite my lip and look up. Lisa is hopeful, and I remember her words all too well about how hard it is to be my friend. "How was the concert?"

"Fucking amazing, but don't change the subject. Go out with him. Try to have fun. You're not doing anything wrong."

I blink away tears. "I feel like I am."

"Why?"

"Because I want to go out with Chase. I'd be lying if I said I wasn't attracted to him."

"That makes me so happy to hear. I want you to be happy, Si. And I know you're a relationship person. You like being with someone."

"I do."

"Now to discuss the important stuff: what are you wearing and where are you going?"

"I don't know. He's going to pick me up around seven-thirty or whenever he's done helping his brother get through the dinner rush at The Mill House. We'll figure something out. There is the tractor-pull tonight."

"The tractor-pull is a step above the school bus derby at least." Lisa rolls her eyes. "Nothing says romance like the smell of exhaust."

"I'm joking, Lisa. But I could give him a tour of Summer Hill: Civil War Edition."

"I honestly don't know if you're joking about that. I know you like the walking tour of the town enough to go every year."

"I think it's cool that a lot of the buildings built in the late 1800s are still here. And it's important to know the history around you."

"You're such a nerd."

I hold my hand up. "Mutant and proud."

Lisa pushes off the counter and untucks her blouse. Dressing office-casual like that every day would drive me nuts. "Have fun tonight," she starts. "And text me with updates. Rob's working tonight so I'll be home being bored and need some excitement."

"Don't hold your breath."

~

WATER DRIPS FROM MY HAIR, splashing onto the hardwood floor. Panicked, I grab my robe, throw it on, and pad to the front door. It's only half-past five, and someone is knocking on the door. Chase isn't two hours early, is he?

"Oh, Mom, it's just you," I say when I open the door.

"Just me? Do I need to remind you of the seventeen hours of labor I went through for you?"

"You do all the time." I step aside and let Mom in, shutting the door behind her. "And hi, Mom."

She gives me a hug, surreptitiously eyeing the house behind me. "You cleaned. Everything looks great, honey. And that smell...is that lemongrass?"

I nod. "My favorite scent. I got a new diffuser too." I motion to the oil diffuser on the end table next to my couch. "The colors change and make shadows that look like a creepy forest at night."

Mom pulls me in for another hug and plants a kiss on my forehead. "It's so you, Sierra."

"Not that I'm not happy to see you, Mom, but what are you doing here?"

"You didn't come home last night." She holds up her hand so I don't interrupt. "Which is fine because you're an adult and I said I wouldn't keep tabs on you anymore, but I wanted to check in before your father and I head out."

Between my siblings and I, I was always granted the most freedom. Which was directly related to the fact that I wasn't interested in the normal teenage rebellion type of things like my brother and sister. Sam went out drinking with friends because that's the normal thing to do and Scott was rebellious just to cause trouble.

My house is about a mile behind my parent's mansion. They can't see into the house or anything but can tell when the lights are on or off. Neither paid much attention to my whereabouts before, but since Jake passed, Mom's been more attentive.

"Head out?" I echo.

"We're going to Indiana to discuss purchasing the wind-mill farm."

"Oh, right." I shake my head. "I remember now. Is Gran going with?"

"Of course. There is no slowing that woman down. I hope you inherited her longevity."

"Me too. And I'll keep an eye on the house. Do you need me to feed Marley?"

"I was just going to ask. I left instructions out in case you need them."

I consider hassling Mom over it, since they've had that parrot since I was a kid, but I'm the same way with my cats. "Okay. I'll hang out with him too."

"Oh, good. Thank you. He does get lonely. Are you and Lisa going out? It looks like you were in the middle of getting ready."

"I was, but I'm not going out with Lisa. I'm going on a date."

Mom doesn't say anything. Her blue eyes widen so much I can almost see myself reflected back in them. Her lips— which are full thanks to lip injections—begin to slowly part yet she still doesn't speak.

"Mom?" I ask. Is she horrified I'm going out? Thinks it's too soon?

"Oh, Sierra." She throws her arms around me. "You have no idea how happy this makes me." She squeezes me tight and leans back. "Your father and I have been so worried. We didn't want you to give up on having a love life."

"There's no love…" I start, feeling awkward. "It's just a date."

"It's a starting point, and one I've been waiting for."

"You don't think it's too soon?"

Mom takes my hands in hers. "Only if you feel like it is. There is no right or wrong time when it comes to things like this. Who are you going out with?" She shakes her head, knowing it's impossible for her to not judge whoever I name. "It doesn't matter. Have fun tonight."

"I will," I say with a smile, but feel empty inside. "Safe travels, Mom. When are you leaving?"

"As soon as your father gets in, we're heading to the airport. We'll be back Monday evening. I switched you to be the emergency contact for the house this weekend with the security company, too." She hugs me again. "It's good to have you back, baby."

12

CHASE

"I got it from here," Josh tells me. "You can go."

"You sure?"

"Yeah. A lot of the regulars are at the tractor pull tonight, so it'll be slow, even for a Friday."

"You say that like it's not one of the most redneck things you go to," I say with a laugh.

"Don't judge it 'till you go. They're fun."

"I'll take your word for it." I change out a few bottles of booze that are running low and clear off one more table before heading out.

"Chase," someone calls right as I get to the door. "Wait up."

Lisa, Sierra's cousin, is hurrying over. She's here alone and put in an order for takeout minutes ago.

"Hey, Lisa. Do you need something else?"

"Just to talk to you."

"Okay."

"Sierra told me what you did. She never would have gotten out of that party tonight if you hadn't helped, but don't tell her I said that. So, thanks for looking out for her. Again."

"I like looking out for her." And looking at her, but I don't say that out loud.

"And she said you guys are hanging out tonight. Did she tell you about her previous boyfriend?"

I nod. "She did."

"That's a relief. And she'll kill me for telling you, but she's looking forward to tonight, even though she's feeling a lot of guilt for moving on."

I find myself nodding again, trying to separate in my mind what Sierra's told me versus what I've learned about her from the voicemails. Fuck. It's blurring together. My lack of response causes Lisa to look at me funny.

"I hope you guys have a good night," she says. "And just remember our family owns a lot of farmland and equipment that can rip you to shreds and scatter the pieces across multiple fields, never to be found again."

"I will keep that in mind. Sierra's lucky to have a friend like you."

"She is." She smiles and goes back to the counter to get her food. I leave the bar, go upstairs to shower, and head to Sierra's. Before I start my car, I find myself staring at my phone, voicemail pulled up. It's like I'm possessed, doing something I know will cause harm.

I have no control.

I press play on the next message.

"I told my therapist that I still call you," Sierra says. "And she said I need to stop. Calling and acting like you're still alive won't allow me to move on, she said. I'm not ready to move on yet and I don't know why everyone acts like that's a bad thing."

I pull the phone away from my ear to look at the date of

the next voicemail. A month and a half goes by before she leaves another, and everything inside me tells me not to listen.

So I don't. I toss the phone onto the passenger seat and start the car, and roll out of the parking lot. The engine revs and I pass a slow truck, crossing over a double yellow line. Oh well. Really, I should be more careful. I have a record, one with a recent arrest. If I get an unforgiving cop having a bad day, a simple speeding ticket could set me back more than a few hundred bucks.

Sierra's house isn't far from the bar and I'm there in less than fifteen minutes. If I'd gone the speed limit, it might have taken longer than that though, to be fair. Her house is off a private drive, and I pass by the large antebellum-style plantation house on the way. The driveway to Sierra's little brick house is gravel, unlike the stone-paved path that leads to the Belmont family mansion.

Being born into a family with money is unfathomable. Being born into one with money *and* history blows my mind. Since internet stalking Sierra's ex wasn't creepy enough, I went and looked up her family history as well.

If it weren't for the Belmonts—the first Belmonts, that is —Summer Hill wouldn't be here. They were the first to settle in this area, and though their establishment in the south was thanks to the slave trade, later Belmonts turned into abolitionists. The original farmhouse that Sierra resides in is rumored to have been part of the Underground Railroad, or so Wikipedia says.

I park next to Sierra's BMW and get out, taking a minute to soak in what I can before going to her door. I know she has cats, likes to be outside and wants to start a garden—or at least she did at the time when she left that message. I have to push all that aside and pretend I don't know anything else about her.

This old house is over a hundred years old and has gone through a series of renovations. The yard is neat but not professionally landscaped like the large white house. Light from the sinking sun reflects off crystals and gems hanging from the trees around the front, and what looks like sea glass is scattered amongst the rocks on either side of the sidewalk leading to the covered front porch.

Planters full of dried and dead plants hang in planter-boxes from the wooden rails of that very porch, long forgotten, but at one time loved. The boxes are hand-painted in bright colors, matching the pillows on the wicker lounge chairs on the porch. Wind chimes and old, metal and glass lanterns hang above them, swaying slightly in the thick, summer air.

I count three birdhouses and even more bird feeders hanging from the trees on my way to her front door. A miniature fairy garden is set up in the weed-filled stone circle around a large Angel Oak. I pause, lifting my head to see the full length of its twisted branches. More crystals and a wind chime made from antique spoons hang, looking out of place yet perfectly at home at the same time.

Is this part of why people around here think Sierra is weird? The eclectic style of the front yard is welcoming to me, though it's hard to narrow down exactly why. Conforming to social norms and doing what you think you should do has never been my strong suit. I have a love/hate relationship with my inability to give a shit about what others think. Finding someone else who marches to the beat of their own drum is incredibly satisfying.

An old carriage lantern hangs by her front door in place of a porch light. My heart skips a beat when I knock on Sierra's door. I'm never nervous around women. No one has ever mattered before. Not like Sierra.

It only takes a few seconds for her to answer the door.

The sight of her takes my breath away. She's wearing a pink dress with her hair down around her pretty face. A gray and black tabby cat is nestled in her arms, sleepily blinking at me.

"Hey," she says and steps aside, welcoming me in, and then closes the door.

"Hi," I say back.

Sierra bites her lip and looks down at the cat. "This is Tinkerbell."

Right. Tinkerbell and Dolly are her cats. I remember that from her messages. "Oh, uh, hi Tinkerbell. She's a good-looking cat."

"Thanks. I think so, of course. But I'm biased. My other cat is super pretty too, but she's not very friendly. She's already hiding, but don't take it personally. She only likes to be around people when she decides it's okay. I can't even pet her half the time."

I nod, looking into Sierra's eyes. She blinks and looks away, shaking her head.

"Sorry. I'm nervous and rambling," she says.

"Don't be nervous." Sierra gives me a half-smile. "No pressure tonight, remember?"

"I remember." She walks away from the front door, going into the living room. Her house is neat, smells amazing, and is decorated in a similar fashion to the front yard. While her walls are painted a light grey, splashes of color pop almost everywhere I look.

"So, what do you want to do tonight?" she asks and sits on the couch. Tinkerbell lazily moves from her arms, stretching and then settling on the arm of the couch next to Sierra.

"Whatever you want to do." Seeing she's barefoot, I take my shoes off and join her on the couch. "Did you eat yet?"

"I ate half a bag of shredded cheese," she says and then laughs. I'm laughing right along with her. "I eat when I'm nervous."

I lick my lips and lean in. "Do I make you nervous?"

Sierra inhales, making her large breasts rise under her dress. God, she's gorgeous. "Yes."

I could push her, have fun with it, and make her squirm. But I don't. Because Sierra is different. So much different. Instead, I take her hand in mine, running my thumb over the smooth skin on the inside of her wrist.

"Don't be nervous."

She nods quickly and pushes her hair behind her ear.

"Did you make those dessert-ish things yet?"

"I actually just finished a batch before you got here. I made the dough this morning with the intention of bringing you some at the bar if you were working. The dough has to chill for a while," she explains and gets up, leading me into her kitchen. "I stuck them in the oven to keep them warm."

"Is that what smells so good in here?"

"It might be part of it. I put lemongrass oil into the diffuser. It's my favorite scent. It has a nice, subtle sweetness to it, don't you think?"

"Yeah," I agree, not really knowing what else to say, which is rather unlike me, but there's something about Sierra's place that's welcoming...and so homey. I've never felt this before, and I've only been here for a few minutes. I don't even want to think about how fucked up that is. "It is nice."

"Do you want anything to drink?" She opens the oven and pulls out a tray of square pastries. "I have wine, but I think I'm going to forgo alcohol tonight, for obvious reasons."

I chuckle. "I'll skip it with you."

She pours two glasses of lemonade and sits next to me at the kitchen table, serving the beignets.

"These are really good," I say, after taking a bite. "I'm impressed with your baking skills."

She waves her hand in the air. "These are easy. My grandma is an amazing cook. She actually grew up really poor and her own mother had to improvise a lot in order to feed her family. She taught us the best of her recipes."

"So, she wasn't born a Belmont?" I ask and take another bite. "I might have looked up your family history on the internet," I confess. "I find that kind of stuff fascinating."

Sierra smiles. "I do too, which is why I live here instead of a new house like my sister. Houses like this don't do well when left empty. And no, my grandma wasn't. She married into the Belmonts but it was because of her my grandfather started doing business with one of those big food chains. It's an interesting tale. I like hearing her talk about it as lame as that sounds."

"It's not lame at all. But what might be lame is that I'm really curious if this house was actually part of the Underground Railroad or not."

Sierra beams. "There's no actual proof, but we think so because of this weird space upstairs with a hidden door. Want to see it?"

"Hell yes."

She brushes powdered sugar from her fingers, takes a drink, and gets up. Excitement gleams in her emerald eyes as she leads me up a narrow staircase.

"A historian came out and evaluated the weird little room not that long ago," she explains. "And she couldn't come up with a logical explanation for it, which is why we think it was used to hide slaves trying to escape to freedom. And one of my ancestors was hanged for helping slaves run away, so it fits the history."

There are two rooms upstairs. One is set up as a guest room and the other has bookshelves along the entire perimeter. A yoga mat and exercise ball are the only furniture. We go into that room and I can't help but admire all of Sierra's books as we pass through. She takes me to what I presume to be a closet, turns on a light, and pushes clothes out of the way. She pushes on a piece of old paneling, moving it to the side to reveal a small door.

"You're not claustrophobic, are you?"

"Not at all."

"Good. Because you have to do a bit of crawling." She drops to her knees and grabs a flashlight that's stashed right inside the little trap door. She's wearing a short dress and her ass is in my face as we move through a narrow crawlspace that follows the roofline of this old house. It's weird to get turned on in a place like this, I know, but I can't help it. Sierra is too fucking good-looking to begin with. Pair that with her interest in history, and I want to fuck her right here in this hidden room.

"We're behind the other room now," she tells me as she stands, shining the light around. The roofline angles down on one side, and exposed beams and insulation surround us. The room looks like an old attic and is only a few feet wide. "There was a cot in here, right up against that wall." She shines the light on the wall opposite us. "But it was full of mice so it had to be taken out. And there was another door leading from the crawlspace to here, but it wasn't in good shape either. Some of the boards had to be replaced, and obviously the little squares of carpet were added. I got splin ters enough times crawling through here that I lined it to save my knees."

"Do you hang out in here often?"

"No. It's hot as hell, as you can tell. But sometimes I come here and just think about who stayed here, praying not to be caught and for a better life. Gives me perspective," she adds quietly.

I step forward and the boards creak beneath my feet. Pictures are carved into one of the wooden beams, along with the name 'Ester.' "It's amazing this has survived."

"It is. There was an old lantern and a schoolbook with

notes written in it under the bed. The book is super fragile, but can still be flipped through. And the lantern is on my coffee table. I like lanterns."

"I noticed," I say with a smile.

Sierra inhales and gathers her hair in her hand, pulling it off her neck. "Want to get out of here? The heat gets to you fast, which makes me feel like a baby when I think about people staying here for days."

"I am very grateful for whoever invented air conditioning."

"Me too," Sierra says and goes back through the crawlspace.

"Do you do yoga?" I ask, mind going into the gutter on its own accord as I imagine Sierra in various poses.

"I used to. And speaking of air conditioning, the upstairs only recently had the ductwork done to get central air up here. It was too hot most of the time before." She closes the closet door and her eyes go to a photo on her bookshelf.

It's of her and Jake.

"I was trying to do most of the renovations myself," she goes on. "So I could only do a bit at a time since, you know, it's super expensive to update old houses. But my parents thought it would be a good distraction, I guess, and paid for everything up here to be updated so I could decorate. I like decorating."

"A distraction?" I ask, though I already know what she's talking about.

She looks away from the photo. "After Jake died, I stopped doing pretty much everything I used to do." Slowly, she shakes her head. "It hurt. A lot. And instead of feeling it, I shut down. It's easier to feel nothing, after all." She blinks and flicks her gaze to me. "I don't know why I just told you that. I've never told anyone that before. If you want to rethink the whole basket case thing, I don't blame you."

I close the distance between us and take her hand. "I don't think you're a basket case, Sierra. You do what you have to do to guard your heart. Life is hard. Sometimes the best you can do is survive."

Her long lashes come together as she closes her eyes in a long blink. "Why do I get the feeling you're speaking from personal experience?"

"Because I am."

I slide my fingers up her arm and over her shoulder. Sierra closes her eyes and leans in. With my other hand, I reach behind her, putting my hand on the small of her back, and bring her in so her hips are against mine. Sierra brings her arm up and rests her hand on my chest, feeling my heartbeat.

I want to kiss her.

I want to taste her.

Feel her.

Love her.

"Chase," she whispers, tipping her head up.

"Sierra," I whisper back, moving her hair over her shoulder. I press my forehead against hers, getting more and more turned on from her touch as each second passes by. She curls her fingers in, bunching my shirt beneath her grasp. I run my fingers along the skin on her back, exposed from the backless dress.

She shuffles closer, taking her other hand and setting it on my waist. Desire comes over me like a wave crashing on the shore and I lose the shred of self-control I was holding onto.

I put my lips to Sierra's, gently cupping her face. She hesitates for a second and then she kisses me back.

And neither one of us can stop.

Sierra's arms wrap around me, holding me as close as she can. I kiss her hard, hands moving down to the hem of her dress. I pull it up, and then take hold of her legs, lifting her up and pressing her against a bookshelf. Sierra wraps her legs around me and moves her lips from mine to my neck. She sucks on my skin and rakes her fingers through my hair.

I move one of the straps of her dress off her shoulders, watching as the fabric slides down, and cup her breast in my hand. My cock hardens against her, and Sierra lets out a moan as she feels it, pushing her core against me.

I press her harder against the shelf, using one hand to bunch up her dress. She widens her legs and throws her head back as I kiss her neck. The shelf wobbles and books fall around us, but that doesn't stop us.

I've never wanted someone more than I want Sierra at this moment. I want to make her feel because it makes me feel, and for once, nothing hurts. Everything feels right.

She reaches down, trying to undo my pants. I slip both hands around her legs and move so she can undo my belt, sliding it out of the loops and dropping it on the floor. She takes my lip between her teeth as she pops the button on my pants. Her fingers are just inches away from my dick, and I push her against the shelf again in order to reposition us.

A picture frame comes crashing down, glass shattering as it hits the shelf below, and then crashes onto the floor. Sierra tenses and turns her head away.

Shit.

The photo that fell was the picture of her with Jake that I saw just minutes ago. I look down at the floor. Broken glass lies in shards around my feet, and Jake and Sierra's smiling faces stare up at us. Jaw tense, I move my gaze back to Sierra's. Her green eyes are wide with horror.

And then she laughs.

"Sorry," she says. "It's not funny at all. I don't know why I'm laughing. It's just…you're the first person I've kissed since Jake died and his photo falls from the shelf and cuts me."

"You got cut?"

"I think so. I felt something fly up and hit me when the glass shattered." She inhales and looks over my shoulder at her foot. Her legs are still around me and I don't want to let go.

"Yep. I'm bleeding."

There's no panic in her voice, no sign that she's in really any pain at all, yet knowing that she got cut upsets me more than I thought it would. I tighten my grip on her, look down at the broken glass. Carefully stepping over it, I move to the rainbow-colored carpet in the middle of the room and gently set Sierra down. Her eyes are on the broken photo frame and a tear rolls down her cheek.

"Sorry," she says and quickly wipes it away.

"Don't be," I whisper, crouching down next to her so I can look at the jagged cut on her ankle. The ache in my heart turns to anger. This isn't how things were supposed to turn out. The Mystery Woman was supposed to find happiness again. She wasn't supposed to struggle and hurt for this long.

"It doesn't look that deep," I go on, gently wiping away a bead of blood with my fingertip. "I'll clean it for you and make sure there's no glass inside the wound."

She nods, still looking at the broken frame. I stand and reach out to her to help her to her feet. "Thank you, Chase."

"Do you have a first aid kit and tweezers?"

Her eyes widen and her nostrils flare. "I do, but I don't like the sound of this. Won't it just work its way out on its own?"

"Maybe. Or maybe the skin will grow over it and you'll have an infected piece of glass inside your body."

"I've had worse things inside me."

I raise an eyebrow. "Really now?"

She quickly shakes her head. "I didn't mean it like that."

"Sure," I say with a smirk. I help her to her feet and follow her into the kitchen. I get her first aid kit from under the counter and wash the cut, then give Sierra an ice cube to hold on the wound for a minute before I go in with the tweezers and pick out the shard of glass.

"Have you done this before?" she asks, looking away as I gently pull her torn flesh apart.

"A few times. Though never from a broken picture frame."

I can feel her eyes on me, and I know she's curious. "Got it," I say, holding up the tweezers. A tiny piece of bloody glass is between them. I put it on a napkin, and then clean up the cut and put a bandage over it. "Good as new."

"Thank you, Chase. There's no way I could have done that myself. I don't mind blood or guts or anything, but digging glass out of my own skin is a giant nope."

"It's harder to do that kind of stuff to yourself. Pain makes most people hesitate, and it can be hard to inflict pain on yourself, even when necessary."

"Most people," she echoes, looking at me as if she can see the darkness within. "But not you?"

I shrug. "I learned a long time ago that you should do what needs to be done." My hands are still on Sierra's smooth leg.

"I should clean up the glass," she says but doesn't move her leg off my lap. "The cats might walk in it. And picking glass out of their paws won't be this easy."

I go with her, helping her sweep up the mess. She puts it in a bag, and we go outside to put it in her recycling bin. She turns to go back inside, and I hesitate. I'm not good with feelings. Being sensitive has never been my thing. The whole situation with being the first man Sierra's been with since her boyfriend died...yeah...I have no fucking clue how to handle it.

But I do know that no matter what, I want to make Sierra happy.

"I can go if you want me to."

Her lips part, eyes mirroring the desperation I feel inside. "I don't want you to."

"Then I'll stay." Stepping forward, I take Sierra in my arms. She rests her head against my chest.

"Okay," she says softly, staying wrapped in my arms. The night is alive and a half-moon shines in the sky, dotted with sparkling stars. It's quiet. It's peaceful. It almost feels like home.

"Is that the river?" I ask, turning my head and looking at the trees behind her house.

"Yeah." She twists and follows my gaze. "The same one that goes by your place. We're not that far apart, actually. If the road went straight from my house to yours, it would only take a few minutes to get to you."

"I'd like that." I inch my fingers along the silky fabric of her dress. "Josh tried to convince me that was the Mississippi River when I was a kid. I believed him."

That brings a smile to Sierra's face. "I told my cousin the same thing. My family on my mom's side is from Connecticut. They hate coming here. My cousins are all stuck-up and judgmental. It was fun making them feel stupid. Which makes me sound awful, doesn't it?"

"Not at all."

"Good. Because they are awful. Trust me."

"I've been running the deer paths along the river. I kind of ended up behind your parents' barn. I didn't realize it ran by your house before."

"When Lisa and I were kids, we'd follow the river and see where we'd end up. Funny story, actually, the first time we made it all the way to The Mill House, your dad was there. I, uh, was always kind of scared of him. And that's not a funny story at all. God, I'm awkward."

I laugh and put my hands on her waist, well aware of my inability to stop touching her. "He kind of scared me too when I was a kid. Well, the few times I even saw him."

She shakes her head. "I'm sorry."

"Don't be."

"So, you've been to Summer Hill before."

"Yeah, but the last time was ten years ago when I was fifteen."

"I would have been thirteen then. Were you here long?"

"No. I came with my mom, who tried to drop me off with my dad for the summer so she could run off to Cabo with her then-boyfriend. I was here for a week before I left."

Sierra wraps her arms around my shoulders, stepping in close. My cock starts to harden again from the innocent gesture. She affects me on every level.

She's dangerous.

"You just left?"

"Yeah. I went home. I had friends there and bounced around for a few weeks until she came back. She didn't even realize I was back early. I still think if I hadn't come home on my own, she'd have never come back for me." I let out a breath. I've never opened up like this about my past to anyone before. "But hey, it all worked out."

She slowly moves her head back and forth, about to say something when a strangled screech comes from the woods.

"What the hell was that?"

"Most likely a coyote. Though there have been rumors about chupacabras."

"You have coyotes and mountain lions here?"

The soft breeze blows Sierra's silky hair around her face. "There hasn't been a confirmed mountain lion sighting in years, but some of the farmers swear that's what's attacking their cattle."

The same high-pitched howl echoes off the house again.

"It's kind of creepy, especially if it's not a coyote," she admits. "Want to come in?"

"Yeah, I've never faced a chupacabra before."

"Me neither and I don't feel like it tonight. I have no weapons."

I take her hand and follow her back inside. She shuts and locks the door behind us.

"What do you want to do?" she asks, and I can feel her discomfort.

I want to kiss her again, feel her breasts crush against me and push her up against the wall. I push my desire to the side. For her sake.

"I don't care," I start, and then spot a book laying on her coffee table. "Is that *Unbroken*?"

Sierra picks up the book. "Yeah. Perks of working in a bookstore. I get early copies. Have you read the others in the series?"

"Yeah. I actually preordered that one on my Kindle."

Lust fills Sierra's eyes for a moment. Her cheeks flush and her lips part. She glides over, fingers clutching the book. Then she shakes her head, and the want is gone. "It's a good series. Emma Stark is a crazy good writer."

"Yeah," I agree. "The first movie was pretty good too."

She hands me the book and we sit on the couch, discussing the similarities between the book and the movie. The air conditioner kicks on and Sierra shivers. I reach for a folded blanket on the arm of the couch and spread it out over her. She yawns and rests her head against my shoulder.

Remembering that she woke up hungover and is running on little sleep, I hook my arm around her and open the book.

"It's signed?"

"Yeah, so don't crack the spine," she says with a smile. "You can read it if you want." Her smile disappears. "Sorry I'm boring and lame. This is the worst date, I know."

I kiss her forehead. "I've had worse."

13

SIERRA

"*S*ierra."

Someone nudges my arm and says my name again. I think. Maybe? Or am I dreaming. I'm tired and don't want to get up. I'm warm and comfy laying on the couch with Chase's body spooned around mine.

My eyes fly open.

Chase is with me.

I'm nuzzled up next to him, with my ass pressed firmly against his cock.

And it feels good.

"Sierra," he says again, reaching over me and picking my phone up from the coffee table. "An alert for your security system just went off."

"Huh? I don't...I didn't hear..." I blink and slowly push up. My brain is all hazy with sleep. I take the phone from him and squint in the dark. It wasn't dark when I fell asleep. Chase sat with me, gently running his hand through my hair as he read. Falling asleep while he read probably made this the most boring first date in the history of dates, but there was something so *nice* about it. So comfortable.

I want to do it again.

I want this to be a routine.

I want more of Chase Henson.

"It's my parents' house." I unlock my phone to see what's going on. "They're out of town and set it up for me to get the alerts. It's probably just Marley setting off the motion detectors again. He does that a lot at night."

"Marley? Is he the family ghost or something?"

I raise an eyebrow and look away from my phone at Chase. "He's a parrot. The ghost is too sophisticated to set off the alarm. Plus, it stays in the attic."

"You really have a ghost in the—never mind. So everything is okay over there?"

"Probably," I say, seeing the cause of the alarm. "The motion sensor in the sunroom picked something up, and that's where his cage is. He either threw something out of his cage or he got—shit."

My phone buzzes in my hand and I reluctantly answer, talking to the person from the alarm system company. I give them the proper passwords and things seem okay, and then I tell them not to alert my parents—the homeowners—because they are out of town. Suddenly, I lose my credibility and the cops are on their way.

I rub my forehead and look at Chase. I don't have a chance to say it before he disagrees.

"You're still not a basket case."

"That's debatable," I mumble and get up, missing the feel of his body against mine immediately. "I'm a boring, lame, basket case."

"At least you're good-looking," he jokes. "Do you have to go to the house?"

"Yeah. I should check if Marley got out or not anyway."

"Let me come with. In case it's not the bird and it's something else. Those chupacabras can be rather unpredictable, you know."

"Ah, right. I do need a big, strong man to protect me."

Chase is behind me, arms wrapping around my waist. I melt against him, eyes closing. I want to go back to the couch, but this time, instead of him being next to me, I want him on me. Kissing me. Touching me. Pushing inside me.

His lips brush the skin on my neck, and my body reacts. Goose bumps break out along my flesh, and heat bubbles in my stomach, spreading down between my legs. I twist in his arms and he kisses me. Hard. Desire explodes inside me and his lips against mine aren't enough. I grab the hem of his shirt and yank it up. Chase raises his arms, letting the shirt slip off easily.

We melt into each other again. Chase gathers my hair in his hand and pulls it to the side, mouth going to my neck. He sucks and kisses, and a moan escapes my lips. My hands explore his back, feeling every pound of muscle beneath my fingers.

And then I feel something else. A little mound of scar tissue and I remember the mark I saw on his back this morning. I run my finger over it, distantly wondering what happened, but more focused on what's currently happening.

Yearning.

Warmth.

A growing need to feel every single hard inch of this man.

We fall back onto the couch, with Chase on top of me. I widen my legs, welcoming him in between. Want swells inside of me, turning desperate with each kiss Chase gives. He sits up, tearing his mouth away from mine, and gathers my dress up around my waist. And then he stops.

"I see flashing lights," he pants. "Through the trees."

"Crap. The cops are almost here then." I put my hands on his chest, admiring the tattoos. "I lost track of time."

"Yeah, it did kind of slip away."

He's still on top of me. I'm still tracing the black lines of his tattoos, following the curves of a sun that's inked onto his flesh. I slide my hands up and over his shoulders, bringing him back down to me. "We should go."

"Yeah," he whispers, putting his lips to mine. "We should."

I'm lying down, but the world is spinning around me. I've never felt like this before. So damn attracted to someone. Hardly able to control myself. Desperate for more.

In the first time in over a year, I'm feeling something other than numbness and pain. I'm alive again, and living feels *good*.

Having more control than me, Chase gets up and picks his shirt up off the floor, turning it right-side out and putting it on. I smooth out my dress, fish my keys from my purse, and put my shoes on. We get into my car and speed down the gravel drive, coming to a stop just in time for the police to turn off the private road and onto my parents' driveway.

Chase and I wait by the front door. The police car stops and I recognize Rob before he's fully out of the car.

"Hey, Sierra," he says, eyes going to Chase. Trying to suppress a smile, he gives me a small nod of approval and comes around the car. His partner, a younger man whose name escapes me, stands outside the car, looking at my parents' house in awe. It is impressive when seeing it up close for the first time. I take the ostentatious curb appeal for granted. It's just home to me.

"Did the security people talk to you?" I ask, turning to unlock the door.

"Yeah. They said a motion sensor picked up movement. Is it Marley again?"

"I think so." I open the door and step in, sliding my hand up and down the wall to find the switch for the chandelier that hangs above us in the two-story foyer. "Come on in and have a look. None of the other motion sensors picked up anything, so it has to be Marley or someone's been hiding in the sunroom for hours and finally decided to get up and stretch their legs."

Rob laughs. "That sounds like the most likely cause."

"I knew it." I shut the door and take my shoes off out of habit. My mom would throw a fit seeing Rob and his partner walk into the foyer with their shoes on, but I'm not asking them to take them off. Chase, however, sees me take mine off and follows suit.

"Holy shit," Rob's partner mumbles, running his eyes up the sweeping staircase. I lead the way to the sunroom in the back of the house, turning on lights as I go.

"Marley?" I call, pausing in the threshold in the sunroom. His cage is open, and the extra clips my mom put on to keep him in, lay in pieces on the ground. "That bird is too smart for his own good." I shake my head. "Well, we know who the culprit is. Unless the person who's been hiding in here also took Marley with them. Which seems unlikely. So you guys can go."

"You need help finding the bird?" Rob asks.

"Nah, he'll turn up, but thanks." I walk Rob and his partner out, closing the door behind them.

"How the hell are you going to find a bird in this big house?" Chase asks, eyeing the large foyer.

"Marley is an African Grey. He's pretty big and if he's not already in the kitchen trying to get into the pantry, I'll make popcorn."

"Popcorn?"

"He's obsessed. But he can only have like one or two pieces at a time because it's not good for him."

We go back through the house and into the kitchen. Marley is sitting on the lip of the fruit bowl, working on an apple. He looks up when he sees us, ruffling his feather.

"Dead men. Dead men," he squawks.

Chase looks at me, eyebrows pinched. "Did he just say what I think he said?"

"Yeah. I tried to teach him to say 'dead men tell no tales' from *Pirates of the Caribbean* but it was too long of a phrase. So now he just says 'dead men' when he sees me."

Amused, Chase shakes his head. "That's not creepy at all."

I go to the counter, holding out my arm. Marley takes another chunk out of the apple and lands on my arm, walking up to my shoulder. He rubs his beak—sticky with apple juice—on my face. I gently stroke his feathers and grab his half-eaten apple.

"Come on, mister," I say and turn. "It's bedtime." I put Marley back in his cage, give him the apple, and shut the sunroom doors. "I can disable that sensor," I tell Chase, pointing to the little detector on the ceiling. "So if he gets out again, he'll be confined to this room and won't set off the alarm again."

"Good idea."

"Thanks for coming with me."

"Sierra, you can stop thanking me."

"Okay." I smile like I do when I'm nervous, becoming suddenly aware of every sensation in my body. We head out after I close up the house, and the whole time I'm mentally going over what I should say to Chase because I know he's going to ask me if I want him to stay.

I do.

I miss having someone next to me. I miss waking up with strong arms wrapped around me. I like not being alone. Saying that out loud will come off lame. Pathetic maybe. Part of me nags away, demanding I just come out and say it.

We get into my car and I haven't said a word.

I drive as slow as I can, trying to muster up the courage.

I say nothing.

The car comes to a stop in my driveway. I look at the time before I shut it off. It's three twenty-one in the morning. Three. Two. One. I can do this. I close my eyes.

"I guess I'll head out," Chase says.

Three. Two. One.

I open my eyes, looking right at Chase. Moonlight dances across his handsome face, casting shadows on his stubble-covered jaw. I remember the texture of his scar under my finger, the way he felt pressed up against me.

Three...two...one. "Stay."

His hazel eyes lighten. "Okay."

He takes my hand as we walk to the front door, but he pauses before we go inside. Sure he's going to tell me he changed his mind, that he'd rather go home and do anything else than sit around being bored with me, I yank my hand from his, closing off my heart before the hurt has a chance to hit.

"I like that most houses here have porches," he says quietly. Thrown from him saying the last thing I expected, I open my mouth, gaping for a second before gaining back the ability to say coherent words. "The historic ones at least."

I blink, brought back to earth when mosquitos swarm around my face. "The porches helped keep the houses cool," I ramble. "That way they could open the windows for the fresh air without the sunlight coming right in."

"Makes sense."

"The back porch is better. It's screened in, which obviously wasn't original to the house. But it keeps the bugs away and you can hear the river better in the back of the house. Sometimes, when I can't sleep, I go out there, lay in the hammock, and just stare into the woods and wish...and wish..."

"You could vanish—in one sense or another—and just simply exist amongst the trees."

My heart is in my throat. I swallow hard, pushing it down. "Yes."

"It would feel free." A chill comes over me. Chase steps in and wraps me in his arms. More bugs buzz around, and Chase waves them away. He slips his hands down my back, stopping on my ass, giving my cheeks a squeeze as he pushes me into him. His mouth goes to my neck. My eyes flutter shut and a soft moan leaves my lips. He brings my dress up, and the rough skin on the palm of his hand rubs over my exposed backside. He pushes his hand down, slipping between my legs. A jolt goes through me from his electric touch.

And then I think of Jake.

"Chase," I murmur, moving away.

"Did I do something wrong?"

"God, no." I turn my head, needing to look away. "It's just…I think we should wait. I'm, uh, not sure if I'm ready."

"Okay. I respect your morals."

"It's not about morals. I haven't been with anyone since Jake died. I want to make sure I'm ready, for your sake."

"My sake?" he asks as if someone doing something for his sake is completely foreign. I don't know how to say it without sounding stupid. I'm already getting more and more uncomfortable as each second ticks by. I don't to be hit with guilt while he's inside me. I want to enjoy sex with Chase—fully enjoy it. And I want him to enjoy it too.

Sensing my discomfort, he moves my hair out of my face and kisses me. "Let's go inside. The mosquitos are eating me alive and I had to put *Unbroken* down after a cliffhanger ending of a chapter."

My heart swells in my chest, and I smile at Chase. "It's good, isn't it?"

"Very."

We go inside, grab blankets, pillows, and the book, then

go onto the back porch and into the hammock. Chase puts his arms around me, and I rest my head against his chest, listening to his heart beating.

"I'm sorry if this isn't how you thought your night would go."

"Don't be sorry. I rarely have expectations for anything, either. I didn't think ahead on tonight. As long as I'm with you, I'm happy."

~

"SO ROB TOLD ME SOMETHING INTERESTING," Lisa comments as soon as she sees me.

"Marley set off the alarm last night?" I suggest, peering over the top of my sunglasses.

"Hah. Hilarious." She takes off her shoes and sits on the edge of the pool to stick her feet in. I came over to my parents' to take care of Marley after Chase left, and decided to stay and lounge around on a giant inflatable pink flamingo floaty. "But yeah, he did mention that. You know what I'm talking about and oh my fucking God why didn't you call me and tell me you slept with Chase."

"Because I didn't sleep with him."

Lisa narrows her eyes, holding her hand to her forehead to shield the sun. "You can't get out of this one, Si. Rob saw you guys together last night at three am."

"Chase was with me," I start and stick my arm in the water, paddling over to Lisa. "He stayed the night with me. But we didn't have sex."

"Oh my God. Do not fucking tell me you friend-zoned him."

"I didn't. I slow-zoned him a bit though."

"What do you mean?"

135

I get closer to the edge of the pool and Lisa catches the neck of the flamingo with her foot, pulling me over.

"Honestly, I'm afraid I'm going to think about Jake when I'm with Chase. And I don't want that. And then I feel guilty for feeling that way."

"Oh." Lisa's face softens. "That makes sense. How did Chase handle the news that he wasn't getting past first base?"

"He was fine with it. And we did get past first."

"You minx," she teases.

"I'm very attracted to him. Stopping was hard for me too."

"Not as *hard* as it was for him, right?"

"It was hard. And big. Like an anaconda in his pants," I say as seriously as I can.

Lisa snorts a laugh. "Charm that snake, Si. Charm it real good."

Now I'm laughing. "We are going out to dinner tonight. Kind of. At four. Maybe that's a late lunch?"

"Why the weird time?"

"He's working at The Mill House tonight."

"Oh, that stinks."

"Yeah," I agree. "But I did tell him to come over after work if he doesn't get out too late."

Lisa wiggles her eyebrows. "His trouser-snake is going to be hungry. Feed it so it doesn't bite."

"Maybe I want it to bite." I smile and lay back on the floaty. Then my phone rings and I shoot up.

"Expecting a call from Chase?" Lisa teases and grabs my phone that's resting on a folded towel behind her. "It's not. It's your sister. Want me to decline the call?"

I make a face but shake my head. "No. I'll answer. She'll just keep calling until I do."

I hop out of the pool, dry off my hands, and grab the phone.

"Hey, Sierra," Sam says before I even say hi. "Are you busy?"

"Not really. Why?"

"Lily is having a difficult time with Sundance. He doesn't want to go over the jumps. Her show is in a few days and she's freaking out."

"Really? She is?" My eight-year-old niece is rather laid back for having two type-A parents.

"Okay. I am. The damn horse keeps stopping as soon as he gets to the jump. She already fell off once."

"Is she okay?"

"Yeah, it was as easy as a fall can be. Can you come help us? You're better with horses than I am."

Sam never admits anyone is better at her than anything. I put my phone on speaker and nudge Lisa.

"I didn't hear you. Can you repeat that?"

"Can you come help us? You're better at this than I am."

"You need my help because I'm better?"

"Yes, Sierra. We all know you're better with horses than me. Now will you please come help us?"

Lisa opens her mouth and puts her hand to her chest, faking shock. Silently laughing at her, I tell my sister I'll meet her at the barn in a few minutes.

"I like seeing you like this."

"Like what?"

Lisa smiles. "Happy. Whatever Chase is doing to you, make him keep doing it."

14

CHASE

I sit on the rock by the river, with my phone in my hand. The battery is at two percent, but I can't get myself to get up, go inside, and charge it. If the phone is dead, I can't listen to Sierra's messages.

I should have told her. Come clean. Confessed the truth and have this whole thing be behind us. I had the perfect opportunity when she asked why I didn't call. I've replayed it in my mind a million times, though mostly because of how fucking hot Sierra looked wearing my T-shirt.

The conversation could have gone a hundred different ways, with the most likely being her running away as fast as she could. Then I'd stay here long enough to help Josh with the bar and be out of here. I haven't been out west in a while. Texas was always good for business.

But I'm so damn tired of running. For the first time in my life, I want to stay where I am. And I know the only reason is because of Sierra.

I exit out of the voicemail and bring up a text instead, writing out a message to send to Sierra.

Me: **I finished Unbroken. That ending came out of nowhere**.

Sierra: **You're a fast reader. And I know!! So crazy, right? I'm glad I have someone to talk to about the book now.**

Me: **I think she set it up to write a spin-off.**

Sierra: **OMG I thought the same thing!**

Me: **I need a new book recommendation, by the way.**

Sierra: **I have a few ;-) I'll bring you something tonight.**

I start typing a reply, but my phone dies. "Dammit," I mutter and get up. I'm tired, and should probably lie down for a few hours before work tonight. Though I was more comfortable than I'd been in my whole life lying in that hammock next to Sierra, I didn't sleep much. Laying down like that—comfortable, content, completely at ease—doesn't happen too often. I wanted to soak up as much as I could, remember every minute I can.

I'm so fucking lame. I know.

~

"Is the voicemail not set up on your phone?" Josh asks. We're behind the bar, serving drinks.

Shit. It's not. Because setting it up will make all the saved messages from Sierra disappear. I think. I'm not sure. But it's not something I want to risk. "I haven't gotten around to it yet." I shrug. "My other phone should be back soon."

"Right. I almost forgot about that." He grabs a glass and goes to the tap, filling it up with beer. "Anyway, I called because Dakota wants you to see her sing in the church choir."

I haven't stepped foot in a church in years. And with all the shit I've done, there is a good chance a lightning bolt will come down from the sky, striking me down before I can go inside. But she's my niece. She's family.

"Yeah, I can go. When is it?"

"Tomorrow morning, at eight."

"Fuck, that's early."

"It must be nice having eight be early."

"Hey, you don't open until the afternoon."

"True. But I do have a four-year-old who gets up with the fucking sun." He gives the beer to a patron. "Is it too early for you?"

"No, not at all. But tomorrow...never mind. I'll be there."

Josh wipes down spilled liquor from the bar. "What's going on tomorrow?"

"Nothing." Most likely nothing, at least. I'm seeing Sierra again tonight. Late. I don't doubt that I'll stay over at her place again. That'll be three nights in a row we've been under the same roof. And three nights of not hooking up. I'd never push her, but there's a good chance I'll get carpal tunnel from all this.

"Really, because it seemed like something. Are you going to Sierra's again?"

"How do you know?"

"You can't take a piss in this town without someone finding out. I knew you were full of shit when you said you two didn't hook up."

I take a drink order and turn my back on the crowd, pulling a bottle of vodka from the shelf. There's no point trying to convince Josh otherwise. Why disappoint him, anyway? Besides, if I keep going out with Sierra, I'm sure we'll eventually hook up. Unless I die from fucking blue balls first.

I make a Dirty Shirley for a college-aged woman and move on to the next customer.

"You know that chick is eye-fucking you hard, right?"

Josh whispers, motioning to the girl who ordered the Dirty Shirley. "If she bends over, her tits are going to spill out of her top. And you didn't even notice."

I look over, and the Dirty Shirley girl catches my eye. She smiles, and then slowly pulls her straw from her mouth.

"Sierra's that good in bed, huh?" Josh heckles.

"Yeah," I agree. I have no doubt that she is, but it's so much more than that.

"You can leave early," Josh says. "I have it covered tonight."

"I can stay. I said I'd be here tonight."

"You are meeting Sierra again tonight, right?"

"I'm going over once I'm done here."

Josh smiles. "You're done. Go."

The whole people-doing-favors-for-me thing is still weird. Really fucking weird. "You don't mind?"

"Not at all. Like I said, I want you to stay. And if Sierra's got you so wrapped up you didn't even notice Tits over there, she might be the one to convince you."

"She just might be," I echo. "I'll do a round clearing tables then take off."

"Chase, just go. And have fun," he adds, raising his eyebrows.

"I can do that." I fill one more drink order then head up to the apartment, needing to wash the smell of the bar off me before going to Sierra's. It's nine-thirty, and she wasn't expecting to hear from me until at least after midnight.

Texting her throughout the day...starting our date hours before we planned...it goes against everything I've done. Breaks all the simple rules I've set up for myself.

Being eager to see her, to just spend time with her, is a new feeling for me. I fucking like it, though in the back of my mind, in the small area that I allow to process emotions, I'm terrified.

I don't want to hurt her. I don't want to be disappointed.

Facing my fears comes naturally. I don't let it hold me back, and I'm not stopping now.

Pausing in the kitchen, I pull my phone from my pocket and stare down at the screen. I lick my lips, heart thumping in my chest as I unlock the device. My finger hovers over the green phone icon. I shouldn't do it. I need to stop.

But I can't.

I need to hear her voice. Feel her pain.

"The therapist asked if I still call you." Sierra's voice is thready, void of any emotion. "She says it's not healthy and that I won't be able to move on if I keep doing this. I hate when people say that. Moving on isn't going to make my life good again. Moving on isn't a magical cure. What am I moving onto? What do I have to look forward to anymore?" She sighs and pauses for a few seconds. I press the phone closer to my ear. I think I hear the river in the background. "I remember being happy. I miss it. But I just don't see how I can ever feel whole again."

The message ends, and I pull the phone away from my face. The next message is from three months later. I guess she took her therapist's advice for a while at least.

"I got into grad school. And my first thought was to tell you."

The bad feeling is back in my stomach, and I curse myself —again—for listening to these messages. I lock my phone, set it on the table, and strip out of my clothes to shower. I'm about to turn the water on when someone knocks on the door.

I roll my eyes. I should have known better than to leave Josh tonight. I wrap a white towel around my waist and stride to the door, yanking it open. Josh isn't standing in the threshold.

Sierra is.

Her mouth opens and her eyes widen. She runs her eyes over me then looks away, only to turn right back.

"Chase. Wow. I mean hi."

"Hey. What are you doing here?" I ask. "Not that I'm not happy to see you or anything. I wasn't expecting it."

She blinks a few times in a row, following the line of hair that goes down my stomach to my cock, before looking me in the eye again. It's turning me on to know she's enjoying what she's seeing, and now is not the time to get a hard-on. I'm only wearing a towel.

"Lisa wanted to go out for drinks, and I thought I'd come see you. Your brother said you just left and thought you were up here."

I step back, letting Sierra come inside, and shut the door behind her. "Yeah, I was going to get in the shower then call you and say I got out early." I hold the towel at my hip with one hand and reach for Sierra with the other. The moment my fingers sweep across the silky fabric of her dress, I'm a goner. My heart speeds up and my lips part. I need to feel her. All of her.

She hooks her arms around my shoulders, and her finger instantly goes to the scar on my back. I press my lips to hers, softly, knowing that if the kiss turns into anything more, I won't be able to stop myself.

"You look beautiful," I tell her. She's wearing a red dress with white polka dots, a red bow in her hair, and yellow heels. "Your outfit looks familiar, which is weird to say, I know."

She shakes her head, smiling. "It's not weird, and it should be familiar." She runs her hand along the dress. "Minnie Mouse."

I use it as an excuse to slowly check her out again. Her large breasts are hidden away, which makes her outfit all the more sexy for some reason. I know what's under there, but I can't directly see it, like a present waiting to be unwrapped.

"Right. I see it now. It's subtle, but I like it."

"Thanks. I like to dress like characters but in normal clothing to see if anyone picks up on it. I have fun coming up with the concepts. Most people think it's strange."

I run my fingers through her hair. "I like strange." I kiss her again. "I like you."

She kisses me back, hands running up and down my back. I push my tongue into her mouth knowing I shouldn't because once I get started, I won't be able to stop. Sierra's hands fall down my back, over my hips, and onto the towel. She slips her fingers inside, slowly, just half an inch, teasing me in the best and worst way possible.

I kiss her harder, dipping her back. Sierra moans when I run my hand down her back and onto her ass, giving it a squeeze.

The someone calls her name, voice muffled through the closed door.

"Sierra? Are you up here?"

I stop kissing her, but I don't let go.

"It's Lisa," she sighs. "She didn't like me going up here alone."

"She's smart."

"I know," she agrees but seems annoyed. Hell, I'm annoyed. But if Sierra is going to cut me off again, this is a good stopping point. I won't push her to do anything she's not ready for.

"You should let her know you're fine."

Sierra nods, sliding her hands back up to my shoulders. I stand her upright and look at the door, keeping one hand on Sierra's waist. I know it's crazy, but it feels like if I let go, if I stop touching her, she'll slip away and disappear forever.

Or maybe I will.

I re-tuck the towel around my waist the best I can one-handed. Sierra turns, pulling out of my arm. She opens the door a foot and sticks her head out.

"Yeah, I'm here."

"Did you find Chase?" Lisa stops by the door, eyebrows raised as she looks me up and down.

"Yeah. I found him."

Lisa blinks, cocking her head to stare down Sierra. "And you stripped him naked?"

"I was already naked," I quip, giving Lisa a smirk.

"Well then," she replies. "I guess I'm not needed here. Have fun."

Sierra makes a face. "I feel bad not getting a drink with you. That's why we came, after all."

Lisa shakes her head. "I'd feel worse knowing you left *that* for me. We can get drinks another time. Like tomorrow. When you give me details."

"I don't kiss and tell." Sierra purses her lips and tries not to smile.

Lisa turns to me and puts her hand next to her mouth. "Yes, she does," she whisper-talks. "So give her something to talk about."

"Now two people have told you that," I say to Sierra. "Maybe you'll take her advice at least."

"She better," Lisa says. "Don't disappoint me, Si."

Sierra rolls her eyes. "Are you sure you don't want me to get a drink with you?"

Lisa checks the time on her phone. "I'm gonna call Rob. He gets off in twenty minutes so he'll be here in thirty. I can play a game of pool with Wyatt until then."

"Let him win," Sierra teases.

Lisa grimaces. "I physically can't do anything bad on purpose. Wyatt can just grow a pair and deal with it."

Sierra laughs, emerald eyes glimmering. "Then don't

complain to me when he stomps around work annoying the shit out of you for it."

Lisa huffs. "Fine. Call me in the morning."

"I will." Sierra moves away to give Lisa a hug goodbye. Lisa eyes me up and down once more, then whispers, "not fair" to Sierra before leaving.

"So," Sierra starts, closing the door.

"So," I echo. "Are you hungry? We could get something to eat."

"I am, actually. I was going to get something here with Lisa. You?"

"I'm always hungry."

She bites her lip and I notice her eyes keep dropping down to the V-line of muscle above my hips.

"I'll take a quick shower," I go on. "And then you can tell me which of the two sit-down restaurants in this town to take you to."

"I like that plan."

"Do you want the TV on or something?"

She reaches into her yellow bag and pulls out her Kindle. "I'm good."

∾

"I'M SORRY," the waitress says, coming over to our table, bill in hand. "We're closing in five minutes."

I tear my eyes away from Sierra and look around. The tables around us are empty and cleared. We're the only ones here.

"Oh, sorry," Sierra says, looking just as shocked as I am. "I lost track of the time."

The waitress gives her a warm smile. "It's all right, honey."

I take the bill before Sierra has a chance to even consider

paying it. After dinner we ordered drinks, and then dessert, and then drinks again.

I always thought the whole 'we can talk for hours' thing was bullshit until today. Because the time went by too fast, and if Sierra and I sat and talked the rest of the night I'd be happy. And saying 'she gets me' is even more of a bullshit line, but she does.

"Every cat I've ever met has been an asshole," I say, going back to our conversation. I pay the bill and leave the waitress a generous tip since we kept her here.

"Then you haven't met the right cats. Mine are nice. Well, Tinkerbell is." Sierra finishes her wine and laughs. "Dolly is an asshole. I'm trying to contradict you and I'm failing."

"Dogs, on the other hand, like people. Even people who are shitty to them."

I stand and go around the table, offering a hand to Sierra. "I know. I like dogs too. Maybe it's the way you have to earn a cat's affection that I like. You just said it: dogs love you no matter what. But cats—" She holds up a finger, pointing at me. "You have to earn their affection."

We step into the thick, summer air, emerging onto the main street that runs through the downtown of Summer Hill. The bookstore is a few blocks away, and while most shops are closed by this hour, people mill about the town.

"I'm not used to this heat yet."

"The humidity is high," Sierra comments. "It's been a humid summer. And you never really get used to it."

"I didn't think so."

"Want to go swimming?"

"You have a pool?" I ask, not remembering seeing one in her yard.

"Not technically, but my parents have one and they're still out of town."

"Then, yes," I say, not caring that I don't have swim trunks with me. I have a few pairs, actually, since I frequented the beach while living along the shore in New Jersey. Sierra says nothing about going to her house to get one either.

"Thanks," she says as I open the passenger door of my Mustang for her. I hurry around and get in, and head toward her house. We park by her parents' house and go around back, Sierra enters a passcode and opens a gate to the back-yard. Crickets sing out as we dash along a cobblestone path to the pool.

My previous line of work permitted me inside a handful of upscale, luxury houses like this. I was there for a job, not as a guest, but I still stood in awe of people who lived that way. The Belmont's historic estate isn't as over-the-top as some of the new mansions I've been in, but they know how to live lavishly. The pool setup is no exception.

Sierra opens French doors to a pool house, revealing a built-in bar.

"Want anything?" she asks.

I close the space between us, standing behind Sierra. I wrap my arms around her, and she presses her ass into my cock. My lips meet the skin on her neck and Sierra melts against me.

I already feel drunk.

I'm struggling to stay in control.

"I want you," I whisper. Sierra takes in a quick breath. I can feel her pulse rise, bounding through her body. "When-ever you're ready."

"Chase," she moans, whirling around in my arms. Her eyes fall shut and she rests her head against my chest. "Thank you."

"Stop thanking me, Sierra."

She doesn't say anything. She just takes my hand and leads me to the edge of the pool and takes her shoes off.

"Float with me?" she asks, reaching for a big, pink

flamingo floaty. I take off my shoes, pull my phone and wallet from my pocket, and toss them all onto a lounge chair. It takes a bit of creativity, but we both get on the damn thing with minimal splashing. I let my bare feet dangle in the water and lay back. Sierra's right next to me, head resting on my arm. We look up at the stars above, not talking. Time passes, minutes, then maybe an hour, and we're still perfectly content and comfortable together.

"How did you get the scar on your back?" she asks quietly, slipping her hand onto my chest.

"I was in the right place at the wrong time," I say after a moment's consideration. There's no good way to tell her I broke into someone's house to take a piece of priceless art.

"Don't give it all away," she teases.

"It was from a piece of glass," I go on. "From a broken window." A window I broke as I snuck into a house that was supposed to be empty. I felt bad for the guy and went easy on him. I left him unconscious on the floor but alive at least, after I allowed him to get one good swing on me. I failed to see the broken glass in his hand, however.

"Ouch," she says. "No wonder you knew to check for glass in my ankle."

"Yeah, I learned from experience." Carefully, I turn onto my side and face Sierra. She hooks her arm around me and closes her eyes, tipping her head up so her nose brushes against mine.

And now we're kissing. Slow, soft kisses. I cup Sierra's cheek with my hand and the kisses turn hard. Deep. Desperate. I move my hand down to Sierra's waist. And then her hip. I gather her skirt in my hand, bunching up the fabric around her ass. Sierra moves closer, bringing her leg up and over mine. My fingers press into her skin, feeling the warmth between her legs as I urge her onto me. Sierra pushes up, fury in her kisses. I slide my hand up to her waist, pulling her close.

She's over top of me now, and, fuck, she's hot. Her breasts crush against me and she's kissing me like her life depends on it. She widens her legs, straddling me, putting us off balance, but it's so far in the back of my mind, I don't realize it until the floaty flips over and Sierra and I both sink into the water.

In the shallow end, we both pop out of the water, Sierra flips her wet hair out of her face, green eyes wide. She looks at me for a beat and then we both start laughing. I reach for her, bringing her against me.

"You did say you wanted to go swimming," I muse.

"True. And the water does feel good tonight."

"It feels very good."

Water laps against us, and I reach out to push Sierra's wet hair away from her face. I've never been a cuddle-after-sex type of guy, but right now I want to hold Sierra to me, wrapped up in peaceful silence as much as I want to fuck her.

Sierra takes my arm, wiping beads of water off my tattoos so she can trace them with her finger.

"Do you want to dry off?" she asks.

"Only if you do."

"I don't mind being wet."

I can't help but smirk.

She flushes slightly but laughs. "Take that how you want."

"Can't I just take you?" I take her around the waist and bring her over.

"I think so," she whispers softly as her long, wet lashes come together. She leans back in the water, spreading her arms and legs out in an attempt to float. "I always sink."

"The wet dress isn't helping," I tell her. "It's weighing you down."

"Chase Henson, are you trying to get me out of my

dress?" she asks with fake shock, standing upright. She backs up to the edge of the pool and hops up, keeping her feet in the water.

"Is it working?" I ask as I join her.

"There's a good chance it will."

Fuck. I can't resist her any longer. I twist and wrap my arms around her, and we're kissing like we never stopped. Water from her wet hair drips down her face, but I don't care. I find the zipper on the back of her dress and pull it down, slipping my hand inside her dress and feeling her wet skin. We lay back on the concrete surrounding the pool, kissing and removing each other's clothing.

"Chase," Sierra breathes. "Hang on."

It takes everything I have to move away. Her finger sweeps across my cheek and then she gets up.

"Come here," she says, taking my hand. We go around the bar and into the pool house, emerging into a living room. It's nicer and larger than probably half the houses in this town and sits empty in the Belmonts' backyard most of the time. The air conditioner is on, bringing a chill to our wet skin.

"You were right about the dress. It is heavy." She bites her lip and turns around, gathering her hand in her hair. "Can you unzip it all the way?"

Fuck yes, I can. "Sure."

Slowly, I pull the zipper the rest of the way down, where it stops right above her ass. She's wearing a bright purple bra and her lace underwear matches. If she were anyone else, I'd strip her out of the dress, pick her up over my shoulder, and throw her down on the couch. We'd fuck, get dressed again, and I'd leave with an empty promise of a phone call.

But she's not anyone else.

She's the only woman who's succeeded at making me nervous about fucking this up. And she's not even trying.

With her back turned, she lets the straps of her dress slide over her shoulders and into a fabric puddle around her feet and onto the floor.

"That's better," she says shyly and turns around, fighting herself to not be self-conscious. Though she has absolutely nothing to be embarrassed about.

"You are beautiful," I tell her and step over, taking a firm grasp on her hips. "So fucking hot." I kiss her neck, and Sierra softly moans, hands going to my chest. She drops them to my waist, popping the button on my jeans. Using her free hand, Sierra fumbles to push my jeans down, but the wet denim sticks to my skin. I help her get them off, then raise my hands above my head so she can remove my shirt.

She shivers as the air kicks on again, sending a blast of cold right at us. This time I do pick her up and take her to the couch, grabbing a blanket. I cover us both and put my arm around her shoulders, bringing her in so her head is resting on my shoulder.

"This place is nice."

"It is," she agrees. "I had sleepovers out here a lot when I was a kid."

"I bet your friends loved it."

"I think they loved it more than they liked me," she says with a laugh. "That all seems so long ago. And so trivial."

"It does."

She relaxes against me, absentmindedly running her fingers up and down my arm. Then she turns and puts her hand to my chest, outlining a tattoo on my chest.

"What does it say?" she asks softly, mouthing the words spelled out in Latin.

"'If you tell the truth, you don't have to remember anything.' Mark Twain said it."

"I love that. It's deep in a very simple way."

"Yeah," I agree, and that's the reason I got it. To remind me to stay grounded despite the crazy shit I got myself into.

"Why is it in Latin?"

I shrug. "I thought it sounded cooler that way."

Sierra laughs softly. "Does each one have significance?"

"Yeah, in a way at least. They're significant because I like them," I offer, making Sierra smile. "I get a new one every time I move."

"You've moved a lot." Nerves tingle under her fingers as she outlines another tattoo.

"I have."

"Can I ask why?"

"You can," I tell her. "And I'll answer, though I don't really have a good answer other than the concept of people staying in one place is weird to me. You work the same job, doing the same thing over and over again only to come home to the same house, surrounded by the same people every day for the rest of your life. It's too easy to get stuck in an endless cycle of going through the motions that way. I wanted to experience life, not just survive because I had to." The words leave my mouth a second before I recall one of Sierra's voice-mails, which said something similar.

"I like going home to the same place and seeing the same people every day."

I shrug. "Maybe if I had people I liked to go home to, it'd be a different story." The honesty in my statement sends a shock through me.

Sierra doesn't speak, but instead tips her head to the side, inspecting me. "Were you looking for them?" she finally whispers.

"Who?"

"People you liked enough."

"No. I didn't think they could exist."

"Didn't? You do now?"

My heart speeds up. "I'm starting to think it's possible."

Her hands land on my shoulders, and I rest mine on the small of her back, gently bringing her in.

"You have no idea how fucking beautiful you are, do you?" I ask.

Sierra just shakes her head, looking a little shy.

"If only you knew what you are doing to me."

The shyness goes away and Sierra flashes a coy smile. "Oh, I know." She drops her gaze to my lap, staring for a few seconds before moving closer. She plunges her hand inside my boxers, feeling the full length of my hard cock. Her slender fingers wrap around it, starting at the base, and slowly pumping up. She circles her thumb over the tip, and it feels so damn good. My head falls back against the couch as she keeps working her hand. I widen my legs and Sierra moves closer, going onto her knees. She keeps jerking me off, and her soft skin is enough to make me come if she keeps this up.

I take her wrist and pull it from my boxers and kiss her hard. My tongue goes in her mouth and I pull her to me, crushing her large breasts against my chest. We lay back, and I cannot stop kissing her.

The glistening tip of my cock sticks out of my boxers, and Sierra reaches for it again, moaning with hunger for it when she feels the wetness.

"God, I want you," I groan, and Sierra's grasp tightens. Her hand on my cock feels fucking amazing. Her pussy is going to destroy me and I'm going to love every fucking minute of it.

"I want you too," she pants and I advance, laying her down on the couch, dick pressing into her tender core. Sierra bends her knees and wraps a leg around me. I can feel the heat of her pussy through her panties. She inhales deep, pushing her tits up into my face.

She bucks her hips, rubbing herself against me, and

moans. I brush her hair out of her face and kiss her, taking her bottom lip between my teeth before I move my mouth to her neck. Sierra gasps and a shiver runs through her. She curls her fingers, nails biting into my skin. The pain turns me on even more, and I'm rocking my hips against hers, feeling like I could come in seconds.

I'm so caught up in her. I want to come while at the same time I want to fuck her all night. I kiss her neck again and start to trail kisses down it. I pause at her collarbone and pull back to admire her breasts. Her bra has no padding —not that she needs it—and I can see the faint outline of her nipples through the wet fabric. It's the kind that clasps in the front, and it's so fucking hot when I undo it. I palm my hand over one of her tits while I kiss my way to the other. I flick my tongue over her pert nipple, and Sierra squirms.

She rakes her fingers through my hair, moaning softly. Keeping one breast in my mouth, continuing to tease her nipple with my tongue, I slide my other hand down and slip my fingers inside her underwear. With one finger, I circle the entrance to her sweet pussy, cock aching to push inside. She's so fucking wet.

I rub my finger over her clit, spreading her wetness from inside. I want to taste her, to lick up every drop she gives and not stop until she's coming so hard she screams my name.

In one sudden movement, I pull away and move down, head between her legs. I look up, smirking at Sierra who steals a glance down. She bites her bottom lip, eyes wide, and breasts heaving as she inhales. Keeping my eyes locked with hers, I take both sides of her panties and slowly roll them down her thighs. She lifts her ass so I can slide them off, leaving them in a pile on the floor.

Then I move back up, putting my lips to hers once more before kissing a trail down her stomach, not stopping until my mouth is hovering over her pussy. Her muscles twitch, and I know she's waiting. Wanting.

I turn my head and take the soft skin on the inside of her thigh into my mouth. I suck it soft, then hard, and then nip at it with my teeth. Sierra groans and reaches down, taking a tangle of my hair in her fingers. I turn my head, warm breath hitting her clit. She's squirming against me now, so fucking worked up she's desperate for the release.

I lash my tongue out against her once, relishing in how good she tastes. Then I pull back again, running my fingertips up and down her thighs. Her grip on my head tightens, and she directs me to her pussy.

There is something so fucking hot about a woman who takes charge. She knows what she wants.

Me.

And I don't disappoint. I move my hands under her thigh, lifting her legs over my shoulders. I spread her wide and go at her clit with my tongue, feeling her core tighten as she gets closer and closer to coming.

I slip a finger inside and moan against her pussy when I feel how hot and tight she is. I press against her inner wall, finding her g-spot.

"Ohhh," she moans, twisting her fingers in my hair. "Faaa…faaa…fuck." She pushes herself against my face as she comes. Her pussy contracts wildly around my finger and my dick aches to feel her tighten around it. I keep my mouth on her, not letting up until she's writhing in pleasure.

Sierra's chest rapidly rises and falls, and she lets her hands drop to her sides. The orgasm brought a flush to her face and it's sexy as hell. I wipe my mouth on the back of my hand and then kiss her again, gently brushing her damp hair back, giving her a moment to catch her breath. Sierra wraps her arms around me, slowly running her fingers down my ass. She grips me tight and pushes me against her.

I pull back just enough to look into her eyes. She's so beautiful.

Sierra lifts her head off the couch and kisses me. She tugs down my boxers with her other hand. I want nothing more than to push my dick into her, but I want to make sure she's okay with it too. She was hesitant only yesterday, after all.

I pull my mouth away from hers, feeling like I'm underwater and just ripped off my oxygen mask.

"We can stop," I pant. "If you want to. Just tell me."

She brings her hand up and cups my face. There's so much emotion in her eyes, and it almost breaks my heart. "I want *you*."

In a mad dash of desperation, she yanks my boxers off. My skin, cold from the wet fabric, burns against her warmth and I fucking love it. She widens her legs, welcoming me between. Her thighs are still wet and warm from her orgasm. She lifts her hips, aligning the tip of my cock against her tender core. I move my gaze down and she opens her eyes, and for a split second, it's like I'm looking into some sort of mirror that reflects only my soul.

My lips find hers again and I kiss her as I push inside. She cries out, eyes falling shut. She's tight and warm and feels so fucking good. I bury my cock in her pussy and kiss her hard. I pull out slowly, not stopping until only the tip is back at her entrance. Then I push in hard. Sierra moans and grips me tight, rocking herself right along with me. I thrust in and out of her hard and fast, then stop and move my hips in a circular motion that sets Sierra over the edge. Her breathing quickens and I feel her core tighten around my cock. Her fingers dig into my flesh and her legs shake as a second orgasm rolls through. I open my eyes and watch her face as she comes.

My breath hitches and I let my head fall forward, resting against hers. My heart is racing, and every nerve in my body is alive. I'm fucking Sierra hard, and it feels so damn good. But it's more than a physical connection, and I've never felt that before.

"Chase," she pants, shuddering from an overload of pleasure. A guttural groan leaves my throat and I come hard, pushing my cock in deep and holding it there, buried inside her. Panting, I rest my head against hers, holding myself up with my elbows. Sierra's breasts rapidly rise and fall and she brings her hands up to my hair. I kiss her gently before I slide out, and then rest by her side on the couch, spooning my body around hers.

Sierra puts her hand over mine, and neither of us speak for a moment. I brush her hair aside and kiss her neck.

"Are you okay?" I ask, so remotely far from anything I've ever said after sex before. Physically, I know Sierra enjoyed it; she came multiple times. But emotionally...that's a different story and a whole new world of concern for me. What the hell is happening? It's strange, but I like it. I like *her*.

"Yes," she whispers back, knowing what I'm asking about. "I'm better than okay."

15

SIERRA

I stand in front of my dresser, close my eyes, and grab the pull. My fingers tremble and my heart aches distantly in the background. The drawer sticks like it always has, but this time it takes a little extra yank since it hasn't been opened in so long.

Not able to look just yet, I blindly reach inside, feeling around for the pair of cotton pajama pants hidden beneath old T-shirts. The tag pokes the flesh under my fingernail, and I know I have the right thing. I grab it, keeping my eyes up, and go into the living room where Chase is waiting.

"You can wear these," I tell him, extending the folded pajama pants.

"Are you sure?" he asks softly, fingers sweeping my wrist as he takes the pants from me. "I can stay in this if it's—"

"No, you're soaked from the pool. You need to change."

He gives me a cheeky grin. "I can get naked."

The heartache quiets and I smile back. "I approve of that idea."

"Really though...it's okay?"

I nod and having him care this much helps. "Yes. Jake

never wore them, actually. I do a lot of online shopping since, you know, Summer Hill isn't exactly filled with tons of stores, and these didn't arrive until after he died. The tag is still on. You'll have to pull it off."

Chase's eyebrows push together, and I know he's struggling to find the right thing to say. I don't even know what I want to hear. Six months after Jake died, my mom, Lisa, and Samantha came over to help me get rid of the rest of Jake's things. I got mad, screamed at them, and even threw a coffee mug at the wall. Having his things here made it feel like he was going to come home. I could close my eyes at night, after looking in on the open closet and see his things hanging up and pretend he was still away at school.

That he was still alive.

They told me I needed to get rid of his things so I could move on. I kept his favorite shirt, his Dallas Cowboys hoodie that I wore more than he did...and those stupid pants.

"What's with the cats?" he asks, looking down at the black pants, with multi-colored cats wearing party hats printed all over.

"It was a joke. He always called me a crazy cat-lady."

Chase just nods then goes into the bathroom to change out of his wet clothes. I shake my head at myself and sink down onto the couch. Tinkerbell jumps up into my lap, immediately purring.

"I make everything awkward," I tell the tabby. "Should I not talk about Jake? He was part of my life, and it's not like he's an ex." I sigh, rolling my eyes. "Fuck."

The bathroom door opens, and a few seconds later, Chase comes back into the living room. I was afraid I'd get hit with sadness when I looked at the pants that were meant for another, but right now, my attention goes to the perfect "V" of muscles on his torso and the bulge from his cock moving slightly with each step.

I want Chase. I want to move forward with him. I want to have sex with him again because the sex we had just an hour ago was amazing.

Dolly dashes in front of Chase, darting between his feet. Chase comes to a sudden halt so he won't step on the cat, and to my surprise, she rubs on him. Chase reaches down and she leans into his touch.

"That cat hates life," I say, blinking rapidly to make sure I'm seeing things right. "I can hardly pet her half the time."

Chase picks up Dolly—and she's fucking purring, that traitor. "No pussy can resist me."

I laugh, finding him all the more attractive. There's something hot about a guy who can make you scream in bed *and* make you laugh.

Dolly growls a second later, and Chase sets her down. "She's a weird cat."

"She is. At least she's pretty."

Chase sits next to me on the couch, slipping his arm around me. "I need a new book to read."

"Oh, right. You do. And I have one for you. It's a romance set in the zombie apocalypse."

"Sounds interesting."

"It is. It's a four-book series, and each book is pretty long. I'm a sucker for long books. I love the way a big, thick spine feels in my hands," I say coyly, narrowing my eyes before smiling.

"I never thought it was possible to get turned on hearing someone talk about a book before."

"Speaking of big, thick things..." I run my hand over Chase's chest and onto his abs, feeling every ridge of muscle beneath my fingers. Chase closes his eyes and leans in, kissing me. Feeling his lips against mine not only turns me on but also makes me happy. Ridiculously happy. I have to stop kissing him because I'm smiling.

"What?" Chase whispers.

"Nothing," I whisper back, wrapping my arms around him so my hands are in his hair. "I just haven't felt like this in a long time."

Chase runs his hands down my back and pulls me tight against his chest. "I've never felt like this." Still holding me, he lays down on the couch, bringing me with so I'm on top of him. I get comfortable, resting my head on his chest. Chase presses a kiss to my forehead. "I don't know what you're doing to me, Sierra, but I don't want you to stop."

"I don't want to either."

Chase squeezes me in a tight hug, kisses me again, and then falls silent, running his hand up and down my arm. Tinkerbell jumps up, purring loudly, and settles on the pillow above us, kneading her paws into Chase's hair. We both laugh, and I reach up, petting the big cat.

"Do you go to church?" Chase asks.

"Sometimes, why?"

"My niece is in some choir thing and wants me to watch her tomorrow. I'm not a church person. Too many rules and stipulations."

"You're in the wrong state," I joke. "I was brought up going to church. Sundays are 'family days,' and if I'm not in church, I get the disappointed glares from my parents and grandma during dinner. We all go over to my parents for dinner pretty much every Sunday. And by 'we all' I mean everyone."

"Do you have a big family?"

"Maybe? I'm not sure what's normal or not. My mom's family is on the small side, I'd say, but they're all up east so we rarely see them. My dad has two sisters and they both have kids, so I have five cousins."

"That's a lot."

"Is it? And my sister has three kids—two girls and a boy—

and then two of my cousins have kids, and another is pregnant right now. My cousins from my dad's older sister are a lot older than me, like nearly ten years older and live like an hour away. I don't see them very often. Lisa and I are the youngest."

"You two have always been close then, right?"

I nod. "My aunt—her mom—and my mom are good friends. And Lisa's older sister and my sister are friends. That's just how it is around here."

"You said you have a brother that lives in Orlando, right?"

"Yeah," I say, not remembering talking about Scott. "When did I say that?"

The tiniest bit of panic flashes across Chase's face for just a millisecond. "The other night."

"Oh, right. And yeah, he's one of the few Belmonts who got out alive."

Chase laughs. "Why'd he move?"

"The farm life wasn't his thing, and he got an engineering job with Disney. He works on building rides and attractions."

"That's pretty damn cool."

"I know! We used to give him hell every holiday to share all the Disney secrets with us, but he never did."

"I've never been to Disney World."

"We've been quite a few times. I love it. Though the last time I went…" I shake my head. The last time I went was Scott's idea, thinking it would be good for me to get out of Summer Hill and into 'the real world' as he put it. I spent a long weekend with him and his then-girlfriend, ping-ponging between emotions. I'd enjoy a ride only to get off and immediately break down crying.

"Maybe I'll take you someday," Chase says, pushing a loose strand of hair back and tucking it into my messy braid. "And you can show me around since you're an expert."

"I'd like that."

"And if you wear your Minnie dress again, I'll dress up like Mickey," he says with a smile.

"You have no idea how much I'd love that. You don't happen to have a tight, red V-neck shirt, brown leggings, tall boots, and mustard-yellow leather gloves, do you?"

"Shit, I did, but I left them behind when I moved. I knew I should have kept them. The gloves were well broken-in at this point too. Whose costume is that?"

"Gaston, the bad guy in *Beauty and the Beast*."

"You want me to be the bad guy?"

"Fictional villains can be rather sexy." I laugh, bringing my face down to Chase's. "I'll go with you."

"I'd like that. But where are we going?"

"Church, to watch your niece in the children's choir. One of my nieces is in it too. Maybe they know—"

Chase kisses me, and my heart skips a beat. "Sorry. I'm failing at resisting you."

I keep my face close to his so that our noses are touching. "I don't mind that one bit."

"What do you wear to church?"

"Most people our age dress rather casual now," I explain. "The older crowd still puts on 'church clothes,' and I usually wear a dress. But I wear dresses because they're comfortable. You could get away with nice jeans and a button-up shirt. If you want to be safe, wear dress pants with that shirt. No tie needed."

"Sounds good. I'm not a morning person."

"I'm not either. If we each set an alarm, we'll be safe."

"I'm going to be tempted to hit snooze and stay in bed with you."

I groan, feeling heat spread inside me. "I can be easily swayed, you know."

"Nothing about you is easy, Sierra. And I like that."

I rest my head on his chest again, listening to his slow, steady heartbeat.

"Are you tired?" he asks.

"I should be, but I'm not. You?"

"Same. Even if I was, I'd stay up."

I close my eyes, feeling my heart swell in my chest. Chase is everything I ever wanted in a man, even before Jake. The things he says, the unapologetic way he lets me know how I make him feel, the way he's honest with me, his patience and understanding of my harrowed past, how he makes me laugh…

"I think I hear the chupacabras in the distance," he murmurs.

"I do too." I sit up, turning to the window. "Sounds like they got a kill. We can go onto the screened-in porch for a better listen if you'd like."

"I would."

We move to the back porch, and Chase takes my hand, listening to the coyotes yip and howl for several minutes before moving on, and the chorus of crickets and katydids envelope us in the night.

"It's so loud yet so relaxing." Chase turns his gaze from the dark yard to me.

"I love it. I missed it so much when I was at college I'd play those relaxation soundtracks at night so I could sleep."

"If I was used to it, I'd miss it too."

I bite my lip, staring into Chase's eyes. His words echo in my mind, about how he never stays in one place for a long enough time for it to feel like home, and I'm hit with a sudden desperation for him to stay. I hesitate, scared he doesn't feel as strongly as I do in this moment. I close my eyes, inhale, and slowly let my breath out.

Three…two…one…

"Maybe you will get used to it."

He steps in, angling his body to mine, and rests his hands on my waist. I hook mine over his shoulders.

"Maybe I will." He rests his forehead against mine, and everything stands still. He gently kisses me, then breaks away, takes a fistful of my hair and pulls it to the side, moving my head over and exposing my neck right where I like to be kissed. He bites and sucks at my flesh, and a shiver travels through me. I bring my hands down to his hips and he takes them both, bringing them behind my back. Holding my hands hostage with one of his, he plunges the other hand inside my shorts, deft fingers sweeping across my hot center.

I moan, wriggling against him, and try to free my hands. His grip tightens, and he puts his lips back to my mouth, kissing me like his life depends on it. He rubs my clit and my breath hitches as desire winds tighter and tighter inside me. Unable to move my hands and touch him, my need for a release doubles and I'm panting, desperate for more.

Chase circles my clit with his finger before pushing it inside me, making me gasp. He presses against my inner walls again and again, then moves his fingers back to my sensitive clit, making my knees weak. I'm getting wetter by the second, and when my muscles start to contract, Chase releases my hands. I grab onto his shoulders, keeping myself upright as the orgasm runs through me.

Chase doesn't let up, and it's almost too much to handle. He hooks his free arm around me, keeping me from falling to the floor. I loudly moan and curl my fingers into his bare flesh, legs trembling. Not giving me a moment to catch my breath, he closes the distance between us, and his hard cock presses into my belly. I groan again, still feeling the effects of the orgasm running rampant in my body.

His arms go around me and he lifts me up, carrying me back a few paces and setting me down next to the hammock.

"Take your pants off," he instructs, voice deep and full of lust.

My fingers tremble and I look right into Chase's eyes as I pull down my fabric shorts. I'm not wearing underwear, but Chase already found that out when he finger-fucked me. Still, the sight seems to take him by surprise and I think he's going to lay me down and have his way with me right now.

Instead, he has me sit on the edge of the hammock and he drops to his knees, putting my legs over his shoulders.

"Lay back," he orders, and my heart starts hammering away the moment I do. The hammock swings forward, bringing my core to Chase's face. His tongue lashes against me and I cry out. Twisting the ropes of the hammock in my hands, I lift my head and watch Chase. Minutes later, I toss my head back as I come again, so hard it makes my vision blackout.

This time, Chase settles next to me, gently stroking the inside of my thigh until my heart stops racing and I can breathe again. I twist in the hammock and kiss him. We're laying sideways on the hammock, with our legs dangling over the edge. I slide my hand down Chase's stomach, pushing the elastic band of the pajama pants out of the way. I pump his cock in my hand a few times before I move over, straddling him.

Chase keeps his feet planted on the ground and his hands on my waist to steady me as I position his cock under me. We lock eyes as I move down, pushing his hardness into me. Chase lets out a moan, which turns me on all over again. He slides a hand up under my T-shirt, thumb circling my nipple.

I lean forward onto him, trying to fuck him but not flip us over in the hammock at the same time. My movements are more of a grind than a thrust, but I don't think Chase minds. His breathing quickens and suddenly he picks me up and moves us to the ground, where he lays over top of me and drives his cock in and out of me hard and fast until he comes.

His head drops against mine. Both panting, we lay there for a minute trying to catch our breath. My wind chimes ring out around us as a cool breeze blows through the night.

"That was fun," I pant, curling my legs up and giving his ass a squeeze.

"I'd do it again." He gives me a cheeky grin and gets up, grabbing my shorts and tossing them to me. I clean myself up the best I can before I stand. We go inside and into my bedroom. Chase sits on the bed while I use the bathroom, emerging in a new pair of pajamas.

"Now I'm tired," I say, sitting on the bed next to him.

"Me too."

"So," he starts, putting his arm around me. "I came inside you. Twice."

"Oh, yeah. Um…" I stopped taking birth control after Jake died. There was no point. I've never had a regular cycle, and keeping track of when my period is due has fallen to the wayside with everything else going on. But I do know it's been at least three weeks. I should get it soon. Fuck. I hope so. "I don't have anything. And the chances or getting pregnant are against us, right?"

Chase gives a grim nod then shrugs. "I don't think I have anything either. And probably. Just, uh, let me know. I don't usually do that. There's something about you that makes me lose control."

I look at Chase, the man who just fucked me senseless minutes ago, and feel shy. Do I need to ask him to stay the night? Is it a given? We talked about getting up and going to church together, which implies going to sleep and waking up together, right?

"We can go to bed," Chase says slowly as if he's reading my mind.

"Do you mind if I shower first?"

"Not at all."

"Okay, and I have an extra toothbrush if you need it. I'll leave it out on the sink. The shower and toilet have their own room in the bathroom, so you can come in and brush your teeth."

"Okay, thanks."

I get up, wondering if I should have invited Chase to shower with me. We've had sex twice, and he's been up close and personal with every inch of me already. But in the heat of the moment, it's hot. When I'm naked and shampooing my hair…not so much. I mentally roll my eyes at myself. I need to stop over-thinking.

I brush my teeth then take a quick shower, then get out and towel dry my hair the best I can before getting dressed. Chase is in bed, under the covers, reading the book I had left on my nightstand from a few days ago.

I'm not sure I've seen anything hotter in my whole life.

Chase jerks his head up, looking startled, most likely from the sound of my ovaries exploding.

"This is surprisingly good," he says, closing the book.

"It's very dirty." I throw back the covers and get in bed next to him. My heart skips a beat and nerves tingles down my spine. I've spent the night with Chase before, just never in this sense.

Deliberate.

"Now I'm even more intrigued."

"Quinn Harlow is one of my favorite authors."

Chase puts the book down and turns off the light. He takes me by the waist and pulls me close, then spoons his body around mine. Physically, I'm exhausted. I haven't had that many orgasms in one day in, well, ever. I haven't gotten much sleep the last few days and my body longs for it, but my mind won't shut off, though tonight, it's not necessarily a bad thing.

Because after over a year of living in the dark, I'm finally starting to see the light. And the sunshine on my face feels so damn good.

~

"You're still getting ready?"

I turn away from the mirror, hair wrapped around my curling iron, and almost burn my forehead. I blink. Once. Twice. Three times.

"Not everyone can just throw on a suit and look as good as you," I finally muster, still taking in the sight of Chase. His button-down shirt is tucked into gray dress pants, belted around his trim waist. His normally messy hair is neat and right now he really could pass for that mega-rich CEO he pretended to be the first time we met. The transformation from rugged bad boy to sexy-man-in-a-suit is making my brain turn into mush.

"You'd look good in anything," he tells me, crossing his arms and leaning on the doorway to the bathroom. He got up this morning and went home to shower and change before church.

I pull the hot iron from my hair and smile at his reflection. "Thanks, but I think we have to agree to disagree."

He raises his eyebrows and crosses the room, stopping behind me with his arms wrapping around my waist. His lips find my neck and I close my eyes, leaning into him. And then I feel the heat of my curling iron not a moment too soon, and jerk it away from my arm at the last second.

"You're distracting," I murmur.

"You say it like it's a bad thing." He slides his hands down my thighs and inches my skirt up.

170

"It's not." I set the curling iron down inside the sink and hold onto Chase's arms. "What time is it?"

He looks over me and down at his wrist. "Seven thirty-two."

"Shit." I'm nowhere near ready and I still have to feed Marley.

"I'm going to take that as you need me to stop distracting you."

"Yeah," I groan, not wanting him to step away. "We don't want to be late. Walking in late is worse than not going to church. If you're not there, you have the chance of the whole 'out of sight out of mind' thing and people might not notice. But if you walk in late, everyone sees you."

"Makes sense." Chase shakes his head. "This town is weird."

"It is. Which is probably why I like it. I fit in."

"You do fit in, but you're not like some of the others."

"What do you mean?" I wrap another section of hair around my curling iron.

"You're not judgmental."

I meet Chase's eyes via his reflection in the mirror. "I'm the worst. I judge everyone and I judge hard. I just don't say anything."

Chase laughs. "I don't believe that for a second."

I smile back at him and quickly curl the rest of my hair, and then we rush out of the door, swing by my parents' to feed Marley, and then speed to church.

"If lightning strikes me, you're going down with me," Chase says, looking at my hand in his as we walk through the parking lot.

I laugh and shake my head. "You're not going to get smote. Smited? Smoted? Whatever. The worse thing that's going to happen today is a lot of questions and a little bit of gossip."

"People gossip at church?"

"All the damn time."

"I don't feel as bad about not going to church now."

We make it halfway through the parking lot before someone stops us, asking how I've been and who Chase is. The same thing happens three more times before we make it into the chapel, and I swear I can feel eyes on us the entire mass. Being the subject of gossip and stares is nothing new to me. I'm well aware that being born a Belmont makes me interesting—to the people of Summer Hill at least. But today it's bothering me. Are people thinking it's too soon for me to be with another man? Jake's been gone for a year and a half. When is it socially okay to get on with my life?

And more importantly, why do I care?

Chase and I take a seat in the back minutes before the service starts. Lisa and Rob come in not long after we do, and slip into the pew next to us. Rob is in his uniform and is either on the clock or going to work right after this. Most of the town, including its police officers, attend church on Sunday morning. It never dawned on me until right now that this is the perfect time to commit a crime.

Chase and I walk out of church hand in hand, and his brother waves him over as we get to Chase's car. Lisa is fast approaching, so Chase goes over to see Josh while I wait by the Mustang for my cousin.

"This is Chase's car?" Lisa asks incredulously.

"It is. You seem surprised."

She purses her lips and looks from the car to Chase. "What did he do before he moved here?"

"I don't know."

"Really?"

"Yeah, it's never come up."

"Interesting."

"Why is it interesting?" I ask.

"Because I know how much a car like this costs, and the fact that he's wearing a designer suit and an expensive watch makes me wonder what the hell he used to do."

"His suit is designer?"

"Yes. I might have taken a minute or two to check out his ass and saw the label. His ass is very fine, but I'm sure you're aware."

"It is," I say and force a smile. I have asked Chase about his previous line of work, and he's declined to comment. In fact, he told me it was a long story. My mind races and I can't come up with anything rational. He said he moved around a lot. He could be a traveling nurse for all I know.

"So," Lisa goes on. "You guys came together. Does that mean you spent the night together?"

That brings a smile to my face. "Yes. And before you ask, *yes*. Twice and it was fan-fucking-tastic."

Lisa beams. "I'm honestly feeling a tad jealous you got to hit that."

I laugh at her and turn my head to look at Chase. He's crouched down, smiling as he talks to his niece.

"And everything went okay?" Lisa asks, and she doesn't have to explain for me to know she meant emotionally, not physically.

"Yeah. It felt right, and we were very much caught up in the moment both times. He's easy to be around, as lame as that sounds. We haven't known each other long, but it's like I can just relax and be myself around him. It's hard, sometimes, not to compare him to...to Jake though."

"I bet that's normal."

I nod. "Yeah. It's a little weird. It's not like we broke up and I have negative feelings toward him. It'd be easier if that were the case. Chase has been really understanding. I think that's the biggest part of why this feels so right."

"Is this more than just a fling?"

"I think so. It feels like it's more." I shake my head. "If it doesn't come up, I'll ask him."

"No, you won't," Lisa says point-blank, raising an eyebrow.

"Fine. I probably won't because that's one awkward conversation waiting to happen. But…" I trail off and look back at Chase. "I think he feels it too. He's coming back over today. We don't have plans other than to lounge around until dinner."

"Fucking, you mean."

"Oh, for sure. I probably want it just as bad as he does."

Lisa laughs. "He's into you. More so than a fling. I can tell by the way he looks at you."

I can't hide my smile. "Good," I say shortly, not comfortable with gushing over Chase like a teenage girl.

"Are you bringing him to family dinner tonight?"

"No, not yet. Mostly for his sake, though. Having your sister, my sister, and all of our parents in one room is overwhelming even when you're part of the family."

"That is the truest thing you can say about our family."

$$\sim$$

"How was your date?" Mom asks as soon as I'm through the door that evening. They just got back into town a few hours ago, but since my mom doesn't actually do the cooking—or the setting of the table, or the cleaning up after dinner—having us all over for dinner isn't an issue.

"You went on a date?" Sam asks, turning around so fast she almost bumps into me.

"Didn't you see them together at church this morning?" Vanessa, Lisa's older sister asks, handing off her sleeping toddler to her husband. "I thought Lisa said you went out with that Henson guy."

"That is him," I tell her.

Vanessa makes a face of surprise. "Really? He looked so...so..."

"Not like a Henson?" Lisa supplies and her sister agrees. "You're such an asshole, Nessa."

"Lisa," Gran scolds, voice coming from across the foyer. I swear she has better hearing than I do. I take off my shoes and take my phone from my purse before the housekeeper takes it to hang up. I look through the sea of my family members for my mother, whose hair and makeup are perfectly done. You'd never guess she stepped off a plane hours ago. Her eyes, more blue than green like mine, sparkle and she's trying not to smile. My mother might be ridiculously posh at times, concerning herself with more than what others think than with what's going on in the world, but I know she cares.

"It was fine," I say simply, but my smile gives it away.

16

CHASE

I fall into bed at three am Friday morning. I smell like alcohol and smoke, but I'm too damn tired to shower. This week passed in a blur, and thanks to Sierra, it was a beautiful fucking blur.

I stayed at her house the rest of Sunday after church until she had to go to her parents' for dinner. Monday, she came over after work and stayed the night. The next day, I brought lunch to her at work and stayed for the remainder of her break before I had to come back here and work at the bar. She had me over Wednesday night and since she didn't have to be at work until the afternoon Thursday, we spend the morning in bed together, reading, fucking, and cuddling.

It's the last thing I'd thought I'd do. Lying in bed with my arm tucked under Sierra, holding a book with my other free hand, having to put it down every time I needed to turn a page because I didn't want to disturb Sierra. It sounds so lame to say we spent the morning in bed together reading, but when Sierra got to a sex scene in her book, she read part of it out loud to me, turning us both on enough to recreate the scene ourselves.

Being close to someone like that isn't something I do often. Or ever. Things are different with Sierra and all that bullshit about finding that one person out of millions who you're meant to be with doesn't sound so shitty anymore.

The more time I spend with Sierra, the easier she is to read. She's scared. Keeps her heart guarded. Sometimes, when she gets too close or acts too comfortable, it's like she catches herself and pulls back.

With Sierra on my mind, I pass out and dream of her, waking four hours later with enough energy to get up and shower. Regretting going another day without grocery shopping, I grumble when I look inside my fridge for something to eat. Settling for stale cereal with the rest of the milk, I drag a chair over to the large window and eat while watching the river.

I move to the couch, flipping through channels when Sierra calls. My heart skips a beat when I see her familiar number on my screen.

"Hey, babe," I answer.

"I didn't wake you up, did I?" she asks.

"No, I was up already."

"Oh good. I was planning on leaving a message for you to listen to when you got up. Why are you up so early? You worked late last night."

"Couldn't sleep. I'll go back to sleep later, though. Are you on your way to work?"

"Yeah. And that shipment of books I ordered Monday is supposed to come in. I'm pretty excited about it."

I can tell she's smiling as she talks. It's fucking adorable.

"While I have you on the phone, I might as well ask you if you'd be interesting in going to a bonfire tonight at Rob's house."

"Do you want to go?" I ask her.

"Kind of," she says after a moment's hesitation. "I haven't been to anything like that in a long time."

"Then let's go."

"Are you sure?"

"Yeah. There's probably nothing else to do around this town anyway, right?" I joke.

"Well, there is me."

Fuck. Me. "You're so fucking hot, Sierra. And I will do you. I'm going to fuck you senseless until you're coming so hard you're screaming my name."

"Oh...oh my," she breathes. "Today's going to go by slow now that I know what's waiting for me."

I chuckle, imagining her pretty face and missing the feel of her body against mine. "How long do you get for lunch today?"

"I'm the only one there today, so I don't really get an official break, but I can sneak into the backroom whenever I want."

"You're the only one there?" I echo, not liking the idea of Sierra being at the store alone. It's not the first time she's worked alone, yet for some reason, a bad feeling starts to rise inside me.

Is it because I'm starting to care—really fucking care—about her?

"Yeah. Friday mornings are always pretty slow. Janet comes in at two. I usually stay for a while to make sure she's good and then I can leave around three-ish. If it weren't for the new books coming in, today would seriously drag. Is it weird to say I miss you? I saw you yesterday."

I blink, forcing away thoughts of all the bad things that could happen to Sierra as she steps into the backroom of the shop, innocently dashing away to get a book. I know because I've done quite a few bad things.

"It's not weird." My voice comes out flat. I get up and go to the window, blinking as the sun shines off the water and into my eyes. "Because I miss you too. I feel like I'm addicted to you."

"Are you worried you'll overdose?"

"That would be the best way to go. I'll see you tonight, Sierra."

"Bye, Chase."

~

"I miss that sound," Josh says, looking at the river below the large living room window. It's a little after noon, and he just came over with pizza and beer, having been kicked out of the house by Melissa, who's in some crazy nesting phase right now and wants to reorganize everything.

"It's relaxing. I've grown accustomed to it at night."

"I didn't sleep for a whole fucking week after I moved out of here." Josh turns away from the window and sits on the couch, taking another slice of pizza. "It was too quiet at the new place Melissa and I bought."

"I do like it at night. Though I sleep just fine at Sierra's."

Josh grins. "You two have been spending a lot of time together."

"I suppose."

"Really? 'I suppose' is all you're going to fucking say to that?"

I bring my beer to my lips. "What do you want to know?"

"Is shit serious?" he asks casually.

"It hasn't been very long," I reply, knowing Josh is hoping I'll say yes because he thinks if I do, Sierra and I will be married with babies not long from now. He wants me to stay, and I believe that he genuinely wants me to be happy.

Besides Sierra, he's the only person who hopes for happiness for me.

It's fucking weird.

"I knew I wanted to marry Melissa on our third date." He puts his fist to his chest. "You just feel it, in here." He shrugs. "At the very least, you're having fun with her, I'm sure."

I nod, letting his words sink in. I do *just feel it* when it comes to Sierra. Not about marriage or babies or anything like that, but feeling like I'm home. "She is fun."

"You two met before," Josh tells me. "The first time you came to Summer Hill. She was only like a year or two old then. I graduated with her brother, and we used to hang out before he moved away. We were at the house and Mrs. Belmont came to pick Scott up. Sierra was with her. I remember because Scott and I caught snakes to scare his sister with. We were expecting Sam and not Sierra."

"I don't remember that at all. It's kinda fucking with my head, trying to think back. I try not to remember too much from my childhood."

Josh frowns. "I'm sorry I didn't say more to Dad about it."

"Don't be. It was a long time ago."

The rumbling sound of a truck drowns out the gentle babbling of the river. I get up to see what's going on in the parking lot.

"Are you expecting a UPS shipment today?" I ask Josh.

"Nope. It must be for you."

I shake my head. "I didn't order anything."

Knowing the delivery guy is going to be confused to have been taken to a bar, we go downstairs and outside, meeting him in the parking lot.

"Chase Henson?" he asks.

"That's me," I say, looking at the small box in his hands. I have to sign for it, and as soon as I see the shipping label, I realize it's my phone, sent back from the Apple store with a new screen. There was a time I didn't think I could live without this thing, now I'm not even excited to get it back. Just how disconnected I was from my previous life didn't hit me until right now, as I feel the light weight of the box in my hands.

I haven't talked to anyone I used to in weeks. I haven't thought about working a job in even longer. And it's really fucking nice. Maybe I won't turn this phone back on. Maybe I should keep it in this box and forget that part of me completely.

Start over fresh in Summer Hill.

With Sierra.

"I bet you're happy to get that back," Josh says as we walk back up the stairs to the apartment. "You can let your friends know you're still alive."

"Hah, yeah." There's only one person I trust enough to consider a friend, and not talking to him for days or even weeks at a time is nothing out of the ordinary. Not talking to him might be a good thing. We tend to get into trouble when we're together.

Josh and I go back upstairs and watch a couple of episodes of *Breaking Bad*—Josh was appalled when I said I hadn't seen it. After he leaves, I do the shit I've been putting off: grocery shopping and straightening up the apartment. I get done a little before Sierra calls, saying she's going to go home to take care of her cats and get changed, then she'll be over.

I shower and throw fresh sheets on the bed, then end up watching another episode of *Breaking Bad*. I turn the TV off and stand, looking at the brown box on the counter. As much as I want to forget about the past, I know I should at least turn on the damn phone and get my mom's number off it. It might be sad I don't know her number off the top of my head. It's changed multiple times over the years, and we rarely talk. There's no point in memorizing it. Still, she's my mother and though she resents the hell out of me, I need to know if something happens.

The phone is completely dead of course and will take a few minutes before it even turns on. I plug it in and forget about it as soon as Sierra knocks on the door. She's wearing a coral-colored dress that shows off her perfect tits and hugs her tight around the waist before flaring out, giving the whole thing a contradicting sexy-yet-innocent look that instantly turns me on.

"I brought you a home-cooked dinner," she says, holding up a wicker basket. The moment she's inside and the door closes, I grab her and kiss her hard. Still holding the basket in one hand, she curls her other around me, fingers going to my hair.

"It smells amazing," I tell her, lips brushing against hers. "You made it?"

"I wish. My parents' personal chef did. I stopped by on my way out and was able to get us something to eat. Are you hungry?"

"Starving." I put my mouth on Sierra's neck, teeth grazing her flesh. She groans and tips her head back, wanting more. I move away, take her hand, and lead her to the table. I've come to realize that getting Sierra hot and bothered and then not immediately having sex leads to her desperately fucking me as hard as she can. Walking away from her is a challenge for me, that's for sure, but the way she'll be looking at me in an hour will make this worth it.

"I was super paranoid about this. One of the side dishes had shellfish in it. So I used a new spoon for everything in case it got cross-contaminated and got food from the opposite side of the dishes. I don't want to kill you. Not yet at least."

I smile at Sierra. "That probably won't affect me. I have to actually eat it to have a bad reaction."

She slowly shakes her head, eyes trained on me. "I'm not willing to risk it. I like you, Chase Henson. I want to keep you around a bit longer."

It dawns on me as she begins to unpack dinner that she's probably hypersensitive to losing anyone she cares about. I take her hand before she grabs a biscuit.

"Thanks, though. For making sure."

"Of course, Chase."

Our eyes meet and my heart does that stupid skip-a-beat thing again. So much emotion is conveyed in under a second it throws me for a loop. She wants her happy ending as much as I want to give it to her.

Not the mystery woman.

Her.

And I want to be a part of it.

Leave it to Sierra to make me have a moment right here and right now, in the most mundane setting.

I get us plates and silverware and go back to the table.

"I grew up thinking these were a family recipe," she tells me, breaking apart a biscuit and putting it on her plate. "And then when I was like sixteen I found out it was from the can. Talk about an existential crisis."

"Your whole life was a lie," I laugh.

"Yes! I mean, I knew my mom didn't cook worth a shit, but I honestly thought my grandma made the best biscuits in the history of biscuits every holiday. Then I found out the truth." She breaks off a small piece and eats it while getting more food out. "And to this day, I can't open a can of biscuits without wincing and feeling shame."

"I've made canned biscuits maybe three times in my life and all three times I had to close my eyes and look away," I admit.

"It's awful! Couldn't they come up with a better way to do that by now?"

"You'd think so."

Sierra shakes her head, smiling, and serves dinner for us both.

"What was it like growing up with a personal chef?" I ask, picking up my fork.

She shrugs. "It all seemed normal to me for years, until I started going to friends' houses and hearing how they'd help their moms cook dinner or make cookies together. It made me kind of sad to realize that I was missing out on so much with my own mother. Which I know…poor pitiful me and my personal chef."

"No, no, I get you. My own mother wasn't involved in the least, so I understand that feeling of letdown when you see other people. Like how the fuck did they get things so… so…*right?*"

It's not the first time words escaped me, the truth seeping out, desperate to finally be set free. It won't be the last time. And for the life of me, I cannot figure out why the fuck Sierra makes me so unhinged.

"I don't want to sound pretentious by saying that upholding the perfect family image was damaging or anything, but sometimes I'd see my friends and wish I had what they had. Because all the glitz and glamour comes with a cost. I still rarely see my father."

"So I take it you don't want to go into the family business, right?" I ask slowly, recalling her voicemail about getting into grad school. I don't know what her focus was, but I doubt it was agriculture.

"Not in the same way my dad runs things. The plan was for the three of us—my brother, sister, and I—to take equal parts. Scott wants nothing to do with farming, obviously, and Sam can't wait to take over." Sierra lets out a breath and spreads butter on her biscuit. "But the Belmonts have been farmers for years, and I like that family history. I'm a part owner of the farm whether I like it or not, and there's no way I'd sell my share. When I was a kid, I wanted to be a farmer, like my dad. My sister wanted to be a farmer's wife. That's the Belmont way, after all."

"That doesn't suit you. At all. You're not the kind of woman who can sit idly by and be a trophy wife."

Sierra raises her head, looking into my eyes. "What kind of woman am I?"

"That's a loaded question," I say with a chuckle. "You are smart and kind. You won't sit around taking orders from someone, and you won't let anyone use your gender as a handicap and play that role of 'farmer's wife.' You want to make the world a better place, even though the last year or so hasn't been kind to you. You believe people are inherently good, and for some unknown reason, you make people like me see it too."

Sierra's eyes gloss over, and for a beat, she stares at me. Then she blinks and looks away. "Sounds about right."

"I wanted to be an Avenger when I was a kid," I tell her, digging into my food. "At least you had more ambition than me."

"Aspiring to be a superhero is pretty ambitious."

"Ambitious but not realistic."

Sierra's fork goes limp in her hand, resting against her plate. "What did you do? Before you came here, I mean."

I lean back in my chair. "A lot of things. I never found anything that stuck." It's a half-truth, but I still feel like shit for saying it. Though I did do a lot of things, like I said, none are things I'm proud of. All are far from anything I'd share with Sierra. I don't want her to look at me differently than she is now.

"I bartended a bit before I came here," I say, which is true.

To an extent again. *Fuck.* I mentally sigh. "At a bar on the shore in New Jersey."

She scoops up rice with her fork and snickers. "You lived on the Jersey Shore?"

"It's not as bad as the show makes it."

"So you're not D.T.F. tonight?"

I raise an eyebrow. "I should be glad I have no idea what you're talking about, right?"

Sierra laughs. "Yes, and I am too. Is that where you're from originally? You don't have a Jersey accent, but you do sound northern."

"And you sound southern. Though not as much as other people in this town."

She nods. "It's because my mom doesn't have an accent."

"Oh, right. You said she's from the east coast."

"Yeah. Though she's picked up on the Mississippi accent more and more over time. Stay here long enough and you'll pick it up too."

"Maybe mine will rub off on you."

"Lisa and I used to pretend we were from New York and see if we could get people to believe us."

"Did it work?"

She shakes her head. "Not at all. But we were usually drinking when we'd play that game."

"I was born and raised in Indiana," I tell her. "Northern Indiana, close to Lake Michigan, to be exact, and not all that far from Chicago, actually."

"Does it get cold there in the winter?"

"Very. With lots of snow since we're by the lake."

"I like snow. It's so pretty."

"Has it ever snowed here?"

"A few times," she says. "It's never much though. I went to Park City, Utah a few years back for a New Year's ski trip and party. It was breathtaking."

186

"You'll have to see the piers in Lake Michigan in the winter then. The ice build-up is insane."

"I'd like that."

"I'll take you someday."

Sierra smiles. "I'm going to hold you to it."

17

SIERRA

I rake my fingers through Chase's hair, and he lets out a soft moan in his sleep. Leaning back into the pillows, I close my eyes as well even though I'm not tired. I know Chase only got a few hours of sleep last night and didn't nap like he intended to during the day. We have time before the bonfire at Rob's tonight, so he might as well sleep.

And he has to be exhausted from the sex we just had. Hell, I am, and I wasn't the one holding me up against the wall the entire time.

We're in his bed, both still naked. Chase's head is nestled against my breasts, and he has one arm lazily draped around me. I hook my leg over him, and a foreign feeling of peace falls over me. It's so pleasant it's almost startling. I didn't think I'd ever be able to get on with my life after Jake, let alone find another person who gets me the way that Jake did.

I'm drifting to sleep when Chase's phone vibrates on the nightstand next to me. Chase jerks awake, eyes wide as he sits up.

"It's your phone," I tell him and reach for it, pulling it off the charger. "Is this new? I thought you had a different one."

"I do," he says and pushes himself up.

"Whoa, that's a lot of missed texts," I blurt when I see the screen. Chase takes the phone before I can get a better look. "Did that say you have thirty-seven texts from someone named Jax?"

"Yeah. This is my phone—my real phone. The one I've been using is a temporary, so to speak."

"What?"

"Dakota, my niece, broke the screen my first day here. I sent it away to be fixed and forgot about it until it came back today."

"Who's Jax?" I ask, trying to get another look at the phone. I can be a bit nosey regardless, and right now I really want to know why Chase has so many missed texts and calls.

"A friend." He sets the phone down and reaches for me.

"Shouldn't you text him back?"

"Nah, it's not important."

"He sent you like forty texts. I think that warrants at least a look."

Chase shrugs and grabs me by the waist, sliding me to him. "Later. We should probably leave, right?"

"Probably. I don't know what time it is." The sun set a while ago, and soft moonlight filters through the window in Chase's bedroom. He presses the home button on his phone to check the time, and I see that has a slew of missed calls as well as texts. How is he not dying to read them?

"Nine twenty-three," he tells me.

"Wow. I did not realize it was that late."

"We're good at losing track of time." He grins and moves closer.

"Very. Maybe we can lose track of time again later?"

His lips graze mine as he talks, his deep voice rumbling through me. "Not maybe. Definitely."

~

DARK CLOUDS BLANKET THE SKY, and the smell of rain sits heavy in the air, mixing with the thick scent of the bonfire. The crackles and pops of the fire fight to drown out the late-night singing of the crickets, and talk and laughter weave between the two, muted by the country music that's coming from the barn. Humidity clings to the night, blanketing us in sticky heat.

This is summer the way it should be. I've spent most of my summers like this, outside with friends, partying in some sense or the other.

"You look lost in thought," Chase says, handing me a can of beer. I crack the top and take a sip. I'm not a fan of beer. The idea of it sounds nice, refreshing even, but I can't get past the taste. It's terrible.

"I am. I was thinking of how these get-togethers have evolved over the years. From innocent slumber parties with my girlfriends to crazy parties in college to this…low-key, more adult fun. I missed that last transition."

Chase puts his arm around me and kisses my forehead. Sometimes saying nothing is the best thing to hear, and Chase knows how powerful his silence can be.

"Siiieerrraaaa!" Lisa calls from across the yard, throwing her hands up.

"I think she missed the transition too," Chase jokes and I laugh.

"Lisa will always be in the crazy stage. She's been in the crazy stage since birth."

"I told you to be here at nine, hooker," Lisa bellows as she rushes over, throwing her arms around me. She's already drunk and the party just started. "It's like ten…ten…something."

"It's ten fifteen. That makes me fashionably late."

Lisa pouts. "But I had no one to tell me to stop taking shots. Or take shots with. Want one?" She turns before I can answer. "Rob! Bring me those tequila shots."

"I don't think Sierra wants one of those," Chase says, eyes meeting mine. He arches his eyebrows and smiles, and I roll my eyes back at him, knowing he's referencing that time I almost had a threesome with Mr. and Mrs. Backwoods.

"Why don't you let Sierra make her own decisions," Lisa slurs.

I love and hate Drunk Lisa. She lacks a filter most days, and when she's been drinking, the filter is completely off and locked away in some repressed compartment in her mind that won't surface again until at least three hours after her hangover wears off.

"I don't want tequila," I say, grimacing. "Do you have any wine inside, though?"

"Of course. Come with me. I have to pee anyway."

I take Chase's hand and start forward after Lisa.

"No," she says, turning around. She holds up her hand, squinting at Chase. "Just the girls."

I shake my head. "Lisa, chill a little."

"Rob!" she calls, turning away from us. He jogs over a few seconds later.

"What's up, babe? And hey, guys," Rob says.

Lisa takes my hand out of Chase's and loops her arm through mine. "I need to take Sierra into the house for some girl stuff. You talk to Chase. Because if we're going to stay together and they're going to be together, then the two of you need to get along."

"We do get along," Rob says slowly, not following Lisa's drunk logic.

"Ugh," she sighs, throwing her head back. "You don't know each other. Go be friends. Start a bromance and become best friends. Come on, Sierra."

I look at Chase, who is amused by the whole thing, and gives me a small nod, telling me to go with Lisa.

"What the fuck?" Lisa blurts as soon as we're inside.

"About what?" I ask her.

She blinks, and then shakes her head. "I don't remember. Wine is in the fridge. I'm going to pee." She stumbles through Rob's house to the bathroom while I open a bottle of wine, trading my beer for a plastic wine glass. I fill it halfway, take a few sips, and lean on the counter while I wait for my cousin.

"Where's my glass?" she asks when she's back in the kitchen.

"I'll pour you one later. How about some food?"

"I'm drinking my calories tonight."

"Take a break for a minute and dance with me," I try, taking her arm and pulling her out the door. I see Chase standing by the fire, talking with Rob and his friends.

"You like him, don't you?" Lisa slurs.

"Yeah. I hope so, at least, since we're sleeping together."

"You know what I mean. Like really like him."

"I'm starting to."

"Good." Lisa gives me a smile and rests her head on my shoulder. If she's getting tired already, there's no way she's going to make it through the rest of the night. "But it is weird seeing you with someone other than Jake. When you guys were out there, backs turned, I thought it was you and Jake for a second. Then I saw you with Chase and it's just weird."

I know she's drunk, but her words hurt. Tears well up in my eyes and I work hard to blink them away. I grind my teeth the rest of the way to the fire, shaking Lisa off my arm as soon as we stop. She goes over to Rob, throwing her arms around his shoulders.

"Sierra," Chase says, smiling disappearing. "What's wrong?"

"Nothing," I lie the same moment a renegade tear falls from my eye.

"I don't believe you," he whispers, wiping my tear away. "Did something happen?"

I shake my head. "Just my drunk best friend saying stupid shit." Chase steps in, wrapping one arm around me. I rest my head against his chest and gather my composure. Chase cups my face, gently moving my chin up so he can kiss me. The guilt intensifies for a brief second before vanishing completely. Chase kisses me harder, tongue slipping past my lips. He slides his hand back into my hair, closing his fingers into a fist. If I weren't holding my wine, I'd throw my arms around Chase and completely surrender to him.

"Better?" he asks, breaking away.

"Yes." I take a few big gulps of my wine, mostly because I want to finish it and not carry a cup around all night. It takes me a while to feel like myself again, and no matter how hard I try, I can't squish the ball of fear that starts to form every time I run into an old friend. Are they thinking the same thing Lisa is?

"Those are the girls you went out with the first night I saw you, right?" Chase asks, watching Katie, Bella, and Heather draw near.

"Yeah, they are. I'm surprised you remember."

"I'm good with remembering faces."

"I'm not. At all."

Katie catches my eye and waves. "Sierra! Oh my God, it's good to see you again!"

She hugs me and then looks at Chase, doing a terrible job hiding her smile. There's no need to introduce Chase to them. They know who he is and that we've been spending time together. Not because I told them, but because this town talks. I go through a formal introduction regardless, for Chase's sake. We talk to my old friends for a while then refill our drinks and go back by the fire. It's already hot out, but the smoke keeps the mosquitos away.

"I feel like I'm in a country music video," Chase quips as we sit on a hay bale.

I laugh. "Nah, all the girls would be wearing cowboy boots and cut-off jeans if we were. And we'd be sitting on a tailgate."

"We're missing drunken fights and someone passing out in the barn, too."

"I'm sure one of those two will happen tonight."

"I think you just jinxed it." Chase sits up straighter, looking over the fire. "Looks like a fight's about to break out."

We stand and see three guys, fists clenched, staring down another guy. The leader of the offensive pack is Justin, a guy I've known since childhood. Behind the guys, who are exchanging heated words, is Francine, who's the world's fakest friend. Her arms are crossed and lips pursed, watching the men shout. Justin lurches forward, shoving the other guy in the chest. He stumbles back but takes a swing, fist colliding with Justin's temple. Justin's friends jump in on the guy, and another joins in on the fight, going against Justin and his crew.

"I'll get Rob," I say but Chase shakes his head.

"I got this." He strides over and shouts, "Hey!" The brawl comes to a temporary halt and all five guys look at Chase. "What the fuck are you doing?" Chase goes on.

"He touched my girl," Justin sneers, pointing to the guy he shoved, that I recognize now as Daniel, who moved to Summer Hill not that long ago and has never quite fit in.

"Take it somewhere else." Chase goes right up to them.

"Stay out of it, fucking Yankee," Justin snarls and I shake my head. Way to further the southern stereotype. I turn, hoping to find Rob. He's a cop in this town, after all. People listen to him. In that split second that I turn away, all hell breaks loose. I look back just in time to see Justin taking a swing at Chase.

Horrified, I stand rooted to the spot, watching everything unfold. Chase ducks out of the way, catches Justin's fist and twists his arm before popping him quickly in the face. Justin goes down and one of his friends moves in at the same time the other jumps on Chase from behind.

Chase flips him over with ease and takes out the other friend in two seconds flat. Daniel and his friend stand there, arms out to their sides, looking at Chase and not knowing if they should fight him or not. Justin scrambles to his feet and pulls out a pocket knife. He flips open the blade and charges at Chase. My eyes widen in horror and my mouth falls open, but no words come out.

Chase turns, grabs Justin's wrist and has him disarmed in the blink of an eye. He twists Justin's arm behind his back, apprehending him until Rob and one of his police officer friends run over. There's a gleam in Chase's eyes, and I can't deny that he looks almost disappointed the fight is not only over but was easy. For him at least.

"What the fuck?" Rob exclaims, seeing the knife on the ground.

"That guy's fucking psycho!" Justin yells, pulling away from Chase and mopping blood from his bleeding nose with the back of his hand. "He just attacked us!"

"Give it a break," Rob says. "We saw the whole thing. You charged at him with a knife. That's assault, Justin. If he presses charges against you, I'm hauling your ass to the county jail."

Chase holds up his hands. "I'm not pressing charges. Just don't be a dumbass anymore."

Justin spits blood onto the ground and glares at Chase. Francine stares daggers at me from across the yard, and now

I know why she was standing there so smugly, watching the fight take place. It was about her.

"Why didn't you tell me your boyfriend is Jason Bourne?" Lisa asks, coming up behind me, unable to look away from the guys.

I'm just as shocked as she is. "He's not my boyfriend."

"Close enough. I wanna learn how to do that," she goes on. "That was badass. God, it's not fair you get to go home with him tonight."

"Yeah...it's not."

"Why don't you have a drink in your hand?" Lisa asks, just now realizing it. "We gotta fix this."

Fights happen at these types of parties all the time. It's a running joke that there's nothing else to do but beat each other up. The spats are broken up, no one is seriously hurt, and we go on with the night. I can't get over the look in Chase's eye, the way he enjoyed fighting.

"Right."

"What do you want?"

"Surprise me."

"I will!" Lisa skips off to the cooler in the threshold of the barn. The guys disperse and Chase comes back to me.

"Are you okay?" I ask him.

"I'm fine. That guy's an idiot."

"He's always been one. You handled that well."

Chase gives me his signature shrug. "I taught a self-defense class in college."

"Really?" I tip my head. It's the first time he's mentioned that he even went to college.

"Yeah. And I've been into martial arts since I was a kid. It was one of the few things my dad did for me. If you can call it that. He sent money for classes. He thought it would make me disciplined. He wasn't there to do shit, so he hoped someone else could."

"Did it work?"

Chase gives me a devilish smirk. "No." His hands land on my ass and he pulls me in. "I lack self-control. Especially when it comes to you."

I bite my lip, grinning right back. "You're a bad influence."

With a swift movement, he picks me up and kisses me. "The worst."

"Get a room," Lisa calls, making her way back with two hard lemonades. "Or at least go in the barn."

"I'm kinda ready to go home," I admit.

"So you two can fuck?" Lisa blurts, handing me my drink.

"That is part of why." I make a face. "You know I'm not much of a party person."

"You're so lame, Si. But fine. Go home and have fun with that piece of man-meat."

"I'm standing right here," Chase says dryly.

Lisa looks him up and down and then winks. "I know."

We laugh and I take Lisa's hand, guiding her across the yard to Rob before Chase and I leave.

"Where do you want to go?" Chase asks, opening the car door for me. "Home or the apartment?"

"We can go to your house." I get in, taking note that Chase never refers to his house as 'home'. He said he's never been anywhere long enough for it to feel that way. "It's closer."

The bar is still packed when we pull up, and we sneak around back and up the stairs before anyone can see us.

"I forgot about that," I say when we step through the door. "How do you sleep with all the noise?"

"I don't. Not well at least until the bar closes. But I'm a night person anyway, so I'm up until two or three most nights."

"I could be the same, but I have to get up for work."

"Why do you work at The Book Bag?" He takes off his

shoes and goes to the couch. I set my purse down and unbuckle my sandals, and join him.

"I have to have a job."

"I know, but you said you own part of the farm. Maybe it's presumptuous to assume you'd make more money doing that than working at a small bookstore."

"I would, but I like The Book Bag. And the biggest thing is not wanting a handout from my parents. I already don't fit in the best and the last thing I want is them holding the fact that they gave me money or a job over my head. I want to be successful in life because I earned it. Not because someone gave it to me."

Chase looks at me for a minute, admirably. "And that's exactly why you'd be a terrible farmer's wife."

"I'd be the worst."

"Always telling him what to do and not taking your rightful place in the kitchen. And I just know you'd have an opinion you'd want to share."

"The nerve of me, right?"

"It's borderline disgraceful."

We both laugh and Chase takes me in his arms. My head rests against his chest and I close my eyes, just breathing it all in. Noise from the bar thumps on below us, yet it's still peaceful sitting here with Chase. I start to doze off until a loud cheer from the patrons below startles me.

"It's quieter in the bedroom," Chase says, then gives me a smirk. "Though if I'm talking about us, it's far from quiet."

"You wanna give them a run for their money?" I ask, biting my lip.

Chase scoops me up and carries me into the bedroom. "Hell, yes."

18

CHASE

*T*he sound of metal rubbing on metal reverberates through the quiet room, waking me from my sleep. The sound is unfamiliar, and I immediately go on the defense, looking for whoever caused the noise. The stakes are higher this time because it's not just me to worry about. Sierra is next to me, and if anyone lays a finger on her, I'll kill them.

The glowing screen of my phone catches my eye, and it takes not even a second to realize the sound was a text coming through, causing the phone to vibrate up against a metal bowl full of change. Sierra didn't stir. She did tell me she's a sound sleeper and doesn't wake easily once she's passed out.

It's my old phone, which sounds weird to say since this one is actually a newer model than the one I got from the Summer Hill electronic store. The text is from Jax, and I know I should read it. I unlock the phone and internally groan at the number of texts, missed calls, and messages.

I go to the voicemails first. There are fewer of them than texts, and Jax would call instead of text if it were actually important. It's like I'm listening to Sierra's messages all over again, except my mystery woman is naked in bed next to me, fast asleep and none the wiser to the shit I'm about to listen to. I press play on Jax's first message and bring the phone to my ear.

"I got a job for us," he starts. "Fifty-grand easy. Call me."

The next message is from over a week later. "Where the fuck are you, Henson? I got fucking arrested and need you to bail me out. I know I flaked on you last time, but I had a good fucking reason. I'm at Stark County."

The next message comes three days after the last. I hit play. "Fuck you, man. Fuck. You. I had to get Weston to bail me out. But really, where the hell are you? No one's heard from you in weeks. If you're fucking dead I'm going to kill you. Don't you fucking force me to ask Beth what happened to you."

I know he did because the next message is from Beth, who was more than a fuck buddy but far from my girlfriend.

"What the fucking hell, Chase?" she starts. "Jax just left and said he hasn't seen or heard from you either. I'm worried. Really fucking worried." Her voice is raspy and I can tell she's sucking on a cigarette as she talks. "Last I heard you were going down south to handle some family shit. Call me, asshole."

The last message is from Jax again, and it was left last night while Sierra and I were at the bonfire. "I'm in trouble and need a place to lay low. You know I wouldn't ask if it wasn't serious. And I'm serious. Beth said something about Mississippi. I'm headed south now to stay out of dodge. If you're not dead, call me back, motherfucker."

"Shit," I mumble, bringing the phone away from my face. Jax has helped me out more than once. I can't walk away from this.

I run my hand through my hair and open the texts. The

majority are from Jax, telling me about jobs, then asking where I am. Three texts are from Beth, with the first being a photo of her new nipple piercing, the second inviting me to come over for the night, and the third asking where I am as well. The rest are from clients, seeing if I'm available for hire. The most recent text is from Jax, asking if I'm alive.

I let the phone drop onto the bed and lay back down, curling my body around Sierra's. In her sleep, she arches her back and moves closer. The sound of the river surrounds us, and my chest tightens when I think about how bad I want this.

Sierra.

A simple life here in Summer Hill.

Together.

Living happily together for the rest of our days.

They say nice guys finish last. What the hell happens to the bad ones?

∼

"You work tonight, right?" Sierra asks over breakfast. We're at Suzy's Cafe, and we're both well aware of the stares we're getting from the other customers. I can only assume half of them are jealous. I'm the one walking hand in hand with someone as beautiful as Sierra, after all. And the other half are probably wondering what the fuck Sierra is doing with me.

"Yeah. I'm closing down the bar."

She makes a face, looking down at her phone. "My mom keeps pestering me to go spend the day shopping with her and Sam."

"Go with them," I tell her, reaching for my coffee. We'd talked about walking the deer path I've been running. Sierra told me she likes to hike, but gets a little freaked out to go alone, which she should. My mind goes to all the bad things that can happen and it makes my stomach hurt. "If you want to, that is."

"I haven't hung out with them in a while."

"It's nice you guys do things together."

"Yeah, it is. My sister and I are total opposites, but we get along for the most part. Same with my mom. I'm way more free-spirited than the rest of my family, and it makes me stick out."

"I don't think there's anything wrong with that," I say and Sierra smiles. "This might be a dumb question, but when you say you're going to spend the day shopping, you can't mean you're going to be around here, can you?"

"No. They want to drive to Eastmont, which is almost two hours away. They have good stores there."

Our food comes, and we talk throughout breakfast. On our way out, an elderly woman comes up to Sierra, smiling as she eyes me up and down.

"Good morning," she says with a thick southern accent. "To both of you." She brings her eyebrows up and smiles again.

"Good morning, Mrs. Williams. This is Chase." Sierra turns, introducing me. "And Chase, this is Mrs. Williams. She owns The Book Bag."

"Nice to meet you," I say and shake her hand.

"I knew Sierra was seeing someone new. I just didn't know he was this handsome." Mrs. Williams winks at me and squeezes my hand. "It's nice seeing her happy again," she whispers to me, loud enough for Sierra to hear. "I hope to keep seeing you around."

"I plan to be here," I tell her, and out of the corner of my eye, I see Sierra smile. I take her hand the rest of the way to the car. We go back to my place so she can get her stuff, needing to hurry home to shower and change in time to meet her mom and sister. She's stuffing her clothes from last night into her oversized purse when she gets a text.

"Lisa's at work," she tells me with a laugh. "She's begging for coffee. I didn't know she had to work this morning."

"She has to feel like shit."

"Yeah. Total shit."

"The bank isn't open long on Saturday, at least."

"Right. She's there until noon. And it's nine-thirty now... yeah. She's gonna need that coffee." Sierra makes a face. "I'm already running late, but I feel bad. I'll get her coffee. And food. I doubt she ate."

Watching Sierra, I remember how I felt last night lying in bed next to her. How I want to start over. Make this place my home.

With her.

"I'll take it to her," I offer. "I need to go to the bank anyway. Tell me what to get."

"You don't have to do that, Chase."

"I'm going to the bank today. It's no big deal."

Sierra looks at me as if it is. "Thank you. She likes black coffee. Easy."

"That is. What to eat?"

"Blueberry muffin."

"Got it. Go shop." I take her in my arms, needing to feel her breasts crush against me one more time. "And if you're shopping for lingerie and can't decide on something, feel free to send me pictures."

The words leave my mouth and intrusive thoughts immediately take over. I have her late-boyfriend's phone. The phone that he held in his hand. She held it too. Did she send him naughty pictures on it? The parallels are too much for me to handle. It's wrong, and I fucking hate myself for listening to those messages.

Those messages that I haven't deleted yet.

"Chase?" Sierra asks. "Are you okay?"

I blink and put my mouth to hers. "Better now."

We kiss once more, and then she leaves. The second she's out the door, I feel relief. Not to be away from her, because I'm missing her already, but because of this sudden feeling that I'm teetering on the edge of fucking up. I let out a breath and go into my bedroom, pulling out a bag filled with cash from under the bed. I take a couple thousand out, stick it in my nightstand drawer, and zip up the bag to take with me. At the last second, I grab my phone—my old phone—from the nightstand.

I get the coffee and muffin first, then go to the bank. Lisa is at the front, head resting in her hands.

"I come bearing gifts," I say, holding up the coffee. The sun is behind me, and Lisa cringes when she looks up.

"Oh my God, I could kiss you." She takes the coffee from me and chugs it. "Where's Si?"

"Shopping with her mom and sister. She was running late so I offered to bring this."

Lisa opens the bag and digs into the muffin. "Seriously, thank you."

"It's no problem. I need to talk to Melissa, actually. Is she here?"

"She is, but that's not what I mean. Well, it is. I needed coffee like it was nobody's business. And I'm fucking starving and this muffin has those big sprinkles of sugar on the top. So damn good. But I mean for making Sierra happy again. I don't even think she realizes it. You know she wears those weird outfits, right? Well, she stopped after Jake died. I think it was like too much effort or something. Now she's back to those damn character-inspired whatever." Lisa waves her hand in the air. "I can never guess what she is, and I hate when I can't do something. But my point is, she's herself again. Part of her died with Jake, and whatever you're doing, it's bringing her back to life."

I swallow the lump in my throat. Suddenly, I realize that's a whole lot of fucking responsibility.

"And," Lisa goes on, "I just want to remind you once again that my family owns a *lot* of farmland in this town. You hurt Sierra, I can kill you and make it look like an accident and scatter your body over the thousands of acres we own."

I smile, liking Lisa more and more. "If you were going to hide my body, you don't need to make it look like an accident. Save yourself the trouble."

Lisa smiles back. "Good point. Then I'd just beat you to death with a shovel."

"Sounds about right. I won't hurt her."

"You better not. Want me to get Melissa now?"

"Yeah, then finish your coffee. You're gonna need it."

I pull out my phone while Lisa goes in the back and open Jax's text. He asked if I was alive. I simply respond 'yes' and hit send.

19

SIERRA

I set my Kindle down, trading it for my phone. I'm supposed to be at the Sunday family dinner in ten minutes and I'm half expecting it to be Mom, asking where I am. It's Lisa instead.

Lisa: **Are you bringing Chase to dinner tonight?**

Me: **No. He's hanging out with his brother tonight.**

Lisa: **Good. We need to talk.**

Me: **Trouble with Rob again?**

She doesn't respond, so I take that as a yes. I read a few more pages before getting up out of the hammock and going inside, opening a can of cat food so Dolly and Tinkerbell come running. They like to sit on the screened-in porch with me, but I won't leave them out there unattended. I might have a slight irrational fear of something tearing through the screen and getting them.

When I get to my parents', I see Rob and Lisa sitting together on the back patio. His arm is around hers and they're animatedly talking with Sam and her husband. No one looks stressed. Rob laughs and brings his head closer to Lisa as they talk. I'm not a body language expert, but those two do not look like lovers in a quarrel. And I know they didn't just have a fight because when they do, they're all over each other for a day or two after making up.

I catch Lisa's eye and wave. She gives me a tight smile and whispers something to Rob. He jerks around, face flat before smiling like everything is normal. Lisa stands, shoulders tense, and starts to make her way inside.

"Sierra, dear," Gran calls. "You look lovely. Did you get a bit of sun today?"

"Too much," I tell her, crossing the solarium floor to give my grandmother a hug. "I was hiking and thought the sunlight wouldn't get to me since I was in the woods."

Gran smiles. "I've made that mistake a time or two. Not recently, mind you. Come, dear. Keep me company while I have my tea."

I shoot Lisa an apologetic glance and follow Gran to the front porch. Storm clouds are rolling in, and the smell of rain on the horizon calms me.

"Have you thought about going back to school?" Gran asks, stirring sugar into her tea.

"Not really." I look into my cup, watching tea leaves swirl around the bottom. Part of me wants to try to read them, but I know Gran would think I lost it for sure. "Getting into the same grad school twice is pretty unlikely. The program I was in is very selective."

"But not impossible."

"I know. Maybe I'll go back and get a second degree in agriculture. Or business. The more I think about letting Sam run the farm, the more I feel we're all doomed."

Gran gives me a wry smile, gracefully bringing her tea to her lips. "You would bring a level head into the equation. Which we need. You would be an invaluable asset to the Belmont Industry."

I almost choke. It's the first time Gran has ever hinted that she wants me to come into the family business.

"I'm not really a business person," I mumble.

Ignoring me, Gran goes on. "There is more to this than men in stuffy suits, my dear."

"Yeah…I know." I set my teacup down and look out at the gray clouds. The breeze picks up and a chill comes over me.

"So," Gran says, changing the subject. "When am I going to meet this gentleman you've been seeing? Gloria Freemont tells me he's quite the looker, even with those tattoos." She shakes her head, clicking her tongue. "I don't see the appeal in that."

I laugh. "A lot of people find tattoos sexy, Gran."

"You know what I found sexy about your grandfather?"

"Do I want to know?"

"The way he treated his inferiors. You'd never know they were inferiors. When I met him, the farm was struggling. There had been a drought followed by a year of nonstop rain. It nearly wiped out everything. And within the next two years, luck changed and he got the first partnership selling to a national distributor. He made his first million the next year. But he still worked the fields. Took extra shifts to give his employees days off. I'll never meet another man like your grandfather," she ends, voice dropping.

Gran married two more times after my grandpa died. She divorced her second husband after six years of marriage, saying she was bored with him. She married six months later to a telenovela star she met in Miami, shocking us all. He wasn't a legal citizen, so the marriage isn't technically recognized. He got into some trouble and got deported. She still keeps in contact with him, but I don't think she ever fully committed to either of those men.

It was my fear after Jake died. I'd never find someone I

loved as much. I'd forever think back to what I had, comparing anyone I had interest in to Jake. And they'd fail.

"Excuse me, ma'am," Melinda, my parents' housekeeper says as she steps onto the porch. "Dinner is ready."

I help Gran to her feet and go inside, taking my usual spot at the dining room table next to Lisa. She's quiet throughout the meal, averting her eyes whenever I look her way. As soon as we're done, she grabs my wrist and pulls me into the living room, away from the rest of the family.

"We need to talk," she blurts, looking nervous.

"Are you pregnant?" I whisper.

"What? God no." She looks down at her stomach. "Do I look pregnant? It's this fucking shirt, isn't it?"

"No, you don't. But if you just found out you wouldn't look pregnant. That's not the point. What the hell is going on?"

"Chase," she says, and her voice cuts through the air like a sharp knife.

"What about Chase?"

"He came to the bank yesterday."

"I know. He brought you the coffee and the muffin, right?"

"Yeah, but he stayed and had a meeting with Melissa to set up an account."

I slowly shake my head. "I don't see why that's reason to sound the alarm. He's living here, so it makes sense to have his bank account here."

"It's not just that though…and I don't know all the details since Melissa handled it. He put a lot of money into his account. And I mean *a lot*. I saw the paperwork at the end of the day. He had cash, Si. Two hundred grand in cash."

Yeah, that's weird, but I don't want to say it out loud. "Maybe he took all his money from his other bank?"

"You don't have to literally take it out in cash like that. It's just weird and gave me a bad feeling. So I...I got his info and asked Rob to run a background check on him."

"Seriously?"

"Yes, and you should be glad I did." Lisa's eyes cloud over with guilt and worry. "He's been arrested before. Many times. And the most recent was three months ago for breaking and entering."

I don't say anything. My heart is in my throat.

"That's not all." Lisa swallows hard before going on. "Rob said some of the charges were dropped but couldn't figure out why. And the same judge wrote them off. He said it seemed suspicious as fuck, so he had his lieutenant look at it, and he thinks Chase might have ties to the mafia or something."

"Chase is not in the mafia," I say, trying to sound like I believe it. "That doesn't even make sense."

"Think about it, Sierra. He came to the bank with a duffle bag full of money. He's been arrested a million times with the charges suddenly dropped, and you saw him fight those guys at the party! Plus, he has that suped up Mustang that had to cost at least fifty grand and he was wearing designer clothes."

"Maybe he likes nice things. That doesn't make him a mobster."

"Sierra, use your head. Something is off about him and he could be dangerous!"

"Nothing is off about him," I hiss, anger rising. "You don't know him like I do. And are you forgetting you were the one who told me to go for him?"

"That was before I knew."

"Maybe you should have run a background check on him first." I let out a huff, shaking my head.

"Sierra, be logical."

"Oh, I am logical. I'm not the one running unwarranted background checks and creeping on someone's bank information. I like Chase. He makes me happy. Oh, right. You said it's weird seeing us together."

"What?"

I raise an eyebrow. "Right. Act like you don't remember telling me it's weird seeing me with someone other than Jake. You remember Chase fighting, but don't remember what you said."

"I said that? Fuck, I'm an asshole."

"Yeah, you are." I spin on my heel, giving Rob a look on my way out. I grab my shoes and head out, pissed because it feels like they betrayed me, going behind my back to get dirt on Chase.

And because I'm struggling to not believe it all to be true.

～

"You should really lock your doors."

Chase's voice comes from behind me, and I jump, heart going a million miles an hour. I'm upstairs in my reading room, lost in thought and grumbling at myself for thinking it would be a good idea to reorganize my bookshelves at nine at night. Or ever. Because I have a lot of books, and now I have a huge mess. But after dinner, I needed to stay busy. It was the only way to keep Lisa's words out of my head. She's called me twice and texted a few times to say she was sorry for saying it was weird to see me with anyone other than Jake. I believe her, and know she does feel bad. Lisa's always been one to spout off when she's drunk. It's not the first time, and it won't be the last time.

"Chase," I say, voice all breathy. "I didn't hear you come in."

"Exactly. Anyone could have walked in. And up the stairs."

I grip my copy of Harry Potter and stand, eyeballing Chase. He's wearing jeans and a white T-shirt, looking sexy as hell. His wavy brown hair is a tad messy, adding to his sex appeal, and the stubble on his face accentuates his good looks.

"I texted you," he goes on, stepping over a pile of books.

"Oh, I heard my phone but thought it was Lisa. She's been texting me all night."

"Dakota wanted me to read her a bedtime story, that's what took so long."

He comes closer and my heart skips a beat. "That's sweet of you to do."

He gives me his trademark shrug. "She's a cute kid. Actually makes me a bit sad I didn't get to know her sooner."

The knot in my chest loosens and Chase takes me in his arms, greeting me like usual. I let the book drop and hold him tight. We kiss and in that moment, one thing becomes abundantly clear to me: I don't care if Chase is dangerous. Who he is…what we have…I don't want to change a thing.

"What are you doing?" Chase asks, looking at the books on the floor.

"Rearranging my bookshelves. I was thinking about doing it by color."

His eyebrows go up. "You're going to split apart your series?"

I laugh at the horror in his voice. "No. I had a plan for that. The bottom shelf will be for series. Most of my books are standalones. I think. Shit. I really don't know and now I have a huge mess."

"I would think working in a bookstore would make you want to organize them by author name."

"That's too logical. And I do that all day at the store. Arranging by color is prettier. Have you seen pictures of rainbow bookshelves? The aesthetic is amazing."

"I haven't but I'll take your word for it. And there is something pleasing about seeing colors gradually change into each other. Though I'm personally a minimalist and prefer whites and grays."

"I noticed. I like color."

Chase smiles. "You do? I had no idea." He pokes me in the ribs, making me laugh. And now that he knows I'm ticklish, he doesn't stop until we're both on the floor. Chase is over top of me, and I drag my hands down his back and grip his waist, moving him between my legs. We haven't had sex since Friday after the party, and it feels like it's been so fucking long.

Chase must be thinking the same thing, and we kiss and rip off each other's clothing in a matter of seconds. We're both lying naked on the floor, surrounded by books. Chase kisses his way down my body, not stopping until his head is between my legs. I gasp, reaching down and taking a tangle of his hair as his tongue slowly rolls over my clit. He licks and sucks, then slips a finger inside me, pressing on my inner walls until I come. Wiping his mouth, he looks up with a devilish glint in his eye.

He stands up, helps me to my feet, and guides me over to the yoga ball. With his hands on my waist, he sits, legs spread and feet planted on the ground. Facing him, I carefully move on top and guide his cock inside. He starts out slow, making sure I'm okay and that we can keep our balance. The ball is up against the wall, sandwiched between that and Chase's legs. I wrap my arms around Chase and arch my back. The movement causes us to bounce on the ball, and I feel every inch of him inside me.

"Fuck," I moan and rock my hips. Chase buries his head in my breasts, as his hands run up and down my back. He takes one of my breasts in his mouth, teeth gently nipping my flesh.

I lean forward, throwing a hand out to catch the wall and keep from tumbling off, and thrust hard against Chase. We bounce on the ball, driving his cock deeper into me. I moan and Chase bucks his hips, then starts fucking me hard and fast. My breasts bounce in his face and his fingers dig into my waist.

"You are so fucking hot," he groans and my muscles tighten. The orgasm starts from deep within, exploding within me and making my toes curl and ears ring. Chase presses me against him, breathing hard as he comes, and feeling his cock pulsing inside me is so hot I almost come again. Panting, Chase lowers us to the floor.

"Fuck," he mumbles. "I meant to pull out."

"I didn't think about it either," I confess. Pulling out has been our method of birth control the last week or so. "I like feeling you come. Is that weird?"

"Fuck no. That's hot." Chase brushes my hair out of my eyes and kisses me.

"I have a doctor's appointment next week to get back on the pill. I tried to get her to just phone in the script but I'm due for my annual so I have to go in."

"Sounds fun."

"Loads." Thunder echoes outside and rain falls down hard against the roof. "Oh, shit," I say and sit up. "I opened the bedroom windows to let in the breeze and never closed them."

Chase gets to his feet and grabs his boxers. "I'll close them."

"Thanks."

He steps into his boxers and rushes downstairs. I take my time getting up and moving downstairs, going straight to the bathroom to clean myself up.

"Want to take a shower with me?" I ask Chase. "Before the storm hits."

"You can't shower in a storm?" he asks, raising an eyebrow.

"You could get electrocuted that way if the lightning hit."

"That sounds like an old wives' tale."

"I'm pretty sure it's true," I say and turn on the water. "So we have to hurry."

"You're lucky I already fucked you." He comes into the bathroom and runs his eyes up and down my body. "You are beautiful, Sierra."

We get in the shower and wash quickly. Since Chase had planned on staying the night with me, he brought clothes. We change into PJs and go into the kitchen.

"I have homemade cheesecake from my parents," I start and open the fridge. "Do you want any?"

"Yeah, sounds good."

I pull the dish from the fridge not a moment too soon. Thunder booms and the power goes out.

"Hang on," I say and feel my way to the kitchen sink, dropping down and opening the cabinet beneath it. I turn on a flashlight and use it to locate my candles.

"Those lanterns come in handy," Chase says after we stick candles in them throughout the house.

"I know, right? I've been told I have too many as decorations, but look at this. So practical. The cats won't get into the flames this way."

The wind is blowing against the back of the house, so we take our cheesecake and a blanket to the front porch. We sit close together on the bench, eating in silence as we watch the storm rage on around us.

I look at Chase as lightning flashes, illuminating his handsome face. Lisa is wrong. There is nothing off about him. At all. And if there were…I don't think I'd care.

20

CHASE

"The twins are measuring a week ahead. Melissa is getting induced Friday unless she goes into labor before then," Josh tells me. It's Monday night and the bar is slow, as expected. The regulars are all here, drinking away their problems like usual.

"Is that a good thing to measure ahead?"

"It's not bad, and actually matches with what we thought was the original conception date."

"You remember the day?"

Josh lets out a snort of laughter. "Unlike you, I wasn't getting it every night. Dakota went through a phase of only falling asleep if she was held and would end up in our bed. Melissa and I didn't get many opportunities. We took what we could get, and it resulted in identical twins."

"They weren't planned?" I can't help but ask. Accidental pregnancies might be on my mind.

"Eh, not really, but we knew we wanted another kid someday. It happened sooner than we expected, though with pulling out being our lazy way of preventing, I'm surprised it didn't happen sooner."

His words hit me and I feel the blood drain from my face.

"Y'all too?" he laughs. "What the fuck are you thinking? You know that shit doesn't really work. I'm surprised Sierra lets you—nope, don't want to go there."

And now I'm laughing. "I can't even fucking think about it."

"I hope you don't have to, but seriously, did you miss sex ed in school? Or maybe you're hoping for a little Chase. You and Sierra would make nice babies."

"Not fucking funny, dude."

"Oh it is. To me." Josh turns and goes to another customer, and a group of middle-aged women come in the doors making a beeline to the bar. One sees me, smiles, and keeps walking, but the other two come to a standstill. Smiles realizes her friends stopped, and turns, wondering what's going on. They shake their heads and look at me, trying to warn Smiles about something. She rolls her eyes and comes up, ordering three beers.

Now that she's in front of me, I recognize her as one of the waitresses from Suzy's cafe. Her hair is down now, and she has quite a bit of makeup on. I bring them their drinks and move away, wiping up spilled whiskey. Over the music, I can hear the women talking.

"Sierra Belmont is dating him," one whispers.

"How did he land a Belmont?" another quips. "I mean, he's good-looking, but—" Her voice is cut off by laughter coming from the opposite end of the bar.

"Sierra's a smart girl, if she feels safe around him, we should too," the waitress says firmly, and I wipe the same spot over again just to listen. They turn their conversation to the upcoming Fourth of July festival. I move on, and the night goes by slowly. Around ten o'clock, Melissa calls Josh and says she's not feeling well. Apologizing more than once for making me close by myself, he leaves in a rush and texts me an hour later to say they think Melissa is in labor and are headed up to the hospital now.

I'm happy for my brother and excited to have two nephews that I'll know from the start this time around. By eleven-thirty, the bar is empty except for the local drunks, and after finding them rides home, I close down and am upstairs by midnight. I text Sierra, not wanting to call and wake her up, then get in the shower.

I check my phone before going to bed. Sierra hasn't texted me back, leading me to assume she's sleeping. Thinking about her lying in bed, eyes closed, looking inno-cent yet still sexy as fuck at the same time brings a smile to my face.

With the image of Sierra on my mind, I open my voice-mail. Sierra and I have a good thing going. I need to delete these messages and pretend it never happened. Or maybe I should listen to them one more time, commit them to memory so I don't fuck up again.

Sierra never told me about her brother in Orlando. I heard it on a message and slipped up. I can't be that careless again. What she's told me and what I've heard from the messages blur together in my brain. I need to forget every-thing I wasn't supposed to hear.

Or better yet, I could come clean. Almost clean? Tell her I listened to the first one then deleted the rest. It doesn't sound as bad. I sigh and look at the messages. There are more that I haven't listened to, and that last message calls to me.

Why is it the last?

What made Sierra finally stop calling?

"It doesn't matter," I tell myself out loud. I need to delete them all. Move on and not bring this up again until Sierra and I are happily married with a kid or two. It'll be a thing of the past and she'll be annoyed for half a day then get over it because clearly we were meant to meet and end up together.

Whoa.

The thought comes so naturally to me it's jarring. I feel so strongly for Sierra already and know I'll never meet another woman like her in my life. I have to delete the messages.

My other phone rings, and I snatch it off the nightstand. I haven't heard back from Jax, and I'm starting to worry. When I see Beth's number and not Jax's, the worry intensifies. Not wanting to talk to her, I let the call go to voicemail. She leaves a message, and my heart is in my throat when I push play.

"Chase, baby," she starts and I can tell right away she's drunk. Beth is usually drunk. "Where the fuck are you? I haven't had a decent lay since the last time we were together. Fucking hell, I miss your cock. You better not be dead."

There was a time when her dirty-talk was a turn on in an I-know-I'm-getting-some sense. Don't get me wrong, I enjoyed sex with Beth, as well as with the previous women I dated or hooked up with. Compared to what I have with Sierra...it's all nothing. Am I finally seeing the difference between fucking and making love? I always thought the latter would be lame, tender, boring sex, but it couldn't be further from the truth with Sierra. I'm fucking her, that's for sure, but it's more than physical.

I put the phone back down and get situated under the covers. After half an hour of lying in bed wide awake, I get up and go into the main living area. The cabinets in the kitchen are dated, with the oak stained a dusty-colored brown. The wallpaper in lieu of a backsplash is ugly and peeling, and the original hardwood floors are in need of some major TLC before they have to be replaced completely.

Dark paneling has been put up along one wall, covering the brick. It's dark, cheap, and makes this place feel like a time capsule back to the early 80s. It makes me cringe every time I see it, and the smell of musk clings to the compressed wood. If I'm going to make this place mine, I need to make some changes.

～

"Wow," Sierra says, stepping over a pile of broken paneling. "You're making good progress."

I rip another piece of paneling off the wall and toss it with the rest. I was up until four am last night tearing shit apart and picked up where I left off when I got up.

"The brick is in good shape," I note, moving to the last section to tear off. "I was a little worried there was a reason it was covered up."

Sierra comes closer and touches the wall. I know her well enough now to know exactly what's running through her mind. These walls have seen so much over the decades. I remove the last piece of paneling and toss it into the pile. Despite the air conditioner being on, the sunlight has warmed up this space and I'm sweating from the physical labor. I wipe sweat from my face and chest, and Sierra goes to the fridge, getting me a glass of ice water.

"Thanks," I tell her and drink it all.

"Seeing you all hot, sweaty, and shirtless is turning me on," she tells me, biting her lip and running her fingers over her stomach, which is exposed from the crop top she's wearing. "Just add a hardhat and a tool belt and I'd feel like I just walked onto a porn set."

"I can roll with that," I say and grab her by the waist. Sierra hooks her arms around me, widening her legs and pressing her hips into mine. "Well, ma'am, I've just finished the renovations on your apartment and need to collect my payment."

"Oh no," she says, shaking her head. "I don't have any money. Is there any other way I can pay you?"

She's naked and on top of me in a matter of seconds, and we end up on the floor between the couch and the large window. We're both sweaty when we're done and get in the shower together.

"What time do you have to go to the bar tonight?" Sierra asks me as we get dressed.

"Around nine. Earlier if it's busy."

Sierra makes a face. "It might be busy. There's a town meeting tonight about the Fourth of July Fest at seven. They usually last an hour or so and everyone needs a drink after."

I laugh as I pull on boxers and sit on the bed. Sierra skips her bra and puts her shirt back on. The faint outline of her nipples is visible, making me want to fuck her all over again. "Do you go to those meetings?"

"I have before. Lisa and I had the bright idea to be on the town council a few years ago. They take that shit seriously. We got off it as fast as we could."

"What's the deal with the Fourth of July Fest? I heard people talking about it at the bar last night."

"The town shuts pretty much down for the day. There's a parade in the morning, a cookout, drinking, and dancing during the day, and then fireworks at night. Last year Josh hosted the after-party in the bar's parking lot. It was a lot of fun. Since the babies are due close to the holiday, someone else is doing it this year. Speaking of babies, have you heard from him at all?"

"The last I heard Melissa got her epidural and was getting ready to push." I make a face at the thought, and Sierra mirrors it.

"That's exciting! But I can't imagine pushing two babies in a row like that. Do you know what names they picked out?"

"They had a few picked out but weren't choosing until they met the boys. We can go visit them tomorrow if you want."

"Are they at Mercy?"

"Yeah."

Sierra's face pales. "I don't think...the last time..." Her eyes flutter closed and she takes a breath before looking at me. "The last time I was at Mercy, I held Jake's hand as he died. I...I don't think I can go back yet. I'm sorry."

Her words bring hurt to my heart. Both at her loss—I didn't know she watched him die, that she saw him take his final breath—and that what we have isn't enough. It's stupid, and probably immature to think I could love her enough to erase the pain of the past. But that's what she's doing to me.

"I understand and don't be sorry. We can see them at home."

"You should go," she says. "I can tell you want to, and I think it's sexy you want to see your nephews."

"I'll make sure to send you pictures of myself holding the babies then."

Sierra gives me a coy smile. "Make sure you do."

I grab a shirt from the closet and put it on. "You said you like to decorate, right?"

"I love to."

"Once I get this place updated, want to help me decorate?"

Sierra's eyes light up. "Um, yes!" I don't have to say it for Sierra to understand, which solidifies how right we are for each other. I don't say it, but she knows.

I want this place to be *home*.

~

SIERRA WAS RIGHT. After the town council meeting let out, everyone came here. I don't quite understand why a town of roughly three thousand needs this many fucking people on the council, either. For a solid two hours, we're nonstop busy.

Almost everyone asks me about Josh, Melissa, and the babies. And they all seen disappointed I don't have any updates. And a handful of them eye me apprehensively, tensing when I come to their table or bring them a drink, similar to the women last night.

I've said it before and I'll say it again: this town is fucking weird.

It's going on eleven when I get time for a break. I hurry up the stairs to Sierra, who's been busy mapping out exactly how she wants to decorate this place. She went home to take care of her cats and get overnight stuff and brought along her computer and several interior decorating magazines to flip through, keeping busy while I worked downstairs.

She's on the couch, wearing sleeper shorts and a tank top, with a blanket draped over her shoulders. The blanket is light pink and has a big rainbow-colored unicorn in the middle. She brought it over as a joke since I don't have throw blankets for the couch. But once we decorate, she'll get a stylish one, she promised.

"Hey, babe," she says, looking up from her computer. "Sounds busy down there."

"It is. Those council members are an interesting crowd."

She laughs and sets her computer on the coffee table. "That's a nice way to put it. Your phone was ringing. Someone called a few times."

I reach into my pocket for my phone, raising an eyebrow. "Oh, the other phone."

"Yeah, the other one. It's probably an old girlfriend begging you to come back to her, isn't it?"

My arms fasten around Sierra's waist. I don't think I'm going to make it back to the bar. "Probably. But she's got nothing on my new girlfriend."

Sierra's eyes light up and she smiles before kissing me. We haven't talked about titles or exclusivity. I think it went unsaid. Though saying the title out loud is fucking nice.

"No," Sierra whispers. "She doesn't."

We kiss again and then Sierra tells me what she has planned. Time goes too fast, and I have to go back to the bar. I grab my phone on my way out and see it was Jax who called. Three times. I step outside by the river and call him back.

"Jesus fucking Christ," he answers on the second ring. "Chase Henson lives."

"Shut the fuck up," I say back, grinning. "What kind of shit are you in now?"

"Remember the set of Lambos we took back in Chicago?"

"That's kind of hard to forget."

"Right? That's the problem. The guys we took them from want them back."

I run my hand through my hair. "Of fucking course. But we don't have them."

"I tried to tell them that. Tried to say why we took them in the first place, and it only made things worse. It was, what, six...seven months ago? Those assholes must have made a couple good deals since then and are putting a cash prize on my head."

"Fucking hell. Did you talk to Jefferson?"

"He's on vacation. In fucking Europe. For three weeks. Who the fuck goes to Europe for three weeks?"

"We did. I think we were there longer."

"Shit. Right. I need to lay low until he's back and can get those assholes properly dealt with. Where the hell are you?" he asks.

"Summer Hill, Mississippi."

"Still? Beth said you went to deal with family shit. What the fuck is taking so long?"

"My dad died."

"Fuck. I'm sorry, Chase."

"Thanks, but it's fine. I was never close to him."

"Yeah," Jax goes on. "But he's your fucking father. So, what are you still doing there?"

"Helping my brother. His wife is in labor with twins as we speak. Where are you?"

"Indianapolis. I'm making my way to Miami to wait out the remainder of the three weeks on a fuck-cation with Jackie Sullivan."

"That chick you recovered the necklaces for?"

"Yeah."

"Isn't she like fifty?"

"Don't talk shit about her."

I laugh. "Easy tiger."

"Only problem is her husband is home for a few more days before going on a business trip. Mind if I stop by for a day or two?"

"No. It'll be good to see you." I give him the address, and before we hang up, Jax asks me one more question.

"What the fuck is really going on? You fall off the grid then pop up in the middle of nowhere in the south. Are you being held against your will by your inbred relatives?"

"Fuck you, and goodnight. See ya later."

I met Jax when I took a job in Reno. Our line of work is solitary, dangerous, and makes it hard to trust anyone. Jax helped me out of a bind, and I returned the favor. We realized how well we work together, and how we could actually get more money by taking on more jobs as a team. He's the only person besides Josh and Sierra I consider a friend. I'd be lying to say a part of me didn't miss him.

But an even bigger part thinks having him come here is a bad fucking idea.

SIERRA

"*S*tay here."

"What?" I mumble, confused why Chase is telling me to stay in bed. Like I had any intention of getting out. The sun is just starting to rise and we left the window cracked so we could better hear the river. I could stay in bed all day and it wouldn't be long enough.

"I'm going to see who it is. Just stay here."

"Who what is?" I reach for Chase as he gets out of bed. My fingers grace the warm flesh of his naked ass. Having him next to me was one of the best things. I pull the blanket up over my shoulder, missing him already yet not awake enough to realize what's going on.

Chase pulls on pants and opens the bedroom door. Then I hear it, and nerves shoot through me. Knocking. Someone is knocking on the front door. A beat passes and a deep male voice bellows, "Chase, are you alive in there?"

By that time, Chase is out the door, and I sit up, dressed in panties and Chase's T-shirt, and strain in the dark to listen. Chase greets whoever is at the door happily. Like he knows him.

I push my messy hair out of my face and pad my way to the bedroom door, peering out.

"How the fuck did you get here so fast?" Chase asks. "You said you were in Indy."

"I was," the guy answers. I can't see his face yet.

"That's a ten-hour drive."

"I flew."

"You hate flying," Chase tells him.

"I hate dying even more," he says and both he and Chase laugh.

"Come in," Chase says. "And be quiet."

"Why?" the guy asks, stepping into the living room. Early morning sun illuminates his face. He's almost as tall as Chase, and just as built. His dark hair is cut short and he has a fresh bruise on his cheek. I step out of the doorway and into the hall.

"Chase?"

"Oh," the guy says, eyeballing me. "Fuck you, Henson. If this is your inbred cousin, I'm jealous."

Chase rolls his eyes. "This is my girlfriend, Sierra. Sierra, this is Jax, an old friend. He's going to stay for a few days until he gets something settled."

I'm by Chase's side now, and he puts his arm around me. I stare at Jax for a few seconds, trying my hardest not to stereotype. He shares few characteristics with Chase apart from being tall and muscular. Where Chase is good-looking, Jax is harsh. Weathered. Chase's hazel eyes soften when we speak and are full of emotions. Jax's are dark, and void of anything you could mistake as a feeling. He has a look about him that makes me not want to trust him, that makes me think he's trouble. *A criminal.*

"Why are you here so early?" I ask.

"I'd love to know the same," Chase echoes, holding me closer to him, like he doesn't want Jax to go near me.

"It wasn't as long of a drive from the airport to here as I expected," Jax tells us and sets his suitcase down. He takes a minute to size up the apartment, then goes to the fridge. Aware that Jax has stared at my breasts more than once in the minute we've met, I go into the bedroom to put on a bra. Chase follows me, closing the door behind him.

"Sorry," he says. "I didn't think he'd be here now. He called last night and said he was on his way to Miami and was going to stop by. I assumed he was driving and wouldn't be anywhere near here until much later. I meant to talk to you about it today."

"It's okay. He's your friend. You don't have to explain it to me."

"I feel bad about it."

"Don't." I yawn and stick my bra inside my top, sliding the straps up over my arms.

"Go back to bed," Chase tells me. "You have to get up for work in a few hours. I'll rub your back to help you fall back asleep."

"I'm not tired right now." I check the time on my phone. "We could go out for breakfast soon. Just let me shower and get dressed."

"If that's what you want."

"Yeah. You know I like breakfast, and I'm sure Jax is hungry if he came in from the airport."

Chase looks at me for a second before smiling, but his eyes don't convey the happiness. He takes me in his arms, muscles tense. I hook my arms around him and he relaxes, resting his head against mine.

Then he suddenly kisses me, hard, fast, and desperate.

"I want you to know," he whispers, pulling back just enough so he can talk. His forehead rests against mine. "How happy you've made me."

His words sound like a goodbye as if he's preparing to go off into battle and we might not meet again.

"You make me happy too," I say and then it hits me. Hard. So hard I'm gripping Chase as if my life depends on it. I close my eyes, bracing for the familiar sinking feeling. I've grown so used to the sinking below the surface, the air on my skin sends a shock through my system as it hits me.

I'm no longer drowning.

Chase has been my life preserver, and so much more than that. He brought me back. Lifted me from the murky depths of the darkest water and breathed life back into me. Tears spring to my eyes and I need to kiss Chase again.

Not want, but *need*.

"I honestly didn't think I'd feel happy again," I confess, voice hardly a whisper. "And I am."

"I always hoped you'd get a happy ending," he replies. His words don't make sense, but I'm not going to overthink it. Not now. We kiss again and fall back onto the bed, with Chase between my legs. His cock starts to harden against me and everything wells up inside. All the emotion. All the pain. It's too much. If we don't find an outlet we're both going to explode.

Chase pulls my shorts off and I yank down the waistband of his boxers. His dick is against me, wet tip rubbing over my clit. I shudder with pleasure and feel even more desperate to have him inside me. His eyes meet mine, conveying everything I'm feeling, as he pushes inside, driving that big cock deep.

I let out a moan then bring my hand to my face, muffling any sounds coming from my lips. We're not alone, and the fact that we both had the sudden uncontrollable urge to fuck turns me on even more.

And makes me realize just how far I've fallen for Chase.

He thrusts in and out with unrelenting strength, and the bed frame hits the brick wall behind it. Neither of us do anything to quiet it because that would mean stopping and if Chase stops, if he takes his cock out of me before I come, there's a good chance I'll spontaneously combust and die.

I wrap my legs around him, holding him tight, and angle my hips up. Chase's breathing quickens and I know he's close to coming. He suddenly flips us over so I'm on top, and once situated, I start rocking my hips, pushing him farther and farther into me. He grabs my hips then slides one hand down, thumb finding my clit.

The sex is hard and fast, but it's so much more. We're both desperate for a physical release, but intertwining our bodies transcends anything I've ever felt before, and as I look down at Chase, I know in that very moment he walked into my life at the exact right time.

We were meant to meet so we could do this, and I don't mean epically fuck.

My orgasm hits me suddenly, and I have to use both hands over my mouth to keep quiet. Chase comes right after I do, groaning out loud as he finishes. I fall forward onto him, and he folds his strong arms around my shoulders.

"That was intense," I pant. "I don't think I've ever come that fast before, and that's including the times I've done it myself."

"That's one hell of a compliment," Chase says with a chuckle. He brushes my hair out of my face and kisses my forehead. "And I'd say same for me, but that first night we spent together when you shot me down...I took care of business myself and it was pretty much instant."

I laugh, feeling his cock inside me as my body moves. "I think that's a compliment, right?"

"It is."

"That wasn't the first night we spent together," I correct and move off of him, trying to lay flat until he brings me a towel to clean up with. "The first night was right in here, actually."

"But I was on the couch. Fuck. Speaking of the couch...I almost forgot Jax is here. What the hell are you doing to me, Sierra?"

"Just the usual Black Magic love spells. It'll only be a matter of days before your soul is mine and I can use your reanimated corpse to do my evil bidding."

"As long as you keep fucking me like that, I'm fine with it."

I act like I consider his words. "I suppose I can work in a spell or two to preserve your body. It would be a shame to waste *this*."

Chase laughs and gets up, grabs a towel from the bathroom, and hands it to me. "Still want to go out to breakfast?"

"I might wait a minute or two before going out there. The door wasn't shut and even if it were, there's no way anyone in the living room wouldn't have heard us. And you know how important first impressions are..."

Chase steps back into his boxers before getting a new pair of jeans from the dresser. "As far as first impressions go, this one has to be the fucking best."

∾

CHASE: **I can't be held responsible for distracting you at work. Brace yourself.**

I smile down at my phone and wait for another picture to come through. I'm at work, and Chase is currently at the hospital visiting his nephews for the first time. One of the babies was a whole pound smaller than the other and needs to be on oxygen. Chase promised me over and over that he wasn't just making shit up to make me feel better, and that both babies were given a good prognosis and should come home by the end of the week.

I admire the photo of Chase holding the newborn for a minute before replying.

Me: **You look so hot with a baby in your arms.**

Chase: **Don't get any crazy ideas now**

Me: **Heck no. Not for years and years and years and years.**

I add a laughing emoji and send, then take another glance at the photo Chase sent. The bell on the door rings as someone enters the little shop, and I look up, startled by who I see walking in.

"Mom?"

"Hello, Sierra, darling."

I raise an eyebrow. "What are you doing here?"

Mom blinks, long, false lashes coming together slowly. "Is it so out of the question I come and see you at work?"

"Uh, yeah. Is everyone okay?"

"Yes, yes, we're all fine. I thought I'd come get a book to read by the pool."

"Sure, Mom. You're the only one here right now so why don't you just tell me what you want."

Mom looks at me, lips pursed, but gives up with a sigh. "I talked to your aunt Kelly today."

My aunt Kelly is Lisa's mom—my dad's younger sister. "Is she okay?"

"Oh, yes, she's fine. We're going shopping later—that's not the point. The point is she told me some startling news."

My phone dings as another text from Chase comes through. I flip it over since I have a feeling I know what this is about.

"She told me about that man you've been dating…that Henson boy."

The way she spits his name pisses me off. Instantly. He's not good enough for her solely based on the fact his family doesn't come from money.

"He's been arrested before! What are you thinking, Sierra?"

"Mom, calm down."

"I will not calm down! I'm worried about you, honey." Her eyebrows push together and I see a rare real-mom moment where her emotions are visible through the layers of foundation and blush on her face. "Men like that are never good news."

"Mom, Chase isn't a bad guy. I promise you that."

"But he's been arrested over a dozen times."

It takes effort to keep my face neutral and act like this is old news. "He's not a bad person," I state again.

"Your father and I talked, and we don't like this." She holds up a hand. "I understand you're an adult and can do as you please, but know how worried this makes us. You're my baby girl and I want to protect you."

"He makes me really happy, and if you met him, you'd feel the same way I do. Well, not the same in the I-want-him-sexually way, but in the he's-not-a-bad-guy way. Unless the whole bad-boy-yet-good-man thing turns you on."

"This isn't funny, Sierra. I wish you'd take things more seriously. You could do so much better, sweetheart. He's a bartender who lives above a bar. What kind of future could he offer you?"

Anger flashes through me and I'm on my feet, leaning across the counter. "I do take things seriously! I spent the last year and a half in *serious* depression. And my future? I didn't know I was even going to have one, let alone look forward to one until I met Chase."

The color drains from my mother's tan face. "I didn't think—"

"No surprise there," I snap, and all the things I've wanted to say to my mother over the years bubble to the surface. "That's how it's always been with me though." I throw my hands up in defeat. "I'm not Sam. I don't have a high-paying, prestigious job like Scott. And now I'm not dating someone you approve of and you automatically want me to cut him off before you even meet him."

"It's not just that, Sierra," she starts.

"Then what is it? I know I'm not what you expected, Mom, and I'm still not sure if I should be sorry for that. My life hasn't turned out like I thought it would, but I found someone who makes me happy, and I wish you'd give him a chance before coming in here and telling me that he's not good enough."

Silence falls over the both of us. "You're right," Mom finally says, voice strained. "Maybe he is a nice man. Maybe he does treat you well. That still doesn't change the fact that he's been taken away in handcuffs multiple times for assault. I'm worried about you, Sierra. And a lot of us feel that Chase shouldn't be trusted."

Assault? Chase? That doesn't make sense. I put my head in my hands. *A lot of us…*That only means one thing. The Summer Hill gossip mill is alive and running with rumors of Chase's arrests. That explains the stares we got at breakfast this morning. I thought it was just because of Jax.

"It doesn't matter," I say out loud to my mother as well as myself. "Whatever Chase did before doesn't matter. He's a good person, Mom, and I really care about him. He cares about me too, and if you'd give him a chance, you'd see what I see in him."

Mom's lips press together in a tight line, and wrinkles form around her pout. "Fine," she finally says. "Bring him to dinner Sunday."

"I will." I sit back down on the stool behind the counter and let out a breath. Chase's words echo in my mind, about how weird it is to always be in the same place with the same people. Maybe if I moved around like he did, I wouldn't seek my family's approval. I let my thoughts briefly wander to traveling the world with Chase, going from city to city, state to state, even to different countries.

"Don't be late," Mom says, needing to get the final word in.

"We won't be." I let out a breath, suddenly feeling sorry for my mother and her concern over the opinions of others. I'm sure a large part of this really is stemming from fear that I'm dating a bad person, but it's not all of it.

Mom opens the door but doesn't step outside. "Sierra," she says, turning back toward me. "I love you. Someday, when you have kids, you'll understand that you want nothing more than happiness for them. I want you to be happy. I hope Chase is who you say he is. And no, you're nothing like your brother or sister, and I've always admired that about you. And wondered where you got your free spirit because it sure wasn't from your father or me."

"Thanks, Mom," I say quietly. "I love you too."

She gives a tight smile then leaves, and silence falls over the store. I stare at the bright sunlit windows for a moment, then blink and look back at my phone so I could read my texts from Chase.

~

AT LUNCH, I realize I left my wallet at Chase's house and need it so I can buy food. I phone an order into Suzy's Cafe and rush to The Mill House. It's one-thirty, and the parking lot is empty. I go around back, slowing when I see the river.

It reminds me of Chase, and not just because it runs behind this place.

Reminding myself I have to hurry, I go up the stairs and knock on the door. A minute goes by and no one answers, and I think Jax is either sleeping or ignoring whoever is at the door. A second before I turn to go, he answers.

"Sierra. Hey. Chase isn't here."

"I know," I tell him, offering a polite smile. He's wearing pajama bottoms and a Metallica T-shirt and looks like he just woke up. "I left my wallet here this morning and need it to buy lunch."

Jax nods and steps aside, letting me in. I go right to Chase's room to grab it. A rush goes through me when I see the messy bed, sheets twisted across the mattress and a pillow on the floor. I cannot wait to mess up that bed again.

"Find it?" Jax says, appearing in the doorway. His large frame takes up most of the space, blocking me in. My heart speeds up.

"Yeah," I say, grabbing the hot pink Coach wallet from the nightstand. I push my shoulders back, not wanting Jax to see he scares me. If Chase trusts him, I can too…right?

"You must really have a hold on him," Jax starts. "I've never seen him like this before?"

"Like what?" I take another step forward and Jax doesn't move. I left my phone in the car and we're the only ones here. My pulse rises.

"In love."

"Chase isn't in love with me," I say and shake my head. Not yet at least.

Jax rolls his eyes. "You don't see it? What, are you fucking blind?"

"I happen to have excellent eyesight, thank you very much." I put a hand on my hip and stare down Jax. "What do you want?"

He tips his head, amused at my unexpected question. "I want to know what you're doing with Chase."

My eyebrows pinch together and it takes me a second for his words to click. "Are you trying to interrogate me and make sure my intentions are noble?"

"Something like that."

"Seriously?" I can't help but laugh. "You're worried that I might hurt Chase?"

"You're a Lannister and he's a —"

"Whoa, whoa, whoa," I interrupt, holding up my hand. "I'm so not a Lannister. I'm a dragon."

Jax makes his face. "Stark maybe. But no Targaryon."

I narrow my eyes. "And you're a Frey."

"Ouch," he says, leaning back like the insult hurt. Then his eyes meet mine and he laughs. "You're all right, Sierra."

"I can die happy knowing you think so."

He leans forward in a deep bow. "Go forth, Mother of Dragons."

"First of her Name…Breaker of Chains…you gotta say the whole thing."

"I wouldn't have taken you to be a Game of Thrones junkie."

"I love it. The books and the show were both excellent. Lord of the Rings is good too. But Harry Potter is the best of all."

"Fuck yes it is. Chase is a Slytherin, just to warn you. I made him take the Pottermore official test a few years back."

"I'll let that one slide. I'm a Hufflepuff, and we see the good in everyone after all." I laugh and go back to the front door. Just a minute ago I was scared that Jax might hurt me, but he turns out to be a fantasy nerd like me and a loyal friend to Chase.

"See you around, Sierra," he says and opens the door for me. The relief I felt is zapped away. On Jax's right arm, just under the sleeve of his T-shirt, is a tattoo of a sun. The same exact sun that Chase has tattooed on his chest. Suddenly, Lisa's theory that Chase is in some sort of organized crime ring doesn't sound too far off.

22

CHASE

"Not that I've ever doubted your skills," Jax tells me later that night. "But how the fuck did a chick like Sierra end up with you?"

I laugh. "I have no fucking clue."

Setting a bag of takeout from the bar on the coffee table, I fall onto the couch. It's two o'clock in the morning, and I'm fucking tired. I had to go straight down to the bar after coming home from Mercy hospital. Dakota wasn't handling the transition from only child to older sister of two very well. She asked if I would take her to get a Happy Meal for lunch, and of course I said yes. There's a McDonalds less than a block away from the hospital and it wasn't too hot to comfortably walk to it.

Josh was fine with it. Melissa was fine with it. Melissa's parents were fine with it. But Judy Henson—low and behold —wasn't. It led to an awkward conversation between Josh and his mother, Dakota crying, and Melissa, who was worn out and in pain, snapping at Judy.

Melissa's father ended up coming with, which wasn't as bad as I expected. The guy was talkative but nice and thanked me more than once for filling in at the bar so Josh could spend more time at home with Melissa and the babies.

"Makes sense why you fell off the grid," he goes on. "But what are you going to do?"

I take a bite of my burger and shoot him a look. "With what?"

"Playing house here."

I shrug. "I like it here."

Jax, who's never been much of a talker, grunts. He opens his bag of takeout and puts his feet up on the coffee table, flipping through channels.

"Want to know something fucked up?" I blurt.

"I love fucked up."

"My phone broke, and I had to send it in to get the screen replaced. That's why I fell off the grid. And I got a temporary in its place. It's Sierra's dead boyfriend's phone."

"How the fuck do you know that?"

"The person who sold it second-hand failed to do a factory reset and deleted shit by hand. But they forgot the voicemails. Sierra kept calling him after he died."

Jax blinks, looks away, then back at me again. "You listened to the messages?"

"A few of them."

"Does she know?"

"No. I listened before I knew it was her."

"That is not the kind of fucked up I was expecting. I thought you were going to say cousins really do hook up here and Sierra's got a hot cousin that joins in with you two."

I make a face. "You have issues."

Jax laughs at himself. "I do. But I'm also enjoying the visual of Sierra having a near-identical cousin. They're really going at it—fuck. Here you come, ruining everything."

I chuckle and shake my head. "I can never tell her, can I?"

Jax takes in a deep breath and pulls his French fries from the bag. "Fuck if I know. Are they sex-messages?"

"No, but it's obvious she didn't want anyone else to hear."

"Yeah, I don't—wait. She has a dead boyfriend?"

I nod, taking another bite of food. "He died almost two years ago. Car accident."

"Fuck," Jax mutters, turning his attention back to the MMA game on TV. I finish eating, take a shower, and fall into bed. I'm tired but can't fall asleep because my damn mind won't shut off and I keep thinking about Sierra. Doing the right thing has never kept me up at night. I've never lost sleep over what someone might think of me.

Sierra changes everything. She's changing me without trying. Or maybe she's not. Maybe she's just exposing who I've been all along and fought hard to cover up.

~

"MY MOTHER HAS FORMALLY INVITED us to family dinner this Sunday," Sierra tells me. I brought her lunch at The Book Bag today, and we're sitting together behind the counter. "I'm sorry in advance."

"It'll be fine."

She purses her lips. "You don't know my family."

"Tell me about them." I put my hand on Sierra's thigh, inching my fingers under the hem of her black skirt.

"Scott's cool. But he doesn't live here. My sister Sam is as type-A as type-A can be. Same with her husband, Brent. My dad talks about two things: work or the New Orleans Saints. My mom and Aunt Kelly are judgmental as fuck, and my Gran knows everything about everyone in the town." She dips her fry in cheese sauce. "They're not bad people though. Very nosey, but not bad. Nothing is off limits either."

"I can handle it." I squeeze her thigh and Sierra moves her

leg, letting me slip my fingers further between. Then the bell above the door dings and I move my hand down to her knee.

"Hi, Mrs. McKay," Sierra says to the woman who walked through the door, greeting her with a smile.

"Hello, darling," Mrs. McKay replies. Her eyes go to me and narrow.

"She works with Judy Henson," Sierra whispers to me once Mrs. McKay walks down an aisle. Sierra rolls her eyes and puts her hand on mine, letting me know she doesn't give a shit what people think.

I stay with Sierra a while longer and then leave to work at the bar. I'm opening and closing tonight and already dreading it. I'm not a nine-to-five guy. Hell, even working evenings and nights at the bar is already getting to me. Maybe Jax was right to think living a life like this is bullshit.

23

SIERRA

"This looks amazing!" I say, unable to keep the smile off my face. "I can't believe it's done already."

"I had a decent designer." Chase puts his arm around me and kisses the side of my head. "And once I got Jax off his lazy ass, the sanding and painting went fast."

"I love it. White cabinets are trendy right now, and it really brightens up this space."

"Exactly what I was going for," Chase teases, taking another look at his renovated kitchen. Jax snores loudly from the couch, half covered with the rainbow unicorn blanket I brought for Chase as a joke.

"How long is he going to be here?" I ask. "Not that I mind or anything."

"I mind," Chase grumbles, eyeballing the empty containers of takeout on the floor. Overall, Chase is a neat person. He doesn't make his bed or vacuum every day, but I've noticed that he doesn't like clutter or things being out of place. "It's been nearly a week and shouldn't be too long. He's waiting for his mistress's husband to go on a business trip before going to her summer house in Florida."

"That sounds like a joke, but you look serious."

"I am serious. She's old enough to be his mother."

"Good for her," I say and take Chase's hand. It's Sunday afternoon and we came back to Chase's from church so he could change into jeans and a T-shirt. He asked me three times on the way if he should stay in his dress clothes for dinner tonight. He says he's not nervous, but seeing him want to make a good impression means more to me than I expected it to. He wouldn't want my family to like him if he wasn't serious about us, right? Chase is a person who gives no fucks. So when he does, it means something.

We go into Chase's room, and watching him unbutton his shirt is an instant turn-on. I bite my lip and reach up, pulling on the silver chain hanging around my neck. Chase catches me watching and grins. Slowly, he undoes the rest of the button and peels his shirt back Magic Mike style. As soon as the shirt hits the floor, I'm a goner.

～

"CHASE?" I ask, reaching for him. "Are you okay?"

"Yeah," he mumbles, pressing his hand to his stomach. "Got a random cramp. I'm fine now." I'm lying in his bed, sheets covering my naked body. He's in the middle of the room, searching for my clothes that were ripped off and strewn about. He keeps his hand on his abdomen and straightens up, tossing me my underwear and dress.

I get dressed and then go to the bathroom, coming back in the room to find Chase balling up the dirty sheets. He has one hand pressed to his stomach again but brings it away as soon as I set foot in the room. I internally roll my eyes. Not feeling well isn't anything to hide.

"Have a stomachache?" I ask, grabbing new sheets from the closet.

"Yeah. I have all day," he confesses and grabs the opposite end of the fitted sheet. We have to turn it twice before getting it on the right way. "I'm fine though."

"You're nervous for tonight," I joke.

"I've never felt sick from nerves," he tells me. "I don't feel nervous often, either."

"Lucky. Nerves go right to my stomach. It's not always pretty."

We head to my house and spend the rest of the afternoon lounging around in the hammock. Tinkerbell and Dolly are with us most of the time, and Dolly's approval of Chase makes me like him that much more.

"You feel kind of feverish," I tell him, pressing my hand to the back of his forehead. "Are you still not feeling well?"

Chase shrugs. "I'm tired."

"I'm going to take your temperature." I get out of the hammock and return with the thermometer. I put it to Chase's forehead. "Ninety-nine-point-two. You do have a fever."

"I'll take a Tylenol and be okay."

"We don't have to go to dinner. Not if you're sick."

"I'm fine," he says again. "And it's just dinner. I'll be sitting there eating, not running a marathon."

"If you say so."

"I do." He pushes my hair back over my shoulder. "My only concern is making you sick."

"I don't get sick very often. I used to eat dirt when I was a kid. My mom jokes it gave me a hell of a good immune system."

"I did not eat dirt as a child," Chase laughs. "Maybe I should have."

"I'm like never sick. I highly recommend it to children everywhere."

Chase takes my hand and gets off the hammock, stretching his arms above his head. His T-shirt rises, giving me a glimpse of his abdomen. We bring the cats in, feed them, and get in Chase's car to drive to my parents' house. I notice him wincing when he gets out of the car, but does his best to hide it.

"Are you ready to meet your maker?" I ask, walking up to the front door.

Chase takes my hand. "I am. Are you?"

"No. I want to get a plate of food then go home."

"We will. In an hour or two."

I make a face and Chase squeezes my hand. He stops before we go up the steps and onto the porch and kisses me.

"Thanks. I needed that."

"I know," he says.

We enter the house and find everyone in the back parlor, no doubt waiting for us to arrive. Lisa and Rob aren't here yet, and I wonder if she's skipping altogether. We haven't spoken since she confronted me about Chase's criminal record. I introduce Chase to everyone, and then Gran pulls us out onto the porch for tea.

"It's nice to finally meet the man who's responsible for making my granddaughter happy again," Gran says to Chase.

"It's nice making her happy," Chase replies.

Gran watches Chase and prepares her tea. "I knew your father," she tells him. "He drove trucks for us for a while."

"You probably knew him better than I did."

Curious, Gran sets her tea down. "He didn't reach out to you over the years?"

"Not very often."

"It must have been hard growing up without your father when he had another son he was quite fond of."

Chase shrugs. "That didn't bother me."

"And you get along with your brother now?"

"Yes. Very well, actually."

Gran takes a sip of tea. "It would be easy to resent him, living the life you could have."

"No, ma'am," Chase starts. "I find resenting anything to be a waste of time. Stressing over what could have been gets you nowhere. What matters to me is what could happen next."

Gran smiles and turns her attention to me. "I like this one, Sierra."

"You won over Gran," I whisper to Chase. "The rest will follow."

The sound of a car engine turns all our attention to the street. A police car pulls in, and I hate the feeling of dread I feel knowing Lisa and Rob are here. She's my best friend, and she's family. I don't want to fight.

I take a drink of tea, knowing I need to put my game face on. It's obvious when Lisa and I aren't getting along, though I do have Chase with me this time to provide a good buffer... expect that he's the cause of the ill feelings.

"You're late," Gran says to Lisa and Rob as they walk up to the porch.

"Blame this one," Rob says, sticking his thumb out at Lisa. "She can't get anywhere on time to save her life."

Lisa rolls her eyes. "I so could."

"Join us," Gran says, much to my chagrin.

Lisa looks at me, then at Chase, pressing her lips together in a tight smile.

"Have y'all met before?" Gran asks, meaning Lisa, Rob, and Chase.

"Yes," Chase answers. "Sierra and I were over at Rob's for a bonfire not that long ago."

"Lovely." Gran settles her gaze on me, giving me a small nod of approval. "I was just telling Sierra what a fine young man she's found. Not to put you on the spot or anything, dear," she tells Chase.

Lisa gives Rob the side-eye, and then shakes her head. Gran hasn't noticed, but Chase does. He's smart enough to not bring it up, at least. Gran asks Chase about his newborn nephews and tells us a story about The Mill House before it was a bar. Lisa avoids eye contact with me the whole time and is on her phone, texting. I'm pretty sure she's messaging Rob because he replies to texts right after she sends. I might not hear their words, but I know they're talking about us.

Tension builds, and the awkwardness starts to hurt.

Dinner isn't much better, but at least my sister likes to dominate the conversation and brag about how well my niece did at her last horse show. The rumors about Chase have circulated through town. I know what everyone is thinking, and are dying to ask. But we Belmonts were raised to have good manners, and asking someone about their shady past over dinner isn't polite.

I'm more of a sit-back-and-listen kind of person at family meals, but make an exception this time whenever there is a lull in the conversation, which doesn't happen often with my family.

"Is Scott coming home for the Fourth of July Fest?" I ask my mom.

"He said he's in the middle of a big project," Mom tells me. "Of course, he won't disclose any details."

Dad looks up from his plate. "You've never been to a Fourth Fest here, have you?"

"No, sir," Chase answers. "This will be my first."

"Why didn't you come to Summer Hill before?" Dad asks.

"I knew I wasn't welcome," Chase answers honestly, surprising Dad. "I'm well aware of the situation my birth caused."

"So why are you here now?"

"Well, I came for my father's funeral," Chase says slowly and I give my dad a what-the-fuck look. "And I stayed because my brother asked me to. We went our whole lives not really knowing each other and thought it was a good time to change that."

"Where were you before you came to our little town?"

"Atlantic City."

"You don't have an accent," Brent, my brother-in-law, says. "I thought everyone on the Jersey Shore had accents."

"I'm not from there," Chase explains. "I was born and raised near Chicago."

"How did you end up in New Jersey?" Dad asks, furthering his interrogation.

"After studying psychology at the University of Chicago," Chase starts, "I decided to throw a dart at a map and go wherever it landed. The world has so much to offer, I didn't want to limit myself to one city. You can learn a lot from people who are different than you."

"It sounds like you've moved around a lot," Mom says, picking up her wine. She looks at my aunt Kelly and widens her eyes. It's a good thing Mom doesn't like to play poker. She's so damn obvious.

"I did," Chase answers. "A year ago today I was in Argentina."

"That lifestyle sounds tiring," Mom quips.

"It's quite the opposite. Waking up not knowing what could happen makes you feel very much alive."

"We must bore you here." Mom smiles as she talks, but the implications of those five little words send a shiver down my spine.

"My tooth!" my niece cries, spitting something into her hand, and then holds up a bloody tooth. "If finally came out!"

I sigh and lean back in my chair, not realizing how tense I was until I relaxed. I've never been more thankful for a kid losing a tooth in my life. The conversation moves to the kids, with my niece unable to stop talking about her tooth and showing us how she can fit things in the new gap in her teeth now.

We have dessert and drinks on the patio near the pool. Chase eyeballs the pool house and nudges me with his elbow. I smile back, feeling blood rush through me at the thought of our first time.

We share a piece of cake, sitting together on the diving board, feet dangling above the pool. Chase makes me laugh so hard I almost fall in the water. He catches me at the last second, arms wrapping around my waist. We steal a kiss, not really caring if anyone sees.

"Sierra?" Lisa calls, standing a few yards back. Her arms are crossed tightly over her chest. "Can I talk to you?"

"Uh, sure."

"Alone?"

"Yeah." I get to my feet and walk up the diving board. It wobbles under my feet and I consider jumping in the pool to avoid this awkward conversation. Lisa turns when I'm a foot behind her and walks to the end of the patio, away from everyone.

"Chase was pretty charming at dinner," she starts.

"I guess so."

She starts down a cobblestone path and sits on the ground, pulling at the grass. "Still, I hope you reconsider."

"Reconsider?" I ask, sitting next to her. "Reconsider what?"

"Being with Chase." She breaks off several pieces of grass and twists them in her fingers. "He has a criminal record, Sierra."

"That doesn't make him a bad person."

Lisa's eyes widen. "Yes, it does. Criminals are bad people.

Chase has a criminal record. I don't see how you can't follow this."

"Because I know Chase."

"Not as well as you think. Why was he arrested? What did he do? And why did the same judge from Indianapolis get all the charges dropped?"

My heart drops. Jax said something about Indianapolis. He came from there...I think. "I don't know."

"You should. If anything, Sierra, just ask him. Maybe there is a good reason—though I sure as shit can't think of one. And don't even get me started on that friend who's staying with him."

"You mean Jax? What about him?"

"Have you seen him?"

"A few times now," I say, working hard to keep the snark out of my voice.

"He looks like a thug."

"Oh my God, Lisa. Listen to yourself! He's a nice guy and is actually a really big nerd. You'd like him if you gave him the time of day before slapping ridiculous labels on him."

"It's not a label. He really is a thug. And Jax isn't his real name."

I throw my hands up. "How in the world do you know that?"

"Rob ran his fingerprints through the system."

I stand up, nostrils flaring. My mouth opens but no sound comes out. There have been few times in my life that have left me speechless, and this is one of them. "I...I can't, Lisa. You don't like me being with Chase. I know that. But I can't —and I won't—deal with you acting like this. It's beyond ridiculous at this point."

Lisa gets to her feet as well, following me when I take a step back.

"His name is Nelson Cole and he's been arrested more times than Chase. And he *has* served jail time."

I blink, slowly shaking my head. I don't know what to say, and I'm battling off throwing up, crying, or screaming.

"I'd go by Jax if my name was Nelson too."

Lisa lets out an exasperated sigh. "Sierra, I don't want to make you mad."

"That's surprising. You're doing an awfully good job at it."

"I have a bad feeling about them."

"Are you sure that's all it is? It's not too *weird* seeing me with Chase?"

"I already told you I was sorry for saying that. And yes, that's what it is. Chase has a shady past, and now this guy shows up out of nowhere with a creepily similar past. It doesn't make sense. You've been through so much, I don't want you to get hurt again."

"Chase isn't the one hurting me. Like you just said, I've been through so much and I'm finally happy again. Chase is everything I could want. He's funny and sensitive and likes to sit in bed with me and read. He's patient and kind and has made sure I'm okay with moving on every step of the way. He understands what I've been through."

"I didn't know that."

"No shit. Instead of talk to me, you go play Scooby Gang and run Jax's fingerprints." I shake my head. "I'm not even going to ask how you got them, but I'm pretty sure stealing his prints like that with no reason is illegal." I put my hands to my head, rubbing my temples. "I have a headache now. I'm going home."

"What's going on?" Chase asks when I come back. "Neither of you looked happy."

"It's nothing. Lisa gets in moods like this from time to time. She'll get over it."

"Can I do anything to help? I know I'm the source of her mood."

"How do you know?"

"I'm pretty good at reading people," he tells me. "It was obvious the moment she got out of the car and saw me."

I push my hair back. "Right. Don't worry about it though. She'll get over it."

"If you say so." Chase doesn't sound convinced. We gather our plates and cups and say goodbye to my family. On the way out to the car, I go over Lisa's words. She is right. Something is off, and all it will take to get to the bottom of it is asking Chase what's going on.

Chase opens the car door for me. All I have to do is ask him. He'll answer with no hesitation. I'm sure of it.

"Fuck," he says under his breath when he sits down. His hand flies to his stomach and his eyes close tight.

"Chase? Are you okay?"

"Yeah," he assures me, straightening up. "Another cramp. I must have eaten something that doesn't agree with me. Good thing we have a mile drive to your place."

I put the back of my hand to his forehead. "You still feel feverish."

"I'm fine."

"We'll see about that when we get to my house." I rest one hand on his thigh and adjust the air with the other. We park in front of my house just moments later, and I take Chase's temperature as soon as we're inside.

"One-oh-one." I show him the thermometer. "Your temp is going up."

Chase sighs and runs his hand over the back of his head. "I'll take more meds and crash. After I fuck you senseless, that is."

I raise an eyebrow. "As much as I want to have sex with

you, I think we should skip tonight. You're sick, babe. You need to rest."

Chase grumbles but doesn't protest, and that's all I need to know he's feeling worse than he's letting on. We change into pajamas and get ready for bed. I bring Chase medicine and a glass of water. He takes it and lies down, falling asleep within minutes.

I'll ask him about his past another time.

~

CHASE WAS STILL in bed when I left for work Monday morning. Tylenol did nothing to bring down his fever, and he was in more pain than he was letting on. Around noon, he texted to say he was going to his place to get new clothes and would come back and be at my house when I got off work. He said he was feeling worn out and wanted to go back to sleep.

I didn't hear from him after that, and the assumption that he was in my bed passed out kept me from worrying. But when I got home around four o'clock and Chase was nowhere to be found, panic set in. I called him three times with no answer. I can't help my mind going to the worst place, and I get a vision of Chase cold, stiff, and dead on the living room floor of his apartment.

"Stop," I say out loud. Most people *don't* die young. I feed the cats, throw a load of laundry into the washer, then get in the car and head to The Mill House. I call Chase again, annoyed that he never set up his voicemail. The phone rings and rings and rings, but he doesn't answer.

There are a few cars in the parking lot, and Cory, the bartender working tonight waves to me as I cut through the bar, taking the faster route to the stairs. The door to the apartment is locked. I knock, anxiety growing by the second.

"Oh, uh, hi," I say when Jax answers the door. He's

wearing a white T-shirt and boxers, and looks like he just woke up. "Is Chase here?"

"Yeah," he starts, and I enter the apartment. Empty beer cans and a spilled bag of chips is on the floor by the couch where Jax has been sleeping. "He's being a pussy and says he's not feeling well."

"Still?"

"I know, right? Go play nurse and make him feel better. I'll put on headphones and try not to listen."

I pull a face but ignore him, striding through the living room to get to Chase. His bedroom door is shut, and I enter without knocking. The blinds are drawn and there's a trashcan next to the bed.

"Chase?"

He mumbles something incoherent in response. I take off my shoes and get in bed, crawling over to him.

"Babe, you okay?" The second I touch him, I can tell he still has a fever. A high fever. "You're burning up!" I exclaim and rip the blankets off him.

Chase starts to sit up but stops, wincing. He looks at me, blinks a few times, and then shakes his head. "Sierra? When did you get here?"

"Just now. You're burning up, Chase. You have a fever."

"Yeah." His eyes flutter and he lies back down.

My chest tightens. Something is wrong. Really wrong.

"I think you should go to the doctor. You're sick."

"I'm tired," he mumbles. "That's all. Lay down with me and I'll feel better."

"No, you need more than a nap. You don't own a thermometer, do you?"

Chase doesn't respond. His eyes are closed and his breathing is slow. I put my hand on his shoulder and give him a shake. He starts to sit up and winces again, hand going to his stomach.

"Fuck," he says hoarsely and reaches for the trashcan. I get it to him just in time for him to throw up. He groans and lays back, hand still on his stomach. "Can you bring me water?"

"Of course, I'll get it now." I take the garbage full of puke out with me, trying hard not to let it gross me out. Chase is really sick right now. He needs me.

I get water after the trash is cleaned out, and hurry back to the bedroom.

"Doesn't sound too good in there," Jax says, raising his eyebrows.

"I thought you were putting on headphones."

"Nah. I'm not going to get laid anytime soon. I need to get my jollies somewhere."

I roll my eyes. "Has he been like this all day?"

"Like what?"

"Kind of out of it."

"Yeah, he has. I thought he was drunk at first. Then I remembered he didn't drink."

I give Jax a dead stare. "And you didn't think anything could be seriously wrong?"

Jax shrugs. "He said he was fine."

I shake my head and go back into the bedroom. Chase is huddled in a ball on the bed, with his hand over the right side of his abdomen. He straightens out when he sees me, not wanting to appear weak or let on that anything is actually wrong.

"Is that where it hurts?" I ask. "The lower right side?"

"Mostly."

"I think you have appendicitis."

"I don't think so." Chase sips the water. I take the glass from him and make him lay down. Gently, I press my fingers into his stomach, on the right side.

"It'll hurt more when I let go," I warn him. "And that means you need to get this thing taken out." I move my hand

and instantly feel bad for him. "You've been feeling sick for over twenty-four hours. We need to go to the hospital. Now," I say through gritted teeth.

Chase doesn't argue, but he doesn't get up either.

"Chase Henson," I say firmly. "Get your ass into the car *right now* or so help me God I will carry you down those stairs and put you in myself."

Chase slowly sits up and nods, looking more and more confused. Certain he's having emergency surgery as soon as we get to Mercy General, I grab a fresh change of clothes for him and rush out the door.

"Dude, you look terrible," Jax says, standing from the couch. His eyes go to me. "Is he okay?"

I shake my head. "I'm pretty sure his appendix is about ready to burst if it hasn't already. I'm taking him to the hospital."

"I'll drive," Jax says. "You should sit with him in the back."

"Good idea."

Jax grabs his pants from the floor and puts them on, then helps Chase down the stairs. We're halfway through the parking lot when Chase throws up again. Jax goes back inside for a water bottle and a trash bag to take with us in the car. I gently wipe his face with a tissue, and Chase looks around like he can't quite figure out what's happening.

That's not a normal symptom of appendicitis. My stomach flip-flops and I grip Chase's hand, practically dragging him to the car. My fingers shake as I pull the seatbelt over him and click it into place.

"Sierra," Chase mumbles. "Where are we going?"

"The hospital. Close your eyes and try to relax."

"Okay." Chase's eyes fall shut and his head tilts to the side. Jax is in the driver's seat seconds later, and I hand him my keys. We speed off, making the hour-long trip in just over forty-five minutes. Chase is admitted right away, and after his blood work comes back, he's whisked away for surgery, leaving me in the ER waiting room with Jax.

"We can go up there." He stands and extends his hand.

"Where?"

"The post-op waiting area."

I take his hand and let him pull me to my feet. His skin is rough and a quick look lets me know he suffered a nasty burn. The thick scar tissue covers the back of his hand.

"You sound like you've done this before."

"I have. And I've been through it with Chase before too. He'll be all right. He's a tough son of a bitch."

I nod and the shock starts to leave me. Everything happened so fast in the ER, and the faces of the doctors and nurses told me everything they didn't say: getting Chase into surgery and removing his ruptured appendix might not be enough.

"Why did Chase have surgery before?" I ask and press a button to get into an elevator.

"Broke his leg flipping over the handlebars of a four-wheeler. He refused to go to the hospital for a week and the small fracture he got in the fall turned into a nasty break. By the time he got seen the bone had to be reset."

"I've seen the scar," I say, recalling the straight surgical line on his thigh. "How long ago was it?"

"Fuck if I remember," Jax says, getting a dirty look from the woman who's in the elevator with us. "Five years ago? Six?"

"You two have been friends for a long time then, right?"

"Feels like a lifetime," Jax jokes.

I nervously pull on my cat necklace, mind whirling. When Chase said he never stayed anywhere long, I assumed he left everything and everyone behind. We get to the surgical floor and the nerves come back tenfold.

I can't lose Chase. I wouldn't survive it. Sitting in the

cold, hospital waiting room, thinking about Chase on the operating table, makes my stomach churn. I close my eyes and get hit with another vision. I'm standing in a graveyard, watching a coffin get lowered into the ground. My heart is inside that coffin, but no one believes me. The dirt falls, burying me deep underground.

I've been through it before.

"Hey," Jax whispers, putting his hand on mine. "It'll be okay."

I open my eyes and realize I'm close to hyperventilating. I blink back tears and nod. Jax pats my hand and leans back in his chair. I wrap my arms around myself and stare up at the TV in the corner of the room.

What feels like hours later, a nurse calls my name. I scramble up and over to her. She gives me a quick rundown —surgery went fine, but the infection was worse than they thought, which was why Chase was so out of it before we came here. He is being moved to the ICU to be treated for sepsis after this. She takes me back to see him, and tears fill my eyes the moment I see him lying in the recovery bed, hooked up to IVs and machines.

His eyes are closed, and he looks peaceful. The nurse warns me he might wake up totally confused and even combative, saying that's pretty normal.

"Chase," I whisper, putting my hand on his, careful to avoid the IV line. I gently stroke his skin, pressing myself close to the bed to stay out of the nurses' way as they check the monitors.

Chase's eyes flutter open and he starts to sit up. "Sierra," he mumbles.

"I'm here. Right here. Don't sit up, Chase. You just had surgery."

His head falls back onto the pillow and a few seconds go by before he opens his eyes again. "Why did I have surgery?"

"Your appendix burst. You're pretty sick, babe. You need to rest." I blink tears back. "But you're gonna be okay."

"Right," he agrees and twists his hand around, interlacing our fingers. "Sierra?"

I lean in, straining to hear what he has to say. "Yes?"

"I think I love you."

I don't try to stop the tears that fall this time. "I think I love you, too."

~

THE LAST TIME I was in the Intensive Care Unit, Jake died. Slight jitters take over when I step through the doors. Everything is the same. The lighting. The smell. Even the nurses.

Jake was at the room at the end of the unit, farthest away from the nurses. It didn't matter by that time. The curtains were drawn around the glass walls. They gave us privacy because that's all we had left.

Chase is in the second room, right across from the nurses' station. The curtains and pulled back, and a nurse is in there now, adjusting tubes and checking on him. He's awake and looks bored. It's easy to convince myself that he's fine and out of the woods. But having an infection turn septic is serious. Very serious.

Chase looks up, smiling when he sees me. I stay to the side, waiting for the nurse to finish, then go in and hug Chase.

"I guess you were right," he says, running his hand through my hair. "I did need to go to the doctor."

"Yeah, no shit," I say back and we laugh. Chase winces slightly. "Are you okay?"

"I'll be fine. Give me a day or two."

I raise an eyebrow. "I think you'll still be here in a day or two."

"We'll see."

"You have a drain in the wound."

"It's turning you on, isn't it?" He wiggles his eyebrows. "Hey baby, want to see my wound drain?"

I laugh and run my fingers through his hair. "Do you know Josh's number?" I ask Chase.

"It's in my phone. You can get it," he replies, then tenses.

"Your phone is at home."

"Good." Chase relaxes, eyes fluttering closed. "Why do you need his number?" he asks a moment later.

"To let him know what's going on."

"No, he just left the hospital with the boys, remember? I don't want to make him worry."

"That's really sweet of you, but he needs to know you won't be at work."

"Fuck. Right. I should call him."

"I'll handle it," I say and continue running my fingers through his hair. Chase closes his eyes again, and within minutes, he's asleep again. I tuck the blanket around him and slip out, filling Jax in on how Chase is doing, and then going into the hospital lobby to make a few phone calls. I get ahold of my mother first and am surprised by her concern. I have to stop her from getting in the car and coming here right away. Instead, I send her on a mission to get Josh's cellphone number, and texts it to me in a matter of minutes.

"Hello?" Josh answers, and I'm so glad he does. I never answer unknown numbers.

"Hey, Josh, it's Sierra."

"Hey. What's going on?"

"I'm at Mercy with Chase. He just has his appendix taken out."

"Shit. Is he okay?"

"He will be. His appendix ruptured and turned septic. He's in the ICU right now."

"I'm on my way."

"No," I say quickly. "He doesn't want you to come. He didn't even want me to call you and make you worry or take time away from the twins. But I knew you needed to know."

"Right. Are you staying there with him? You sure he's okay? People die from sepsis."

"I'm not leaving, and the nurse seemed confident he's going to recover." I sit on the bench right outside the entrance doors. Night has fallen, and the city is far from asleep. "He was really out of it when I got to his house this evening, and his fever was high. The ER doctor told me we got here just in time." Tears fill my eyes and I don't know why I'm telling this all to Josh. "It was scary."

"I'm glad he has you. He's lucky, you know."

"Yeah," I say and sniffle. "I think I am too."

A baby cries in the background. "Call me if anything changes?"

"I will. Bye, Josh."

The crying gets louder, drowning out whatever Josh said. I hang up and call Mrs. Williams, and then call my mom back to make sure she'll feed the cats. Back inside, I tell Jax to go back home, and he takes a taxi so I have my car. Chase is still sleeping, so I sit in a chair next to his bed, resting my head against the wall. Before I know it, I'm asleep too.

24

CHASE

*T*here must be some unwritten rule stating that hospitals have to be cold and uncomfortable. I wake up freezing and I'm the one covered up with a blanket. Sierra is curled up in a chair, goose bumps broken out on her arms. Her head is resting on her shoulder as she sleeps.

Carefully, I sit up and swing my legs over the side of the bed. I'm hooked up to so many damn lines it takes a minute just to stand without pulling something lose. I take the blanket and a few steps to Sierra when someone knocks on the door.

Sierra jerks up, blinking as she looks around the little room, trying to remember what's going on.

"Chase?" she asks. "What are you doing?"

"Good question," the nurse echoes, standing in the doorway.

I give Sierra a smirk and hold up the blanket. "I was going to smother you in your sleep."

She smiles right back. "I thought we already established blankets don't make good murder weapons. I'm actually disappointed. We're in a room full of objects you could use to kill me and you go for the blanket."

"That's my girl." Aware the nurse is staring at us like we're crazy—and probably wondering if she should call security—I go to Sierra. "I thought you were cold."

"I am, but you shouldn't be up, right? It's only been like six hours since your surgery." She turns to the nurse.

"Right. Well, not alone. Getting up and walking is good for you, but with assistance."

I roll my eyes and sit back in bed. I'm still tired, and in more pain than I expected. Sierra leaves to use the bathroom while the nurse assesses me. She brings me pain medicine and two extra blankets. I move over as far as I can in bed, making room for Sierra when she returns.

"I'm not hurting you, am I?" Sierra asks, covering us up. "These beds aren't made for two."

"It feels good having you next to me."

"Good, because I'm going to be here with you for the next few days."

"Go home. You'll be bored sitting here. I'm already bored."

Sierra shakes her head. "I'm not leaving."

"I could be here for a week."

"I'm staying right here for the next twenty-four hours at least." She tips her head my way, and I see tears in her eyes. "I need to make sure you're okay," she whispers. And then it dawns on me just how hard this must have been on her...and how hard it still is. Going to the hospital to see my nephews created too much anxiety, and here I am in the ICU, with IV antibiotics, trying to fight off a serious infection. When I really think about it, it even freaks me out.

"I'm not going anywhere," I promise and take her hand, moving the IV tubing out of the way.

"You better not." She lets her head fall against my shoulder, and I feel a weird sense of peace, despite the discomfort I'm in.

"Sierra?"

"Yeah?"

"When I woke up after surgery...I told you I thought I loved you. That was a lie."

She sits up, eyes widening. "A lie? So you...you don't?"

"No. I don't *think* it. I know it. I do love you."

~

"MORNING," the nurse says, opening the door the moment after she knocks. Sierra opens her eyes, blinking a few times, and sits up. She's not a light sleeper, and it takes her a full minute to wake up. I find it amusing yet adorable. Seeing her get up with ease lets me know she never fell deep asleep last night.

"Morning," I respond.

"How are you feeling today?" she asks and shuts the door behind her. She pulls the curtain around the bed, preparing for a full assessment. I grumble and start to sit up. Sierra gets out of the bed and smoothes the blankets over me. She stretches her arms and rolls her neck. I know she was uncomfortable all night, worrying about squishing me or pulling out the IV. Selfishly, I liked having her next to me all night.

"Good. Can I go home now?"

The nurse laughs. "Not quite. You're going to be here with us for at least another day."

Sierra goes to use the bathroom while the nurse checks me over. I'm in the middle of getting more blood drawn when Sierra comes back.

"Want me to get you anything from the cafeteria? I'm gonna head down for breakfast."

"Sure. Whatever you get is fine. And a black coffee."

The phlebotomist shakes her head. "They probably won't let you have that."

"I won't get the coffee," Sierra says and shifts toward the door. She hesitates, looking back at me, eyes full of unspoken worry.

"I'll still be here when you get back," I assure her, offering a small smile.

"You better be," she replies quietly and walks out the door, not returning for nearly half an hour.

"Sorry," she says as soon as she's back in the room. Empty handed, I might add. "Turns out I'm not allowed to bring food in here and whatever you eat has to be approved by the doctor. You're on a 'special diet,'" she tells me, making quotes with her fingers.

"Are you fucking with me?"

"I don't fuck with food. They had good biscuits and gravy downstairs too."

"I've never liked that. Maybe it's a good thing you didn't bring me any."

Sierra laughs and sits at the foot of my bed. "I ate yours anyway. Do you want me to get the nurse and find out about breakfast for you? Are you hungry?" She gets up and inspects the monitors. "I have no idea what any of this means."

"Neither do I." I sigh. "But I do know I want this shit off so I can go home."

Sierra half smiles, giving me a weird look.

"What?"

"You've never called it home before."

She's right, I haven't. I never intended to, and saying it right then was a slip. But it's true. "It never felt like it before." I take her hand. "I'm realizing I was wrong."

"About what?"

"I was looking for a place to call home, but now I know home is a feeling. When we're together, I am home."

"I love you," she whispers, eyes glossing over.

"I love you, too."

She leans over the bed and kisses me, and I want nothing more than to pull the curtain and fuck her hard. Never mind that my body is weak, I'm fighting off a nasty infection, and I was cut open a few hours ago.

Sierra's phone rings and the Game of Thrones theme song fills the room. She frowns when she picks it up, silencing the call.

"It's Lisa," she explains.

"Are you going to answer?"

"I don't know."

"You should," I encourage. "I know it upsets you to fight with her."

Sierra nods and answers the phone. "Hey," she says and pauses, listening to whatever Lisa has to say. "Yeah, last night. And I think so. I hope so." She pauses again. "It's okay. Well, it's not, but I can't worry about that now." Another pause, this one longer than the others. "Uh, well I don't think they'll let you in the room or anything since you're not family. They're strict in the ICU. I was worried they wouldn't let me in since I'm just his girlfriend. But if you do come up, I could use clothes, my phone charger, and a toothbrush."

Just his girlfriend. I play her words over in my head. She didn't mean it as an insult, no, not at all. So why does it feel like one? I watch Sierra talk on the phone, pushing her messy hair out of her face. She has on the same clothes she did yesterday, barely slept at all, and hasn't once complained.

The words are insulting because she's everything to me, and the stupid label implies a lesser bond. According to the hospital, anyway.

"Lisa is going to come up here," Sierra tells me and sets

her phone on the bedside table. "I think she feels bad for being a dick yesterday. Two days ago? What day is it? I don't even know."

"Lay down next to me," I tell her. "You need to sleep."

"You need to more and I know you're not comfortable with me in bed next to you."

I smile and shake my head. "You're impossible, Sierra Belmont."

25

SIERRA

"Ms. Belmont?"

A hand lands on my shoulder and my name is repeated. I slowly sit up, back aching. I fell asleep sitting in the chair next to the Chase, bent forward with my head and arms resting on the edge of the bed.

After breakfast, Chase got sick from one of his meds. Throwing up caused him pain, so he was given more medicine to combat the nausea along with the pain. He's been passed out for the last few hours.

"Yeah?" I ask, rubbing my eyes. Dried mascara crumbles off my lashes. A shower sounds nice right now.

"There's someone in the waiting room for you," the nurse tells me. My eyes slowly start to focus and I get a flash of the nurse's face. She was the same nurse who put her arm around my shoulder and consoled me after Jake's heart stopped beating. I wonder if she remembers me. It was almost two years ago, and I'm sure she sees a lot of people and a lot of tragedy.

"Thanks," I say and stand. My legs are cramping and my right foot is asleep. I shake feeling back into it and limp my way out to the waiting room. My mom and Lisa are standing there, and Mom throws her arms around me right away.

"Oh, sweetheart," she says, voice heavy with emotion. "Are you all right?"

"I'm tired, but I'm fine. Chase is going to be okay."

She gives me one more squeeze. "I packed your bag. If you need anything else, let me know."

"Thanks, Mom."

"Do you want coffee or anything to eat? I tried calling before we got here but your phone must be dead."

"It is, and coffee would be great. The coffee here isn't that good."

"There's a Starbucks around the corner. I can get you something. Do you still like their caramel frappuccinos?"

"I do."

"I'll go get it. It shouldn't take me long." Mom blinks away her tears and pulls me in for one more hug. "Love you, baby," she whispers and goes, leaving me alone with Lisa.

"How are you holding up?" she asks.

"Okay. I think. Chase was awake this morning and acting normal. It's easy to think he'll be better soon, then I remember they wouldn't have put him in the ICU if it weren't serious. He had a bad reaction to his medication this morning, which was scary. He's sleeping now."

Lisa grinds her jaw and looks at the floor. "I'm so sorry, Sierra. I mean, I still feel like you should be careful, but for right now, I'm sorry. I made Chase out to be the bad guy and didn't think anything like this would happen to him. I know he needs you, and you need him. I won't press the issue anymore."

"Thanks, Lisa." I pull my arms in around myself. "I'm glad you came."

"I would have come with you last night too," she tells me. "If you called."

"I know."

Lisa shuffles her feet and takes a Harry Potter backpack off her shoulder. "Your mom was pretty much horrified to see this was your luggage."

I take the bag and chuckle. "She'd be even more horrified to see my real suitcase."

"It's the Star Wars one, right?"

"Yeah. It's in the creepy basement."

"Right. I didn't think about that. Though I suppose you don't need a full suitcase now."

"Yeah." I unzip the bag and pull out my phone charger. "I'm gonna go charge my phone and let the nurse know I'll be out here. Just in case." Twisting the charger around in my hands, I go back into the ICU. Chase is still sleeping under the watchful eye of the nurses. I plug in my phone, let his nurse know I'm going to be right outside, and go back into the waiting room.

"Are you mad at me?" Lisa asks timidly.

"I'm too exhausted to be mad," I tell her and sit down next to her. "I don't want to fight."

"I don't either. And remember when we were eight and promised we'd never fight over a boy? I guess this is a little different, but it's still a boy causing us to not get along." She loops her arm through mine. "So Chase is doing okay?"

"Yeah. The doctor said if he got here any later it would have been a different story." Tears fill my eyes and all the emotion that's been stirring inside of me bubbles up. Lisa wraps her arms around me. "It's like I'm cursed," I say through my tears. "People I love get hurt. They end up here."

"Shhh," she soothes. "You are not cursed. You are not causing this. Chase is going to be okay. If anything about his track record is true, it's that he's resilient. Nothing seems to stop the guy," she tries to joke.

"It keeps playing out in my mind," I confess. "I've been through it once. I know how it is and I can't keep it away."

"Keep what away?"

"Seeing Chase die. Remembering how it feels to watch the casket get lowered into the ground. Waking up alone and feeling like all the happiness inside of me turned to ash. I don't think I can survive it again. I don't *want* to survive it again."

The depth of my words hits Lisa and a tear rolls down her face. "Don't ever say that, Si. You can survive anything and I won't let you not get through it." She takes my hands. "And Chase is going to be okay. He's a fighter, and he's got you to fight for."

"I hope it's enough."

"Are you kidding me? It's more than enough. You are enough." She lets go of my hands and brushes away her tears. "You said you love him."

"I do." I grab a tissue from the box on the side table and mop up my eyes. "And yes, before you ask, he told me he loves me too."

"I can't deny that it's obvious he cares a lot about you. Maybe he has redeemed himself from his past. The first time you guys ever met, he saved you from that drunk. And the next time, you were the drunk you needed saving from. I'm going to try to be more like you and let his actions speak for themselves."

"You're totally judging him on his past."

"Oh, completely," she says and we both laugh. "But I'm going to try. For you."

"Thanks, Lisa."

With a smile, she nods. "He's going to be okay."

I nod and wipe my eyes again, and then lean back in the chair.

"Do either of you need anything? We packed what I would bring for myself. Except for the sex toys."

I smile and unzip the bag, pulling out face wash and a change of clothes. I go down the hall to change, and Mom is in the waiting room with coffee in hand when I get back. She and Lisa stay a while to keep me company for a while, then offer to get pick up lunch for me while I sit in the room with Chase.

He's getting his blood drawn again, and is sitting up looking much better this time. The color is back in his face, and he's joking around with the guy taking his blood.

"He doesn't believe that I don't like needles," Chase tells me.

I smile. "I don't believe you either."

"There's a difference between getting tattoos and this," Chase continues.

"Yeah, this is over already," the guy says, pulling the needle out of Chase's arm. "That's hours and hours of work, right?"

Chase nods. "That one," he points to a detailed star on the inside of his arm, over the vein the blood was drawn from, "took three hours."

"I couldn't sit still for that long," I say.

"It gets broken up," Chase explains. "The writing on my chest was done over several weeks." I sit on the edge of the bed and kiss Chase once we're alone. "Are your mom and Lisa still here?"

"Yeah. They're going to get lunch and bring something back for me."

"Go with them."

"I don't want to leave you."

"I'm fine, Sierra. I promise. I feel a hell of a lot better now that I'm on a medication that doesn't make me throw up. And if this blood work comes back showing improvement,

273

the nurse told me I'll go to the regular floor. Even I don't think I need to be here," he says, rolling his eyes. "Then I'll be home in a day or two after."

"You sound so sure."

He brings his hand to my face, cupping my cheek. "I am sure. Go get something to eat. It'll be nice to get out of here."

"I'm pretty sure they already left."

"Things between you and Lisa seemed pretty tense last time you saw each other."

"They were."

"How are they now?"

"Better. We had a bit of a heart-to-heart out in the waiting room."

Chase gives me a cheeky grin. "I guess getting sick was good for something, right?"

Feeling like he knows more about the situation than he's letting on, I smile back, not getting into it. "Yeah. I guess it was."

~

"I HAVE GOOD NEWS," the nurse tells us the next day. "I just got orders from the doctor to have you moved to the non-critical floor."

"Don't look too sad to get rid of me," Chase jokes. What a difference a good night's sleep did for him. He's been up and moving around today and looks almost back to normal. He's been removed from all the tubes and wires except for one IV line, which is currently disconnected with the port on his arm covered with gauze.

"This is the one time saying 'I hope I never see you again' is a good thing," the nurse jokes back. "Your blood work is showing great improvement. We'll run some again in the morning and as long as your counts are good, you can go home."

"Thank fucking God," Chase mutters under his breath. Another hour later, and he's moved into his new room. Jax had come for a visit that morning, bringing Chase his phone and wallet. I left for breakfast while he was there, returning not long later to find the men talking in hushed voices. They immediately stopped when I walked into the room.

I can't think about it. I don't want to start suspecting Chase of anything. Not right now. Not ever. Lisa finally agreed to let the issue go. Now's not the time to see merit in her argument.

There's a recliner chair in the new room, and Chase sits in it to watch TV, telling me to lay down in the bed and take a nap. I've never been much of a napper, but I fall asleep almost instantly. I haven't gotten much sleep the last few days, and none of it has been quality sleep.

When I wake up, a little kid is staring at me.

"Hi," she whispers and moves closer. Her hazel eyes are familiar, peering at me through slats in the bedrail.

"Koty," a man says. "Let her sleep."

"She's been sleeping for hours, and I'm bored."

"Leave her alone."

"Daddy, she's awake. Her eyes are open."

I blink, mind slowly waking up, and realize that the little girl is Chase's niece.

"Sierra?" Chase calls softly.

"I'm awake," I say, though I wish I had pretended to be asleep. Now I feel awkward. I do my best to smooth out my hair and say hi to Josh and Dakota. They've been here a while already and are getting ready to go.

"Thanks for looking after my brother," Josh tells me. "I have a feeling he wouldn't have taken himself to the hospital."

"He wouldn't have. How are the twins?"

"Exhausting," he says with a laugh. "But great. They're good sleepers, thankfully."

"That's good to hear. I know Chase wants to go see them again. We'll come by once he's feeling better."

"I am feeling better," Chase says. "I get to leave tomorrow. I'll be back to normal and at work the next day."

Josh just shakes his head and looks at me. "Have fun with him."

"Wish me luck."

Josh laughs. "You'll need it."

~

"You're on strict orders to rest, mister," I tell Chase, pulling down the comforter on my bed. "Starting now."

"You know," he begins and gets into bed, "I'm more likely to listen to you if you're wearing a sexy nurse costume. I'll take you seriously when you're dressed as a healthcare professional."

"Nice try. The doctor said no sex for two weeks."

"Like I'm going to listen to that. And are you going to be able to hold out that long?"

"Yes," I say, trying to hold onto my resolve. It's a losing battle, but for Chase's own good I have to resist. "You don't want to pop a stitch out having sex. Then it'll be even longer. It's almost been a week already, which is kinda crazy to think about. Time went by in a blur." I pull the blankets over his legs and hand him the TV remote. Tinkerbell jumps up on the bed, purring instantly. Even asshole Dolly was happy to see me when Chase and I got home from the hospital minutes ago.

"I'm going to drop off your prescriptions and go grocery shopping. You need to sleep, and when I get back, we can talk about possibly a blow job."

"You can't tease me like that, Sierra."

I lean in, lips brushing against his. "Who says I'm teasing?"

Chase grabs me and gives me a kiss so good I want to say fuck being careful so I can fuck him. I leave before I crumble, shaking myself as I walk out the door. I go to the pharmacy first, which is located downtown on the same street The Book Bag is on. I park in between, planning on going in and saying hi to Mrs. Williams and thanking her a million more times for giving me almost a whole week off so I could be with Chase.

With fewer than three thousand people in Summer Hill, it's expected to run into someone you know no matter where you go.

I smile at Mrs. Matthews, my fifth-grade schoolteacher.

"Oh, Sierra," she starts, looking startled. "Hello, dear. How are you?"

"I'm pretty good," I reply, happy that I can say that now and be totally honest.

"Are you sure?" She looks around then leans in. "Judy's very concerned about you."

Judy? I blink, mind racing as I try to process what the hell Mrs. Matthews is talking about. *Son of a bitch.* Judy Henson is Josh's mother, and she works at the school with Mrs. Matthews.

"Yes, I'm sure. And you can tell Judy she has nothing to worry about. Chase and I are happy together."

"She says he's nothing but trouble. And after what he did to Josh—" Mrs. Matthews cuts off with a huff. Her blonde hair is curled and teased several inches above her head.

"What did he supposedly do to Josh?" I cross my arms, feeling the angry Southern woman in me start to come out.

"He up and left him to work the bar after his twins were born."

I imagine myself stomping my foot and yelling about what a fucking liar Judy is. Instead, I keep my cool, narrowing my eyes every so slightly. "Chase has been in the hospital the last week. He had surgery, and we just got back today. I'm here to drop off prescriptions for him. He actually wants to get back to the bar tomorrow but Josh won't let him." I shake my head, fighting the urge to break things.

"You can't believe everything you read on the internet, and you can't take all gossip as the truth," I say and storm away. I'm never catty, but right now, I'm pissed. I pull Chase's insurance card and prescriptions from my purse and give them to the pharmacist, more thankful than ever for HIPPA. At least she won't get into personal details with anyone else.

Still seething, I head for my car instead of The Book Bag. Mrs. Williams is going into the store just as I cross the street, and she catches my eye and waves. Now I have to go in, and I internally grumble the entire way. As soon as I step foot inside, all my negative emotions melt away. The scent of ink and paper, the familiar rows of books...even the creaking of the floorboards beneath my feet is comforting. I pause in the threshold and inhale, feeling loads better in just seconds.

"Sierra, dear," Mrs. Williams says warmly. "How are you, darling?"

"I'm good," I tell her. "Tired, that's for sure, but glad to be home. How are you? And the store."

"We're both the same: old but still standing."

"I'll be in tomorrow morning."

Mrs. Williams waves her hand in the air. "Take another day. Spend time taking care of that handsome man of yours."

"You know you're probably the only person in the town besides Josh Henson who hasn't told me to stay away from Chase."

"Why would I?"

"You haven't heard the rumors about him?"

"Oh, I have. Let me ask you this: do you feel you should stay away?"

"No," I say with no hesitation. "And if people got to know him, they'd know he's one of the good guys, which are hard to find nowadays, I hear." I sigh. "Chase might be a bit complicated, but he's not dangerous. He loves me. He'd never hurt me."

"There's a thrill to loving a complicated man. Thrill...and danger. And that danger can be just as addictive." Mrs. Williams smiles. "I know because I loved one too. The world has a never-ending supply of opinions and advice on what you should do. Don't listen to them. We're all complicated in the end."

"We are."

"Now, go on and get out of here," she orders, eyes twinkling. "That handsome man is waiting for you."

26

CHASE

*T*he book in Sierra's hand slips from her grasp and onto the bed. Her head is to the side, and her eyes are closed. Careful not to wake her, I move the book aside and pull the blanket up to her shoulder. I've been home from the hospital for two days now and am feeling a whole fucking lot better. Being confined to the house is starting to get to me though, and I'm actually looking forward to going back to work.

Jax filled in for me a few nights since I got sick, enabling Josh to go home after opening, which makes me not feel as shitty. The whole reason I said I'd stay here was to help him run the bar after his twins were born, and literally days after they make their arrival, I'm out of commission. Though I won't be for long since I don't plan on listening to the doctor's recommendations on when to return to normal activity.

Having sex is number one on my list, but so far Sierra has been serious about following the doctor's orders. It won't take long before she caves though. I know she wants it just as much as I do. I was hoping to try to break her walls tonight and have her give me a very thorough checkup, but she fell asleep just minutes of opening her book once we were in bed. She's still catching up on the sleep she lost last week, and she has to work in the morning.

I put an arm around her and kiss the back of her neck. Having laid around doing nothing all day, I'm not tired. It's only ten o'clock, hours before my normal bedtime. I hold onto Sierra a bit longer then sit up, getting a book from the nightstand.

I think back to the day I rolled into Summer Hill for my father's funeral. If someone had told me this is the way things would unfold, I'd laugh right in their face.

In bed by ten, reading to help myself fall asleep. Next to the most beautiful woman in the world.

It's the last thing I thought would happen. And sometimes the least expected things are the most needed.

~

"Babe, your alarm is going off."

"One more minute?" Sierra grumbles.

"You already hit the snooze. Twice." I reach over and get her phone from the nightstand. It's nine o'clock, and Sierra slept for almost twelve hours. I don't know how she's still so tired. Hopefully she's not coming down with something.

With a groan, she gets out of bed and starts getting dressed. She still looks rundown when she comes into the kitchen.

"Thanks," she says, taking the mug of coffee I made her. "What are you gonna do today?" She sips her coffee and starts looking for something for breakfast. I've noticed Sierra tends to follow her habits, and in the morning, she goes straight for yogurt and granola and some sort of fruit. She moves the bananas aside and goes for cookies instead.

"I'm going to my place. Not to work," I add. "But to make sure Jax hasn't burned the place down."

"I thought you weren't supposed to drive yet."

"I'm not, and I won't be. Jax has my car."

"Right. I forgot about that. Can I ask you something?"

"Always."

"How did you and Jax meet?"

"We worked together," I tell her.

"You have a degree in psychology, right?"

I shake my head.

"But you said you went to the University of Chicago."

"I did," I explain. "And I did study psych. But I left before I graduated."

Sierra finishes her cookie and takes another drink of coffee. "Smooth with your wording."

"That's just how I am, baby."

She laughs and takes another drink of coffee. "Why did you leave?"

"It's a long story," I say softly. "And you're already running late."

"I am? Shit. I didn't feed the cats yet."

"I'll get it. I'm slowly trying to win them over anyway."

Sierra chuckles. "I think you already are."

~

"WHOEVER SAID no news is good news is a fucking cunt," Jax huffs, pacing in front of the large window that overlooks the river. "I knew Mason was a useless twat. Fucking unreliable piece of shit."

I sit back, waiting for Jax to end his rant. This is what he does when he's pissed, and it's best to stay out of his way and let the obscenities flow. Though this time, I want to join in with him.

"I said I wanted to stay out of it. Keep my hands clean." Jax balls his fingers into fists. He whips around to face me. "Once you're healed and your guts won't spill out, I say we get out of here and get there first. Beat them at their own game. I can get the paperwork by then too. Show everyone what fucking loser cocksuckers they are."

There was a time in my life, not long ago in fact, that I would have jumped at the chance to right a wrong and to bring not just one, but two, assholes to justice. I jumped because it didn't matter where I landed or if I stuck the landing. I had nothing. No one. I lived my life for me, and it wasn't until I met Sierra that I realized how fucking lonely I was.

"I think I'm done with that shit," I tell him.

Jax falls silent. He blinks, slowly shaking his head. "So you're going to stay here and fucking bartend the rest of your life?"

"Maybe. I don't know, but I'm not leaving Sierra."

"You're in love with her."

"I am," I admit right away.

Jax looks out the window, and I expect him to let out another string of swear words. Instead he smiles. "I never thought I'd see the day when Chase fucking Henson is pussy-whipped this hard."

"It's good pussy."

"Jesus fuck, man. I'm happy for you. She's a good woman."

"She is." I press my hand to my stomach, putting a bit of pressure on the incision site when I sit. If I'd gone to the hospital earlier, the surgery would have been simpler with less healing time. Screw up and learn shit, right? Next time I'm sick, I'll listen to Sierra from the start. "Are you leaving then?"

"Yeah. I'll get ahold of Mason and start the paper trail. I'll be out of here in a few days."

Jax and I have parted ways many times over the years. It was never more than a 'see ya later' because we'd always meet up for another job in a matter of time. This time is different. I'm not going to take another job with him. I'm done with that shit, and while a big part of me is relieved, it's affecting me more than I thought it would knowing we might never see each other again.

"You better invite me to your wedding," Jax heckles as if he can read my fucking mind.

"You'd be the best man."

Jax grins. "That means I can plan a bachelor party in Vegas."

"Definitely."

～

"DON'T FORGET you have a doctor's appointment tomorrow," Sierra tells me that night during dinner. I tried cooking for her for the first time, and things turned out halfway decent. Granted, it's just spaghetti, and the meatballs were frozen and only had to be heated in the oven. But the sauce is home-made. Kind of. I used canned tomatoes instead of fresh because that's all Sierra had.

"I remember, and I don't need to go. I make it one more week and I'm in the clear to do whatever I want again. Besides working out." Sierra gives me a glare. "Fine. I'll go."

"I have the afternoon off so I can go with you."

"You don't have to. It's far and it'll be boring."

Sierra twirls noodles around on her fork. "I'm kind of using it as an excuse to get Panda Express. I've been craving it bad since I had it like daily when you were in the hospital."

"Then I don't feel bad dragging you along."

"I'm going to dream about orange chicken tonight."

"Sounds erotic."

"Oh, it will be. If you hear me moaning in my sleep, I'm dreaming about eating. And speaking of eating, dinner is really good. Is there parsley in the sauce?"

"There might be. I added it by accident and tried to scoop it all out. You can taste it?"

Sierra shakes her head. "I can smell it. It's good though, don't worry."

"I don't even know what parsley smells like. You must have an incredibly good sense of smell."

"I guess so. That's such a lame superpower to have."

"Unless you use it to find dead bodies."

Sierra makes a face, and then considers it. "I bet I'd get my own show on the Discovery Channel."

I laugh. "I bet you would."

We talk the rest of dinner, and she tells me about the new books that came into the shop. My mind keeps going back to Jax and how he's going more or less solo on a job that has a high risk. Am I a shitty friend? Going with him would make me a shitty boyfriend, that's for sure.

Sierra and I clean the kitchen together, then go onto the screened-in porch and relax in the hammock. I've never been in a long-term relationship like this. I never stayed anywhere long enough to even give it a go. Sierra and I joke about being one of those couples that stop having sex, falling into the stereotype of a boring, married couple. Sierra's insists on waiting at least until tomorrow to see what the doctor says, not wanting me to get hurt. But all it takes is one kiss to get her hot and bothered enough to throw caution to the wind.

Still, she won't have sex with me. Instead, she pleasures herself while I watch and then she gives me a blow job. If this is what it takes to get through the next week or so of no sex, I think I'll make it.

~

"OH MY GOD," Sierra sighs. "This is so fucking good."

I shake my head, smiling. "It's all right."

Sierra stabs a piece of orange chicken with her fork and holds it up. "It's better than all right. I could eat this all day, every day."

"Speaking of doing something every day…" I look across the table and wiggle my eyebrows. "The doctor did say he's impressed with how fast I'm healing."

"I have been horny all day," Sierra whispers with a devilish smile. "I might just let you. But you have to lay there and let me do all the work."

"I don't know, Sierra, that sounds pretty terrible."

"I know, right? How will you survive?"

"It's going to be a torturous next week."

"Or two."

We finish our food and hit the road. I offer to drive home since Sierra drove me here, again with the strict following of the doctor's orders, and am surprised when she says yes. She's tired again and dozes off by the time we get back to her place.

"Maybe you should see a doctor," I tell her when we walk into her house. The scent of lemongrass fills the air, welcoming me home.

Because that's exactly what this feels like.

"I'm just tired," she says. "I don't feel sick or anything." The cats come running, rubbing on Sierra's legs. She scoops up Tinkerbell and goes into the kitchen to feed them a can of food. "I know we just ate but I'm already craving more fried rice," she says with a laugh, but the humor dies really fast and she pales.

"What's wrong?" I ask.

"I just realized something. I, uh…" She trails off, eyes going to the floor.

"Sierra?" I reach for her, feeling alarmed by the horror on her face.

"I canceled my OB appointment when you were in the hospital. I haven't had my period in a long time. I've been craving fried rice for days and can't seem to catch up on sleep. I've been having cramps all week and I keep thinking it's going to start, but it hasn't."

Holy.

Fuck.

She looks up, face mirroring the same trepidation that's on mine.

"There's only one way to know for sure. Let's go get a test."

"Yeah. It might be nothing. Just PMS."

"Right. Want to go now?"

"Yeah. I have to pee anyway."

"Good thing the drugstore isn't far."

Sierra nods then quickly shakes her head. "I can't go there! People will see me buying a pregnancy test and you know how this town talks!"

"I'll get it for you."

She cocks an eyebrow. "They'll still know it's for me." She puts her hand to my mouth, eyes wide. "I'll order from Amazon and pay for next-day shipping."

"You can wait a full day without knowing?" I ask. I can't. Not at fucking all.

"You're right. It's killing me now."

"Isn't there a Wal-Mart on the outskirts of town?"

"Yeah, there is."

"They have self-checkout."

Sierra lets out a nervous laugh. "You're a genius. Let's go. But we have to be sneaky with how we grab it. Let me make sure no one I know sees."

"I'll use my ninja skills."

"Right. Just slip it in your pocket or something."

Sierra grabs her purse, fingers trembling. We keep making lame jokes the whole way to the store, trying to deflect the *we're fucked* vibe we're both feeling at the moment. Silence falls over us when we get to the store. Sierra gets a basket and fills it with random things. I go down the aisle with the pregnancy test for her only to come back a second later.

"There are a million different types," I inform her. "What kind do you want?"

She shakes her head. "I have no idea. What's that one in the commercial?"

"I need more to go on than that."

"I...I don't know."

"It's okay. I'll just grab one."

She nods, nervously pulling on her necklace and paces up and down the vitamins on the opposite side of the aisle. I add a pregnancy test to the basket and we make a beeline for the checkout.

And then we run into the last person I want to fucking see: Judy Henson.

27

SIERRA

"Oh, hello, Sierra," Mrs. Henson says, stopping short, holding onto an empty shopping cart. Her eyes linger over Chase, resentment obvious on her face. Then she looks back at me and for a second I think she's going to pretend he's not there. Chase told me she's done that before when he's around. Panic flashes through me and I look down at the basket I have clutched in my sweaty hand. I hid the test under a plaid shirt I grabbed off the clearance rack as we walked by. It's a 3XL, but I doubt she can notice that from where she's standing.

"Funny," she starts, flicking her gaze back to Chase. "You can go shopping but can't work. Convenient too, since my grandbabies were just born."

"A five-minute shopping trip isn't the same as an eight-hour shift," I snap and Chase grabs my wrist, pulling me to him in an attempt to curb my temper. It's not the first time this week I've uncharacteristically snapped at someone. "And it's Chase's friend who's been helping until Chase is better."

Mrs. Henson doesn't know what to say. Her nostrils flare and she narrows her eyes, looking at Chase.

"If only you could see what he's done to you," she harshly whispers. "So many people in this town look up to you, Sierra. You're disappointing all of us."

Chase steps forward. "Get over yourself, Judy. Sierra's more of a role model than you'll ever be. She's smart and kind and knows when to let shit go. Every time you see me, you're reminded that your husband cheated on you. We all fucking get it, but it's time to get over it, leave me alone, and stay the hell away from Sierra." With that, he walks forward, tugging my hand so I follow. Out of the corner of my eye, I see Judy sputtering, and then shaking her head as she pushes her cart forward.

If there weren't a more pressing issue on hand, I would have been upset over Judy's harsh words and the fact that she's going to go run her mouth to everyone about Chase telling her off...and will make it ten times worse. Though right now, all I can think about is whether I'm pregnant or not. And how bad I have to pee.

I read over the instructions as we drive home, though it's not like I need to. You pee on the stick, wait, and read your fate. Nervous, I read every word. Even the words in Spanish. Chase doesn't say anything on the way home and stays quiet when we go into my house and into the bathroom.

"It says to wait three minutes before looking," I tell him. "So I'm going to pee on it then flip it over."

"Okay." Chase lets out a breath and steps outside the bathroom door. "I feel like I should tell you good luck."

"Right? I think I need it." I shut the door and sit on the toilet, thinking about the past week. I chalked the tiredness up to the stress of Chase getting sick. I get cravings every now and then, and it's actually irritated me before when people jump to the 'are you pregnant' question whenever I mention I want a certain food. The moodiness and height-ened sense of smell...yeah, that's out of the norm for me.

I cap the test, flip it over, and put it on the closed toilet lid. I wash my hands and open the door. Chase is already looking at his watch. My fingers tremble and I feel sick.

"It's going to be okay," he tells me. "Whatever it says, we'll get through it."

I nod, trying hard not to let myself get ahead. Being pregnant with Chase's baby is the last thing I thought would happen, but actually isn't the worst. I look at him, admiring his physical beauty. Then it hits me how there's still so much about him I don't know.

"What's wrong?" Chase asks, then quickly shakes his head. "Stupid question. You're anxious, I know." He looks at his watch again. "Two and a half minutes to go."

I cross my arms, consider letting the issue go. But if there's a chance I'm actually pregnant...I look up again. "Why did you steal the boat?"

"What boat?"

"The first night we met, you told me you went to Scotland to steal a boat. Why?"

Chase takes in a deep breath and I'm pretty sure he's going to deflect my question and tell me we can talk about it at another time. We have a situation on hand right now, anyway.

"I was paid to."

"You were paid to steal a boat?"

"Basically. But the boat was already stolen...in a way. I was getting it back."

I sit on the edge of the bathtub. "I don't understand."

"The owner of the boat defaulted on his payments. I was hired by the man who sold it to him to get it back. So I did."

"Is that why you've been arrested before?"

Chase doesn't look surprised that I know. "I didn't get arrested that time." He pauses, waiting to see if I'm going to ask him another question. When I don't, he checks his watch again.

"Lisa told me you came to the bank with a lot of cash. She thought it was weird and had Rob run a background check. She told me that you've been arrested more than once." My spine tingles with anxiety, not just from the unknown results of the pregnancy test, but out of fear this conversation isn't going to go the way I want it to. "I told myself that it didn't matter. I love you. I trust you. The past is in the past." I close my eyes, feeling tears well behind the closed lids. "I've been feeling guilty lately because it does matter, and I do want to know. I don't want to judge you. I don't want what happened before me to influence what we have or what's to come. But there's so much about you I don't know, and no matter how hard I try to tell myself to get over it, I can't, and I'm sorry."

"Don't feel guilty. And yes, I've been arrested more than once." He gives me a half-smile. "I've lost count of how many times, to be honest. I left college because I was presented an opportunity. In college, I was good friends with a guy who had very wealthy parents. They were investors or something…I don't remember the details. They had a huge penthouse in downtown Chicago and a garage full of expensive cars. My friend liked to take them out and pick up women." Chase leans on the doorframe.

"One night he got too drunk and somehow lost the keys to his father's Aston Martin. I was able to track down the car and get it back with no trouble. My friend's father was pretty fucking pleased he didn't have to go through insurance or anything and could keep covering up the fact his son was a dumbass. Word got around and one of his friends contacted me, saying he has something stolen too and needed it back, and would pay me ten percent of the item's worth if I got it back. I recovered twenty-thousand dollars in jewelry, then found out he lost it in a poker game."

"That's why you left college?"

"That was the start. The rich businessmen in Chicago talk at the bars after work, and just a week later, someone contacted me about being an 'independent contractor' for his clients. When expensive items showed up missing, I'd get them back. Most of the time I recovered items that money was owed on. Lots of money."

"So, you repossessed things?"

"Yeah. In a way, but a lot less legal, which is why I've been arrested so many times. It's more like bounty hunting for million-dollar items. And I got paid a percentage of the item's worth. Fifteen percent was my usual rate. And that's how I met Jax. I was hired to recover a yacht and he was hired to recover a helicopter. That was on the yacht."

I blink, taking it all in. Chase isn't a bad person. A knot in my chest loosens, and I feel guilty it was even there in the first place. "Why were the charges dropped?"

"Once we get to the station and both sides of the story are hashed out, things are ruled in my favor. Like the helicopter-yacht guy, once you stop paying for your items, the bank technically owns them. And when people from the bank hire me to go get them, it's clear I'm not stealing for my own personal collection. It takes a while to get to that point though. And a lot of cops seem to enjoy arresting people. Don't tell Rob," he adds with a smile.

"And that's why you moved a lot too, right?"

"It's part of it. I'd go where I was needed and enjoyed seeing the different parts of the world."

People don't take kindly to having items repossessed or foreclosed. That explains the assault charges and makes me realize he's used to a certain level of daily danger. "Do you miss it?"

"No," he answers right away. "I enjoyed the thrill of the hunt, but even when I'd find what I was looking for, it never felt like it. I was onto the next, searching for something I couldn't explain. Something I didn't know I needed until I met you."

My heart skips a beat and more tears well in my eyes.

"It's been three minutes," he says softly.

"You do it."

He steps forward and picks up the test, trying to stay calm. I cover my face with my hands, unable to look. My heart starts racing and I feel sick. Maybe it's morning sickness.

"Just to be sure, one line means it's negative, right?"

"Right." I move my hands and look up. One line. Thank God.

"Then you're pregnant." Chase flips the test over and two dark pink lines stare up at me. I blink and look at the test again. There are two lines. Two obvious lines. We probably didn't need to wait the whole three minutes for those suckers to show up. "Sierra?" Chase asks softly, setting the test down. "You okay?"

"I…I…I don't know. Are you?"

"I'm in the same boat." Chase takes my hand and leads me to the living room. He slowly sits and I go into overdrive making sure he's okay.

"You didn't take your medicine yet tonight." I spring up and go into the kitchen, returning with his pills and a glass of water. "Take it."

"Sierra," Chase says calmly, knowing that I'm desperately looking for a distraction. He takes his pills and then pulls me into his arms. I rest my head on his chest and lay still, listening to his heart beating. "At least we know why you've been so tired."

I sit up so I can look at him, not knowing if I should laugh or cry. It comes out as an awkward mixture of both. "I don't know what to do. I'm not ready to have a baby.

Chase wipes away a tear. "Neither am I. I don't know anything about babies. Or pregnancies." He rests his forehead against mine. "Let's take a day or two and let this sink in before we make a decision, okay?"

"Okay." I exhale and melt into Chase. My mind is running a million miles an hour and I'm working hard to resist getting up and Googling all things pregnancy. I always knew I wanted to get married and have kids. I didn't expect either of that to happen anytime soon...or at all, after Jake died.

I'm still getting used to the fact that I was able to fall in love again.

"Are you tired now?" Chase asks.

"Kind of. Mentally, I'm not, but it's like my body can't keep up."

"You're growing a human. Fuck that's weird to say. Weird, and amazing. You have a little person inside of you." Chase slides his hand down onto my abdomen. "Our person."

"Our baby."

As the words slip from my mouth, everything clicks into place. The timing is all wrong, but is there ever a perfect time for things like this? Won't I always find some reason to prolong starting a family, even after marriage?

I know the truth about Chase's past and am so looking forward to telling Lisa. I'll try not to gloat too much about being right that he's a good person.

"I don't want to tell anyone yet," I say. "Let's just keep it between us for a few days."

"That's fine with me." Chase kisses my neck. "I'm still in shock."

"Me too."

Chase keeps his hand on my belly and lays back. I get hit with another vision, though this time, it's not about death or dying. It's this: Chase and me on the couch, with his hand on my belly. Though in my mind, I'm close to my due date and we're both feeling the baby kick.

"I love you, Sierra," he whispers and I get an over-whelming sense that things are meant to be. That all the heartbreak and tragedy I went through before shaped me into who I am today.

"I love you, too."

~

I LOOK DOWN THE AISLE, shoulders hunching forward as I reach out. Pausing, I listen for any signs of life. The store is empty, and Mrs. Williams is in the back, going over inventory. She never goes over inventory. Most of what's in stock is on the shelves anyway. I take the time alone to grab the book *What to Expect When You're Expecting*. I randomly open it to a page about mucus plugs, read a paragraph and feel entirely unprepared. With a shudder, I put the book away and move on, dusting the shelves.

The cramps continued throughout the night, worsening today. Chase kept me from asking Dr. Google what's wrong, and instead I'm calling the doctor today. I never rescheduled the appointment I missed when Chase was in the hospital. It would have been too late then anyway. I was already pregnant at that point.

I call the doc on my lunch break and am able to get an appointment Monday morning. Since I don't know when I conceived—holy shit that's weird to think about—they can do an ultrasound that day as well. It hasn't been a full twenty-four hours since we found out I was pregnant, but it already seems like so much has changed.

I finish dusting and go back to the register, sitting behind the counter. Chase has been texting me throughout the morning, making sure I'm okay, and vice versa. I can use his recovery as a good excuse to lounge around and do nothing, giving us more time to come to terms with everything. Though I will have to think of something good to say when my family notices I'm not drinking any wine.

Mrs. Williams leaves for the day around eleven, and I'm alone in the store until tonight. Customers trickle in and out, and I entertain myself with texting Chase, mindlessly scrolling through Facebook and Instagram, and reading. Around one, Chase comes in with lunch.

"Orange chicken and fried rice," I say before I even open the bag. "You drove two hours to get me food." My eyes gloss over proving that this obnoxious display of emotions is due to hormones.

"I did," Chase says and kisses me. "I came home and heated it up so it'd be warm. Hopefully it's still good."

I open my to-go container and take a bite. "It's the best."

"Are you crying over Chinese food?"

"Yes! Don't judge me."

Chase laughs and comes around the counter. His hands land on my hips and he gives me another kiss. "Does this make you horny enough to have sex tonight?"

I laugh, shaking my head. "Oh, I want to. Trust me, I do. But it's too soon to risk hurting you."

"What about this?" His arms slip to my back and he kisses me, deep and passionate. My knees weaken and if it weren't for Chase holding me up, I'd be on the floor right now. The bell rings and we break apart.

"Are you fucking kidding me?" Lisa says, making a gagging noise. "I came in to buy porn to read, not see."

"I should charge you extra," I say back with a smile. "And you don't read."

"Not very often." She gives Chase a wave. "I'd ask how you're doing, but I see you're getting along just fine."

He chuckles. "I'm getting there. Sierra's been taking good care of me."

"Ew. You two make me sick."

"Should I be sorry?" I ask, making a face.

Lisa waves her hand in the air. "Nah. I'll just hate you in secret."

I laugh. "How's work?" I ask.

"Meh, the same. Francine came in today." She dramatically rolls her eyes. "Which is why I came in here on my lunch break. I cannot fucking stand her and need to gossip."

Chase takes his arms from around my waist. "I'll leave you two to talk. I'm gonna go see my nephews." He kisses me again.

"You're supposed to go home and rest."

"I'm bored resting. And I feel fine."

"You won't feel fine if you pop a stitch."

"The stitches are halfway dissolved by now."

I shudder. "That's kind of gross to think about."

"Don't think about it," Chase says with a laugh. He kisses me again. "I love you," he says quietly.

"Love you, too."

He leaves and Lisa waits until he's out the door and down the street to talk. "So, you two are acting like a normal couple?"

"We are a normal couple."

She looks away, eating the words she wants to say, then looks back with a smile. "Right."

"I talked to him," I blurt. "I asked him why he has so much money and why he was arrested."

"And?"

"He repossessed items for the super-rich. They paid him cash and he got arrested more than once because he looked guilty until things were explained. And people sometimes got violent with him, hence the assault charges. But everything was dropped once the dust settled and it was clear what he was doing. He said he worked a lot for banks."

"And you believe him?"

"I do." Not believing him isn't an option. Chase wouldn't lie. The first night we met, he talked about taking that boat. Why would he lie then when we had nothing between us? "It makes sense, Lisa. That's how he met Jax too, and why his record is similar to Chase's. They're basically bounty hunters, which is actually really hot to say out loud."

"It's not like he's saving the world or anything," Lisa quips.

My brow furrows. "I know. And he's done with all that. He's happy here, with me." *With us.*

"Assuming it's all true, then I'm sorry. He's not a bad guy."

"He's not. And he's going to be around for, well, forever. So please go back to liking him."

"Fine. So you wanna hear the latest Francine drama?"

"Always."

28

CHASE

I gently cradle my nephew to my chest, looking down at his tiny little face. He blinks up at me, opening his mouth as he lets out a soft coo. He yawns and his eyelids get heavy. I rock him back and forth, and he falls asleep.

"I don't know what you're talking about," I tell my brother. "This baby thing is easy."

Josh gives me a dead stare. "He was exhausted from crying nonstop before you got here."

Amusement plays on my face and I sit on the couch, moving as slow as possible to not wake the baby. I'm holding Noah, who's the bigger of the babies. Josh has Aaron and is trying to get him to take a bottle. I lean back, letting Noah rest against me. My mind is on Sierra and the little life inside of her.

We sure as shit didn't mean for it to happen. We were careless, getting caught up in the moment pretty much every time we fucked, and now we're paying the price. Though right now, I don't feel as panicked as I did before. Sierra will be a good mom, hands down. And me...I at least know what *not* to do thanks to my own dad.

"This is kinda nice," I admit, looking down at the sleeping baby.

"Is it making you want one?" Josh jokes.

"Someday," I answer, feeling the urge to blurt out that Sierra is pregnant.

"Wait until they wake up. You'll think twice."

"I will admit I want one at a time, though."

"Going from one to three is quite the adjustment. When Dakota was a newborn, we were able to take turns. You're still tired as fuck, but it's one-on-one. Having two...it's hard. But worth it. So fucking worth it."

Josh pulls the bottle from Aaron's mouth and sets it on the couch next to him. He turns on the TV, volume so low you can hardly hear it.

"How are you?" he asks. "You look a lot better."

"I feel better. I'm sore," I admit. "And kinda rundown. But I'm alive. Thanks to Sierra."

"She seemed pretty upset when she called to tell me you were sick."

I nod. "I guess things looked bad for a while. It's weird having someone care like that."

"So I take it you're staying in Summer Hill?"

"I am," I say casually. I'm never fucking leaving this place unless Sierra and our child come with me. Wherever she is—wherever *they* are—is where I'm meant to be. It's home. "I never thought I'd end up here."

"I'm glad you did."

"You and Sierra are the only ones who think that."

Josh raises an eyebrow. "Her family likes you though, right?"

"Hah," I say with a snort of laughter, causing Noah to stir. I shush him back to sleep. "I'll just say they're not my biggest fans. I have no trust fund or background in farming. I'm their last pick for Sierra."

Josh shakes his head. "I don't get people like that. You two are happy together, right? Isn't that enough?"

"You'd think so."

~

"TAKE CARE OF YOURSELF, MAN," I say to Jax and hand him his bag. Heat from the sun melts down on us, and mosquitos swarm around my face. I swat them away, squinting in the bright light. "Don't get killed."

"Rule number one," Jax says with a toothy grin. "Same goes for you. It seems pretty dangerous here." He raises his eyebrows and looks out at the water. "There aren't crocodiles in there, are there?"

"Alligators," I correct. "You're going to fucking Florida. You should know that shit. And no. Sierra said it's too cold for them up here, thankfully. Those fuckers freak me out."

"You and me both."

The taxi bumps along the country road, pulling into The Mill House parking lot. Jax claps me on the back, giving a curt nod before getting into the cab. His plan is to go visit his mistress in Miami for a few days before heading up north again. Mason, another bounty hunter, has been keeping an eye out for the Haynes brothers, who are after Jax's head. He hasn't seen them lately, making Jax think they gave up and moved on to something else, but I think they're pissed enough to not let this go anytime soon.

A few months ago, the bank repossessed their matching pair of foreign sports cars and Jax tracked them down to collect on the cash. Since there were two cars, I drove one while he drove the other, taking them back to the dealership. The brothers, who owned a nightclub, weren't happy. The matching cars, however douchy, were their pride and joy, and made them look legit when they pulled up to their club.

Having their cars taken back by the bank was an ego blow, plus proved that their club wasn't doing as well as they claimed. Too stupid to understand that by not paying, they lost their cars, they blamed Jax, and think he still has the cars just sitting in a garage somewhere.

Once Jefferson gets back from Europe, he'll get the proper paperwork along with a restraining order against the brothers. It's the simplest way to get assholes off our case. Matt Jefferson is a lawyer turned state judge who resides in Indianapolis. Jax and I helped him out when his teenage daughter decided to have a party on their family boat, resulting in her twenty-three-year-old boyfriend 'borrowing' the boat, two jet skis, and a brand new Chevy Silverado to pull it with. He doesn't understand what we do but appreciates it. The law can only go so far, and I wish we had more politicians like him...or maybe not.

Once Jax is gone, I go into the apartment and grumble at the mess. Even when we were working the same jobs, I could never live with Jax. He's too much of a fucking pig. Not long into cleaning, I start to feel shitty. The skin around my incision is tight and itchy, and I'm overall tired. I lay down in my bed, and with the river in the background, I pass out, not waking again until Sierra calls me on her way home from work.

"Lisa wants to get drinks tonight," she says, panic-stricken. "I can't drink or sit in a smoky bar."

"Tell her to come here," I suggest. "Sit in the restaurant side where there's no smoking. I'll make you something with no alcohol and she'll never know."

"That's a good idea. But you can't work yet."

"I can help out for a bit while you two are here at least."

"You sound like you just woke up," she says, and I hear her

start her car. "Are you feeling okay? The doctor said to be on the lookout for signs of the infection coming back."

"I was asleep. Jax left and I had to clean up his fucking mess. I laid down and fell asleep."

"Oh, sorry. I didn't mean to wake you."

"Nah, it's fine. When are you going out?"

"Seven. We'll go to The Mill House. Stay there and get some sleep. I'll bring you dinner at six. And Chase?"

"Yeah?"

"That picture you sent me of you holding baby Noah…I know we said we'd take a few days to really talk about it but I already know. I knew as soon as I saw that second pink line, actually."

"What do you know?" I ask, needing to hear her say it out loud.

"That I, without a doubt, want to keep this baby."

I'm grinning ear to fucking ear. "Me too."

～

"These would normally be served in a copper mug," I tell Sierra and Lisa. "This bar is not equipped for hipster drinks, apparently."

Sierra laughs. "I'm not surprised."

"It's strong, you'll probably only want one," I say, making sure Lisa hears. The less Sierra drinks, the better. It'll lessen the chance of her getting caught sans alcohol. "I'll come back and see if you need a refill though."

"I like that you're fucking the bartender." Lisa takes a big drink. "We get to drink for free."

Sierra shakes her head. "Don't work too long. I mean it. You're supposed to take two to three weeks off."

It's Friday night, and we're busy. "I'll stay behind the bar. I won't move around too much then."

Sierra stares at me flatly. "I've seen the bar. And you behind it. You're on your feet the whole time." She takes another drink then makes a face, hand going to her stomach.

"Are you okay?"

"Yeah. I have cramps again."

"I hate that," Lisa groans. "You're so lucky you have a penis," she tells me.

I nod, hiding the concern on my face. Sierra's been having cramps on and off for a week now. She thought it was her oncoming period before, but now that we know she's pregnant, it's freaking me out. Cramps can't be a good thing. I tried to keep her from Googling her symptoms because nothing good comes from that, though according to the internet, slight cramps like she's been feeling aren't anything to worry about.

Sierra's friends Katie and Bella come to The Mill House not long after, and are trying to get Sierra and Lisa to sit at the bar and then dance. Not consuming alcohol is easy enough, but avoiding the smokers at the bar isn't possible. Sierra meets my eye across the room, smiling and putting her hand over her stomach. I smile back as I bring drinks to another group of young women.

Cory is getting a better handle on running solo but is still struggling. I'm glad Jax was able to come down here this past week and lend a hand. I take a tray of drinks to Sierra's table, hoping I can keep her friends happy with being away from the main part of the bar for a while longer.

Katie and Bella are drunk already, and *ohh* and *ahh* when I give Sierra a kiss. I slide into the booth next to Sierra for a minute, wanting to get my fix of her and needing to get off my feet for a minute.

"You still should go lay down," Sierra tells me, resting her hand on my thigh. "Before you overdo it."

"I'm fine," I assure her. "I need to get back to my routine

in order to feel better."

"I'm not going to get you to listen, am I?"

"Nope."

She rolls her eyes and squeezes my thigh.

"You guys are like the cutest couple ever," Katie slurs. She drunkenly points at Sierra. "You're like the prettiest, and he's seriously hot. Physically, you look good together. And mentally, you look happy."

"That doesn't make sense," Bella giggles. "You can't see someone's mental...mentalness."

"But she looks happy."

Bella considers her words. "Yeah. She does. You do look happy, Sierra."

Her friends start to gush again, and I almost don't hear what's going on behind us. Almost.

"Where's the big guy?" someone demands.

"I...I don't know," Cory stammers. I turn, not in the mood for a fucking bar fight. But what I see isn't some drunk getting agitated. It's the Haynes brothers. Both of them, surrounding Corey, fists clenched, looking pissed off as fuck.

"Shit," I mutter and get up.

"He was here yesterday," one of the brothers says. They're not twins, but they're both big, ugly brutes. "We saw him."

"He...he left. I don't know where he went." Corey's eyes dart to me. Fuck.

The bigger of the two whips around. I only saw them once before this, but I never forget a face. Beady blue eyes, spiked blonde hair, too-tight polo shirt with the collar up, and enough cologne to choke a horse...classic asshole apparel.

"I know you," he says, narrowing his eyes. "You fucking stole my car!"

I roll my eyes. "I didn't steal your car. I wouldn't want it anyway. I'm a Ford guy."

"Jay!" Big Haynes calls to his brother. "Look who I fucking found."

Jay's there in seconds, glowering at me. "Where are the fucking cars?"

I shrug. "Probably in the garage of someone who could actually afford them."

At that, Big Haynes takes a swing. I catch his fist and twist his arm behind his back. Country music blares from the speakers above us, but a hush falls over those around me. They step back, anticipating a fight.

"Easy now." I twist his arm hard, knowing it hurts. "You're not starting shit in my bar," I hiss. "Get your brother and get the fuck out before I kick both your asses and take whatever piece of shit you drove here."

"Give us the fucking cars."

"I don't have them," I say through gritted teeth and shove him into the bar top. "You lost them when you stopped making payments. The dealership took them back, dumbass. If you want the legalities of it, take it up with the judge who signed off on it. Now get the fuck out of here."

"Fine," Big Haynes grunts. I let go of his arm and step back, ready for him to come at me again. He gives his brother a look, and he nods. They storm out of the bar, tension hanging in the air.

Corey looks at me, unblinking. "You're kind of my hero," he half jokes. "Those guys were looking for Jax...who are they?"

"No one. Just two assholes looking for a fight."

"It seemed like you knew them."

"We crossed paths once."

"And you stole his car?" Corey's voice gets high-pitched with nerves, and I have a good guess what he's thinking. If I'm the kind of person who steals from those assholes, there's nothing that I won't do.

"No. He stopped making payments on it but refused to give it back to the dealership. I was the one who went and retrieved it."

"Wow," Corey says, taken aback. "No wonder they're pissed."

"Yeah. Just pissed at the wrong person."

"Are they gone?"

I glance at the door, knowing they didn't come all this way just to let it go after a stern talking to. They're going to be even more pissed to know they're one step behind. By now, Jax is already in Florida fucking his cougar. "For now. I'll handle it. Get back to work. If everyone here sees you looking rattled, they'll leave. Give one free round to that group over there. Make them look back and think this was an exciting night."

Sierra rushes over, pushing through the small crowd around the bar. "Are you okay?" she asks, eyebrows pinched together. Her hands fly to my waist and she starts to lift up my shirt.

"Now you want to fuck me? Right here with everyone watching?"

She purses her lips, trying not to laugh. "Good news. You're not bleeding and your organs haven't popped out of your cut."

"It's healing, remember? I'm fine."

Sierra moves in closer and my arms go around her slender body. "I know. I just...nothing can happen to you, okay?"

"It won't. I promise."

"You don't know that." She takes in a shaky breath. "Promise me only one thing."

"What?"

"Promise you won't make promises."

"I can't do that," I tell her and run a hand through her

hair. "Because I promise you that I'm going to love you—and our baby—forever."

"I can live with that one." She inches closer, hooking her fingers through my belt loops. "Who were those guys? I've never seen them before."

"They're not from around here. Remember when I said people more times than not weren't happy to see us? Those are some of the unhappy ones."

"How did they find you?"

"They're looking for Jax. He isn't the best at covering his tracks."

"Are they coming back?"

"Probably," I say and Sierra's face pales. "So I think you should go upstairs and lay down."

"You mean you want me out of the way."

"Yeah," I admit. "I don't want you to get caught up in the collateral damage." I move my hand to her stomach. "Either of you."

"What are you going to do?"

"I'll start with calling Jax. He started this mess. Usually when this happens, we're able to get a restraining order issued and as soon as it gets violated, the unhappy parties get arrested."

"Doesn't that make them even more mad?"

"Oh, for sure. But most of the time that anger is redirected at the person or company who reclaimed ownership of their stuff."

"So 'don't shoot the messenger' isn't foolproof?"

I laugh. "Not at all."

"Sounds dangerous."

"It is. That's part of why I liked it. I need to make one more promise. I promise that I like this more than the danger."

Sierra smiles and flattens her hands against my chest. "I'm glad you're okay."

"It takes more than a couple of assholes like that to hurt me. Are you tired?"

"I am," she says with a laugh. "I know I'm getting old here, but it's barely eight o'clock and I'm ready for bed."

"That's all the more reason to go upstairs. Watch TV and rest. I'll come up in a bit and check on you. Are you hungry?"

"Not really, but fries with cheese dip sounds good." Sierra smiles, shaking her head at herself. "I'm going to gain a hundred pounds before this kid is born."

"You'll still be hot." I kiss her neck. "I'll get the key. Lie down and wait for me. If you're still up, I'll rub your back."

"You're too good to me, Chase."

I shake my head. "I can never be good enough." I go behind the bar to get the key to the apartment for Sierra. I get into the break room, grab them, and pick up my phone to text Jax and tell him about the shit storm he started. Then a scream comes from the bar. I drop my keys and the phone and sprint to the bar.

The Haynes brothers are back, blue eyes full or rage. Big Haynes is holding a gas can and a lighter, and Jay grabs Sierra by the arm, jerking her forward. My entire body seizes up. Nothing bad can happen to Sierra. Nothing. She is my everything. Sierra tries to pull away but Jay holds her tighter.

"Your bar for our cars," Big Haynes growls. "And I need something new to ride tonight." He gives a sideways glance at Sierra, then flicks the lighter and shakes the gas can. The world is spinning and all I can think about is how bad I'm going to hurt them both. The entire bar is watching, and I see two of the locals weaving their way through the frozen crowd. The people in this town might not like me, but they love this bar.

"Touch her and die," I say, through gritted teeth. Sierra's

eyes meet mine, and I've never felt so helpless in my life. Sierra looks at a beer bottle on the table next to her, then back at me. Unspoken words pass between us, and I give her the smallest nod.

Big Haynes is a foot from me. I bring my fist back and hit him hard in the face right as Sierra grabs the beer bottle and hits Jay with it. The bottle doesn't break, but hits him hard in the mouth, clicking against his teeth and causing his lip to bleed. It's all that's needed to make him lose his grip on Sierra. She jumps back, and Lisa grabs her arms, bringing her behind a table.

I hit Big Haynes again in the side of the head. My knuckles collide hard with his temple, knocking him out. He stumbles back, lighter falling from his grasp and clattering to the ground. Two of the locals who have been here drinking since we opened hours ago, take him by the arms and drag him outside.

Jay growls and kicks the table Sierra and Lisa are behind, shoving it into them. Lisa loses her balance and falls into Sierra, who stumbles back and trips over a chair. They both land hard on the ground. I don't think. I just act. Consumed by rage, I grab a bottle of whiskey and bring it down over Jay's head. The glass breaks, and blood streams from his skull. He wobbles but comes at me again, throwing punches. The smell of alcohol permeates the air. I turn away to check on Sierra. Lisa helps her to her feet, pulling her away from the fight.

In that half-second my head is turned, Jay hits me in the face. My vision blurs for a beat, and the pain adds to my anger. I charge forward at Jay, punching him in square in the nose. I feel his nose break along with hearing the sickening crack, but I don't stop. I hit him again. And again. Until he drops to the ground.

"Chase!" Sierra calls. I kick Jay hard in the dick and turn, rushing to her side.

"Are you okay? Did he hurt you? I'm going to fucking kill him."

"I'm scared," she says and grabs my arms. "But I'm fine."

I run my hands over her, needing to make sure. Behind me, Jay stirs, slowly coming to his feet. Lisa grabs the first thing she can get her hands on, and swings a dirty broom at Jay. "Move again and this handle is going up your ass," she sneers. "No one hurts my cousin."

Jay slumps back to the ground. No one says a word, and if it weren't for that damn music, you could hear a pin drop. Sierra is safe in my arms, but rage still sears through me. I'm so fucking pissed.

I'm pissed at myself for not taking Sierra behind the bar with me to get the keys.

I'm pissed at Jax for creating a trail leading to Summer Hill.

And I'm pissed at these assholes.

"Are you okay?" Sierra asks softly, hands wrapping around my arms. "You just had surgery."

"I'm fine. I'm more concerned with you. You fell. Isn't that bad for the...the you know what?"

"On my ass. I'm okay. *We're* okay." Sierra closes her eyes and rests her head on my chest. She lets out a shaky breath then looks up and out at the bar. Everyone is still frozen, staring at Jay on the floor. Everything happened so fast, and if I would have been one minute faster, Sierra wouldn't have gotten involved like that. She'd be upstairs, safe and sound.

"You should go up," I tell her. "Get away from the smoke."

She nods but doesn't step away. "The cops are on their way. Lisa called when that guy grabbed my arm."

"Good. That was quick thinking." I pull Sierra to me, never wanting to let her go.

The cops show up minutes later, and with the entire bar

as witnesses, the Haynes brothers are arrested right away.

Wanting to get out of the smoke, Sierra goes upstairs while I give a statement, explaining everything I know about those cocksuckers. The bar is slowly going back to normal, with people talking and laughing again.

I help Corey clean up the mess made from the fight, and get things back in order again. He's frazzled, having never been involved like that in a fight before. Hearing the threat of someone burning down the bar sent him over the edge.

Lisa, Katie, and Bella are sitting at the table in the back. Katie is so drunk there's a slim chance she'll remember any of this.

"You guys okay?" I ask.

Bella's eyes widen. "That was insane. But yeah, we're fine. Sierra's okay, right? She said she was going upstairs."

"Yeah. Just shook up. Nice work with the broom," I tell Lisa.

"Thanks. I realize it's not the most lethal weapon, but it was the first thing I could get my hands on."

"I think you're wrong there. That thing has swept up the unimaginable. All it takes is one sweep across face and you're infected with God knows what and it's only a matter of time before you turn into a zombie."

"So that's how the apocalypse starts," Lisa jokes. She's looking at her phone, feverishly texting someone. Then her screen goes black. "Mother fucker," she swears. "You don't happen to have a charger, do you?"

"Not for that type of phone."

"Dammit. Rob is freaking out right now and I need to tell him to chill the fuck out."

"You can use my phone," I offer.

"Thanks. He's going to keep freaking out until I call. He's at the station tonight and not being out here is killing him. He's not convinced we're okay yet."

Wanting to get upstairs to Sierra, I pull my phone from my pocket and unlock the screen. "It's quieter in the back," I say and hand the phone to her.

Lisa takes the phone and disappears behind the bar. I mop up a spilled drink and take an order for a burger and fries to the kitchen. The bar-goers have settled back into their usual routine of drinking, talking too loud, and dancing along with the music. I fill another drink order and clear one more table before Lisa comes back out, holding my phone out like it's the missing piece of incriminating evidence in a murder trial.

"I opened the phone app to dial Rob's number," she starts, "and it went right to your voicemail. You must have been on that page last time you shut off your phone."

My blood runs cold, and each heartbeat echoes loudly in my ears. Fuck. No. It was the last screen I had open. Knowing Sierra and I are going to have a child together in the coming months, I knew I needed to delete all the messages. Pretend it never happened and move on.

But I didn't because I looked up from the bar and saw Sierra walking through. And with my mind on Sierra, it didn't even occur to me that the voicemails would be the first thing anyone sees when they use the phone.

"I saw all the messages."

The messages. No. Fuck. Fuck, fuck, *Fuck.*

"I was going to make fun of you for being lame and keeping all of Sierra's messages. Then I realized some are from over a year ago. What the fuck? I mean, how is that possible?"

I inhale, and in that moment, everything changes. I don't want to lie my way out of this. I don't want to build the foundation of my family on a lie.

My.

Family.

My stomach twists and I feel like I'm going to puke. What

the fuck have I done? I look at Lisa, her face full of accusation. I need to come clean and get it out in the open. Sierra and I are having a baby after all. I need to tell her everything.

"When my niece broke my phone, Josh felt bad and got me a temporary one in its place in its place. He went to that secondhand electronic store in town. When I got it, I realized that the memory wasn't properly cleared out. Out of curiosity, I listened to the first message before I deleted them all."

Lisa's mouth opens. She keeps her eyes on me and shakes her head. "Wait...what?"

"That phone...it belonged to Jake. The messages from Sierra are for him."

Things start to click into place for Lisa. "I knew she called and left messages after he passed. We all tried to get her to stop and it took months. You said you listened to the first one before you deleted them. But they're still here."

"I know."

"So you listened to them?" she asks.

"Some of them."

"Does Sierra know?"

"No."

"You have to tell her."

"I will," I say. "I want to. Hell, I've wanted to. I didn't know it was her when I heard the first few. They were so...so tragically beautiful I kept listening. I hadn't even met her yet when I heard the first one."

"Then you did meet her and still listened to the messages she left for her dead boyfriend."

Fuck. When she says it out loud, it sounds awful. I cringe. "Yes."

Lisa rubs her temple. "This is all kinds of fucked up. And Sierra has no idea at all?"

"No."

"You need to tell her. Or I will."

29

SIERRA

"*L*et me look at it one more time," I tell Chase and turn on the flashlight on my phone. We just got out of the shower, and I'm not convinced he is 'fine' like he says he is. I make him lay down on his bed so I can inspect the incision site.

"See? Told you it's fine. I didn't split my skin open."

"You're lucky."

"Yeah," he agrees. "I probably am." He pulls the blankets down and waits for me to get in bed next to him, spooning his body around mine. He's been quiet since he came up from the bar, which was why I thought he might be hurt and didn't want to tell me. He said he felt bad for what happened, was pissed at Jax for not being more careful, and was worried I was hurt, if not physically, then mentally. That asshole did grab me, after all. I was really shaken up. Seeing them go after Chase and make threats against me was upsetting. And scary. Very scary. The moment he grabbed my arm and yanked me forward, terror filled me. Yet I knew Chase was there to protect me.

It wouldn't be the first time he saved me.

"I love you, Sierra," he whispers, nuzzling his lips into my neck. My heavy eyelids close, and I'm asleep in minutes.

At three in the morning, I get up needing to pee. "I thought this only happened when you have a big belly," I grumble and slowly get out of bed. The cramps are back and the moment I get up, I know something is wrong. "Chase," I say sharply. "Chase!"

"What's wrong?" he asks, shooting up from a dead sleep and reaches for my spot in the bed. "Sierra?

I move my hand down between my legs and feel wetness. I've never in my life wished to have peed my pants before, but right now, I do. Though I know what it is, and my full bladder reminds me that I haven't yet gone.

"I'm bleeding," I say, voice a hollow whisper.

"Where?" Chase asks before he gets it. "Fuck. No." He's out of bed, turning on the light, and in front of me in just seconds. I hold out my hand, fresh blood on my fingers. The sight of the shiny crimson on my fingertips makes me dizzy. I wobble on my feet and if it weren't for Chase, I'd pass out onto the floor.

"We need to go to the hospital," Chase says. I nod but don't move. He helps me to the bed and goes to his dresser, pulling out a pair of clean pajama pants. He leads me into the bathroom and brings me a towel. I pee, clean myself up, and get redressed.

If I hadn't taken that test a few days ago, I would have thought this was my period. I would have been relieved, although embarrassed, to wake up in a puddle of blood in Chase's bed. Though if I didn't know I was pregnant, I might have gone out drinking with Lisa tonight and not be in Chase's bed right now at all.

Chase helps me into the car and fiddles with the radio on the long drive to the hospital. My cramps intensify, and I hope the folded-up washcloth is enough. I didn't bring any pads or tampons to Chase's, and he, of course, doesn't have any.

Chase takes one hand off the wheel and grips my thigh. "It'll be okay. Whatever happens, it'll be okay," he says, echoing the same words he said when we were waiting for the test.

"Yeah." I close my eyes and look at Chase. "It will."

~

"LET'S GO HOME," Chase says softly, standing and coming over to the hospital bed. After an hour in the ER, we were told there was nothing that could be done. I had an early miscarriage. The doctor was surprised I even had symptoms and said many women who lose a pregnancy this early don't even realize it, thinking they just had a late period. Medically, I'm perfectly healthy. The doctor even said we could 'start trying again next cycle' if we wanted to.

Falling didn't make me lose the baby. I didn't fall hard enough to hurt myself, and this early in pregnancy, there's nothing yet to come detached, like there is with a baby further along. Still, Chase was overcome with guilt and needed to be assured again and again by the nurse that me tripping over a chair and landing on my butt wasn't the reason for this.

I take Chase's hand and get up, not talking as we go back to his car. He opens the door for me and gets in the driver's seat with a sigh. I look down, arms wrapped tightly around myself.

"Sierra," he says gently and takes my hand. "I love you. I want to make sure you know. No matter what, I love you and always will."

Tears fill my eyes. "I love you, too." I squeeze his hand and pull my seatbelt on. My head is spinning. I'm tired, which always makes me emotional. And I'm not sure how to feel right now. I'd only known I was pregnant for a few days. We didn't try for a baby. We didn't want this to happen. Having a baby right now would have fucked up our lives in more ways than we could think. Chase and I haven't been together that long, and there's a lot to be worked out before having a child together. *Not* having a baby should be a good thing. We can consider it again when the time is right. Years from now. After a wedding or once we move in together.

But I'm sad.

Really, really fucking sad.

I wish I hadn't taken that stupid test.

I stare out the window the whole way back to Chase's house.

"Are you okay?" he asks when we park.

"I think so. Are you?"

"No," he answers, and it jars me. "I know the timing was all wrong, but I was starting to become okay with it. I'm sad. More than I thought I'd be."

"Me too," I say. And then I start crying. Chase helps me out of the car and wraps his arms around me, holding me as I sob. We're in the parking lot of The Mill House, and the rushing water from the river echoes through the silent early morning.

"I love you," he whispers. "I always will."

"I love you too," I say back between sobs. "I'm sorry I lost...I lost..." My words dissolve into tears.

"I never once thought it was your fault," he goes on. "You heard the doctor. Sometimes it just happens and there's no real reason. Don't be sorry."

I inhale sharply. "I don't understand why this keeps happening. Lisa said I'm not cursed but I think I really am."

"Curses aren't real," he soothes. "You're not cursed."

"It feels that way."

"It might now, but it won't forever," he whispers and cups my face with his hands. He brushes away my tears and kisses me. "Let's go to your house. It's been a long fucking night." We go around back and I sit on the rock overlooking the river while Chase gets his stuff from inside. I don't say a word on the short drive to my house. The sun is up and I pull all the shades once we get inside.

"We need to talk about it." Chase opens the fridge and pulls out a bottle of wine. "Maybe not now, but tomorrow."

"Yeah. I know."

He sets two glasses on the table and fills them. I pick mine up and take a gulp.

"You know what's weird?" I start and take another drink. "If I didn't take that test, we wouldn't be sad. If I would have waited another few days to see if my period started, I would think this was all it was."

Chase nods. "Yeah. That's true."

"I wish I hadn't taken it. Because I did think about us together with a baby. I felt something for whatever I thought was growing inside of me." I bring the glass to my lips and drain it. I set it down on the table and exhale, waiting for the alcohol to kick in and numb the pain.

"I did too. When I was holding my nephews today…" He trails off and finishes his wine. "Let's go to bed."

I nod and follow him into the bedroom. We snuggle close together, and the booze hits me. My lashes are wet with tears and my eyes feel swollen from crying. Chase pulls me onto his chest and runs his fingers up and down my arm until I fall asleep.

~

HAVING CHUGGED a big glass of wine before bed, I once again wake up having to use the bathroom. Chase is still sleeping, and I worry about him overdoing it. He's still recovering and getting in a fight was the last thing he needed.

It's early in the morning, and we've only been asleep for a few hours. I go into the bathroom and turn on the shower. I strip from my clothes and pull my hair into a messy bun on the top of my head and look at myself in the mirror as I wait for the shower to warm up.

My hands land on my abdomen and my bottom lip quivers. Dizziness crashes down on me, brought on by a whirlwind of emotions. The fact that I had gotten pregnant hits me, and all the consequences of an unplanned pregnancy play out in my head.

Telling my parents.

Going to church with my growing belly.

Making room in this small house for Chase and our baby.

Figuring out how to work and raise a child.

Would I have a wedding? I've dreamed about and planned my wedding for years. Small and intimate. Whimsical but not over the top. We'd have the ceremony in the church and an outdoor reception at the family farm, with big white tents set up and our horses grazing in the background.

I get into the shower and sink down, letting the warm water wash over me. I thought about my wedding a lot before Jake died. We'd been together almost two years. I assumed a proposal was in the making. Jake was a practical person, thoughtful but not exactly romantic. Still, I did quite a bit of pinning on Pinterest, and my dream wedding is still in the back of my mind.

I cover my mouth with my hands, muffling a sob. I don't want to wake Chase up. The image of his face flashes before me, and my heart lurches in my chest. As hard as I try not to compare Jake to Chase, I can't help but feel the difference between the two. Everything with Jake was logical and calculated. Our relationship made sense, the sex was good, and we got along in most aspects. There is no doubt in my mind that we didn't love each other with all our hearts.

But Chase…I love him with all of my heart and every piece of my soul. Chase is unpredictable. Wild. *Dangerous*. There's no logical reason for us to be together.

And yet we are.

I close my eyes and lean into the water, feeling it drip down my face. Having a baby with Chase right now would be terrible timing. Sometimes the most terrible things are the most beautiful.

A shudder goes through me and I mourn more than the loss of the little life I had inside me. I mourn the loss of what could have been. The unconventional start to a family. The awkward family dinners and even the judgmental stares from people as we walk through town, pushing our baby in a stroller as we walk.

I feel like my body betrayed me and wasn't enough. I know what the doctor said—and what Chase reminded me—but it does little to comfort me. No, this pregnancy wasn't planned, but it doesn't make losing it any easier.

When my fingers start to get wrinkly, I get up and wash myself, and then get out and dressed. I feed the cats and take an Advil for the pain. My cycles have never been regular. Ever. I'll go weeks without a period and then get hit with a horrible heavy one, getting practically bedridden from pain. Then the next will be twenty-eight days later and super light. I started taking birth control as a teen to regulate my cycle and to deal with the pain. I pour myself another glass of wine and down it, and then get back into bed with Chase.

"Hey, babe," he says sleepily. "Are you okay?"

"I don't know," I say, being completely honest. "Physically, I'm fine."

"What about emotionally?" Chase pushes himself up. His hair is messy and there are pillow creases on his cheek. I'm so damn attracted to him even now, though sex is the last thing on my mind.

"I keep thinking of what could have been. I mean, I know this wasn't what we expected. At all. It would have been hard and trying, and yet I'm sad it's not going to happen."

"It still can," Chase says and puts his arms around me. "Maybe not right now, but later. And next time we can do it on purpose. It hurts now, but it'll get easier. I know you've heard that before."

"I have."

"You're not alone, Sierra. You will never be alone. I'm here. I'll always be here."

Tears fall from my eyes and Chase pulls me to him, cradling me against his chest. I relax against him and feel the wine hit me. I'm half-asleep only moments later.

And someone is knocking on my door.

"I'll go," Chase says, moving away. On an empty stomach, the wine gets to me harder than before. I'm drunk. All I want is to succumb to the darkness and fall back into sleep. Time slips away and what feels like just a second later, Chase is in the room. "Your mom's here."

"Why?" I grumble.

"She heard about the bar fight."

"Mother fucker," I say into the pillow. Chase helps me to my feet and I wobble as I walk, grimacing from the sunlight. Mom is standing in the living room, perched on the edge of the couch. Her hair is done and she's dressed in designer clothes.

"Sierra," she gasps when I stumble into the room. "You look terrible."

"Thanks, Mom. Tell me how you really feel."

"Lisabeth DeGraw told me about the fight at The Mill House last night. And how you were involved. Are you okay?"

I shrug, trying to copy Chase's signature move. In my mind, it was a flawless copy. But in real life, I looked like I was having some sort of convulsion. "I'm alive, right?" I sit heavily on the couch.

"What happened?"

"There were some guys. They got mad. And Chase stopped them." I look at Chase, realizing for the first time that he's only wearing pajama pants. My mother hates tattoos and is getting a good display of Chase's inked skin.

"I heard they were there because of you," Mom says pointedly, looking right at Chase.

"Mom," I whisper through clenched teeth.

Chase's brow furrows and he nods. "They were."

"Sierra could have gotten hurt," Mom snaps. "One of them grabbed her."

"They didn't hurt me, Mom," I snap. Something else hurt me, and the hurt is running deeper than I ever imagined. I spring to my feet. The wine paired with bleeding from the miscarriage makes me dizzy. My eyes flutter and I sink back to the couch.

Mom is too busy staring daggers at Chase to notice. "They could have hurt her. Easily. None of this would have happened if you hadn't come to this town. I knew you were bad news the moment I laid eyes on you. If you care about my daughter at all, you'll stay far away from her."

The pain etched on Chase's face breaks my heart all over again. I turn to my mother, eyes blurring with tears.

"I will talk to you later," she says to me and then walks out the door. I take in a shaky breath and clutch my heart. Chase is next to me in seconds, and I bury my head in his neck.

"You're drunk."

"I'm not drunk enough."

"You have more wine in the fridge."

I pull back, staring at him quizzically. "You're not going to tell me to lay off the alcohol?"

He shakes his head. "Not now." He kisses my forehead and leaves, returning with a bottle of sweet red wine.

"Nocturne Acres," he reads. "I've never heard of that."

"My family owns a vineyard in California," I say and take the wine from him. I don't waste time with a glass. I chug it right from the bottle. Chase takes the bottle from me and brings it to his lips. He sets it down on the coffee table, out of my reach.

"I'm sorry for all the shit that happened, Sierra."

"Don't be. And don't let my mom get to you. That's how she is to everyone. Manipulative and judgmental. You're not bad news."

"Maybe I am," he says so softly I almost don't hear him. "I never meant to hurt you, Sierra."

"I know. You didn't know those guys were going to show up."

"Right. Those guys."

I lean over Chase, reaching for the bottle. I have a sense he's talking about something else, but in that moment, my brain goes to self-preservation mode. I need another few swallows of wine so I can pass out.

"You need to take your medicine," I say and move away from Chase. I wobble when I stand, having to put my hand on the wall to steady myself as I move into the kitchen. Chase isn't supposed to take the antibiotics on an empty stomach. I open the fridge and pull out eggs.

"What are you doing?" he asks, standing in the threshold of the kitchen.

"Making breakfast."

"I'll do it. You can lay down."

I shake my head. "I want to stay busy."

"Okay." Chase comes into the kitchen with me, and we

work together to make breakfast. I drink half the bottle of wine as I cook, and make it through a plate of scrambled eggs before I'm feeling sick. Chase takes me to the bedroom and tucks me in. The world spins around me and I close my eyes.

Chase sits next to me, giving me a kiss before he gets under the blanket too. "When you're ready, we need to talk," he says softly. "And remember my promise. I will always love you."

30

CHASE

*M*aybe I should have cut her off and not let her have that second glass of wine. I don't know how to handle this, and my mind is all fucking over the place.

I need to tell her about the voicemails.

My heart breaks to see Sierra hurting.

I wish we were still having a baby.

I rub my temple and look at Sierra. She's sound asleep—as she's been for the last three hours—next to me in her bed. She looks at peace now, and I wish so fucking bad that same peace will carry on into the day when she wakes.

I don't know what to do from here. I had no fucking clue losing a baby you'd only known about for two days could hurt so damn much. Do we keep this to ourselves forever? When is it okay to try and have sex again? I'm going to assume we'll both agree to better birth control than pulling out since that worked out so well for us last time.

Thinking about the physical toll this is taking on Sierra, however 'normal' the doctor says it is, makes me want to throw up. She said the bleeding slowed, but she didn't say it stopped. My heart hurts for the loss of what could have been but hurts even more knowing what Sierra is going through.

It's not fucking fair. This shouldn't have happened to her. She's already dealt with a loss. Why does she have to go through it again?

Sierra stirs in her sleep and I hug her, wishing I could take away her pain. If there were a way, I'd do it, no matter what the cost. Sierra is everything I never knew I always wanted. I hold her tight in my arms, ignoring the pain it's causing me to feel around the area that was sliced open not that long ago.

I'm asleep and dreaming about Sierra when my phone rings. I jerk up fast and feel a painful tug on my flesh. Wincing, I grab my phone and see that it's Josh. Instantly. I feel like shit for not calling him and letting him know what went on last night.

"What the fuck?" he asks as soon as I answer.

"Shit. Sorry, man. I should have called you last night."

"You're not supposed to be working," Josh says. "Let alone getting in fights. What the hell were you thinking?"

"That I wasn't going to let some assholes lay a finger on the bar. Or Sierra."

"Is it terrible to say I wish I was there so I could see it all go down? I heard the guys you took out were twice your size and jacked on steroids."

"So this town likes to gossip and expand the truth. The steroid part might be true. I wouldn't put it past those guys, actually. And it was easy to take them out. They're a classic case of all brawn and no brain. If they hadn't threatened Sierra, it would have been fun."

"Makes you miss the old days?"

"No," I say honestly. "You know I enjoy a good fight or two. But this…" I look at Sierra's pretty face. "This is better." Even now, with a constant ache in my heart for what we lost.

I look out the window, wondering if it would have been better to have not met Sierra at all. We wouldn't be in this situation right now. Would she be better off without me?

I've been changed for the better. I didn't know how much was missing until I found her.

"How are my nephews?" I ask. "And Dakota."

"Wearing us out of course, but great. Dakota is having some jealousy issues. I'm taking her fishing after church tomorrow. That clearing behind The Mill House is a good spot."

"Are there a lot of fish in the river?"

"In the deeper parts. I'm hoping not to catch a lot," he admits with a laugh. "It's easier. Though Kota likes to throw 'em back so there's nothing to take home and gut."

"I've never been fishing."

"Ever?"

"Nope. Don't forget I grew up in Chicago. You wouldn't want to get in any bodies of water around there."

Josh laughs. "Come with us then. That would make Dakota happy. Are you going to be home?"

"I've been staying with Sierra. But I can stop by."

"Great. See you tomorrow then."

"Tonight. I'll be at work."

"I thought you weren't supposed to go back to work until next week."

"I'm not," I say. "I'll take it easy."

"Come in at ten," Josh says, knowing better than to argue with me. "I can leave early and you'll only have to work half a shift that way."

"Sounds good." I hang up and lay back down, holding Sierra. I wanted her to have a happy ending. It's not too late, is it? She rolls over in her sleep, feebly reaching for me.

"Chase," she mumbles and curling into my arms. I close my eyes feeling more determined than ever to make this woman happy. Her phone rings and I reach over to her side of the bed to silence it.

Lisa is calling, and seeing her name on Sierra's phone makes a chill settle in the room. She's going to tell Sierra about the messages if I don't. It wasn't an empty threat. Lisa has proved more than once that she's not my biggest fan and feels that she needs to protect Sierra…no matter what the cost.

I admire her loyalty and fierce friendship. That kind of bond is something we all long for. To have that best friend stand up for you even when you're wrong. To risk pissing you off because they know it's for your own good. To care about you more than you care about yourself.

Except Lisa gets too caught up. She acts before she thinks. And she doesn't like to be wrong. Sierra told me that Lisa already dug up dirt on me. She'd love another chance to prove how bad I am.

Maybe I am bad. I did listen to the messages. The intimate words weren't meant for me to hear. They weren't meant for anyone but a ghost. And I listened.

"Morning," Sierra mumbles and pushes herself up. "Or maybe afternoon?"

"It's afternoon. Want anything? I can get you breakfast. Or lunch. You probably want water, right?"

"Yeah." Sierra rubs her eyes and sighs. "I should be taking care of you still."

"You are."

She brings her knees to her chest and closes her eyes. "I did a lot of thinking between passing out from too much wine."

"Yeah?"

"And I still can't come up with a reason why this happened. I like to think things happen for a reason. Maybe it's bullshit we tell ourselves so it's easier to deal with shitty situations. Losing Jake..." Tears fall from her eyes. "I didn't find a reason for that either." She turns, and the pain in her eyes breaks my heart. "But then I met you. And then this happens. I...I...don't know why."

"Don't look for a reason," I tell her softly. "You won't find one."

~

I GRIP Sierra's hand tightly as we stand for the final prayer in church. We're in the back, and the lack of emotions coming from Sierra is worrying me. We spent the rest of Saturday in bed, talking about what could have been. It was harder on me than I'd ever admit. I'm not the kind of person to play out the what-ifs in life. I'm more of a repress-and-move-on type of guy, but Sierra needed to talk about it.

Mourn it.

Miss it.

And start to heal from it.

This time, she has me to help.

I went to bed Saturday night with Sierra wrapped in my arms. As I was drifting to sleep, Sierra softly whispered my name.

Maybe this happened to bring us closer together, she had said. *If we can get through this, we can get through anything.*

This morning, Sierra was quiet and calm, going about her normal routine but void of any emotion. She wasn't sad. She wasn't happy. Tinkerbell walked back and forth on the table, sticking her paw in Sierra's coffee during breakfast. And Sierra just sat there, petting the cat as if she were unaware of everything else around her.

I'm not good with stuff like this. The loss of the pregnancy is hitting Sierra hard, and she's not coping in a normal way. She's been down this dark path before, and I know all too well how easy it is to fall back on old habits.

The prayer ends and the choir starts singing again. The children are in the front, and Dakota catches my eye and waves. I smile back and give Sierra's hand a reassuring squeeze.

On the way out, her sister catches up to us. Sierra told me more than once how uptight her sister is, and how it's made it hard for the two of them to get along. Though right now, her sister's eyes—which are the same shade of green as Sierra's—are full of worry.

"Mom told me what happened at the bar," she starts. "I'm sorry."

Her apology shocks me, but Sierra only blinks.

"Thanks," I tell Sam.

"Our mother can be difficult. Ignore her. I know you two are happy."

"We are," Sierra says, voice flat.

Sam looks at her sister, eyes narrowing. "Are you okay, Sierra?"

"Fine." Sierra's eyes are on the ground.

Sam shifts her gaze to me. "She's tired," I tell her.

Sam nods but doesn't look convinced. "I'll see you guys tonight, right?"

"Right. We'll be there for dinner."

"Okay. Bye."

Panic starts to rise in my chest. Sierra is hurting and I want to make her better. I want to take the pain away but I don't know how. We make it outside and into the parking lot when Dakota runs over, throwing her arms around my waist.

Sierra blinks in the bright sunlight and smiles at my niece. It's just one smile but it makes me feel much better.

"Are you going fishing with me, Uncle Chase?"

Before I answer, I look at Sierra. Yesterday, the plan was

for me to go fishing while Sierra hangs out at home. But now I'm not sure if I should leave her alone.

"He is," Sierra answers for me. She's still smiling. It's forced, though I don't think anyone else could tell. "Did you know your uncle has never gone fishing before?"

Dakota's mouth falls open.

"So you're going to have to teach him."

Dakota jumps up and down with excitement. "I can do that! We're going to have so much fun!" She skips back off to Josh, who's talking to his in-laws. He gives me a wave and puts his hand on Dakota's shoulder to keep her from running away again.

"Are you sure you don't mind me going?" I ask Sierra.

"Not at all. I think I'm going to lie down and read the rest of the day. Or clean. The house is due for a good cleaning." Her voice is flat, and the way she's just going out things isn't right.

"Okay. I won't be gone long."

She presses another smile and takes my hand again. We're almost to the car when we're stopped again by Lisa. She's with her parents and sister, all of whom I met at the last family dinner. Sierra's aunt is talking to her, and Lisa slips away, moving close to me.

"Did you tell her?" she whispers harshly.

"Not yet."

"You have to tell her."

"I will," I promise. "Now's not a good time."

Lisa shakes her head. "When is there a good time to tell your girlfriend you not only listened to, but kept all her messages meant for her dead boyfriend?"

"There's not a good time. But trust me, right now is not the time to do it."

Lisa narrows her eyes. "Trust you? I hardly like you. I'm

giving you the benefit of the doubt for Sierra's sake. You tell her, or I will."

Anger surges through me. "If you care about Sierra like you say you do, you'll fucking wait," I say through gritted teeth. "Give her some time." I glance up, making sure no one can hear us. Sierra says something to her aunt that makes her smile, and my heart softens.

"Give *her* time?"

"Yes. Don't like me. Don't trust me. But fucking listen for Sierra's sake, who you say you care about. It's not my place to go into details, just…just be there for her."

Sierra comes back and I put my arm around her.

"Hey, Lisa," she says sounding a bit like her old self. "Are you coming to dinner tonight?"

Lisa looks right at me. "I wouldn't miss it."

~

MY FIRST FISHING experience was interesting, to say the least. Doing anything with a four-year-old has the potential to end up being disastrous, and when you throw in live bait, yards of tangly fishing line, and a muddy riverbank, you're playing with fire. Still, spending time outside with my brother and niece was nice. Needed, even. It was a good way to decompress, and now that I'm showered and changed and headed to Sierra's house, I feel I have a clearer head to offer her.

I park in front of Sierra's house and get out of my car, squinting in the bright sunlight. Lisa's car is parked next to Sierra's BMW. We have to be at her parents' in an hour for dinner, and I was hoping to have some alone time with her before then.

The screen door opens and smacks shut. Lisa emerges from the porch and stops short when she sees me.

"Hey," I say, trying to be civil. Not getting along with her best friend will upset Sierra. "Did you two talk?"

"Yes," she says, the word leaving her mouth like a hiss. "We did."

"Did Sierra tell you?"

"She told me everything."

A knot loosens in my chest. Sierra needs to talk about this, needs to let her friends and family know what she's going through. "She's hurting more than she lets on."

"Of course, she's hurting."

I run my hand through my hair. "I am too," I say quietly.

Lisa lets out a snort of laughter. "You did it to her."

The harshness in her words shocks me. "We did it to each other."

"You are unbelievable." She rolls her eyes. "Don't act like you're so hurt by something you did for your benefit."

"It's not like I meant to get her pregnant, but I certainly didn't want her to lose it either." I shake my head. "I've met some nasty people in my life, and you're taking it to a whole new level."

"What?" The color leaves Lisa's face.

"You don't like me. Sierra's mom doesn't like me. Judy Henson doesn't like me. This whole town wishes I would leave. I get it. I fucking get it. But who the fuck are you to say I'm not allowed to be hurt by this? It was my baby too."

Lisa's hands go to her chest and she struggles to breathe. "Sierra had a miscarriage? I...I didn't know. Oh my God." Her eyes widen and she looks like she might puke. "That's why you said to wait."

My heart drops out of my chest. Lisa doesn't have to say it for me to know: she told Sierra about the messages. That's what they talked about. Sierra hadn't told her about the baby. Instead of being allowed to heal, Lisa came in and ripped her heart into even more broken pieces.

I run past Lisa and into the house. "Sierra!" I call, but she doesn't answer. She's not in the living room or the kitchen. I check her bedroom. She's not there. I race to the back porch, but she's not there either. My head spins and my heart is going to explode. I need to find Sierra. I need to make things right. She's hurting so fucking bad already.

Sierra isn't in the house. I stand at the top of the stairs, panic rising in my chest. Where the hell did she go? I whirl around, remembering the hidden room. In a fury of desperation, I go into the closet and move the trapdoor.

Sierra is sitting cross-legged on the ground. Her back is to me and she's clicking the flashlight on and off.

"Sierra?"

She doesn't turn around.

"Sierra." I emerge through the crawlspace and stand, going over to her. I sit on the dusty floor and put my hand on her thigh. She clicks the flashlight off and then on again.

"Lisa told me you have Jake's old phone. She said all the messages I left him are still there and you listened to them. It sounds too crazy to be true."

I want to tell her yes, it's too crazy and Lisa is making up shit, but it's okay because we have each other. I can delete the voicemails and give her the phone. She'd never know.

But I can't lie.

"It is true."

Sierra turns to me, and the hurt and betrayal on her face is the worst thing I've ever seen. "I don't understand."

"Whoever cleared the memory on his phone didn't do it properly before selling it," I slowly explain. "They manually deleted things but forgot to go in and get rid of the messages. I didn't know it was you at first. Not until you gave me your number that day at the bookstore."

"But you still listened to them after you knew?"

"I did." The confession is like a knife to my heart. "I shouldn't have and I'm sorry."

The light turns off and when Sierra turns it back on, tears are streaming down her face. "I struggled so much with the guilt I felt about wanting to know about your past. I knew you had been arrested and I told myself it didn't matter because the person you are right now is all that matters. And you...you knew everything about me. The things I said in those messages..." She shuts the light off again. "Why didn't you tell me?"

"I didn't want to risk hurting you. Or losing you. I love you, Sierra."

"You haven't deleted them."

"No, and I have no good reason for that. I'm so sorry. After I heard the first one I had to keep listening. Your words spoke to me in a way I never thought was possible."

She clicks on the light. "The words weren't for you."

Silence falls between us, and I hear my rapid heartbeat in my ears. "It's hot up here. Let's go downstairs and talk."

"There's nothing to talk about," she says and her voice breaks. "I figured it out." Her eyelids shut and a river of tears pour down her cheeks. I reach out to wipe them away and kiss her lips, but she pushes me away.

"I know the reason," she goes on with a shaky voice. "All of this happened...losing Jake...meeting you...getting pregnant just to lose it...it was to remind me that I'll never get a happy ending."

"No. Sierra, no. That's not true. That's all I've ever wanted for you. A happy ending. Before I even met you, I wished for you to be happy."

"You need to go."

"Don't say that. Please, Sierra." My breath catches in my chest. My throat tightens and I think I'm dying. "You don't mean it."

"I do." She closes her eyes and wraps her arms around herself. "I can't do this, Chase. I trusted you and this whole time you…you had this information on me and kept going like things were normal."

"I didn't know what to do. I wanted to tell you. I *was* going to tell you. Just not now. Not after the loss."

"I have a hard time believing you. What if we hadn't lost the baby? Would you have waited until it was born? And then waited again?"

"I…I don't know. All I know is that I love you more than anything, Sierra."

"I need some time alone."

"I'll go downstairs and wait. I'll be there, whenever you're ready."

"No. Leave. Please. If you love me like you say you do, then go."

Tears fill my eyes. I've never cried in my adult life before. "I do love you."

"Then go."

I look down and feel a tear roll down my cheek. I angrily brush it away and go through the crawlspace. I leave the trapdoor open, hoping to get some fresh air inside the hidden room to keep Sierra from getting overheated.

I stand, feeling dizzy. I want to tell myself things will be okay. That Sierra will be upset and mad at me for a while but will understand. I didn't do anything on purpose to hurt her. Yet the betrayal and invasion of privacy is blatant and I have no excuse for what I did.

I fucked up, and it cost me the love of my life.

The world spins around me and my vision blurs from the tears that are pooling in my eyes. Somehow, I make it down the stairs and onto the porch. Lisa is sitting on the bench, holding one of the many decorative pillows Sierra set out. Her eyes are wet from crying.

"Chase," she starts and stands. "I didn't know."

I turn to her, unable to hide the incredible pain on my face.

"No," she says and starts crying. "I'm sorry."

"It's too late," I croak out and turn away. I get into my car and lose the battle against my emotions. I pull out of the driveway and speed down the private road, not stopping until I'm in the parking lot of The Mill House.

I get out and look at the familiar brick building. The sound of the river, once calming, sounds foreign.

This place is no longer home.

31

SIERRA

I flip open the pocketknife and look at the blade. It's dull from use over the years but still gets the job done. I bring my finger to the tip, feeling the sharpness of the metal. I press it into my skin, welcoming the pain.

My head drops and I close my eyes. Tears rain down on the box in front of me. It's Monday morning, and I'm alone at The Book Bag. A big shipment of signed books just arrived, and I should be ecstatic.

I cannot stop crying.

I miss Chase.

I miss his arms around me. I miss the way he made me laugh. I miss how safe I felt with him snuggled up next to me at night.

I miss the way I trusted him.

I miss the lie he led me to believe.

I just miss him.

My body shudders from a sob, and the dull blade slices into my skin. Warm blood pools on the tip of my finger, dripping down onto my hand. I watch it, knowing I should get up and wash the cut, yet I'm unable to move.

My phone rings again, for the tenth time this morning. Chase keeps calling, and I haven't answered. He leaves a message every time he calls, and I don't know if he's trying to be ironic or not. I haven't listened to a single message. It's like the rug's been pulled from beneath my feet, and the man I thought I knew and loved is a different person. The betrayal runs deep, and it's not something I can look past. Not yet at least.

Everyone warned me about him.

They said he was dangerous.

I guess they were right.

My finger starts to throb. I set the knife on top of the box and get up, going through the store to the backroom. I wash out the cut, watching the water push the flap of skin back. I'm too numb inside to react. I wait until the water running off my hand goes from red to clear, and then I bandage my finger up and go back to the storefront and open the box. Burying myself in work is what got me through the aftermath of losing Jake. As long as I have the store, I can keep my mind busy enough to get by.

Maybe.

Doubtfully.

Because it feels like everything inside of me is dead. It won't take long before it starts to fester and rot away.

I take a stack of Scarlett Levine's latest book and start putting them away on the shelf when someone comes into the store.

"Sierra?" Lisa calls. "I brought you coffee." She comes around the aisle and extends a to-go cup.

"You can put it on the counter," I answer flatly.

"Okay." She sets it down and picks up my phone. "Chase is calling you."

"Yeah," I say and move books around and feel Lisa's eyes on me. She came in after Chase left yesterday and told me about their talk. How he said he'd come clean but wanted to wait. How sorry she was because she had no idea I'd gotten pregnant…and then lost it.

"Are you not talking to him?"

"No."

"Maybe you should. You should deal with the loss together."

Something inside of me snaps. "Stop telling me what I should do."

"I just think—"

"Stop!" I throw my hands up. "Just go."

"Sierra, please. I'm so sorry."

"You should be!" I spit. "What Chase did was wrong and I'd feel the same no matter when he told me, but he asked you to wait because he knew what I was already going through. You were so hellbent on making him be the bad guy you didn't listen. You didn't care about anyone other than yourself."

"That's not true." She shakes her head back and forth. "I was worried about you. I didn't want you to get hurt and that's exactly what he did."

"But I didn't need to know right now!"

"Then when? You had to know, Sierra."

"Did I?" I ask as the tears start to fall. I wrestled with this all night, wishing that I didn't know the truth and could have fallen asleep in Chase's arms once again. Painful cramps kept me up all night, and the hurt ran so deep I wasn't sure if I would make it through the night.

I wasn't sure I wanted to.

"If I could take it back, I would. Please, Sierra," Lisa cries. "I'm so sorry."

"You can't take it back," I say slowly and turn, going back to my box of books. My entire body hurts from how much I wish things could go back. The man that I love kept a detrimental secret from me. My best friend was so blinded by hate she hurt everyone in her path.

"Chase is hurting too," Lisa reminds me as if I forgot. "And I know he feels bad. I really think you should talk to him. What happened, happened to both of you."

"So now you're Team Chase?" I bring another stack of books out of the box and whirl around, glaring at Lisa.

"No, well, yes. I…I just—"

"You want to make yourself feel better," I snap. "But it's too late for that."

"I want you to feel better! I didn't know. I was wrong. I should have listened to Chase when he told me to wait. I should have trusted that he would really tell you. It's so much at once, and I'm worried about you, Sierra."

I close my eyes, trying to stop more tears from forming. I believe that Chase loves me. I know he regrets keeping the messages once he knew they were mine. If he listened to them all before he knew me, would it have been different?

If I got a phone with messages still on it, I'd listen too.

Should I answer the next time he calls? I miss him. I need him. Yet I feel so betrayed. I look at Lisa and another wave of heartache comes over. These are things we'd have a heart-to-heart about.

It's like she betrayed me too.

And it's too much. I don't know how much longer my heart can take this pain before it gives out.

"Don't you have to be at work?" I ask her with no emotion in my voice.

Her bottom lip quivers and she cries as she turns to leave. As soon as she's out the door, I break down sobbing. I'm crying so hard I don't hear the bell ring as the door opens, or hear someone come into the store. A heavy hand lands on my back, and for a split second, I think it's Chase.

My heart flutters and I feel relief. I need him. I turn and see Wyatt.

"Sierra?" he asks. "What's wrong?"

"Oh," I say and sniffle. I close my eyes and turn away, using my T-shirt to dry my face. "Sorry. I didn't hear you come in."

"Are you okay?"

I force a smile. "I will be." I try to compose myself and fail. Wyatt takes me in his arms, which only makes me miss Chase even more. It's a strange, painful feeling. When Jake died, I longed to hug him one more time.

But I couldn't.

I wish so badly to feel Chase's embrace. He can wrap his arms around me.

But he shouldn't.

I suck in a sob and take in a steadying breath. Wyatt holds me tight and I have to push to break away. "Thanks. I'm okay. I, uh, I was reading a really sad book."

Wyatt looks at me unblinking. Then he smiles. "Wow. I wish I could get into books that much."

"Yeah, they're powerful. Can I help you with something?" I walk past him to the counter, getting a tissue and the coffee Lisa brought.

"My grandma wants more books by the same author."

"Sure. What's the author's name?"

"I don't remember. It was that book you recommended for her birthday."

"Ah. I remember now." I blow my nose and take a sip of coffee and cross the store, picking up a book from the box. "This just came in this morning. And this one is signed."

"Great. You're making me the most popular grandkid, you know."

I fake a laugh and ring Wyatt up. He looks down at my phone when a text comes through. "Someone misses you," he teases, seeing the missed calls and texts from Chase. My heart aches.

"Yeah. He does."

～

"Ah, Sierra, dear," Mrs. Williams says, shuffling into the store. She uses a cane when she walks now, and her bad hip seems to be getting worse and worse. I'm just about to close down for the day and wasn't expecting to see her.

"Hi, Mrs. Williams. What are you doing here?"

She smiles, brown eyes gentle. "We need to talk, honey."

"That's never good."

"You're not being fired," she goes on with another smile. "But I am putting the store up for sale."

My mouth opens and it takes a second before the words come out. "You are?"

"It's time for me to retire, dear. I've been trying to convince JJ for a while to take over the family business, but he wants to follow in his father's footsteps instead and reopen the garage. I'm going to use the money I get from the building for this new business venture." She lifts her gaze. "Nothing would have made him happier than seeing that car shop open again."

I smile right back at her, and it's my first genuine smile of the day. "He would have loved it."

"I've already gotten things in order, and the official listing goes up tomorrow. You know how real estate is around here. It might be a while before we find a buyer, but I wanted to tell you before the for-sale sign goes up. I know you love this place."

The words sit on the surface of my mind but haven't sunk in yet. I need to keep them there, or else I'll break down. And there's nothing else to break.

"It's been a long time coming," Mrs. Williams goes on. "I've been considering this or well over a year now but kept finding reasons to hold on a while longer. Seeing you happy was the final push I needed."

"Me?"

"Yes, you. You love this place just as much as I do, and before…before I couldn't do that to you, dear."

I work hard to keep the tears from flowing. I was happy, and it all got swept away in an instant.

"You shouldn't have put off retirement for me."

Mrs. Williams looks around the store. "It's been hard for me to let go. Bringing books to this small town was a dream of mine when I was a child."

"Maybe the buyer will keep it as a bookstore."

"Maybe. But not if they're interested in making money," she adds with a laugh and pats my hand. "You look tired, honey."

"I am."

"Busy getting in more bar fights?"

"You heard about that?"

Mrs. Williams laughs. "Who hasn't? And I heard how that boyfriend of yours is quite protective of you."

I can't think about it or else I'll cry. "He is," I say and feel the switch flip back to where it was before I met Chase, back when I thought I was broken and incapable of feeling joy ever again.

A deep sadness comes over me, not because of recent events, but because this time I know that switch is never going the other way ever again.

CHASE

I sit on the rock looking out at the river. Sunlight reflects off the shiny surface, blinding me. My eyes water from the harsh light, my legs ache from sitting still, and my head pounds. Yet I don't move. I stay here, hot, hungry, and uncomfortable with no plan to move.

I deserve this punishment and more. I fucked up. I didn't just lose Sierra, I hurt her even more than she's already hurting. My whole life has been filled with moments I'm not proud of, but I've never regretted anything like I do right now.

I want to make things right.

Blinking, I look away from the water and down at my phone. Sierra won't answer my calls, not that I really expected her to, and hasn't texted me back. I call her, and her phone rings once before she declines my call. My heart lurches at the sound of her voice, telling me to leave a message and she'll call me back as soon as she can.

"Sierra," I start. "It's been over a day since I've seen you, and it already feels like a lifetime. I miss you. I'm sorry." I close my eyes, imagining she's in front of me.

"I got the scar on my back when I broke into a lake house in Utah to take a portrait that was supposed to go to the wife in the divorce. Her ex-husband wasn't supposed to be there. I felt sorry for him. His wife married him for his money, cheated, and took him to the cleaners at court. He was no match for a fight, so I let him take one swing at me unguarded but didn't see the broken piece of glass in his hand. He apologized after he cut me. I still feel bad for taking that painting to his ex."

I hang up and stand, legs asleep from sitting so long. I shake out the pinprick sensation and go into the bar. It's a typical slow Monday night. Josh is working and doesn't need the extra help tonight. It takes a while to convince him to go home to his wife and kids. He feels bad since today was my day off, and only agrees once I tell him Sierra is busy tonight and we're not seeing each other anyway.

I don't approve of drinking on the job, but fuck it. The bar is slow and I fucking need it. I pour whiskey into a glass and down it. I haven't eaten all day. My appetite has been gone since yesterday afternoon when Sierra told me to leave.

I add ice to my glass and more whiskey. I try to sip it slowly but pour it down my throat instead. I need to numb the pain. In no time at all my mind swirls and I lean on the bar, rubbing my forehead.

I can't stay here without Sierra in my life. This town is too small. We'd run into each other and seeing her without being able to be with her would be worse than putting food just out of a starving man's reach.

I'll be reminded of Sierra no matter where I go in this Godforsaken place, making everyday hell on earth. Will seeing me do the same to her?

I bring the bottle of whiskey upstairs with me after I close the bar for the night. I drink enough to pass out, but not enough to keep the nightmares away. I wake at dawn fighting off the image of Sierra's body floating in the river, lifeless eyes staring up at me. Her belly was large and swollen, and a baby cries from deep inside the forest. No matter how hard I try, I can't get through the water to find the child.

Our child.

I don't attempt to go back to sleep until I chugged enough whiskey to kill a whale. I wake up in the afternoon feeling like complete shit. The first thing I do is check my phone in case Sierra called.

She didn't.

I stumble to the kitchen and get a drink. Then I shower and force myself to eat. I get a text on my other phone. It's from Jax, and I forgot that I was still fucking pissed at him for the shit that went down Friday night. It seems like nothing now.

Jax: **I know you said you were done, but I heard of a job in Jackson. 75k if you get it done in 24 hours**

I look at the screen, reading his words over and over again. Not because I'm not getting the message, but because I need to occupy my brain. I shouldn't take a job. I'm not even supposed to be working in the bar yet.

But I don't care anymore.

The only thing I care about is Sierra. I drop the phone and march out the door. Giving up isn't something I've ever done. I fight and I fight until I get what I want. Sierra isn't mine for the taking, but I'm not going to walk away.

I love her, and I know she loves me. I'm going to fix this.

I park in front of The Book Bag and go inside. The familiar dinging of the bell rings out when I step inside. The smell of books takes me back to the first time I walked inside and saw Sierra sitting behind the counter.

"Hi," someone calls from inside the store. It's not Sierra. "Can I help—" She cuts off when she sees me, and I'm not sure if it's because she's afraid of me like the rest of the town or if Sierra told her we broke up.

"She's on her lunch break," she says. "She just left but shouldn't be gone too long."

"Oh, okay." So she's afraid of me. Sierra hasn't told her coworker yet. "I guess I'll go."

"I'll tell her you stopped by."

"No, I wanted it to be a surprise," I lie and turn to go. Then I notice the red and white sign in the window. "The store's for sale?"

"Technically, just the building. I suppose if the new owner wanted to keep running it as the store, they could."

Sierra has to be devastated. She loves this place and what it has to offer the people of Summer Hill. I don't want this taken away from her, and I wish I could convince her to ask her parents for the cash to buy it and make it hers. She'd never do that, and I respect the hell out of her for not falling back and relying on her rich parents.

"What's the asking price?"

"A hundred grand, but between you and me, Mrs. Williams said she's hoping for seventy-five thousand. It's just enough to retire and have money left open to give to her son."

Seventy-five grand.

If that's not fate, I don't know what is.

33

SIERRA

I look down at my lunch, moving my salad around the bowl with my fork. My stomach grumbles in hunger, but the thought of putting food in my mouth, chewing, and swallowing seems like too much effort. I flip a page on my Kindle and force myself to take another bite.

My lunch break is almost over, and I've barely eaten a thing. I make myself eat at least half the salad and toss the rest. My shift at The Book Bag is halfway over, and I successfully made it through the first part without breaking down or showing that I'm sad.

Or showing any emotion at all, really. That part of me is off, and in order to survive, it has to stay that way. It's Tuesday afternoon, and I sat in the alley behind the store to eat my lunch. It's hot and sunny today, just how I like it.

"How was lunch?" Janet asks when I get back into the store. She's only here for a few hours today, helping me log everything in the store and to cover my break.

"Fine," I say softly and immediately get back to work. Janet hands off her notes and takes off. I keep my mind busy by making a detailed list of every item in the store. Mrs. Williams might need it whenever the time comes to move.

Minutes before I close the shop, Janet comes back in. She left her phone in the break room and came back for it.

"Did your boyfriend ever come back?" she asks, looking down at her phone screen as she walks.

"Come back?" I echo.

"To the store. He came when you were on your lunch break."

Chase was here. For me. "Uh, yeah. I saw him," I lie.

"Good. All right, then, night, Sierra!"

"Good night."

I lock the door behind her, mind going a million miles an hour. It's clear Chase cares, and I want so incredibly bad to go to him. Is this something we can get past? Can I forgive him for betraying my trust? I'll have to learn to trust him again. It might take time, but it's worth it…right?

I mull it over the entire time I put back books, and I have to count the cash in the register twice because my mind is on Chase. Once the money is stashed away, I pull my phone from my purse and lean on the wall, sinking down onto my butt. My fingers tremble and my heart aches.

I have over a dozen missed calls and texts from Chase. I open the voicemails and listen to the first one.

"Sierra," he starts and the sound of his voice does something to me. Calms me. Soothes me. Turns me on, even now. "There's no excuse for what I did, and I can never say sorry enough. I kept listening to the messages because I wanted to know you were happy. It doesn't make sense and makes even less after I met you. It wasn't right to listen to words that were meant for another. The things you said…they were so beautiful. I fell in love with the Mystery Woman from her words alone. And then I met you, and I fell even harder. I don't know how to make it right. What you said was personal...not meant for me. I want to make it up to you, and the best way I can think to do that is to leave you messages too."

The voicemail ends and I play the next one.

"I liked to brag about how I wasn't afraid of anything, but there is one thing that always freaked me out. I never wanted to die before I was buried." He pauses and I try to figure out what he means. "I've seen too many people live but not be alive. I thought I was living because I took risks and was surrounded by a certain level of daily danger. But I was wrong. I never felt alive until I met you. And right now... right now I feel like I'm dead inside but my body refuses to die."

I replay the message, soaking in every one of his words. I play the following one, which was left only half an hour later.

"When I was sixteen I purposely ate lobster so I could get out of a math exam I wasn't ready for. I ended up in the hospital for a week and missed my junior prom. I would have been pissed, but my mom stayed with me most of that week I was in the hospital. It was the most time we'd spent together since she legally wasn't allowed to leave me unattended. And when I looked at the test and saw those two pink lines, I knew you'd be a good mom, giving our baby everything I didn't have but wanted from my mother. Any child you have will be lucky."

I find myself smiling at his words, and my heart longs to beat against his. There are more messages. I play the next.

"If you asked me a year ago if I believed in love, I would have laughed. The last thing I thought I'd find when I came back here, was a reason to stay. Maybe that's the reason for all of this, and I keep thinking about the reason I came here, and how our paths crossed. I came here because my dad died. Loss brought us together, and it's crazy how something so beautiful—even if it was short lived—came out of the darkness. Maybe we were always meant to be."

Tears fall from my eyes and I get up, yanking my purse from the shelf behind the counter so fast it catches on a hook and knocks down a box of cleaning supplies. I hastily shove them back and race to my car, driving as fast as I can to The Mill House. My heart is beating outside of my chest.

Chase hurt me.

He didn't mean to, but he did.

Yet that doesn't mean we need to walk away. We can start again, right? My fingers shake when I get out of the car.

Chase isn't working tonight, and Corey hasn't seen him. I go up the stairs, taking two at a time, and knock on the door to the apartment. When Chase doesn't answer, I try the doorknob, surprised to find it unlocked. Chase always got on me for not locking my doors.

"Chase?" I call and step inside, feeling along the wall for the light. Right away, something is off. The air conditioner isn't blowing out freezing cold air. "Chase?" I hold my breath, waiting for him to wake up and rush out of the bedroom.

He doesn't.

I set my purse down on the kitchen table and cross the room, going into the bedroom. The bed is neatly made, and all of Chase's personal items are gone. I whirl around desperate to find something that proves he's still here.

Then I see it, leaning up against the large windows in the living room. Chase's phone. Jake's phone. My heartbeat echoes in my ears and my hand shakes as I pick it up. I hit the home button, and see there is one missed call and a voicemail. Chase set this up for me to find.

I start to feel sick as I unlock the phone and open the messages. All my old voicemails have been erased, and the only message left is from three hours ago. I don't recognize the number, but I press play anyway.

"Sierra," Chase starts. "Hopefully you found the phone and knew to listen. I know you will, as weird as that is. It's a feeling, I guess. I'm sorry for all the pain I caused you. All I ever wanted was for you to have your happy ending, but I'm starting to think you won't get that with me around. I still love you. I will always love you. I promised you that I would, and I've never broken a promise."

The message ends and I press the phone to my ear, waiting for more. There has to be more. Because if not, then that was goodbye.

"No," I whisper, and my words turn into sobs. Chase is gone. Moved on to the next town, searching for somewhere to call home. I fall to the ground, crying. I cry and cry until there is nothing left. Until I fall asleep. I wake at dawn, cold and stiff from lying on the ground. I sit up, and movement outside the window catches my eye.

It's the deer. She's creeping toward the shallow part of the river for a drink, and she's not alone. Her baby is close behind, curiously sniffing at the water. I watch them, transfixed, and know seeing them is some sort of sign. I just wish I knew what it meant.

~

"HEY," Lisa says and apprehensively steps into my bedroom. She's holding a coffee and has brought me one every morning as a peace offering. It isn't working. "Rob told me he was on patrol this morning and saw you leaving Chase's house wearing the same clothes you had on last night. Does that mean you guys—"

"No," I snap, and pull the blankets tight around my shoulders. I don't have to be at work until later this afternoon, though right now I'm not sure I can go at all. Getting out of bed is too much effort. I have no energy. No drive.

"But you were at his house."

"He wasn't there."

"But you…what do you mean?"

I sit up. "I mean he wasn't fucking there. He's gone!"

Lisa's face breaks and I almost feel bad for snapping at her. "He's coming back, right? He has to."

"Why would he?" I shake my head. "You all have made it abundantly clear he's not welcome here and I…I…I pushed him away."

"No. Don't you dare blame yourself. Call him. Tell him you miss him and he'll come back. I promise you, he will."

"I can't. He left his phone. The messages are all gone. He left it so I could see he really did delete everything."

"Sierra," Lisa says and sets the coffee on my dresser. She climbs into bed and puts her hand on my shoulder. "Let's not fight. Be mad at me later, okay? I just want to be here for you."

"Okay," I say and the anger leaves me, immediately replaced by raw, painful grief. I cry into my pillow, and Lisa tries to soothe me by running her hand over my hair. She wears rings on every finger, and they catch on loose strands, which pull and snap.

"You're going to be late for work," I hiccup.

"That's okay. Being with you is more important."

I squeeze my eyes shut and steady my breathing. "I'm okay."

"You're not, and it's okay to not be okay, Sierra."

"I know. And you're right. I'm okay enough for you to go to work though. You've been late enough this summer already."

"Yeah. Write-ups for being tardy don't count. If they did, I would have been fired years ago." Lisa hugs me. "I don't want you being alone. Maybe we should get your mom or your sister to come over. Even Gran."

I shake my head. "No. I'll call Scott. I haven't talked to him in a while anyway."

"He'll try to get you to fly out to Orlando again," she says with a half-smile.

"Maybe I'll go."

Lisa squeezes my arm. "A change of scenery is nice sometimes. Are you sure you're okay by yourself?"

"Yes. I'm exhausted and want to sleep before I go to work."

"Okay. I love you, Si. I'm here for you, no matter what."

I just nod, trying hard not to be mad at her. She didn't mean to set off the shitstorm, and it all goes back to Chase anyway. It was only a matter of time before I found out.

Lisa leaves, and the cats jump up in the bed, meowing until I get up to feed them. My eyes are swollen and red from crying. I hope a few hours of sleep will give them enough relief. I don't want anyone to ask me what's wrong. There's no way I can keep it together then.

~

WEDNESDAY NIGHT COMES and passes with no word from Chase. Josh called, asking me if I'd seen his brother, which makes everything seem so much more definite. Chase is gone.

Scott was working when I called during the day and called me back late Wednesday night. I poured myself a big glass of wine, drinking it fast to give me the courage to tell Scott everything.

And I did. We stayed up until three o'clock talking. I miss my brother. He has this cool calmness to him and is always able to see things rationally without being too cold like Sam. He's the middle child and is literally the perfect blend

357

between Sam's uptight personality and my sometimes-over-the-top free-spiritedness.

The moment I told him about the miscarriage, he wanted to get on a plane and come here. I'm still not sure he's not on a plane right now. Scott didn't give me infinite wisdom, but just talking about everything made the weight on my shoulders a little lighter.

I fell asleep on the couch around four in the morning, and got up just an hour or so later and dragged myself into my room. Thunder rumbles in the distance, and light rain starts to fall.

At eight-thirty, my phone rings. It's on the nightstand next to my bed, and it wakes me up. There have been many times where I've slept through phone calls, but my hyper vigilance to hear from Chase wakes me from a dead sleep.

Only, it's not Chase. It's Mrs. Williams.

"I'm sorry to wake you, dear," she says when I sleepily answer. "And I'm sorry to ask this of you since it's your day off."

"Ask what?"

"If you could open the store today. It might be the last time."

"The last time?"

"The real estate agent just called. We got an all-cash offer and the buyer is willing to pay more if we can get everything settled today."

"Oh. Wow."

"It's sudden, honey, I know."

"Yeah." I close my eyes, feeling guilty that I'm not sharing any excitement. "I'll be at the store."

I'm tired, but I know trying to sleep for another half-hour is pointless. I can't shut off my mind either. What am I going to do when the store closes? The family business has always been a backup plan, just one I never thought I'd have to execute.

~

THE FOR-SALE SIGN is gone by the time I get to the store. Fat raindrops fall down in a fury, and storm-thick clouds gather overhead. I take my usual spot behind the counter and look around. Being inside a bookstore on a stormy day is heaven. I'm really going to miss this place.

With the rain, business is slower than usual. I'm okay with that because I'm not in the mood to talk to anyone. I'm teetering on the edge of bursting into tears, and I'm starting to get annoyed with myself.

I don't like being sad.

Around one o'clock, Mrs. Williams and Jackie Lewis, one of the two real estate agents in Summer Hill come in. Mrs. Williams is beaming ear to ear. I guess that buyer paid the extra cash to get this place today.

"Everything is taken care of, I see." I notice the stack of papers in Jackie's hand that she's keeping dry inside her raincoat.

"Almost," Mrs. Williams tells me. "I sold the building. In two days. For more than my goal. I never thought I'd see the day…" She trails off, laughing.

"That's great." I force a smile. "So, what does that mean for the books?"

"That's up to you dear."

"What?"

Mrs. Williams looks at Jackie and smiles again. "The buyer has a proposition for you. He'd like to know if you'd be interested in buying the building from him."

I cock an eyebrow. "But he just bought it."

"Exactly."

Jackie steps forward and slides the paper in front of me on the counter. The confusion leaves me when I look down. My hand covers my open mouth.

"My client is very motivated to sell," Jackie tells me, sounding professional as if this is an everyday occurrence. "As you can see, his asking price is very reasonable. He's covering closing costs as well."

Thunder crackles above us and the lights flicker. I blink and look down at the paper again. The building is for sale for a dollar. One. Dollar. My eyes scan the paper, heart skipping a beat when I see the seller's name.

Chase Henson.

"Is he here?" I ask, voice nothing more than a hollow whisper.

"He might still be at the bank," Jackie starts. She pulls a pen from her purse and extends it to me. "If you could just—"

I don't hear the rest of what she says. If there's a chance Chase is in town, I need to take it. I push open the door and step into the pouring rain. Life doesn't hand out do-overs. You don't always get a second chance. Sometimes, it's now or never.

I close my eyes as thunder claps loudly above me.

Three...two...one.

"Sierra!"

I open my eyes and see Chase standing across the street. Rain pelts down on me, and lightning flashes above us. The whole world stops and everything fades. The wind. The rain. The pain.

I have to get to him. Now. My heart lurches in my chest and I take off, feet splashing in puddles as I leap off the sidewalk. Chase runs for me too, and we collide in the middle of the street. He takes me in his arms, lifting me up off the ground. My arms go around him and he puts his lips to mine.

I melt into him, bringing my hand to his cheek, cupping

his face and kissing him with everything I have. He kisses me back even harder, slipping his tongue into my mouth. My heart swells in my chest and tears are falling from my eyes, mixing with the rain. Chase holds me tight, and the feel of his muscles under his wet T-shirt sends me over the edge.

"Chase." I move my head back just enough to look at him, needing to see into his hazel eyes and make sure this is real.

"Sierra." My name pours from his lips like velvet, and it's suddenly my favorite thing for him to say. He looks into my eyes, and so much emotion plays on his handsome face.

Sorrow.

Love.

Regret.

Passion.

Rain comes down in sheets and the wind picks up. Chase pulls me to him and kisses me again, and jolts of electricity shoot through me. Time stops, and we forget that a storm is raging on around us. Lightning strikes the stoplight near us, sending sparks flying down onto the pavement.

"You came back," I whisper.

"I never left," he tells me. "Not really."

"I went to your house and you weren't there. I found the phone. I thought you were gone forever."

Chase's brow furrows and he kisses me again. We're both soaked from rain but neither of us care. It feels so good to be in Chase's arms again. He moves his mouth from mine to my neck, kissing and sucking my skin. We're standing in the middle of the street, surrounded by the wind and the rain, as thunder and lightning loom directly overhead.

None of that matters.

Chase is here. The dark abyss inside me fills with light. He sets me down and runs his hand over my arms, feeling the goose bumps on my skin.

"I'm sorry."

"It's okay."

"No," he says. "It's not."

"You're right." I move closer, fingers curling under the hem of his white T-shirt. It's rain-soaked, and I can see his tattoos through the wet fabric. "I'm mad and I'm hurt, and it feels like you went behind my back listening to those messages. But I don't want it to tear us apart. We're going through something hard and painful together, and I need you, and I think you need me too."

"I do, but it's more than that. I never believed in fate or things being meant to be before, and I still don't think I do. No matter what is thrown at us, how many people keep saying we shouldn't be together, I keep going back to you. And I always will. I choose you, Sierra. I love you."

"I love you, too."

He grabs me by the waist and kisses me again. Another clap of thunder booms, this one louder than before. We look up, noticing the broken wire from the traffic signal swaying in the wind.

"We should go in," he says and takes my hand. "That doesn't look safe."

"Right." My fingers go between his. "We have paperwork to fill out."

Chase puts his arm around me and we hurry to The Book Bag, stopping under the awning in front of the door.

"You bought the store."

"Yeah," he says. "I did. But I'm in the market to sell."

"Why?"

"You've already lost so much. I didn't want you to lose anything else. You deserve a happy ending, even if it's not with me…I still want to do whatever I can to give it to you."

"I want it to be with you."

The wind picks up, blowing rain into our faces. Chase

pulls me to him, shielding me from the storm. "I fucked it up, didn't I?"

"No. Not so much we can't get past it."

"I'm so fucking sorry, Sierra." He bends his head down, resting his forehead against mine. His fingers press into my waist.

"I forgive you. It might take me some time to get over it, but I forgive you."

Chase kisses me again, and I shiver. "Let's go in." I nod and he opens the door for me. The bell rings and the calming scent of books surrounds me. Mrs. Williams is sitting behind the counter, smiling.

"That's one way to thank him," she says with a wink. "You found one of the good ones, Sierra."

I turn to Chase, taking in everything about him, flaws, mistakes, and all. "Yeah. I did."

34

CHASE

I reach down, grabbing a blanket off the floor. The hammock swings and Sierra leans back to balance us out, keeping us from falling to the ground. The wind howls and mist blows through the screen on Sierra's back porch.

The storm knocked the power out. Sierra signed the paperwork in the dark inside the bookstore—her store— using the flashlights on our phones to read the fine print. We came back to her house to dry off. We're together, and I'd love nothing more than to put this all behind us and move on, but I know we can't.

There's a lot unspoken between us, and the scab needs to be scraped off and scrubbed out so the wound can heal properly this time.

"Where did you go?" Sierra asks, hooking her leg over me. I tuck the blanket around us, keeping the mist from getting on us. "You were gone for more than a day. Josh didn't even know where you went."

"Jackson. For a job."

Sierra, whose head is resting on my chest, looks at me. "Why?"

A smile plays on my lips. "I guess you could call it fate. Jax texted me about it. Seventy-five-thousand-dollar payout. And that was the amount Mrs. Williams needed to sell the store."

Sierra closes her eyes and puts her head back down. I wrap her tighter in my arms. Thunder rumbles in the distance, reverberating off the trees.

"What was the job?"

"A politician's mistress took off with his wife's horse. He needed the horse back before his wife found out…about the horse and the mistress. Contacting the police would have blown his cover, and he paid extra for discretion."

Sierra pushes up again, eyes meeting mine. "You never cease to amaze me, Chase."

I laugh. "You wouldn't think so if you saw me trying to get that horse into the trailer."

"It's a bit of an art form for some horses."

"I get that now. I'm not the equestrian I like to pretend I am."

Sierra laughs. "I can take you to the barn. I used to ride all the time. But I just kind of…I lost interest in almost everything I used to enjoy." Her breath leaves her in a shaky sigh. "You said you fell in love with me from my messages," she says slowly. "How is that possible? I was a shell of a person. There was nothing to fall in love with."

"There was. Your words…the pain…it was so raw. So real. It hurt to listen to yet it was beautiful. I haven't lost anyone like you did, but I related to your words more than I realized. I'd been living in denial for a long time, and hearing your messages made me realize it…that I wanted more in life. The love you had…I wanted to find someone to love me like that, and I wanted to love that person back just as hard. It's fucked up and doesn't make sense, I know."

Sierra doesn't speak. I gently move so I can see her face. Tears are in her eyes and my heart sinks. Did I say the wrong thing? Was the brutal honesty too much?

"It does," she whispers. "It does make sense." She blinks and tears fall from the side of her eyes, dripping down into her hair. She reaches up, hand landing on my cheek. "Did you find what you were looking for?"

"I found more."

~

THE RAIN CONTINUED to fall the rest of the afternoon. Sierra fell asleep, nestled in my arms. Exhaustion tugged at me, and I fought it as long as I could, wanting to soak up every second of this.

The sun is setting when I wake up. Tinkerbell is on my chest, purring and kneading the blanket with her paws. Dolly is sitting on the table next to the screen, laying in between a collection of colorful lanterns. Humidity clings to the day, and the setting sun takes away the heat.

I brush Sierra's hair out of her face and kiss her cheek. Her eyes flutter open and she smiles as soon as she sees me.

"I didn't mean to wake you."

"It's okay," she yawns. "I didn't mean to fall asleep. I, uh, haven't been sleeping well."

"I haven't either. We both needed to nap."

She looks at the setting sun. "Yeah, I guess we did."

"Are you still in pain?" I ask carefully.

"Not really. It feels like a normal period now. What about you? You should not have worked a job like you did."

"I know," I agree. "I felt it the next day."

The hammock sways as Sierra sits up enough to look at my wound. "It looks bruised, Chase."

"It feels like it is. I'll take it easy now."

"You better."

"Can Sexy Nurse Sierra—sorry."

"What's wrong?" Sierra tips her head.

I run my up her arm. "I'm not sure how to handle having sex again after everything."

"I don't either," Sierra tells me, and brings her arms in around herself. This is a hard topic to discuss. "We're both on sex restrictions right now. For another week at least."

"I'll wait. However long it takes, I'll wait."

She smiles. "I know."

"Are you hungry?"

"Starving."

"Good. Me too. I can attempt to cook for you again."

"I'd like that."

We stand and stretch. Sierra picks up Tinkerbell, and Dolly trots along, weaving in and out of our feet.

"I have to ask one thing," I tell Sierra and reach down to scoop up the calico cat. "What's with the cat shelf?"

Sierra turns, and in the millisecond it takes her to respond my heart races. Then she smiles. "They like to climb on things and be up high. You know they'd love it if we put up a system of shelves around the house."

I'm smiling right back. "I did help Josh put up floating shelves in Dakota's room. I can see the cats hanging out up there."

"I know, right?"

"Where do you want to put them?"

Sierra looks at Dolly in my arms, and her smile turns into a grin. "I've sketched the whole thing out. Let me show you."

I follow her to the stairs. We make it up when someone knocks on the door. I set Dolly on the ground and jog down the stairs to see who's here. Sierra is behind me, still cuddling Tink.

Lisa stands on the porch, holding a bag of food and a bottle of wine. Her eyes go from me to Sierra, and her shoulders are timidly pulled in. It makes sense things are tense between the two of them.

"I brought tacos," she says, holding out the bag. "I hear we have reason to celebrate tonight."

Sierra takes the bag and steps aside, welcoming Lisa in. "We do."

Relief washes over Lisa's face. Sierra takes the wine and tacos into the kitchen, and Lisa grabs my arm.

"Chase," she starts, looking at the ground.

"It's okay," I say, surprising myself. "We want to move past everything."

"Right, and okay. Good idea." Then she looks up with a smile. "And about the bookstore...Sierra told me what you did. Thank you."

35

SIERRA

*M*y father leans over the table, eyes drilling into Chase. It's Sunday evening, and we're all sitting around the table for dinner. The first course has been served, but Dad hasn't taken a single bite.

"What's the most valuable thing you've recovered?" he asks Chase, completely fascinated by Chase's past as a bounty hunter.

"That depends," Chase says and rests his hand on my thigh, "on what you consider valuable."

"You should tell him about the boat in Scotland," I say and take a drink of wine.

"That was fun," Chase says and goes into detail, starting with the sketchy plane ride in a small aircraft. My entire family is enamored, not eating as they listen to Chase talk about his crazy adventures.

Across the table, Lisa catches my eye. She picks up her wine and gives me a small toast. I relax in my chair and put my hand on top of Chase's. He's still not 'ideal' as my mother told me just hours ago, but knowing the truth behind his record has cleared the tension. And now Dad won't leave Chase alone and keeps firing off question after question.

We have dessert on the patio and the kids swim while the adults sip drinks. I watch my nieces and nephew splashing in the water, laughing and having the time of their lives. My mom and sister are in the pool with them, laughing just as much. It's one of the rare times I see my mother let loose and act like a normal human being, not caring about her hair or makeup, or the opinions of others.

Will I be able to interact with my mother like that when I have kids? Maybe we'll get along better when we can bond over the baby. It might be wrong, but I feel like she'll like me better if I give her more grandchildren.

"You'll have one someday," Chase says, reading my mind. He's not supposed to go swimming yet, so we're sitting by the edge of the pool with our feet in the water.

"Someday," I repeat, feeling the painful tug on my heart. What could have been weighs heavily on me, and perhaps it always will. Though this time, there is a promise of happiness in the future.

He puts his arm around me and kisses my forehead. "I hope we have a girl. And she looks just like you."

I smile. "I'd like that. And if we have a boy, I imagine him looking just like you. But no tattoos until he's thirty."

Chase laughs. "You won't be happy to know I got my first tattoo when I was fifteen."

"That's not legal, is it?"

"No. A friend's brother did it in his garage. It was terrible."

"Can I see it?"

"Kind of." He pulls the sleeve up his left shoulder. "It's been covered up. That's how bad it was."

I laugh and bring my face to his, running a hand through

his wavy hair. We stay at my parents' until everyone leaves and go back to my house for the night.

"Now that you're the owner of The Book Bag," Chase starts, pulling down the sheets and getting into bed, "are you going to set different hours? You're not exactly an early riser," he teases.

"I totally would. But I think most people would argue ten o'clock isn't early."

"It's not. I'll come in with you. As your business partner, I'll make a sacrifice and get up along with you."

"You better, or you're fired." I get under the covers next to Chase. The Book Bag is going on, business as usual, just with a new owner. Chase is going to help me get things started and will work the register so I can handle the legal parts of becoming a shop owner.

He reaches over and takes two books off the nightstand and hands one to me. I take a minute to admire him and let this moment sink in. We've been through a lot together in a short amount of time. I might never find a reason to explain why the bad things happened, or why the good ones continue to come. The loss is still painful for the both of us. The mistakes we've both made saliently sit just below the surface, reminding us that we're both human.

Bad things happen.

But good things do too.

There are no reasons. No way to know why life unfolds the way it does.

All I know is right here, right now in this moment... things are as close to perfect as they are going to get. Chase is in my bed with a good book. I don't think I'm ever getting out.

And I'm okay with that.

36

CHASE

"What about this one?" I ask Dakota.

"I have it."

"This one?"

"Uhhh. Have it."

I pick another book from the shelf. "There's no way you have this one."

Dakota laughs. "I do!"

I'm purposely picking books she already has because she finds it funny. It's Monday evening, and Sierra is getting ready to close the store for the night. She's standing at the front of the store, holding baby Aaron as she talks to Melissa.

"You pick one," I tell my niece, who's giggling like crazy. She gets very serious and thumbs through the books, picking one about a princess who fights dragons at night when the kingdom is sleeping. I pull a twenty from my wallet and give it to her, making her even more excited that she gets to pay for her own book. She skips her way to the register.

"As far as grand romantic gestures go," Josh starts, walking down the aisle, trying to get Noah to sleep, "you've set the rest of us up to fail. There aren't enough stores for sale in Summer Hill."

I laugh and stand, putting the books Dakota and I looked at back on the shelf. "I'll consider that more next time. Though next time, I'm going bigger. Like a house."

Josh laughs. "I don't know what happened." He looks at Sierra and back at me. "But don't let it happen again."

My eyes settle on Sierra. "It won't."

∾

FOUR MONTHS LATER...

"YOU WERE RIGHT," I tell Sierra as we walk hand-in-hand along the sidewalk, stopping in front of The Book Bag. "Halloween is an even bigger deal than The Fourth of July."

"Just wait until Christmas," she says. "It's like the early holidays are just warm-ups. Halloween is my favorite."

"Mine too."

We stop in front of The Book Bag, setting up a table. In half an hour, the kids of Summer Hill will fill the streets and trick-or-treat from shop to shop, showing off their costumes as they collect candy.

I go to the edge of the sidewalk and look up and down the street. Every storefront has been decorated, and Sierra told me each year people become more competitive to outdo each other.

"What are you thinking?" she asks me. "You have that deep thought look going on."

"Is it turning you on?"

"It is," she says and wiggles her eyebrows. "But your costume is too."

I look down at myself. "It's the tights, right? It highlights my cock."

"Don't talk like that!" she whisper-yells and laughs. "Someone might hear you."

"They don't need to hear me. They can see this monster."

Laughing harder, Sierra walks over to me. It was her idea to dress up as Belle and Gaston.

"And I was thinking about how weird this town is."

"You always say that."

"I do. But remember, I like weird."

"Weird is good."

I put my arm around her. "Weird is very good."

And now, weird is home.

SIERRA

"This is overkill, you know," Chase tells me, turning away from the table with an eyebrow raised. It's Thanksgiving, and we're at my parents' waiting impatiently to start dinner.

"I want to make sure you don't eat it."

"You can just tell me what has shellfish in it. You didn't need to make a sign."

I smile and nod. "I did. Just to be sure."

"Everything with shellfish is on that table," Sam says. She takes Chase's food allergy as seriously as I do. "Don't go by it."

Chase rolls his eyes, acting more annoyed than he actually is. I laugh and move around the large island counter to him. He snakes his arms around me and steals a quick kiss.

"Happy Thanksgiving," I tell him and then turn back to the kitchen. "Is everything ready?"

"I think so," Mom says, opening the oven to check on the turkey. Sam and I exchange looks, silently laughing. Mom doesn't know how to cook a turkey. Her personal chef prepared most of the meal, while we handled the side dishes.

"I'm going to run home and get changed," I say. I've been in leggings and a T-shirt all day, knowing it was pointless to get dressed while cooking. "I'll be back in like fifteen minutes." I turn to Chase. "You can stay here and hang out with the guys if you want."

Scott, my brother-in-law, and my dad are in the den watching football. Chase had been in there with them, but keeps coming into the kitchen to 'check on me.' It's a bit odd, and it's almost as if he's nervous, which doesn't make sense. Chase isn't shy and doesn't care what others think about him. He's been around my entire family before. Well, except for Scott. But Scott got here two days ago, and he and Chase get along great.

"I'll come with you," he says.

"You don't have to. I'm going to change and probably fix my makeup."

"Probably?"

"Okay, I will fix it."

Chase's hands land on my waist and he leans in. "I'm coming with you. Because I want to fuck you." He kisses my neck.

"Mhhh," I moan and let my head fall back. "Yeah, you're coming with." I take his hand and go out the door. He insists I do my makeup first, and says he has to go to the car to get something.

He's still outside when I'm done with my makeup. Wondering what's going on, I look out the window and see a single lantern light near the edge of the forest. I grab my jacket and go outside to see what the heck Chase is up to.

"Babe?" I call, picking up the lantern. I hold it out in front of me and look into the trees. Another candle flickers next to the river, and I see Chase crouched down by the water. "What are you doing?" I ask.

He stands, and candlelight flickers on his face. "I was

going to wait," he starts and holds out his hand. I pick my way over tree roots and uneven ground, coming to a stop by the side of the river. "I had this whole big thing planned."

"Wait for what?"

Chase pulls something out of his pocket, not taking his eyes off me. "To ask you to marry me." He drops down to one knee and opens the box. Firelight flickers off a giant diamond ring.

My jaw drops and my hand flies to my chest. Tears fill my eyes and I look from the ring to Chase.

"Sierra, I love you more than anything. You've made me a better person and have given me everything I never knew I wanted. Will you marry me?"

"Yes," I say, hardly able to find my voice. "Yes, yes I will!"

Chase gets to his feet and puts the ring on my finger. "I love you so fucking much," he whispers and then kisses me. "Do you like the ring?" he asks nervously.

"Yes!" I assure him with a laugh and bring my hand up. "It's beautiful."

Chase kisses me again, and then grabs me by the waist, grinning. "We should hurry so we can get that quickie in before your family comes looking."

~

"You have to have a June wedding," Mom says.

"No." Gran shakes her head. "May is better."

"June weddings are classic," Mom persists.

"June is overrated," my aunt chimes in. I look at Chase and smile. I warned him this would happen. The wedding planning started the moment I walked back into the house and showed off my new ring.

"I like May," I say to Chase. "June is good too. October is my favorite, but that's too far."

"I'm good with May," he agrees.

"We're getting married in May," I announce.

"Not this May," Mom and Gran say at the same time.

"There's hardly any time to plan!" Mom exclaims. "Venues are already booked."

"I've always wanted to have the reception here," I go on. "I don't want a big wedding."

"You could always do a wedding in Disney," Scott suggests. He winks at me. "It would have to be small that way."

"I like that idea," Chase tells me with a smile. "I'll marry you tomorrow in Vegas if that's what you want. As long as we're together."

"What?" Mom practically shrieks. "No one is getting married in Vegas! Though I am open to the idea of a Disney wedding."

"Don't worry about what you want, Sierra," Lisa jokes. "You're lucky enough you got to pick your fiancée and not have an arranged marriage."

"I'm not that bad," Mom insists. Sam and I laugh. "I just want to make sure things are perfect."

Chase takes my hand and smiles. "They already are."

EPILOGUE

CHASE

"*E*than?" I look around the living room. "Where's Ethan? Where'd he go?" Wild giggles come from under the pile of pillows in front of me. "Mom, have you seen Ethan?"

"Oh my goodness," Sierra says, slowly walking into the living room. "Dad, did you lose Ethan again?"

"Here I am!" our son says, popping up from the pillows.

"Whoa!" I say and bring my hands to my face. "Where did you come from?"

"Again, Daddy, again!" the toddler giggles. He puts his face into the pillows and chants *you can't see me* over and over.

I bury him in pillows again and sit on the couch. "I'm tired and need to lay down. This pile of pillows looks comfy." I pretend to fluff up the pillows, and Ethan erupts in laughter. "Wait a minute. Why is my pillow laughing?"

"I'm not a pillow! I'm not a pillow!"

"Why are the pillows talking? What is going on? Hey!" I move the pillows and lift Ethan up in the air. "You're not a pillow!" I kiss his cheeks and he tries to blow raspberries on my arm, which just leaves a trail of slobber. The second his feet hit the floor he takes off, running full-speed at Sierra.

"Mommy!"

"Careful, buddy!" I say. "You don't want to hurt your sister!"

"Maybe you'll make her come out," Sierra says with a groan. She's two days past her due date and is miserable. She kisses Ethan's cheeks and hugs him tight. "Dinner's ready, boys."

I hold out a hand and help her to her feet. Not a second after she's up, Sierra sits back down again.

"Ow." Her hands fly to her large belly.

"Did you just have another contraction?"

"Yeah. We should probably eat. Now."

"Maybe we should call your mom. You had a fast labor last time."

"Not yet. They're still too far apart." She takes my hand and lets me help her to the table. She doesn't make it to her chair before she pitches forward. "Okay. Call her."

In somewhat of a panic, I rush around the house. We moved a few months ago into this house. It's big and brand-new, built on the Belmont family property. The river runs through our backyard and it's perfect.

I get Sierra's hospital bag, Ethan's overnight bag, and the bag packed for our daughter, Emma. I call Mrs. Belmont to let her know to meet us at the hospital. Then I pack up Ethan and help Sierra to the car. I'm more nervous than she is and am half convinced we waited too long and Sierra's going to have this baby in the car.

She's contracting every two minutes by the time we get to

the hospital, and Ethan cried the last quarter of the drive, not understanding what's going on or why Mommy is in pain.

Only three-and-a-half hours after getting checked into labor and delivery, our daughter is born. She's nineteen inches and six-and-a-half pounds of perfection.

"I don't remember Ethan being this little," I say, taking my daughter in my arms.

"I was thinking the same thing," Sierra agrees. "She's so little and cute." Sierra's eyes fill with tears. "She's so perfect."

"She is." I kiss her soft cheeks and put her back in Sierra's arms, going into the waiting room to get Ethan. Holding his hand, we go back into the delivery room. He stops at the foot of the bed, staring at the little bundle in Sierra's arms.

Then he smiles and climbs up, eager to meet his sister.

"Hi," he says. Emma opens her mouth. "She said hi! Can I hold her?"

"Let me help you," I say and pick Ethan up. We sit on the bed, and I put a pillow in his lap. Carefully, Sierra lays Emma on his lap, keeping a hold of her head. Ethan grins and bends down to kiss her.

"She tastes like a baby," he says and we laugh. I lean in, putting my arm around Ethan and Sierra. I look down at my family. We're an hour from our house, but sitting here together, I feel at home.

ACKNOWLEDGMENTS

Chase and Sierra have been begging me to write their story for well over a year now, and once I finally set out to write it, I couldn't stop. I love this story so much, and am so thankful for my amazing friends in the book world who share the love of One Call Away right along with me.

Christine Stanley, TL Smith, Kristin Mayer, Erin Hayes, and Crystal Gizzard Brunette: thank you for your abundance of support and optimism over this book. You never lost patience with me and my (many) moments of panic while getting this book ready for publication.

Felicia, Theresa, Michelle, Paige, Lisa, Debby, Paula, Colleen, and Franci: You ladies are the best beta team an author could ask for. There are no words to express how grateful I am to have you on my side.

To all the bloggers and bookstagrammers who took the time to read, review, and post about One Call Away: Thank you times a thousand. I'm blown away and humbled each and every time you decide to pick up my book.

And to my family and friends: thank you for helping me

follow my dreams, for offering encouragement, and bringing me wine when it's most needed.

ABOUT THE AUTHOR

Emily Goodwin is the New York Times and USA Today Bestselling author of over a dozen of romantic titles. Emily writes the kind of books she likes to read, and is a sucker for a swoon-worthy bad boy and happily ever afters.

She lives in the midwest with her husband and two daughters. When she's not writing, you can find her riding her horses, hiking, reading, or drinking wine with friends.

Emily is represented by Julie Gwinn of the Seymour Agency.

www.emilygoodwinbooks.com
emily@emilygoodwinbooks.com

ALSO BY EMILY GOODWIN

First Comes Love

Then Come Marriage

Outside the Lines

Never Say Never

Stay

All I Need

Hot Mess (Luke & Lexi Book 1)

Twice Burned (Luke & Lexi Book 2)

Bad Things (Cole & Ana Book 1)

Battle Scars (Cole & Ana Book 2)

HOT MESS

Chapter One

Someday, I'll get my shit together. Today, however, is not that day. I bring my coffee to my lips and whirl around, tripping over the dog. The mug hits my teeth, and hot coffee sloshes down the front of my ivory blouse.

"Really, Pluto? You have to lay in the middle of the kitchen during rush hour?" I glare at the little mutt who looks at me, and then at his empty bowl. "I didn't forget to feed you," I say and grab a towel from the kitchen counter. It's damp from drying last night's dishes, but it'll work. I rub the front of my shirt, swearing under my breath. I'm going to have to change, and I'm already running late.

I take a sip of my coffee and fly to the pantry. "Son of a bitch," I say when I stick my hand into the big bag of dog food. I only feel crumbs.

"Mom, you said a bad word," Grace points out, little feet slapping on the cold tile as she comes up behind me.

I let out a breath. "That's a mommy word. Only mommies

can say those words." I grab the dog food bag and look at my six-year-old. "Did you feed Pluto last night?"

"I did," she says proudly.

"How much did you feed him?"

She shrugs and looks away, a move she mastered years ago. "I don't know."

"You fed him all of it," I say with a shake of my head, closing my eyes in a long blink. I had it mentally planned out to give him the last of his food this morning and pick up a bag on the way home from work. "He's on a diet, remember? We have to only give him one scoop in the evening."

"But he was hungry!" Grace says, and her shoulders sag. "I'm sorry."

"It's okay, baby," I say and smile. She's as sweet as she is sassy. "Thank you for helping last night. You take good care of your puppy."

That brings a smile to her face. "Can you do my hair?" she asks, holding out a brush.

"Yes, let me find something for Pluto first. Did you brush your teeth?"

She nods and pulls out a bar stool, climbing up to wait for me. I get three-day-old chicken and rice from the fridge and stick it in the microwave. While the food is heating up, I fly over to Grace, taking another drink of coffee as I walk. I set the mug down and pick up her brush, running it through her brunette locks.

"Your hair is getting so long," I tell her, carefully brushing through her tangled curls. "And so pretty."

The compliment makes her sit up a little straighter, and I can tell without looking that she's smiling. "I want a bun like you," she says and I internally cringe. My own dark blonde hair — a shade or two lighter than hers — is up in the usual messy bun. I'm not talking the cute and stylish kind. I'm talking the if-I-put-on-a-hoodie-I'll-look-like-adrug-dealer kind of messy bun. But hey, at least my hair is clean.

"What about a braid?" I ask and lean back, looking into the living room for my three-year-old. Paige is curled up on the couch watching cartoons. A wave of sadness and guilt hits me when I see her. Like her mother and older sister, she's naturally not a morning person. Yet she's up, dressed and fed before seven a.m. so I can drop her off at daycare before work.

"Okay," Grace says to the braid. I turn my attention back to her, heart aching. I worked part-time when Grace was little and did the majority of my work from home. She didn't have to go to daycare or get up early. I spent my mornings and afternoons with her, playing and snuggling, living out the life I always imagined.

And then I got divorced, and everything changed.

I carefully braid Grace's hair and then grab the leftovers from the microwave, taking them to Pluto's dish.

"I'll get you dog food tonight," I promise him. "But don't act like you don't prefer this."

He gets up and trots over to his bowl, scarfing down breakfast. I pat him on the head, glad I got to keep him. Russell, my ex, and I adopted him for Grace's birthday three years ago.

"Okay, girls," I say. "Coats and shoes, please!"

Grace hops off the stool and goes to the hall tree by the back door. Paige needs a little more coaxing and asks me to sit and snuggle her for a minute. I can't resist. I sit on the couch, turning off the TV, and pull her into my arms.

"I love you to the moon and back, sweet pea," I whisper in her ear. She looks up at me, golden brown hair falling into her eyes.

"I love you too, Mama," she says back and hugs me. "Can I stay home with you? Please, Mama?"

My heart breaks. "What about your friends? Don't you want to see them?"

"Oh, yeah. Friends!" She perks up and climbs off the couch, jibber-jabbering away about her friend Olivia from school. That's my saving grace about this whole thing. The girl is a social butterfly, though I don't know where she gets it from. I'm not exactly what you'd call a "people person" most days.

I let Pluto out into our small fenced-in backyard while we go through the process of dressing for the cool spring weather, putting on shoes and loading backpacks and lunches into the car. The girls start fighting over who gets to hold the stuffed monkey that was discarded on the floor of the car and forgotten about for weeks. Well, until now.

"Take turns," I say, putting the monkey in Paige's hands. "When Paige gets to school, you can hold it," I tell Grace, too tired to tell her kindergarteners shouldn't be bickering like this over a plush monkey.

I glance at the clock, cringing when I see that we should have left ten minutes ago. Dammit. I snap Paige in her carseat and check Grace's seatbelt. Then I fly back into the house, let the dog in, grab my shit, and slide into the driver's seat.

"You smell like coffee," Grace says after we've backed out of the driveway and made it two miles down the street.

Dammit. I look down, tears threatening to form, and see the caramel-colored stain on my blouse. I can't go into work like this, and I don't want this stain to set in and ruin the shirt. I don't have a choice, seeing there isn't time to turn around. How the hell did I forget to change? An even better question might be how the hell did I forget my shirt was sopping wet? Am I that much of a hot mess having some sort of food or beverage spilled on me is the norm? This is going to be a long day. Hell, it's already been a long week. And it's only fucking Monday.

"Mommy?" Grace asks, leaning forward in her booster seat. "Are you okay?"

"Yeah, honey," I say and blink back tears. "I'm okay." I flick my gaze to the rearview mirror and see both of my precious daughters.

And I really do feel okay.

~

"Long night?" Jillian asks me as I rush into the office.

"You could say that again." I set my purse down at my desk and hesitate before taking my coat off. I had left a black cardigan in the car at least a month ago. It was a little wrinkled and smelled like the stale Cheerios it was piled on, but it was better than my stained blouse. I buttoned it up the top and hoped no one would notice I didn't have a cami on underneath. "Paige has been having nightmares again." I sink into the rolling chair and fire up my computer, looking up at Jillian, who's perched on the edge of my desk.

Her hair is brushed to perfection, falling over her shoulders in a wave of blonde curls, and her makeup is flawless. She's been at Black Ink Press almost as long as I have, and we've become good friends as we bonded over books.

"I was up late reading my last submission. The book is great, by the way, a little slow in pacing, but nothing I can't fix. As soon as I laid down, Paige woke up screaming about the man in her doorway. I know they say it's a phase, but this is starting to creep me out."

I unzip my coat and brace for Jillian to say something. Books are her first passion, and fashion is a close second. She's always put together and doesn't hesitate to point out those who aren't. But in the year since my life fell apart, she's gone soft on me. I kind of hate her for it…as much as I love her for it.

"You need to get that place blessed. I swear Russ is sending voodoo vibes your way to make you want to leave."

I shake my head. "I wouldn't put it past him." Who got the house after we split caused more grief than anything. Well, other than who got the kids. He fought tooth and nail for them at first, and swore he'd be in their lives as much as possible. He did great for the first six months, and then he started dating again.

If only he acted like a deadbeat dad *before* the divorce, we might have ended things sooner and spared the heartache. Though, if I left the first time I thought we were broken beyond repair, I might not have Paige. Or Grace. Or have gotten married in the first place.

Having hope that things will work themselves out is my biggest flaw. Live and learn and all, right?

"I don't know how you take care of your kids and work full-time," Jillian says, as we walk to the break room. I can't start the day without a bagel and some coffee. "It's just me, my cat, and sometimes my boyfriend at my house. And I don't have to commute from the suburbs. Seriously, I don't know how you do it."

I shrug and fill a paper cup with coffee. "I don't either. But I just do. I have no choice but to keep going, and it's only by the sheer grace of God I've gotten this far." I spread cream cheese on a bagel and shake my head. "And to be honest, I don't feel like I'm doing a very good job. I'm struggling so much, Jill."

She puts her hand on my arm. "Besides that rat nest on your head and your interesting choice of clothing, it doesn't look that way. I don't know if that's helpful or not, but know the rest of the world can't tell."

"Thanks."

"You're doing great, Lexi. Don't be so hard on yourself, and don't forget to take care of yourself either. You deserve some happiness."

"Are you talking about masturbating again?"

"Not this time, but don't forget to do that either. I know how long it's been since you've had sex. What I meant was you should go out and have fun. Maybe think about dating again."

I pour creamer into my coffee, shaking my head as I stir. A million arguments rush into my head, listing out reasons why I'm not ready to start dating. I open my mouth to spit them out but stop. Because I do want to date again. I wanted to date again before the divorce was official. I spent the majority of my last pregnancy avoiding my husband, the father of my unborn child, because being around him was more painful than being alone.

No one warns you how painful falling out of love is.

"You're right," I say.

"Now I knew you'd—wait, did you just agree with me?" Jillian flips her hair over her shoulder, long lashes coming together as she blinks.

"I did. You're right. I think it is time. I'm ready." We snap lids on our coffee cups and slowly make our way back to our offices. "I'm lonely," I admit. "I've been lonely for a long time."

"I know," she says softly. "Let's go out on Saturday, just for fun. You can practice your flirting skills and let off some steam. Russ has the kids this weekend, right?"

I carefully sip my hot coffee. "He does."

She smiles, blue eyes going wide with excitement. "I got a new top that's too long for me—the curse of being five-foot-two strikes again—but it will look *killer* on you. Come over Saturday, let me do your hair and makeup, and you'll be turning down hotties left and right."

I laugh, snorting into my coffee. "Sure I will."

"You're a MILF, Lex. Don't sell yourself short."

"So, when I meet these hotties, do I tell them I have kids or not? Because they need to know I'm a mom to be one they'd like to fuck, right?"

"Yes. But make sure to tell them you had your vagina stitched shut extra tight each time you pushed a baby out."

Gerry, one of the assistant editors, raises his eyebrows as he walks past. I sigh. As much as I want to find a partner again, the thought of dating scares me. Russell and I met in college, were married at twenty-two, and got pregnant just months after the wedding. Flash forward to now, and it's been a while since I've been on the market.

"Don't stress," Jillian says, reading my mind. "This is just for fun. Find a hot guy to go home with and use him as practice."

"I've never had a one-night stand before."

"I'm well aware."

"If I did, would you think I'm slutty?"

She stares at me, unblinking. "No, and you know how I feel about that. You're a grown-ass woman. If you *want* to sleep with a different man every night, more power to you. You own your body and your sexuality. Do what you want."

"I love it when you talk feminism to me."

She smiles. "I'll text Lori and Erin and see if they want to come too. The four of us haven't been out like this in a long time. It's so overdue."

I can't dispute that. Lori and Erin were also involved in the book world, like us. Lori works in marketing for Black Ink Press, and Erin recently made the move from being an editor like me to a literary agent. She has kids as well, and though they're in high school, it's nice to have another mom to hang out with.

We go into our small offices and get to work. I pick at my bagel while I open my email, shuddering when I see my growing inbox. I skim through, flagging the important ones, move them into a folder, and then check Twitter and Facebook as I finish my coffee. I get sucked into a public temper tantrum between two agents from rival agencies, wasting fifteen precious minutes of my morning.

Then it's back to the emails, replying to authors and agents about the projects I'm working on. I open a document from Quinn Harlow, an author I've worked with since my start at Black Ink Press, happily surprised she sent over changes to her novel already. I lean back in my chair and start reading through them, getting pulled into her romance novel about a billionaire heiress and an ex-convict all over again.

Before I know it, it's time for lunch, and the number of emails in my inbox has doubled. Again. I stretch my arms over my head, refusing to let it stress me out. I'm going to stay on top of things this week, so much I'll be able to either leave early on Friday or take the whole day off and spend it with my favorite three-year-old.

I load Quinn's book onto my Kindle so I can read while I eat, and after checking Twitter and Facebook again, head out, meeting Jillian in the lobby.

"Erin's in the area," she says, not looking away from her phone. "She's at The Salad Bar. Want to go?"

"Sure," I say but feel guilty. The food is good, but I hate paying over twenty bucks for a bowl of lettuce with light toppings. It's healthy for your body but not for your wallet. I didn't bring a lunch for myself today, anyway. I had time to make the girls' lunches or mine, but not both. They trump me every time.

The bright sun has warmed up the day enough that we get a table outside, soaking up the cloudless day. Erin hugs us when we see her, and I can't help but smile at the sight of my friend. We order our food and swear we won't talk about work, but just minutes later, Erin is telling us about a new author she signed.

"She has a few self-published books that did really well," she tells us. "And has a decent fan base already, but…" She shakes her head and pulls up the author's Facebook fan page. "She'll be a hard sell to marketing. She posts a lot of drunk videos on her fan page." She holds up the phone so we can see a video of the author talking to the camera, waving a drink around. "And she doesn't play nice with the other indies in her genre. I found a lot of other authors posting that she uses them to get ahead, then throws them aside like garbage."

"Ugh," I say. "No one likes a bully."

"She'd have to have a fucking amazing book to make me take her on," Jillian admits. "Have you tried talking to her?"

"Yes, and it's gone nowhere. Like I said, great writer, but an asshole of a person." Erin sighs and sets her phone down. "Enough about work. How's life. Did Aaron propose yet?"

"Not yet," Jillian says, shrugging. She acts like it doesn't bother her, but after five years together, the lack of commitment gets under her skin. "How are your kids?" Her deflection only proves how much it upsets her.

"Driving me fucking insane," Erin admits. Her eyes meet mine. "People say it gets easier as the kids get older. It's a lie. Don't buy it. They just get moody and mean, and Mom is the last person they want to be seen with. I'll trade you."

"There's no way I'm giving up my babies. They're hardly even babies anymore."

"It goes fast," Erin says. "Savor it. Before you know it, you have two teenagers who only care about what you're making for dinner and how much money they can con out of you."

We laugh and the subject changes to books and publishing again. We say our goodbyes, and go back to work. Back in my office, I answer a few more emails and lean back in my chair to hopefully read through the rest of Quinn's changes. One of those changes is an added sex scene, and oh my God, it's hot. I don't realize I'm biting my lip and leaning closer and closer to my Kindle screen until someone knocks at my office door.

I blink, feeling a bit disoriented—Quinn will be happy to know that—and look up, expecting to see Gavin or even Jillian. The smile on my lips freezes in place and my cheeks flush even more than before. My stomach flutters and I momentarily panic that I have lettuce stuck in my teeth. I didn't check, after all, so it's entirely possible.

"Cole," I finally say, still smiling like an idiot to my boss. "Hi." Getting caught reading a naughty sex scene is one thing. Getting caught reading a naughty sex scene by someone you've fantasized about acting out those naughty sex scenes with is another.

Especially when that person happens to be your boss.

"Hi, Alexis," he says, smiling right back at me, his brown eyes shining in the afternoon sunlight. He's one of the few people who always calls me by my full name. It annoys me when others do, but it's sexy when it's coming off his lips. "How are you?"

"Good. I'm just going through what I think are the last changes for Quinn Harlow's latest book."

"Perfect," he says and comes into the office, leaving the door open. "That's actually what I wanted to talk to you about. I just got out of a meeting with the marketing team and they wanted to bump the release date up." He leans over the desk, staring down at my Kindle. Black Ink is one of the biggest publishers in the business and is no stranger to erotic or taboo novels, but I suddenly feel shy that my Kindle is open to a page—the entire page—devoted to oral sex. Maybe it's because I've wondered what Cole's head would look like between my legs?

Stop it.

He's right fucking in front of me. I'm already hot and bothered from the sex scene. I don't need the image of Cole's handsome face slowly trailing down my body as he kisses my neck, my breasts, the soft skin on my—*stop!*

"How soon?" I ask and clear my throat. "When do they want to release, I mean. And how has that changed the marketing plan? Quinn will want to know."

"They want to move the release date up by a month, and the marketing has already started."

"I think we can do that, then."

He smiles at me, and my panties melt right off. "I knew you'd be able to handle this. And between you and me, I'm glad it's you working on her book. You're one of the best we have here."

I shake my head. "You're too kind."

"Really," he says and moves in a little closer. "Do I need to bring up *The Fake Wife?*" he asks with a laugh. I blush and shake my head. I took a gamble on a debut author's thriller not long ago, and the book blew up. The movie came out over the summer and was a hit. "You've yet to advocate for a bad book. How do you do it?"

I shrug, looking up at him. "I just know what I like and go for it." I don't mean for it to sound as flirty as it does. I'm about to divert my eyes and blurt out something random to take the tension away, but Cole speaks before I have the chance.

"I like that about you," he says coyly, giving me a sexy-as-hell smile. "You'll talk to Quinn Harlow or her agent today?"

"Yeah. I'll email them both right away."

He goes on to tell me the details of everything, and I do my best to listen. I even jot down notes so I can explain everything in perfect detail when I talk to Quinn's agent.

My mind starts to drift to Cole's perfect cheekbones and

the alluring way he smells. Cole Winchester is the Editor-in-Chief at Black Ink Press, and is the subject of many office fantasies. The moment you meet him, it's obvious as to why. Besides his looks—tall, athletic, handsome-yet-rugged face that's covered in a perfect five o'clock shadow all day—Cole is a diamond in the rough. He's respectful of his employees. He's responsible and always has his shit together. He's an overall nice guy but can still command the room without even trying. Cole meets all the criteria on my to-date list.

Yet, he's made it abundantly clear that he'll never date anyone from work. Don't shit were you eat and all, I guess. Though I like to think I could be his exception, like one of the leading ladies in the romance novels. And there's that hope again rising in my chest. I've been told that not all is lost when you have hope. But enough of that optimistic bullshit. Having hope only prolongs the heartache.